Spanish Rose, Yorkshire Thorns

MARTA CARDONA

JEREMY MILLS

PUBLISHING LIMITED

Published by Jeremy Mills Publishing Limited
www.jeremymillspublishing.co.uk

First Published 2008

ISBN 978–1–906600–01–3

CONTENTS

BOOK
ONE

MARIA SALVANS HAD been ready on time. Now, standing in front of her was Ben, wearing his best suit, to perform the ceremonial delivery of orange-tree blossom, and she felt impatient. 'Never mind the rhyme Ben, let's go,' she said, taking the bouquet from his hands.

Tolomeu, her brother, was to give her away. He was there – her mother was also waiting to lock the door behind them and the rest of the family were already in the cars. Maria was not going to make a fuss – not nervous, she told herself. But at that moment she wished everything was already done. She wanted to be as happy as any other bride. For months during her engagement she had had doubts, fears and nightmares. But now she wanted them vanished, forgotten, replaced with her enthusiasm and faith in her own strength; she would make good what wasn't. After all, they loved each other and when they were away she would teach him – he said he wanted it so. Everything would be all right, she was sure.

The bride did not look at her mother. She wouldn't have noticed if there were traces of sorrow in her face, she who had been against her daughter's marriage; she had since tried to make things go the best possible way. She helped in the making of the bridal gown – she said, 'any dress looks good if it is well cut.' So they went to a professional for the cut and they themselves did the sewing. Mother and daughter did all the stitching, and the dress looked like a perfect model and fitted Maria well – the white satin shone in her dark complexion and the long gown made her little figure look slim and elegant.

It was summer – a hot and bright August day. The cars left the village going across the river towards the chain of mountains at the other side. Maria had chosen to be married at St. Peter of Reixach. She was born there in Reixach, being baptised in St. Peter's Romanic Church, and all her childhood memories were bound up with these lovely places.

The cars were getting near the top, what a marvellous view! Looking down the hillside she could see the scattered farms, the summer residences – all the houses she knew so well by name. There was 'Can Salvans' – it was built for her father and although the family had moved some years back, the name still remained and the ghost-like memories of the eventful years of her childhood would remain too, Maria thought.

Still the cars drove up – the sight enlarged, reaching the far-away Montserrat mountains and in between a good extension of that beautiful warm and dry dear land she was preparing to leave. She was pleased now that the cars, big and luxurious, were inadequate for this mountain path, so their advance was very slow and gave her the opportunity of contemplating this panoramic view in a quiet goodbye.

The car stopped – and her thoughts too. A radiant bride descended graciously from the car – there were no bridesmaids, only her brother taking her to the altar. The mountain air held her veil, the pinewoods were soft green all round and the monotonous sound of the harvest fly her background music. She walked under the blazing August sun that made her white figure glare as light and purity. Petite, dark haired and with Chinese-like eyes, she seemed vulnerable but resolute. Inside the church it was dim and cool. A tall handsome man with unsteady big eyes was waiting for her.

James had spent part of his childhood in these mountains too, but at the side towards the sea. A son of a peasant labourer who hadn't much time for education, he grew up untamed and extravagant. He never went to play with the Salvans children, whose father was then a distinguished doctor, much respected by the country folk. James's main ambition in life was to make money, yet never finding the right way, but he liked to show it off. He had also a selfish child-like inclination to do good that captivated Maria's attention. Of course, she had been touched by the magic wand of love, besides she believed she knew what she was doing; that is why she smiled at the priest's question and said 'Yes,' without hesitation.

'It's a grand view from here,' she said, opening her arms, 'and what a big piece of blue sky we can see.'

From here, from Can Salvans, for more than twenty years she had been looking at these lovely shapes against the sky and the fields which lay at their feet, but never tired of it; down at the plain, the wide flat river bed with broken threads of silvery water, the fields squared up in brown, ochre and yellow. Towns, villages and more hills, then the ethereal blue silhouette of the Holy Mountain. All the eye could see was her homeland, beautiful land; who knew if she would see it again.

'*Terra beneida*,' she murmured.

'Maria, face the camera please,' James said, pressing her waist to turn her, 'you will take that photo with you.'

And certainly she would, no matter what the picture; many years after she needed only to close her eyes and the view of the valley would come to her as clear as it was on her wedding day.

Le Devesa is an inn, folded inside the lap of the mountain amongst the pine forest. It is famous for its spring of mineral water and its spiced chicken roasted on a wood pine fire in the open air. The water was by that time bottled and carried by cart over the hilltop to be sold in the town of Badalona. In here the reception lunch had been prepared. Later, Maria could not remember if they ate fowl and drank the mineral water, probably neither, but there was champagne in abundance and the wedding cake,

which was a surprise present from her mother, on the top of which two little dolls were dressed as a Bride and Bridegroom. Now, with her back to the landscape, she faced her family. All were there, all showing sincere goodwill.

Maria was the fifth of her father's nine children; some of them were already married, counting sixteen in all. She was a bit like the black sheep of the family, deserting her clan by her marriage and her forthcoming emigration. But, how wonderful they all were to her and they didn't seem to mind. Among animated conversation James and Maria were cutting the tall white cake.

'Be careful with the couple,' said someone, 'your marriage happiness will last as long as you keep them.'

'Oh, nonsense, that is only superstition,' said someone else.

Maria did not reply but moved them carefully away. 'I will keep them as long as I can,' she thought.

Now it was a joyful time, full of excitement and everyone's exuberance.

'Do you have the tickets?'

'No,' they answered, 'but the Work Permit has arrived.'

'When do you leave?'

'We don't know yet; as soon as we receive the passages in three or four days,' James assured.

The luncheon finished, the newly-weds were to go, waved goodbye, lightly saying, 'See you at the airport...'

Whilst getting into the car Maria said, 'Even if we do not see all of them this is better than a farewell at the airport, isn't it James?'

Through the pine forest down the mountain side the car was taking them across the dry river bed to the village, until it came to a stop in front of the modest, much-in-need-of-painting door of her mother's house. There she began to take off her bridal dress with slowness near to regret, for such a pretty gown that took mother and daughter so many hours of sewing and only such a short time to have been worn. She folded and wrapped it. 'I shall take it with me, after all it won't take much room, will it James?'

'No darling,' his arms around her, his lips seeking the kiss, 'anything you say,' his embrace becoming dangerously intense.

'We had better go now, they will be coming back here in a minute,' she said, moving reluctantly away from him.

'All right then, let's go to collect the motorbike at my parents' home,' and taking a small case, 'is this what we need for now?'

'Yes, and that is the key to the flat of my brother Tolomeu. He says it is ready for us.'

That summer afternoon of 1957 Barcelona had not yet experienced the tourism which in later years was to transform the city so much; it was then quiet, drowsing in the heat and very domestic. James and Maria sat in the park sipping an iced drink. Maria was indeed enjoying the afternoon rest after the hectic previous hours, days and even weeks. Now she felt perfectly happy just sitting there doing nothing, not even thinking of the next step she was to take. But James was restless, like someone who dare not miss an appointment. He could barely hide his impatience and soon had her on the back of his motorbike, driving fast out of town. It was pointless to tell him of the beauty the sunset gives to the perspective of the large avenues with their pink-mauve colourings, unique to this Mediterranean capital – he would not hear; he would not see.

The flat where they began their honeymoon was only a few kilometres away from Barcelona. Her brother, his wife and son had gone on holiday; they would stay there until their departure. The house was small and cool. The open balcony had a lace trimmed curtain that let in all the sounds of carts rolling and dogs barking, all the smells of cattle and dusty soil, which this farming village emanated. In the bedroom a large four-poster bed looked generously inviting; James began to take off her clothes one by one, gently with tenderness, anticipating the delight of the fulfilment of their mutual complete possession of each other.

The next morning, her waking was the most wonderful in Maria's life. She opened her eyes to see close to her the shining face of her husband looking at her with big ecstatic eyes, overflowing with happiness; she felt a pang of deep emotion, for such an expressive bright light she had never seen in anybody's face.

'Don't move, darling, I'll get your breakfast.'

She let her head drop again onto the pillow with a sweet smile; she had given everything, her will too. A few moments later James came in carrying a glass half-full with a dark yellowish liquid.

'My breakfast? What is it?'

'Drink it, this will make you feel fit for the rest of the day.'

'All right...ugh!...wine and...?'

'A beaten egg, finish it up.'

She knew a good wife should be obedient so she swallowed this raw egg and sweet wine, for a good start in her role. That first day was Sunday, and joyfully they went about – seeing their parents and to Mass – and from place to place in an elated state as if they had wings. Maria's stomach felt slightly sick since the morning, nevertheless, she was completely captivated by her husband's happiness and she couldn't take her glance or herself away from him. In years to come the memory of that shining gaze would comfort her.

They had their Work Permit and their passports ready, their tickets, it was hoped, would arrive very soon from England; in the meantime they went for a day trip to Montserrat. Maria's wish was to give her bridal bouquet to the Virgin according to the tradition – 'No marriage is well done, until the couple have paid homage to the Virgin that is Brown.' The mountain itself is unique and exceptional in its construction. It is said that in the beginning this was only a uniform peak in the middle of the Catalan plain, when one day descended from heaven a host of angels carrying golden saws and soon they made a marvellous temple for the Mother of God, whose dark-coloured image has a sweet enigmatic smile, inspiring the faith of the Catalan people.

It was another glorious day. Maria sat sideways on the pillion seat, her arms around James and her head resting on his back. Enjoying everything, the landscape so blue and green, the motorbike roared up the hill, passing enormous polished rocks, rocks that seem light but are strong. The air which bit into her was warm, and so was her husband's body, and the young woman felt overflowing with love towards the man, the land, and the sheer joy of living. Inside the Basilica, though, she felt that she was very insignificant, perhaps insecure, she began to pray fervently to the Virgin for guidance and help in her new life. Both were kneeling hand in hand, Maria had the solid faith that a protective Christian environment had given her, with a long life routine of churchgoing. Her character had developed as strong and straight as those rocks of Montserrat. Against this, James's convictions were very faint, neither his family nor he ever went to church, apart from the social necessities of christenings,

First Communions or weddings and funerals. His eyes were wandering about the temple, the richness it contained and the people around. Couldn't he pray? Maria hoped he would learn, she couldn't believe anyone was an absolute unbeliever; only that some people just hadn't the right knowledge. She was sure her influence and example would bring him to the right path.

On the third day a letter arrived. 'This will be the tickets,' said James opening it hastily, only to let the envelope drop in disappointment. 'There are no tickets Maria, read this and see what they say,' and he handed her a sheet of typewritten paper.

'It is from the employer's secretary.'

'Go on, translate.'

'She says that Mr G. is on holiday abroad but wants us to be in England by the end of August when he comes back. We should go by plane to Manchester and someone will meet us there.' She paused, then, lifting her eyes from the letter, in a bewailing voice continued, 'we have to pay now for the tickets, although he will repay the fares as soon as we arrive in Leeds, but James, what are we going to do, we haven't got the money.'

He had quickly recovered and replied, 'Oh, don't worry, I'll find some.'

James, with his erratic jobs and his easy spending manner, never possessed any money but somehow he always managed to look as if he had a pocket full. Maria had been using her savings pursuing a musical career, and the last few pesetas had been spent on clothes. Their only prospects for the future rested on the job in England.

Without delay James set off to find the means to overcome this problem. At the end of the day he had seen and talked to all his friends but no-one could help with money.

At last his sister, a soft hearted girl, was able to lend them the money, although unwillingly, as she said to Maria, 'Look Maria, I'm sorry about this, I didn't want to tell you but I have lent money to my brother many times and he has never repaid it. This is a lot more now and my husband is complaining. Four thousand pesetas is a lot of money! This amount is all we have in the Savings Bank.'

'Please Carmen,' Maria said with an effort to hide her profound dislike of begging to her, 'we will send it back straight away, I promise you – I will do it myself.'

Added to her disappointment was the discovery that James's motorbike, the sale of which she had hoped would provide some money to start them off, was on hire purchase and was owing as much as its actual value. She soon realised they had nothing – absolutely nothing – no house, no furniture, not even a peseta in their pockets, and worse than that, for her, they were in debt. In fact, their only valuable possession was a paper – that Work Permit, with a promise of well-paid jobs for both of them by a man they did not know, in a foreign country, far away from their homeland, and their families and friends. Nevertheless, the light in her husband's eyes was still shining, and she was herself full of eagerness and confidence.

That evening, whilst both were cleaning their teeth in the Wash Corner, James said 'Look Maria,' indicating with his outstretched hand the few toiletries lined up on the shelf, 'All that is ours, quite a lot, isn't it?'

Maria looked at the objects, then at James in astonishment as she realised he was not joking. As she thought how few belongings he must have had in his life, an overwhelming wave of love filled her and, embracing him with tenderness she replied, 'Yes, darling, it is quite a lot. We'll pack tomorrow.'

She was very much in love with her husband, yet deep in her soft voice there was an echo of compassion. She did not know how profound this sentiment was in her or how much part of her being, but what really had driven her so close to him was perhaps not alone the woman's love to her man, although to analyse her feelings was not an exercise akin to her impulsive nature.

The next morning Maria was at her mother's, packing. As it happened, and in spite of what everyone had been telling them for the past few months about being so foolish to marry penniless, they did possess quite a lot. She didn't know how to get everything into the cases. The trunk was almost full of winter clothes, blankets, sheets – useful presents.

'Mama, I shall have to leave something,' she said to her mother who was following her traffic up and down, 'Will you keep all these for me?'

'Yes dear. What are they? Books, papers? The mandolin as well?'

'Oh, no. I'll take it with me and some music papers too. But not all of them.'

'But, do you really think you are going to have time to play?' and her voice broke in disillusionment. So many hopes had been built up in the artistic career of this daughter and now she had married, and what a marriage and for what? To start work! When any other girl would go into marriage prepared to leave work. But Maria, she was different. Her mother could not understand her and even less in the way she believed she would still be able to keep up with her music.

Maria took the black case from the chair and before placing it inside the trunk opened it; there was her mandolin, lying inside wrapped in red velvet like a precious jewel. Looking at it she was quite still – as if her heart had lost a beat – then she gently touched a cord producing a single round – RE. That note alone lifted her into the land of dreams. The sound of music was magic to her – in a second she could see the vast distances of a wonderful life. Did she see herself past the stage from girl to womanhood, playing nursery rhymes or teaching precious infants? We do not know.

The sound died away and she closed the case, proceeding then to finish the packing.

'What were you saying Mama?' meeting her mother's bewildered look she added, 'Oh, yes mama, you'll see how I can find time for everything. Besides, if I leave my mandolin here, I certainly shall not be able to play it. Look, I am also taking the couple from the wedding cake for luck. And this picture of Our Lady de Montcada; she will protect us from evil.'

'You will have to pay a surcharge for your luggage.'

'Sure, but that doesn't matter – well that is all then.'

'What time did you say the plane leaves?'

'After midnight at two o'clock. But mama, you are going to bed.'

'No, no! Blanca also wants to come and Joan is taking us in the car – the boys are going by train. Your mother-in-law says they have hired a car and are all going, even the baby.'

'Well...' Maria said with impatience, wishing the farewells were all said.

It was midnight when the cars were going by the Grand Via de Barcelona. Throughout the city it was never completely asleep. Barcelona rested quietly under its own light which did not come from the sky, but always this beloved city was enchanting.

Waiting at airports was and is always nerve-racking – 'Mother, we shall come back to see you for holidays,' said Maria, and after a short silence she added, 'don't worry mama, everything will be all right.'

Now she was embracing her. No tears there, although someone else was weeping – James's mother and his father blowing his nose alternately with his recommendations –

'Don't lose your documents or your passport.'
'Son, keep your coat on, it is always cold and foggy there.'

The old man seemed really worried, as if the sun never shone in England and summer never arrived there either.

A voice through the loudspeaker was calling their flight – they had then to move away from their sad families. The young couple, who had been happy all the time, now at the last moment, showed some emotion, saying goodbye with trembling lips. Maria looked at her mother but couldn't speak – then turned her back away. How cruel can one be! She didn't realise how sad a farewell is for those who are left behind. Their adventure absorbed them so utterly there was no thought at all for others. As soon as they were out in the open, the dark sky over them, the stars had descended upon the earth, to escort the large airliner, that magnificent steel bird, waiting to take them on its wings to other lands, and new experiences; there was no more looking back to the little people left behind; very dear, yes, but not so important.

Well fastened in, with belts on their seats, the plane took off. Our stomachs have roots, invisible but deep growing in the soil which bore our first steps. The pull of the plane was now up-rooting them, and Maria felt slightly sick. It was the pain of the immigrant whose roots exposed, sensitive, will not grow deep in any other soil, not even back in its own. It is also the anguish of the exiled that he is a foreigner forever to the people of his adopted land, and hence becomes a stranger in his own.

IT WAS ABOUT six o'clock in the morning. The plane had been flying above the clouds, through glorious sky, and was now abandoning the clear dawn as it plunged into a mass of cotton-wool like clouds.

'It is raining' said James, looking through the little window.

'Yes, it can be said that summer is finished by the end of August.'

'How are they going to know that we are the ones?'

'By our frightened expressions, surely,' she said, with a glance to the other passengers, 'how strange, they all look English now, don't you think so? When we left Barcelona it was not so obvious.'

They landed. He unfastened his belt and proceeded to unfasten hers.

'Where will we find our luggage?' asked James.

The wet air touched their tired faces like refreshing balsam. They followed all the other travellers to the customs.

James was nervously carrying his papers, and seemed ready to relinquish them to Maria, as he said, 'You understand this people, see what they are saying here,' and he gave the documents to his wife, pushing her forward.

The officer took their passports with the permits, looking at them carefully, and kept them while explaining to the couple that they were in order, but, he said, it was necessary for a medical check up before proceeding further into the country. At that early hour the doctor had to be fetched, so they must wait.

Left alone, Maria commented, 'He is very attentive. We can have coffee in the meantime.'

'But why the doctor in Spain made a certificate of good health if it is not valid here?' James complained.

'You see dear, it will be in case we have contracted any illness while flying,' answered Maria, accommodating herself into an easy chair well disposed to waiting. 'Some coffee will be served there.'

'Oh, yes, how do you think I'll pay for it?'

'Ah, yes, it is true we don't have any English money. But maybe they will change pesetas. How many do we have?'

She had none. Since their marriage she carried no money in her purse. He took out his wallet and, showing two hundred peseta notes, said, 'My father, poor man, gave them to me at the last minute, he said they will come in handy.'

'Oh, that is good.'

'But now we better not move from here in case the officer comes for us.'

The place was quiet, nevertheless the time passed easily enough for the couple. A young woman came in the waiting room, trying to be casual. She was glancing over everyone there until her eyes fell on them. 'Are you Spanish?'

'Yes.'

'Mr and Mrs Martines?'

Both nodded.

'I work for Mr Gill. I am to take you to the station. I am sorry you had to wait.'

James was smiling with relief whilst Maria replied, 'Oh no, we were not waiting for you. The doctor has to see us yet, we are told not to go away from here.'

'Very well then, I shall look after your luggage, if you give me the tickets, please? Yes, it will be put into my car.'

And in a flash the girl was gone. 'What a decided Englishwoman, are they all the same?'

'Yes they are very resolute,' Maria affirmed.

Then a man from the immigration office arrived. James was taken to one apartment and Maria to another. The medical examination was thoroughly done, when asked if she was pregnant, Maria blushed as she had been married only one week. She was worried, fearing the doctor would think she was lying. But they came out clear and their passports were returned duly stamped. The young secretary had been waiting impatiently, and said that the train was due to leave for Leeds at nine-thirty and there was little time. Whilst driving, she said she worked in Manchester, where Mr Gill had a branch of his men's tailoring business. The train journey from Manchester to Leeds seemed very long to the couple, despite their interest in the landscape. They could see nothing but monotonous rain and rows of stone houses with an extraordinary quantity of chimneys. Not just one per house, but fifty to a dozen, woods of chimneys, and there were no trees. The country appeared little inhabited, and many open spaces seemed bare, smooth old green, grey and mauve, yet freshly wet. They were told the train would take an hour and half. Not a minute later, or a minute earlier. Exactly on time the train carefully chased its way through the spread net of rails and entered the station.

'We are in Leeds, James, have you seen those enormous fat chimneys there? What could they be for?'

'It must be a very big city. It has taken its time to enter. Come, get ready, the train has stopped.'

'Someone will wait for us. Better if we don't hurry. It'll give them chance to see us.'

But the couple stepped off the train immediately.

'Look, this man will carry our luggage.' Maria called the porter.

Then, out on the platform, looking for someone who would be looking for them, they felt a bit lost as nobody was there; everybody had gone except for the porter who followed them up and down.

'We shall have to wait,' said Maria.

'No dear, no, we have the address, do we? So we take a taxi and that's it.'

'It is better we wait here. We have no English money, remember.'

James was not listening, impatiently wanting to get out of the station.

'Lets remain here,' Maria insisted, 'we have been told that someone will fetch us.'

'You are an ignorant,' he replied, 'it's you who are...'

The porter wanted to know where to leave their luggage, but Maria didn't know what to tell him. Whilst James was insisting they go, the porter went to consign their cases and left the pair.

Then James took Maria by her arm and ordered, 'Let's go.'

She shook off his hand replying, 'Where do you want to go?'

'To a bank, to change some money. What do you think? Let's go. You know nothing of the world.'

'I do,' she replied, very annoyed.

She didn't consider herself ignorant, nor did she think for a moment that her decision to wait was wrong. She was sure she was able to decide for herself in any given situation, as she had managed on her own before. Well, why did he have to tell her that she was ignorant? She felt very vexed, but all the same she had no option but to follow him. They left the station. Outside, there were many streets leading from the square. The Post Office building was on the left. Two or three banks showed their signs. They went to the first on the right.

'Come on Maria, do not pull that face.'

To James, all the irritation of a few minutes ago seemed forgotten. Inside the bank he passed her the passports and the money to get changed. It was easy, and in a short while they were out holding hands and smiling. The weather had cleared, the sky was bright, the old grey stones were shining and people were dressed in vivid colours, which gave the city a pretty look.

'Now we can take a taxi and go to Mr Gill's house,' said James with conviction.

They were walking around the square towards the station, when a man dressed in navy blue began to follow them. He carried something in his hand to which he addressed frequent glances, his eyes anxious to recapture the sight of the couple walking around the crowded pavements. At last, he caught up to them and touched James's arm. Maria looked at him and noticed that he was out of breath, and unable to speak.

Instead he stretched out his arm and Maria immediately recognised a photograph of them both and exclaimed, 'That's us, well. Have you come for us?'

'I am happy to find you,' the man answered, his breathing returning to normal. 'If you allow me I'll take you to your destination.'

So they all went to the station for the luggage. Inside the car, James commented with the smug satisfaction of one who always get things right. 'You see Maria, everything goes all right.'

'Yes, of course,' she gave in, 'but we could have saved this man the worry of having to look for us all around the square.'

Passing the centre of the town they took an avenue where the houses no longer stood in rows at each side of the road, but were detached with individual gardens full of flowers. The chauffeur kept driving, immutable, on the left side of the road. As they got further from the centre the houses became larger and the gardens more luxurious. James and Maria were trying to guess which one would be the one they were going to. But the car suddenly cut to the right and proceeded along a narrow lane, leaving the handsome villas behind. Now there were fields, groups of trees, and here and there a house with its roof popping out above the woods.

The car continued steadily, turning bends.

'It's going to be one of those, very large, you'll see.'

'It'll be very far from Leeds.'

Then the chauffeur said, 'We are here,' and turned the car into a drive, past a spotless white open gate flanked by pink and red geraniums, bordering a lodge and up to the main entrance of the residence. The house was a big, irregular construction of new brick-stone without any sense of style, or maybe it had. Two Victorian lamplights hung solidly in the wall each at either side of the door.

Somebody had been waiting for them, because the door opened before they reached the threshold. A woman dressed in white, small, fair and rosy, with little sky blue eyes which wandered like those of a child, showed the couple in.

They stepped onto the thick carpet and both at once looked down to their feet, searching for the cause of the surprising softness under their shoes. Then their eyes followed its length to the wall and rose slowly to the ceiling, whose luxury was equal to it. Plastered leaves centred towards the crystals of the hanging chandelier, sparkling like myriads of chiselled diamonds. Unexpected, it was more breathtaking, and they gazed at each other with some apprehension. Meanwhile, unnoticed, the woman in the white overall disappeared without a sound. Then another person in that carpeted mansion appeared. The woman who now stood in front of them was no doubt the mistress of the house. Her composed air was agreeable, but her word was not.

'I know nothing about you. It is my husband who engaged you and now he is away.'

To that unexpected affirmation followed a pause. Maria thought she ought to reply, but she was so perplexed that she could not think what to say. They had obviously arrived at a very improper time and it was inconvenient to the lady. Perhaps it was true that she knew nothing of them, but then who sent the chauffeur for them?

Mrs Gill seemed to enjoy the uneasiness of the newly arrived couple, and she asked with cold politeness, 'Have you had a good journey?'

'Yes, yes, very good,' answered Maria promptly, 'thank you.'

'Doesn't your husband speak English?'

'No, not yet,' Maria replied.

'He must learn it quick,' and now in the intonation of her voice was authority.

In the meantime, another character appeared. A girl of six or seven, dressed with shorts and a yellow jumper, her abundant chestnut hair in a ponytail. Slender and vivacious, she was curiously observing the foreigners and even circled round to see them from all angles.

'Penelope, go away and play,' Mrs Gill said in a curt, imperative tone so disagreeable that Maria thought the little girl must be a servant's daughter. She disappeared instantly. 'You wait here,' the mistress said to the couple, and she left too.

'What a big nose has that woman,' James commented without any sign of respect, 'what do we do now?'

As an answer, the door opened and the woman in the white overall motioned for them to follow her. They passed through the kitchen into a dining room where the table was laid. They sat.

'Mrs Gill said that you can now have lunch with us, and afterwards we'll take you to your flat. I am the cook, my name is Anne Ross,' the woman explained, her little blue eyes surrounded by tiny freckles. Then a tall man entered, with very white hair which gave him a distinguished look, diminished by a waiter's jacket that was clearly not made to measure. 'My husband Paul,' introduced Anne, 'what are your names?'

'James Martines...Maria.'

'Very nice, we have been waiting for you, we knew that a driver from the factory would bring you here. Mr Gill is travelling but is due to come back tomorrow, so that means you can rest today.'

The man was explaining all this very kindly, whilst the woman was very briskly serving potatoes, vegetables and meat together in a large plate, although everything had been cooked separately. The young pair felt very hungry. Maria was translating, and everyone was trying to make it easy for James. His work was going to be the maintenance and driving of the family's cars, of which they had three. He would also have to clean the windows on the outside of the house, as Paul was doing the inside, and he was to wait the table on Paul's day off.

As soon as James heard the latter he protested vigorously, 'I am not going to put on a white jacket like this one, no, I am not. I will not do that, I have come here to be a chauffeur, not a waiter.'

Maria looked at him, alarmed, 'Darling, we have come to do whatever we are told to do, don't forget that from now on we are servants. Don't you understand? Please don't create problems from the beginning.'

'What is the matter?' asked Mr Ross.

'My husband doesn't know how to wait at a table,' replied Maria, worried, 'can I do it?'

'I don't think so, Mrs Gill will not like it because you are to cook for me when I am off,' explained Mrs Ross.

'Well we'll see,' said Mr Ross, who had adopted a patronising attitude, 'I'll speak to Mrs Gill. Wednesday all day and Saturday afternoon are our days off, and yours will be Sundays and Thursday afternoons.'

Lunch finished, Anne Ross gave them some victuals, continuing her instructions: 'Maria, you have to make your own meals and do your own shopping. You must be here by nine o'clock in the morning, and you'll have one and a half hours for your lunch. In the evening if there is more work you must stay later, although otherwise until six o'clock; here, eggs, sugar, bread, tea and milk to start with, and if you need anything else come and ask me.'

'Look James, here help me to carry these, she is giving them to us, she says they are showing us our house now. Is that the one?' Maria was pointing to a little house on the left side of the gate, some one hundred metres away.

The girl with the ponytail joined them, wanting to carry things. They all went up to the flat. The stairs there were luxuriously carpeted too. In the landing was their luggage, although it seemed to belong there, and not a thought entered their minds as to who brought it up.

Maria and James went quickly from one room to another, eagerly inspecting their home. It was delightful. It had a modern kitchen and a complete bathroom in pink. The sitting room had two windows, and one looked out over the vegetable garden whilst the other faced the house. There was a fireplace and nice furniture. Anne Ross asked if they had any sheets, and Maria replied yes, they had. Mr Ross said he would bring some coal so they could get the fire going, and the two servants went out.

The little girl was following the couple, charmed by the Catalan prattle. She said its sound had some familiarity, yet she couldn't catch a single word with meaning. Then Mr Ross came up with the coal and some short little pieces of wood and proceeded to prepare the fire. But Maria protested that it was not cold.

'Ah, but, yes. The house has been empty for two weeks and needed airing,' he said, leaving it and turning to the girl. 'Penelope, does your mother know you are here?'

Penelope put up her chin with an insolent gesture and didn't even look at him or bother to answer. Kneeling in front of the grate, she started to manipulate the newspapers so she could make a fire. Taking a sheet, she spread it on the floor, then proceeded to curl one corner and rolled it tightly along forming a long strip, which she then folded and tied in to a neat knot, putting it on the fire grill and beginning to make another.

James and Maria watched, fascinated by her ability. 'Who has taught you to do that?'

'I have seen Mr Ross doing it. It's easy, see? Look, and if you make a pile of them well, you have no need for any wood. I'll show you how we get the fires going in England.'

In a little while the flames were sneaking up the chimney fast and the coal began to burn.

'Now, shall I help you unpack?'

'No thank you, we shall do it later, now we like to rest, our journey has been a long one.'

'I am going then, bye, bye. I'll see you after.' And she skidded down and out of the flat.

'What a clever little girl. Do you think she belongs to the family?' asked Maria.

'I would think so,' affirmed James, 'she has a big nose like Mrs Gill's'

But instantly they forgot about the others and turned to each other in a tender embrace.

Putting her head on her husband's shoulders, she said sweetly to him, 'Let's go and see our bedroom...there are two beds!'

'We'll join them.'

'But the blankets will not reach.'

'Perhaps, yes, we'll try.'

Soon the beds were set in such a manner that they could sleep together. Pleased with the work they had done, the desire to sleep overcame them completely. True, the journey had been a long one, their night without sleep, and surely they could have a rest now. James moved to draw the curtains, and then went close to Maria.

'My little love, how well shall we live here,' he said softly, taking her into his arms, 'let me make love to you.'

Some time later, the couple, in their renewed vitality, began to unpack. All their belongings, scattered about the flat, became obviously insufficient.

'We need many things,' said Maria, 'we don't even have a pot to warm water or milk, so we shall have to ask Anne Ross to borrow one until we can buy ours. I'll go now.'

She went, walking up to the big house in an elated state of joyous expectation. Little by little they were going to buy all they needed for the house. They would have a lovely home. The first wages would buy the things they had borrowed, the second another pot, and some plates and teacups, then next a frying pan.

When she came back to the flat they prepared supper together. Eggs, milk and bread, very simple but it tasted delicious. Not a thing around them, nor the lack of things was inconvenient or worrying to them. Everything seemed perfect and happiness shone out of their eyes. Like two birds, they ran and jumped through the flat in incessant chatter, arranging objects, furniture, planning the future. It was long past midnight when they finally sat down to write letters telling their families the news of their arrival.

The following morning, Maria opened the curtains to look out; it was a beautiful sunny day. She could see the greenhouses, and laid in two rows were vegetable plots. Further on were

the woodlands, with the city of Leeds nowhere to
be seen. She had no idea which direction it could
be or, she thought, Barcelona, left so far away.
It had definitely been left behind, as was the
warm weather, she reflected, whilst making the
bed that, with two blankets, had not felt too
warm. Her thoughts went to James; how would
he manage at this moment? He had left the
flat at eight o'clock quite happy, although he
could not yet understand a word of English, so
how was he to know what to do? She found
herself impatient to go but did not dare to make
an appearance before her time. Nevertheless, her
mind took her there already, and her legs took
her down the stairs and out. The door to the flat
was at the back of the house and she had to turn
half round it to go to the larger house.

Looking towards the garage where her
husband would be, she didn't notice a person
coming out of the house she had just left,
advancing towards her. A man, tall and thin,
stood beside her. She stopped, startled.

'In future you mustn't make so much noise.
We have not been able to sleep all night.'

Maria's eyes rounded with surprise. She
glanced up to the man's face, netted with creases,
his longish fair hair covering half his eyes, which
were big and sad like a fish out of water. Maria's
glance went to the windows of her flat, then to
the window below it and then back to the man
with a flush of comprehension.

'You live there,' more affirmation than
questioning.

'Yes, and me wife and children. We have not been able to sleep at all!' he repeated.

'Oh, I'm sorry, forgive us. We didn't know anybody lived here. No one told us. We never thought...we had been unpacking...I am sorry, we.'

'I shall speak to Mr Gill,' interrupted the man, 'this will not happen again,' and he abruptly turned his back on her. She remained still for a few seconds, staring at this tall figure, and became suddenly depressed as if she had broken the first cup from a new tea set.

When she reached the big house her husband was in the garage polishing a black car, the shine from it rivalling that in his eyes.

'You'll see,' he said to his wife, 'how pleased they will be with me, I am going to look after their cars better than anyone else has ever done. This one is the Rover, I think it's the everyday one. The Rolls Royce is in the garage below our flat, for grand occasions, Mr Ross says he'll show it to me later. The other car is a Bentley, it is fantastic!' and to collaborate his enthusiasm took Maria by her waist, lifting her up into the air and dancing around the car.

'Let me down, please, let me down. What they'll think if anyone sees us?' she escaped her husbands caresses and quickly passed the door into the kitchen.

She asked Anne Ross who the man was who lived under their flat. 'He is the gardener. Yes, I know he is very cross. He has been here complaining, he says he's going to tell Mr Gill.'

'But we knew nothing. Is it because they are ill or something?'

'I think he doesn't like foreigners,' continued the woman, lowering her voice. 'Mr Gill is very pleased with him because he is an excellent gardener. His wife is very young and she often runs away from him. Mrs Gill can't stand her,' her voice becoming a whisper, her little eyes moving continuously from one door to another, 'she does not like her at all.' Suddenly Anne Ross changed her tone and said, 'Now, I will show you your work Maria, come with me.'

They went upstairs, and she began to instruct Maria in her job. This person was intimidated by the personality of her mistress, reflected Maria, she was full of servilism and petty nosiness, but she couldn't be bad with those transparent clear eyes, and perhaps was only jealous of Maria's place in this household.

Anne Ross was opening drawer after drawer, and when she opened the shoe cupboard Maria's admiration turned to astonishment. There were rows of them!

'Is it possible,' she began to count, 'twenty...thirty two... thirty four pairs of shoes. What ever for? There is no need.'

'Of course she needs them,' replied the servant with a sympathetic tone, 'you have to learn a lot of things, Maria.'

How did a person with only one pair of feet need at one time over thirty pairs of shoes? With so much footwear, the lady could walk around the world and see half of humanity barefooted, and happy to have just one pair. What had Maria to learn? The variation of people's needs or how people call their greediness need, thus covering with a cloak of respectability what is selfish covetousness and gross injustice to one's neighbour. No, at that moment Maria's ideas about social justice and Christian thought for others were cemented,and she made no further reply. She inwardly decided to fit into her role well, and to try to be a servant under a servant for the sake of her husband and her own happiness.

When Mr Gill arrived, he at once took care of his new employees. He spoke to Maria deferentially, and explained what he was expecting from them. The large Rolls was taken out of the garage to James, who was given a test and instructed in the special care of the car. Mr Gill also confirmed the immediate payment of their ticket money. This gentleman seemed just and prudent, although slow in his outward manners; Maria became well aware of his cold and distancing correctness. Not a word was said about the gardener.

The weather was now cold. It was a long walk from the house to the end of the lane to the main road, then the bus stop. James and Maria went to the town on their days off. They looked at the shops, and buying something to add to their home was wonderful, whilst dreaming about what they would buy the next week. They still needed so many things! Their days off were fun, but the long walk back home was not, especially for James, who never liked to use his legs, preferring wheels as transport. He wished they had a car.

So, one day at the end of October he entered the flat and shouted triumphantly, 'I have bought a car!'

In the kitchen preparing dinner, Maria turned suddenly as if thunder had struck. 'Good heavens, what do you mean? Impossible!'

She looked at him in disbelief and he repeated his affirmation. Her mind debated anxiously, a car was so far from the scope of her dreams, the upsetting of her scale of priorities, a car was utter extravagance, nonsense.

'There is no sense in it...it can not be.'

'The Rosses have a car!'

'But they have been working for some time.'

'We need one more than they do.'

'We need a lot more other things before a car!'

'You don't know what you're talking about!'

'I do. You do not know what you are doing!'

'We are going to fetch it tonight.'

'No, we are not. I don't want a car. We can't afford a car.'

'It is done.'

'How have you done it? How could you? Without saying a word to me. Oh, no, no, and no. Why do you have to spend the money we both earn? We do not want anything we can't afford yet. Don't you understand? Why didn't you consult me? Why? The money is mine too. Don't you realise it?' She couldn't believe he'd do anything without telling her. Since their marriage they were doing everything together, why, then, did he do it?

'Oh, you are stupid James, very stupid, you are an idiot, you shouldn't have done it, we don't have enough money.'

'The idiot is you,' he shouted back, 'you are an ignorant, it makes no difference if we have the money or not. We buy it on hire purchase, and it is not nonsense to have a car. Here, everyone has a vehicle.'

'I do not want to acquire anything by this method,' now she was sobbing, 'I am not coming tonight, I am not,' and she rushed to lock herself in the bathroom.

There she remained, waiting for him to call at the door and beg her to come out. But the minutes passed, and, holding her sobs, she listened intently wishing he'd come to his senses. Presently she heard him descending the stairs; he had served himself, eaten his lunch and gone without a word to her. She burst into loud cries. As her wretchedness became more bearable she opened the bathroom door, as soon she had to be back at work.

In the evening, Maria went to the flat feeling bewildered. James was waiting for her and said in a careless tone, 'No need to take your coat off, we are going to fetch the car. The garage people are expecting us, we have to fill out some forms.'

With the calm desperation of the inevitable, she continued to take off her coat. When he made a gesture of impatience, she didn't answer and proceeded to unbutton her white overall.

'Come on, are you going to be all evening?' he asked, and took her coat in one hand and grabbed her arm with the other, pushing her downstairs and out of the flat. The night was black, dark as a wolf's throat. All was still and frozen, and they could not see whether they trod on grass or ground. All had the same solidness. Maria dragged a pace behind, crossly and silently.

'This long walk is terrible.' His voice was now mild, almost tender. 'You see, in this country nobody walks, every family has a car.'

'The gardener has not,' muttered Maria.

'He has a bicycle,' passing his arm over her shoulder and leaning gently added, 'besides I can't walk so well, you know.' The young wife continued walking in silence, but her heart was gradually melting with warm compassion.

The car was bought, paying by instalments. It was an old 1940 Ford, dirty and scrappy. James said confidently that he would soon have it transformed like new. He began the task the same evening, and nothing could deter him. No freezing temperatures, nor lack of good light, as he used the interior roof light of the car. He stripped off the rotten upholstery and decided they would go tomorrow to buy plastic material to recover the seats. His thrill was great, now he had his own car he could manipulate it. For him it was like an extension of himself, the indispensable compliment of his life. A machine where he could exercise his skills and impose that power every man's soul pains to possess. To his glazed eyes, this Ford was as fantastic as Mr Gill's Rolls Royce. James had the ability to isolate the impulses of his wishes, maintaining them alive and disentangled from other reasoning alien to his ego.

So it was that the time he'd lost for work did not count. The going around garages when looking for the object of his desire when he was supposed to be helping Mr Ross to clean the windows, or cutting firewood did not count. The anxiety with which his wife waited for him, dreading Mrs Gill's questions on his delay in coming back from the factory where he took Mr Gill every morning. No, that did not count either. His interest could not be roused outside the image of himself as a chauffeur-motor mechanic. It was an irksome struggle for Maria to admit this. She repeated Mrs Gill's complaints to him in vain, as he would not be affected. She herself was. She was always looking anxiously through the windows in between dusting and making beds, wishing with all her might to see the car stationed in front of the door exactly where Mrs Gill wanted, and dreading her questions.

'Has your husband come back from the factory yet?'

'No madam,' Maria would answer timidly, 'perhaps he had to do some errand for Mr Ross.'

She worked hard to please the mistress. She kept the bedrooms spotlessly clean and tidy. On the cook's day off she cooked the meal and served so well that no one remembered that it was actually James's job.

Yet Mrs Gill often complained to Maria about James's work. The house work he was supposed to do and also the lack of attention in the work he did do, how he failed to put the car rug over her knees on cold days. To this, Maria explained that he was not doing so because it seemed to him a lack of respect and excess of familiarity, but told Mrs Gill she would mention it to him. Yes madam, the chauffeur would tuck her knees under the blanket. She would always speak up for him.

The ten pounds a week of shared wages was quite good money, notwithstanding the expense of the car. They managed, spending little on food because James thought about catching birds for their meat. He skilfully made a few traps with wire fastened to a string which, when tied to a stone, stopped the bird from flying away when caught, but did not kill it. He placed the traps on top of the Rolls garage, which could be reached through the sitting room window. With a good bait, camouflaged by sand, the birds came, lots of them, and bite they did to the unexpected death. They were fat little things, inhabitants of a land with humid and soft soil that is rich in worms. Where people could afford to throw away not only scraps of bread but full slices. Rich, carnivorous people who slaughter cattle and big birds for their table but have an odd tenderness towards little animals.

For some time the couple enjoyed their meals of little birds. It was agreeable in the evenings to sit together plucking blue tits, fat thrushes, blackbirds and sparrows. The soft feathers were carefully put away by Maria, and in time she would make a pillow for her first baby.

They also saved money on vegetables. The garden produced enough for the residents of the estate. The Catalan couple were supposed to have had some from the beginning, but owning to the unfriendliness of the gardener did not get anything until Anne Ross happened to find out. She told her husband, who then told Mr Gill, who advised the gardener to supply the couple with some of the garden produce. From then on, once a week the gardener went to the door of the upstairs flat and left a box containing potatoes and other vegetables in season. Never asking what they required or liked, he simply left the box at the bottom of the stairs.

Anne Ross often gave them the leftovers from their master's table. Many a time it would be a full meal for them both. She used to do it in a manner of great secrecy so exaggerated that Maria thought everyone must know what she was doing. Maria would take the covered plates and rush to her flat. The following morning, feeling the shame of it, she would take pains to hide the plates. But of course that was helping them save more and she was very determined to put more money aside in case of any special event. She had her list of priorities, although her husband did not always agree with them.

One day, after a discussion over the need for saving, Maria thought she had convinced him to put twenty-five pounds into their bank book. The next week they went back to take it out, as James wanted to buy annual insurance on the Ford and something else the car needed. That was, he said, much more important than their savings.

He was very pleased with himself and therefore happy. He was the husband, the master, the one who commands his wife. To him it was logical and natural that the woman was the one who gave in and obeyed him. From boyhood he knew, 'one has to overpower women; if not they will overpower you,' and this and 'man wears the trousers' he had drilled into the marrow of his bones. He could not imagine any other kind of relationship between husband and wife. During their courtship Maria thought it could be different, and she was encouraged in this hope because then his manners and his conduct were of compliance in doing what she liked. Then, he was always seeking her opinion, ready to adapt his wishes to hers and learn her ways. The girl was sure (too sure of herself) that their marriage would be good.

Nonetheless, it is one thing when courting to give the girlfriend some privileges of choosing, deciding and acting, but once a couple have married the relationship must change radically, so that the wife is no longer a person with her own free personality. She is subject to the will of the husband, who, in order to obtain his kind of subjection has the right to use any means he chooses to employ. Some men even believe it is good to give the wife a beating, convinced that women like to be bashed by strong men and will consequently behave in loving submission.

For the time being the conflict between James and Maria was due to their adjustment to the relationship. It is not easy to give one's own privacy in favour of shared intimacy. It is even less easy to give in one's own judgement and reason to mould them into another's criterion. The physical, sexual union is the knot of the matrimonial bow. The intellect remains in the loop and is much more fugitive.

CHRISTIANS CELEBRATE THE coming of the Messiahs on Christmas day. It would seem logical that Jewish people did nothing. Yet it was difficult to discern what the Gill family was celebrating. Maria and James assumed that distant attitude adopted towards them had its base on religious grounds, rather than because they were foreign servants. More so because the master was a mason. Anne Ross would tell them, lowering her voice to a whisper, how there were meetings of the Gran Logia that were so secret not even Mrs Gill was allowed to enter the room. They used to lock themselves in and no woman ever knew what the men did in there.

Some Jewish ceremonies were not so secretive. One day when Maria was on duty she cooked dinner, or, rather, she only had to finish it. Anne Ross always left everything started, with the meat in the oven and the vegetables prepared, and that day it was not a very special meal. Yes, it was good and abundant, but it was invariably so. When she went into the dining room to serve the first course there were candles burning, Mr Gill was standing at the head of the table wearing a black silk cap, and his male children also wore little black bonnets. Maria stopped suddenly, not knowing whether to remain still. The father was cutting the bread and mumbling something, Hebrew prayers no doubt, and then he proceeded to share the pieces of bread with his family. Immediately after he opened a bottle of wine, filled everyone's glasses and they all drunk it and prayed or toasted in a foreign tongue. Afterwards, the father took his cap off and sat down. At this instant they all broke into laughter and merriment. Maria started to serve in silence. It was evident that her presence had been ignored, as no one said a word to her, and she felt deeply that she was a mere machine, and not even an intruder.

The next day she went to the shops, and there was a woman there who sold chickens that were slaughtered properly for the Jewish table.

She was plump and very English looking, and that day her pink, round face was glowing, as she said with a big smile, 'Happy New Year!'

'Many thanks,' replied Maria quickly trying not to show her surprise, as it was only October.

She has taken me for a Jewess, Maria said to herself, Of course, she doesn't know I come here because in Spain we also bleed the animals to death, and we do not just wring their necks off like the English do. Now Maria understood, the Jewish New Year! That's why Penelope had a new dress and the family a ceremony at dinner.

Like Christmas without the Messiah, like a Last Supper without transubstantiation.

Yet the Christian Christmas was common, and the Jewish family were preparing to celebrate. The commercialisation of the feast dominated all over and did not spring suddenly on the twenty-fourth of December. The climate started to build up weeks and weeks before with all sorts of propaganda enticing people to buy, reminding them that the society we live in is for consuming goods only, and that nothing else matters but to buy enough food, drinks and presents to enjoy.

November had just begun when James and Maria went shopping in Leeds and discovered the shops already decorated with bright balls and trembling tinsel. Maria remarked how early it was.

'Oh, the English do things right, do you think they are like us?' replied James. 'Now we are going to do things the same way and we are going to send presents home too, they will be pleased.'

'Yes, but if you buy presents for your family, I want things for mine, there will be too many presents to buy. Why don't we get one of these pretty calendars for each family, eh? And that will not cost as much.'

'No, only a calendar, it's not enough.'

'It is! Think, James, we have a lot of other expenses.'

Nevertheless, he bought presents for each one of his family and calendars for his friends, whilst Maria, who always worried about spending more than they could afford, bought nothing for her family and felt very sad about it. She soon overcame it, engaged as she was preparing for their own Christmas, the first she would spend in her own home. One that was going to set the pattern and be a continuation of her family's tradition. It did not matter where home was, for it was important for Christmas to be as Catalan as she could make it. Now the time had come to put in practice all she had learned when she was growing up. Who had taught her how to peel a potato or dress a turkey? She could not recall, and surely it was not at school in those days, nor with books. She could only remember watching grown ups do things, as the eyes are like a photographic camera and the mind a storeroom that needs to be filled up. Now she looked into it, and joyfully found what she needed. At home we used to do this, Mother used to do that or the other, Maria remembered, and soon she had her shopping list completed. To find the things required in a foreign country was not as easy. Luckily, a parcel came from her mother with the traditional Christmas sweets. Another came from James's family containing the appropriate salamis.

A few days before Christmas James came in carrying a tree, a silver fir, tall and beautiful.

'It is bigger than the gardener's,' he said, 'he has a misery of a tree. When you see the one the masters have! It is fantastic.'

'You have bought one too big for us. Our house is only small, and besides, I want a Pessebre.'

'We'll make one also, you'll see,' he said as he left the room. He came back seconds later with boxes, lights, papers and several objects which he scattered about the room. He opened up some paper decorations. Maria shrank back.

'No, I do not like these fancy papers.'

'Everybody has them up, and balloons, look.'

'It is bad taste. Why don't we go to the woods and pick some greens? I have seen some pine trees.'

He settled himself down to manipulate his little lights. He began to make a small screen with little figures that could move. Meanwhile, Maria was finishing the Christmas cards. How was she to get her way without having to get cross? She did not like the paper strips, she was not having them up! She didn't care if the English homes were thus decorated, but not hers. No, she did not want a pagan fair. A knock at the door startled them both. Who could it be at this late hour of the evening? James went to see.

'Good evening and happy Christmas!'

On hearing Mrs Gill's voice, Maria jumped off her seat. James was asking them in. Maria's glance went over the room in alarm and met with Mrs Gill, who entered followed by Mr Gill, who was carrying a large box.

'Excuse the disorder; we are in the middle of our decorating,' Maria said, worried that there was no clear space for Mr Gill to place the box.

He deposited his load on top of the scattered cards. A short silence followed, and the unprepared couple did not know what to say to their visitors. Maria was obviously embarrassed.

'What is that?' asked Mr Gill, pointing to the screen cardboard.

'Oh, it is a pretend television. As we have no television my husband is making one,' she answered, and immediately regretted saying it, because only a few days ago Mr Gill had given them a radio set he was not using any more, and now she thought they may think it was a hint for wanting a new television.

'Very good, very good,' Mr Gill was saying, and another silence followed.

'I hope you like the presents,' announced Mrs Gill, pointing at the box and making a gesture for their departure. Maria followed them to the top of the stairs repeating, 'Thank you very much, thanks indeed we are grateful.'

When she went back inside, James was already inspecting the contents of the box.

'Good God, who would imagine they would bring the presents themselves!' exclaimed Maria, almost throwing herself over the table, 'how lucky we are!'

'Look, a chicken, a bottle of wine...tins of food...we are going to have a wonderful Christmas!'

They started dancing for joy.

In the town, everybody was in holiday mode, and there was no need to enter their homes to enjoy the festive period. Going about the streets when dusk came, James and Maria could see the illuminated windows, all decorated, the tinsel hanging, the Christmas tree facing out, as if the dwellers of the house wanted to make the public aware that they believed in Christ. Fanciful thought. The reality could be seen in the Jewish family that did the same, and certainly it was just a social gesture bare of all Christian feeling. How many homes, joyfully illuminated, were only inhabited by the commercially and socially-minded?

Yet, it needs to be said, some sparks of the Christian love spread all over the place, if only with the effort made to remember friends and relations, wherever they may be, and send them a card. To Maria, who could only see the ridiculous part of it, it seemed absurd to pay for a stamp and send by post a card that was only destined for the people next door. She laughed heartily when the postman brought the card from the gardener below, and then came the one from the Rosses and then from the masters. That too was difficult to understand, considering they had themselves brought the presents up to the flat.

Well, what were they to do? They say, 'When in Rome do as the Romans' so Maria sent all the cards by post. She also had to resign herself to seeing her home foolishly decorated with paper hangings and balloons. In the large house, preparations were going on for a big party. There was even more work than usual.

On Christmas Eve, Maria had already done all of the ironing, and cleaned the three bathrooms with their profusion of mirrors. Mrs Gill's bathroom had the walls mirrored from top to bottom. Then Maria had to change her overall and start helping Mr Ross serve drinks all around to the people at the party. Anne Ross had been very nervous all day; her little blue eyes never stopped giving signals of excitement.

'The missus is very hmmm…' she would repeat, and,'everything must be in perfect order or else…'

Maria had been looking forward to Midnight Mass at Leeds Cathedral. Would she have time? It was past nine o'clock and she was still carrying trays in and out of the kitchen.

She mentioned it to Mr Ross and the good man said, 'All right, you go…we'll manage.'

'Thanks Mr Ross, goodnight,' she said and went out, hiding a plate of leftover food under her coat.

It was freezing. The cold, the sudden darkness, and her tiredness all at once enveloped her like lead, paralysing all movement. She stood still in the middle of the path as if she had lost her way.

What am I doing here? she asked herself. Why am I here?

The bright lights she had just left behind, the softness of the carpeted floors, the smell of good tobacco, the perfume of the women, well dressed, polished and smiling, engaged in conversation with educated men, a way of conversing that Maria longed for as she was now completely excluded from it.

Why am I here? I am a foreigner. Oh, how much of a stranger I am!

Slowly, she raised her head towards the sky, her eyes looking for the friendly stars. None were watching her. The sky was a warren of hope. Suddenly, a light appeared not far ahead, like a calling star. Her husband, he had finished work earlier and would be waiting for her. Then she noticed the warm plate on her hands, and her legs began to move forward. Yes, she was bringing supper for James, and he would be waiting for her.

James greeted her lovingly, kissing and embracing her. The little flat was so warm. Sitting by the hearth, they both ate the food from the table of the rich. As she was eating and resting, Maria's heart was regaining its natural warmth, and they talked in the meantime about their distant homeland.

'I remember how my mother used to sew the skin with a needle and thread. To prepare the turkey, she stuffed the bird with prunes. What a pity we have no pine nuts to put in too. You think almonds will do, James?'

As Maria prepared the chicken for the next day, she thought what a strange sensation it was to prick the skin and pass through it with dumb cotton.

'Look,' she continued, 'it is ready, isn't it nice? I'll leave all the vegetables prepared so tomorrow we can sleep as late as we like.'

'I have offered to take the gardener's wife to mass,' James said, 'she is Catholic, you know.'

'Oh, is she?' Maria replied, thinking she would prefer to go without company, 'did she understand you?'

'I think so, we'll ask them to come up for a drink after.'

'Oh, well we'll use our new glasses.'

When they came out of the flat, the gardener's wife, Rose, was waiting. She was very young, with black hair and a freckled face, along with a quick and easy laugh and short conversations. Mrs Ross knew many tales about her, but Maria wasn't that interested. She had two children, and the boy was a little thing and as miserable looking as his father. The little girl, whose hair was neither fair nor dark, always had a ready cry. The poor things were forbidden to go near the big house because Mrs Gill had no patience for them.

The Cathedral was warm, and there were lights and colours. Only Maria wore a black mantilla, and the hats of the other women made the place look like a garden in full bloom. Maria prayed, missing High Mass and Communion very much. As soon as Mass was over James and Rose went outside. When Maria came to the car, both were cleaning the windscreen, peeling the ice off. Maria looked up at the sky, again without stars. She got into the car shivering. The old Ford pulled all right, although they had to stop to clean once more because it was so cold that ice was forming on the windows.

'Are you warm enough, women?' asked James, turning his head stealthily, 'you'll see how big a fire we'll find at home.'

And so they did, as he'd piled so much coal up on the grate that the glow was splendid. Rose had been to fetch her husband and both came up.

'There, Bill,' Maria was offering him a glass of wine, 'and try this special sweet – it is Catalan.'

The man drunk his wine but refused the 'turrons', whilst his wife ate a large piece. What a contrasting pair they were! Her eyes were bright and sparkling, and she looked at least twenty years younger than him, with his a sunken and sad look.

'James, give him another glass of wine, see if we can cheer him up,' said Maria, 'but leave her, I think she had enough.'

Rose was looking earnestly at James, but Maria, remembering Mrs Ross's tales, made it her aim to entertain Bill. Yes, his attitude and manners portrayed tragedy. Perhaps he was now recalling his other wife, and his other children, somewhere in a land out of his reach. He soon got up to go, leaving no smile, and Maria thought that he may no longer know how to. His wife reluctantly followed him.

James and Maria were in bed a few minutes afterwards. She curled herself into her husband's arms for warmth and rest and immediately fell asleep. She would sleep without dreams or nightmares. That evening, she had only wondered what she was doing in England for a small moment, and that was only a prickle of anxiety, and was soon forgotten. Her spirit was not troubled.

On Christmas day Maria woke up rested and happy. She went to put the pot on and the bird in the oven, and then looked out of the window. She had to scrape off the patterned ice, and could only see a colourless outside world. No white snow, no blue sky, everything soaked in heavy grey; she ran back to bed.

Later on, James got up and lit the fire. Maria laid the table neatly and tastefully. The radio was broadcasting classical music. How funny, she thought, that she had spent so many months not thinking about her music. Maria turned around to tell James, but could not find him. Where was he? He had gone downstairs to fetch some coal. To reach the coal, one had to pass the gardener's window. Only, to say good day to the gardener's wife always took James longer than anyone else. Maria used to think it was very amusing, 'did you understand what she said to you?' she would ask him.

'She was not there today,' he replied this time, 'she is probably still in bed, after last night, she is a lazy slut. I am sure he is making dinner today. I think he has told me to go down for tea tomorrow. You'll have to ask them to make sure.' He moved over to the radio and turned the knob, adding, 'we do not want this sad music now.'

Maria's ears felt the shock of striking new sound and lost the vision of her music, yet in her mind remained a purpose; to see her mandolin again.

Christmas dinner was good. It really had the flavour of home. The couple fed themselves plentifully and joyfully. James liked abundance, and to complete his happiness only needed an audience that would admire his full table. He could not restrain himself and repeated several times, 'if your family could see us now they would be green with envy.'

'And if you do the washing up for me even greener they will turn,' she replied, laughing.

'Why not?' he said, and leaving his seat, he kissed her and went to the kitchen.

Maria looked at him in rapture. Her first impulse was to follow him, but she refrained and, breaking her course, went in the opposite direction, to the bedroom. Where had the mandolin been put? At the very top of the wardrobe! She piled up two chairs, climbed them carefully and took the instrument down; she would not ask her husband's help. With shaking fingers she caressed the strings, and the sound of music, aroused her spirit like warm air. She was playing, her fingers becoming more agile as she played. The music came, rising up, lowering down, and smiling at her. She was smiling too, transformed, and at that moment James entered.

'I have done all the washing up for you,' he said, and then saw her beautiful, her eyes bright with passion.

This passion he wanted for himself. He moved close to her, and, stooping, he kissed her on her lips, a long kiss, whilst taking the mandolin from her hands. Gently, without interrupting the pressure on her lips, he took her in his arms and transported her to the room where he laid her on the rug by the fire. With her arms around his neck she responded to his kisses, her passion now turned to her man, the music left behind again in the past. She was giving and feeling happy.

The next day she put the mandolin away, back on the top of the wardrobe, without thought or sentiment. It was St. Steven's Day, or Boxing Day for the English, and a day off for the Ross couple. Maria needed to be in the big house all day and work hard. James would perhaps help her that day. But no, all he did was kiss and embrace her and leave her to work. Then he disappeared and Maria worried, wondering what excuse to give to Mrs Gill if she requested him. She would say today that he was cutting wood, as she invariably did because the woodshed was at the other end of the tennis court, and Mrs Gill never went there. Not even Maria went, afraid of being missed. James would come back after a while, with or without wood, laughing at her.

'You really are silly, you are making yourself a slave, don't let the Rosses influence you, the cook is fearful. Besides, they get out a lot more than we do from the Gills'.'

'Yes, I know that they have been promised a good retirement if they serve faithfully. Poor people! They will be nothing else but servants all their lives. Yet that has nothing to do with us, we have to comply with our duty all the same, we have a contract for a year and you know very well we can't do anything else here.'

'I have said to Rose, we can not go today and will go next Sunday,' he informed Maria as the only reply to her worried admonition.

Maria, dropping the subject, said, 'Well at least you have managed to understand each other, haven't you?' then went back to the kitchen, light hearted. Maria thought that at least this time she knew where he had been, although that was not an appropriate excuse to give Mrs Gill, as she had no liking for Rose.

In the gardener's flat the table was ready, with the food spread over it, cakes, sandwiches, jellies, pork pies and biscuits. Rose was sitting, arms folded by the fire. Bill was also sitting, holding in his hands a sock and a needle. Maria and James entered the room, and Rose asked them to sit down, but Maria remained standing, her eyes fastened on the movements of the thick fingers passing the thin needle skilfully across the sock. How astonishing, the gardener was darning!

His wife, noting Maria's wonderment said, 'I can't sew.'

'Why not?' asked Maria with concern, glancing at her hands, sure she would find a physical handicap.

'Because I don't know how,' said the gardener's wife, laughing but very precise.

'It is not difficult,' Maria assured her, 'you can learn.'

'Oh, no I can't!' she laughed again, whilst the man continued sewing.

Then Maria turned to him.

'I have never seen a man darning before, Bill, you are doing it very well indeed.'

The man's face softened a fraction and he proceeded to fold the sock and put it away. They all sat at the table, and ate and drank tea. Bill and Rose seemed good humoured and friendly, thought Maria, and it seemed there would not be any more reason for complaints, as they were going to be friends after all.

A few weeks passed by. January was near its end. Snow fell often and the cold was intense. James and Maria bought an electric heater and were taking it from room to room without still managing to warm the flat. They were only comfortable when they sat near the fire.

One day, when Maria finished her work and was getting ready to go, Mr Ross came to tell her that Mr Gill wanted a word with her. Instantly her mind moved quickly, searching for something her husband could have done wrong. She was always on the alert, although this time she didn't expect any complaints from the gardener.

Mr Gill was holding a paper in his hand. 'Maria, how do you use the electricity?' he began.

'Well...I don't know, normally I suppose.'

'How many heaters do you have?'

'One.'

'Tell me, do you use it a lot?'

'No, only when we are in.'

'You must have something else. Look, this is the invoice for the electricity of your flat, it amounts to twenty-three pounds and that is too much. Tell me, what are you doing?'

The bewildered girl was making an effort to think about what could have happened, and remembered what they had done.

'One day we forgot to put the water heater off,' she finally offered, 'I am very sorry sir, I promise it will not happen again.'

'I am paying the electricity for your flat. You must try not to use as much from now on, you understand?'

'Yes sir,' and Maria withdrew, almost in tears. She ignored the cook's staring little eyes, passed her and ran to the flat.

She immediately told James, but he remained very cool, and said that she was a silly girl because, even if the emergency heater was on every night for a whole week they could not use so much.

'What you have to do,' he continued, 'is to tell Mr Gill, yes you go now and tell him we have not used all that electricity, tell him it must be the gardener.'

'I'll tell him then.'

The next day she found no chance of addressing Mr Gill. But James took the opportunity to approach the gardener and began to tell him that he was using too much electricity. Maria watched them from the big house, and the expression on the long man's face was not agreeable at all. That faded face could not understand the foreign words, yet by James's manners he could sense himself accused and didn't like it. Maria came out of the house too late; the gardener, wearing his enormous wellington boots, was trotting away through the snow.

'This man is a sour soul, and an idiot on top,' James said.

'Why don't you leave him alone?' complained Maria, turning her back without waiting for his reply, her mind now keen on talking to the master and finding the answer to the electricity puzzle.

However, it was not until the following day, when serving dinner, that she dared to bring the matter up.

'Mr Gill,' she began, 'about the electricity, my husband says it's impossible that we have used all that much, we think it must be an error.'

'Yes, Maria,' he said calmly, 'the electricity used to warm the greenhouses passes through your meter,' and, perhaps noticing the girl's great relief he continued, 'do not concern yourself any more.' Maria continued changing the plates and, when she was going to withdraw, Mr Gill said, 'try to be friends with the gardener.'

She could only manage a nod before leaving the room.

Be friendly with the gardener, that was the master's recommendation, or was it an order? Maria did try. Whenever she happened to meet him she gave him a smile as soft as she could, but the thought of the man mending his socks still shocked her and the smile turned into a compassionate grin, much misunderstood. He would only mumble a 'mo'nin" or 'ev'nin", refraining from any other gesture of communication. He seemed a completely drained man, nevertheless something somehow must be able to stir him up and brighten his life. Would it be his plants?

One windy day as cold as cutting knives, Maria came out of the big house, running towards her flat with her arm over her face in a protection effort, and she almost bumped into him as he was going to the greenhouse.

'How cold it is,' she said, 'are your plants warm enough?'

'Yes,' he answered, 'would you like to see them?'

'Oh, yes please. Show them to me.'

They went in to the glasshouses, and were suddenly far from the cold wind. Surrounded by a calm and balmy atmosphere, they walked along the gravel path edged by a low brick wall, and there were the pipes that robbed the electricity through their meter. On top of it were rows and rows of well groomed pots, plants arranged by colour in beautiful order and artistic sense. There were geraniums, were they the same she saw on the day of her arrival? Yes, of course, and it was a lot of work to plant in and transplant out and then in again in order that there would be flowers for the master's home all year round. Bill explained this to Maria, and his voice warmed.

That is what gives him satisfaction, Maria thought. Does Mrs Gill appreciate how much alive those flowers are? She discards them too soon.

Maria admired the splendour and exuberance inside the glass sheds. She could easily believe Bill talked to the plants and that the plants and flowers would listen to him and grow only on his love.

She left him there surveying his entire kingdom and went to the little house. James was standing in front of the gardener's door chatting with Rose. She was laughing, and he had a bucket full of coal at his feet.

'What are you doing here? It is freezing,' Maria exclaimed.

'I was waiting for you, what were you doing talking to Bill so long?'

'He was showing me the flowers,' she replied, gesturing a greeting to Rose, who quickly disappeared inside, 'such a quantity.'

Both went up to the flat to have their dinner.

'James, try not to be seen by the gardener when you are working on your car. I seemed to sense that he believes you are doing less of the proper work than he does,' said Maria.

'Proper work, what do you mean? I am who does more work.'

'No, James, you are having it very easy, that is the truth. You spend a lot of time out. You are having it easier than anybody else here. Even Mr Ross, and he is a good man, says he doesn't understand why you need so long to take Mr Gill to the factory and back.'

'Oh, shut up. They never had so good a chauffeur and so good mechanic before me.'

'I am not saying you do not look after their cars well, what I am saying is that you spend many hours doing things for you. Have you seen how well looked after are the plants?'

He made no reply and she continued, 'Why don't you wait for your day off? What were you doing last night? Why you came up so late? And besides, I don't know how you can stand this terrible cold weather. You make me suffer so much.'

'I had to adjust the brakes.'

'Well, are we going? It's late. I'll do the washing up after, what are you doing this afternoon?'

'I have to clean the boiler room.'

Maria put on her coat.

'Are you giving me a kiss?' James stopped her, embraced her, he was in no hurry.

'Oh, please leave me, I am late already,' and she fled down the steps without waiting for him.

The next day was not so cold. The sun was out, shining timidly, a February sun, but sun at last. Maria, preparing dinner in her little kitchen, felt happy. Suddenly, the sound of heavy footsteps startled her as it was something very unusual.

James, coming up the stairs furiously banging his feet, shouted, 'That gardener, that gardener, he is so stupid!'

'What is happening?'

'You'll see what is happening' he said stamping his foot repeatedly on the floor, 'from now on we shall make as much noise as we like, there...there!'

From the window they could see the man with his thin face raised up towards their flat, and he was not shouting although his attitude was angry. James raced out of the kitchen to the dining room, and, there, forgetting the carefully laid bird catches, he trod over one which jumped with a shriek as if alive. He then kicked it and *trap*, the string and stone went down and reached the feet of the gardener standing below. Now the man showed great rage and in a flash picked up the stone, flanking it back to James, together with a jet of insults. There was no time for him to take aim but the stone found its target on James's leg, turning him wild. Insults poured out angrily, and, with his fists clenched, James swore he was going to kill the gardener. Both men were insulting each other fiercely, one in English, and the other in Catalan.

Maria extremely worried, was calling her husband back into the house. From the big house out came the servants. One of them went to the gardener, and with gentle persuasion managed to calm him. Then Maria was able to get James in and closed the window. The place was cold, the dinner too.

'Why? Why did you carry on like this?' she cried, 'why don't you let him alone?'

'Because he is a jealous man. Well, what the hell he thinks he is, that wretch, that peevish ...old fool.'

He started his dinner not noticing that it was cold, nor that Maria was not eating. After each mouthful there was an insult to the gardener, and then another.

Maria sighed and, head down, went quietly out of the house to her work. Thinking about the jealousy of the gardener, she wondered what could have caused it. Could it be caused by them having a car? Because of their pink bath? Because James seemed to get away doing less work? Because they were foreigners? Why were they disliked so much?

In this manner she was sharing her anxieties with Anne Ross, her eyes fixed on the carpet as if she was responsible for all the upsetting.

If she could have dared to raise her head she might have seen the flick of mischief in the clear eyes of the woman in white when she asked, 'Have you seen the gardener's wife lately?'

But Maria moved her head from left to right, not lifting her sight from the floor.

CHAPTER FOUR

A FEW DAYS passed by, and no-one mentioned the incident. Maria anxiously expected Mr Gill to summon her, to request once more that she and James befriend the gardener. She was sure that the masters must have heard about the quarrel between the two men. She dreaded the day she would have to serve the table. She racked her brains in search of a reasonable explanation of what happened, finding nothing.

Friday came and Maria set off for the big house, having reached the mental state of endurance she would need to be in to put all the blame onto herself, as she proposed to do. On entering the kitchen, she was seized immediately by a feeling of anguish. Anne Ross was not prepared for her day off. In her clean white overall, she was busying about the place, and then she met the look of surprise in Maria's eyes and explained.

'No, we are not having our day off today. There is a lot of work to do, as today is the day the important visitor arrives.'

'Important visitor, I know nothing, tell me.'

'Don't you know? Haven't you noticed how excited Mrs Gill is?'

Maria had not, as she was so preoccupied with her own worry, and now she understood why she had not been reprimanded yet.

'It's the Duchess of Burma who is coming,' continued the cook, 'she is a very important person, a cousin of the Queen. It is a great honour for the Gills to have her here, you know?'

Her little eyes were jumping up and down, clear and transparent, like marbles.

'Look, Maria, you go upstairs and start polishing the boys' bedrooms, I'll come up after to help,' said Anne, then, seeing Maria still standing in the kitchen, she urged, 'run quickly before Mrs Gill comes and sees you doing nothing!'

Upstairs, Maria found Mrs Gill looking at the boys' bedroom as if she had never seen it before. It was a very large room. There were three beds, modern and comfortable looking, one on each side of the wall. The bedsteads extended as night tables where boyish objects stood. The room had two big windows and a magnificent fitted carpet, which matched the bedcovers and curtains in warm, toasted colours.

Whilst waiting for Mrs Gill's orders Maria was considering how beautiful the room was, although not appropriate for a Duchess. Surely a Duchess required a double bed, a double mattress and a hanging canopy?

'We will put her in here now that the boys are away, as this room has its own bathroom and shower. The guest room only has a wash basin,' Mrs Gill explained, as if trying to convince herself, whilst Maria was wondering if Duchesses take a bath in the evening and a shower in the morning, or vice versa. Mrs Gill left the room, then returned a few minutes later with the bed linen, which was pure Irish cotton, hand embroidered – really fitting for royalty.

'Beautiful sheets!' exclaimed Maria, 'which bed shall I make, madam?'

'That one,' said Mrs Gill, pointing to the far end of the room, by the window. It was certainly the bed farthest from the bathroom door. Perhaps the Duchess would like the view from that window, with the extensive gardens, the tennis court, the rows of greenhouses and the woodland surrounding rolling hills in the far distance.

Later, when observing the finished room, Maria thought it was not welcoming enough, and then the mistress came in with towels and exotic soaps for the bathroom.

'What do you think madam, if we take some of the boys' objects and put some flowers instead?'

'No, flowers cannot be put into the bedrooms.'

'But...' Maria dared to say, 'the room is so big.'

'No, it is all right as it is. Listen carefully Maria, when the Duchess arrives you will be at her service exclusively. Be attentive to anything she needs or wishes. Do you understand? And do it right!'

Maria panicked, instantly imagining that she would have to help the lady to undress, or perhaps to do another service she had not been trained to perform.

'Now go downstairs,' Mrs Gill continued, 'and help Mrs Ross in the kitchen.'

In the kitchen, poor Anne Ross was melting away, as if the nervousness of the mistress could pass through and be manifested in the little person with infant like eyes.

'But do not worry so much,' Maria tried to soothe her.

'It is because another cook was supposed to come and help, and has not arrived.'

Mr Ross came in, asking, 'Maria where is your husband? Tell him he must do an errand.'

Maria went to look for him. He was in the garage attached to their house, polishing the Rolls Royce.

'In there everyone is spirited, I am scared too,' she said. 'Do you know? I have to be her maid and servant. You, James, polish your shoes. Will you know how to do it? I mean to open the door for her and take off your cap and bow. You'll have to imagine that she is General Franco himself!' she started laughing, but stopped suddenly and added, 'quick James, Mr Ross is waiting for you, you have to go somewhere.'

What he went for, amongst other things, was a hot water bottle for aristocratic feet.

At mid afternoon it was already dark, and Paul Ross lit the two Victorian lamps outside the entrance. James placed the Rolls in front of the main door, waiting to take Mr Gill to the station, and everyone was ready but no one had yet eaten a meal.

'Come to the kitchen James,' called Maria softly, 'you have time to eat a sandwich, here, have a tomato one. If you could see what is in there for the guest, caviar and all. Paul says that if there is any left he will let us taste it.'

'Wine girl, wine is what you have to hoard if you can.'

To honour the Duchess all the important people in town were invited to the house, and soon cars started to arrive. Mr Ross was opening the doors, Mrs Gill greeting everyone and then Maria taking their coats from them. It was almost like a film, pompous and magnificent, where romance and drama could be added if fancied.

At last the great madam arrived, and Maria gazed at her, so that she could see what distinguished an aristocrat from an ordinary person. This relation of the Queen was tall and slim with dark hair, a dry complexion and deep set eyes. She was not pretty, decided Maria regretfully. She had the air though, of a person who knows what to do in all situations, and never feels perplexed. She let Maria take her fur coat, and her face was changed slightly by a shade of smile. She had acknowledged her.

Well, that is it then, said Maria to herself, she has seen me, she knows I'm a person, and none of the other ladies ever notice me. I am for them a functional object, one of many in this house, and, considering the quantity of beautiful objects in that place, I am one of the least interesting. She is a great lady indeed, sighed Maria with relief, surely I'll not have to help her get to bed.

The first reception was not very long; some people only came to greet the Duchess, and had a drink then went away. Others were coming later for the Gala dinner. Meanwhile, the lady went up to her room and Maria was called.

'What is your wish, my lady?' asked Maria. She had to say that, and she managed it quite naturally.

'Would you like to iron this dress for me please?'

'Yes, madam!' and in the next instance Maria was out in a rush, too fast, really. If the lady wanted to ask something else she did not have the chance. Maria ran downstairs, and started quickly to iron the dress. It was an evening gown of pink satin and tulle, and very pretty, so Maria eagerly began to iron the creases away. She knew it would be done better with less precipitation, but she could not refrain from her haste, as the thought of the Duchess waiting for it worried her. When Maria was barely finished, she ran upstairs, tripped over the last step and almost fell over the dress. She gazed at it in panic. If it were damaged, she would have to be longer to get it right! She carefully looked at the gown, deciding it would pass, and thought that nothing was more important than haste. After all Maria's hard work, it did not seem as if the Duchess had been waiting for it, and she praised the speed with which Maria had finished her task.

Some clothing was scattered over one of the beds and Maria, noticing it was not the one made with the finest linen said, 'it's not this bed that is prepared for you madam, but that one.' She pointed to the other side of the room.

'Oh, yes,' the Duchess calmly answered, handing Maria a pink object, 'later you can put in this hot water bottle, as I always carry it with me.' Noticing that Maria's mouth was going to open, perhaps in surprise, the Duchess added, 'my feet get cold very easily, even when the room is warm. I like this with a cover, so it remains hot for a long time,' she finished with a smile.

Maria closed her mouth just in time, as she was going to say they had bought a new one for her. This had obviously been in much use as it was soft and a bit grubby, with pink ribbons that were faded and unravelling.

'Anything else?' Maria asked.

'No, thanks.'

'Thank you, madam,' Maria said, and left the room.

Once she was in the corridor she realised she had not curtsied, as the rank of the lady required. She shrugged her shoulders, then, looking at the hot water bottle, felt that she could burst into laughter, but did not dare.

That evening, very late, James and Maria walked to the small flat shoulder to shoulder, both tired. Maria's legs ached so much that as soon as she passed the door she let herself drop on the first step. Why make the effort to climb up if there is no warmth in the empty house, no supper prepared, and no fire to quit their shivering cold? They had eaten nothing but the crumbs left on the plates; no caviar, no canapés, no sweet wine. All had vanished before reaching their hands, between the guests and the hired service who were much more experienced in profiting at a banquet.

'Come on, get up girl, do you want me to carry you?'

'No, no, you are tired too. How many cars have you moved up and down from the entrance today?'

'Oh, hundreds.'

Maria put her hands on the third step and crawled on all fours up the stairs, to fall flat on her bed.

With all the fuss of the gala evening, Maria hoped the problem regarding the gardener and James had passed. The master, however, did not forget. On Monday morning she was summoned to the presence of Mr Gill. He was a man who lost no time with preliminaries.

'I know Maria,' he began, 'what happened the other day. So you will move to another place, find a house or flat not far from the factory where Martines will work. There are machines that need maintenance, and he will carry on as my chauffeur, as now, you could...' (here Maria did not understand any more, as her mind was struck by the magnitude of the problem ahead, and, feeling the anguish of the rejection, she could no longer distinguish the words Mr Gill was saying). Out of their flat, thrown out, yes, of her dear little house! Her first home was only an illusion, and was to be hers no longer. Mr Gill continued talking, and was handing her a paper. She took it with trembling hands and tried hard to focus her eyes. Mr Gill said something like, 'they are to let you go and see then let me know.'

Still holding the paper, Maria stood, unable to utter a word or move a step. Mr Gill, who had said all he wanted to say, unfolded his newspaper. She had to withdraw. She had spent so many days thinking about how to explain the fight between the two men, how could she take the blame away from James, preparing herself to withstand the reprimand, and now she stood frozen, with not a chance of a word coming out of her mouth. It was worse than an argument, but, unexpectedly, the argument had been argued without her. Why give her opinion? The masters would have arrived at a decision to solve the problem. She was told what to do and that was it. There was nothing for her to say, nothing at all.

She went slowly up to her flat thinking about how James would take it. He was so much attached to their home, and he had sent so many photos with long letters to his family praising all they had around them, including the pink bathroom. They had only lived here for six months, and now they would have to leave. When Maria entered the flat, James was sat by the fire, and she threw herself into his arms, sobbing.

'Mr Gill says we have to go...in one of those places to live in!' she cried, showing him the paper.

'What is this?'

'Some addresses, three for us to look at, see which one we like. That is because of your quarrelling with the gardener. I told you to leave him alone. You see what has happened?'

'It is him, is he who has to go. He is stupid and jealous. Remember Mrs Ross said he could not stand anybody here didn't she? So, why they don't send him away? He should go.'

'Because it is *we* who gave motive for it. You should have left him alone.'

'*Leave him alone, leave him alone*, shut up, silly.'

'No, I won't! It is your fault, and you do not seem sorry we have to quit the flat. Well, I am, I don't want to go!' She started to cry again.

Then James took her back in his arms and said, 'Maybe we shall like one of those houses. We shall go tomorrow to see.'

When their work was finished the next evening, James and Maria went out in the grubby Ford. They said nothing to no one, as they were sure there was no need to ask where the places were. James said they could find them easily as he often passed by the district. Maria could not bring herself to tell Anne Ross because she was too deeply upset, and she could feel that the woman knew something about it and could not understand why she was not commenting on it. Maria found it difficult to assess how much of a friend the cook was.

They decided to start looking for the one that seemed easiest to find, number five Headingley Crescent. They knew Headingley Road, and thought that the two streets must be connected. It was dark and raining, and James was driving fast as if he always knew where to go.

'Don't go so fast, you don't give me time to read the street names!' cried Maria.

Then James would stop and make her get out to ask passers by. There were far too many Headingleys, – the Drive, the Close, and the Terrace. Which way would the Crescent be? Logically, they should all be more or less connected, yet they had run from one end to the other looking at all the leading streets and alleys, and no Crescent was in sight. There was no logical distribution of names, and no logic in the tracing of the streets. Far from a spider's web, it was a labyrinth, and the rain kept covering the Ford with tears.

At last, James turned the car towards the Town Centre, leaving Headingley Road behind, and a few streets after that they became lost in a cul-de-sac, where, as they left the street, Maria saw the sign they needed. 'La lluna creixent!' she exclaimed with good humour.

The name didn't resemble the moon, nor could it be seen anywhere, as it was covered by the clouds that night. Only the shape of the street, a semicircle that was broken sharply, resembled a moon. Number five was in front of them. Maria and James knocked hard, and after a while a woman opened and, without answering their greetings, said,

'What do you want?'

'We were told this house is to let, can we see it?'

The woman, puffing on her cigarette, did not reply. The rain fell into the beam of light from the door and formed a curtain, so she could not see properly who was callous enough to disturb her at this hour.

'We are sorry is so late, but we could not find the place,' Maria apologised, stepping forward into the light.

The woman moved aside, and they went in. There were steps leading upstairs, and a door at the left led to a living room, with a fire burning in the grate, the television on, a kitchenette with kettle boiling, sofa, armchairs, chairs, table, rug on the floor, and a cat and dog.

'The coal place is outside,' the woman was pointing to a door at the right, 'bathroom on the first landing and the bedroom at the top of the steps.'

'That is no good, no good at all,' James was saying in Catalan, 'let's go.'

'Would you like to go upstairs?' asked the woman, suddenly polite.

'No, no need to, thank you very much, and sorry we have disturbed you,' said Maria, as James was already outside. 'Goodnight,' she added, going out quickly as her husband, starting the car, gave her no time for more.

'To see this, it was not worth to get wet, and the petrol,' he complained.

'Let's go home,' murmured Maria, feeling all at once very tired and shaky with cold.

Soon they'd left all the Headingleys behind and were glad to reach the little flat which was still their home. Maria was silent, whilst James spoke incessantly, complaining or cursing, hoping or despairing, fleeting senselessly from one to another. Maria knew well how pointless it was trying to put a clear idea in his thoughts when he spoke like that. She had tried many times to reason with him and she would try again, but for now she let it be.

They had decided to go see the other two houses during a day off, in daylight, when they would be easier to find. And the next house was, despite being situated in the same quarter of the town where all the houses were exactly the same, slim and stuck to each other as if needing the comforting proximity of their neighbour at hand. Built in rows where the streets slanted, the houses climbed, one above the other, like gigantic steps. The next house they went to see had four rooms; one in the basement, a kitchen on the ground floor, a living room, and, up the stairs, a bedroom, with the second bedroom up another flight of stairs.

'How fond of steps are these English people, it is absurd to have it like that,' said James. He didn't even care to climb up to the first bedroom, and soon he was out. They never asked where the bathroom was.

The third house they visited was different, as the district seemed better and the houses were not as narrow. One could see from the outside that they had at least two rooms on the same level. A young man opened the door and began to show Maria and James the house. A somewhat dark entrance had four doors; kitchen, bedroom with a high window looking out on to a grey wall, a bathroom with a two inch window, and a sitting room that was blessed by a splash of light coming through a large window, and a French window which opened to a garden which was on a higher level, three steps up. The view was of other houses and back gardens.

'Is nice isn't it?' Maria was saying, 'is nice to have a bit of garden. What you think James?'

At that moment, the sunshine laid squares of colour across the floor just where the three people stood.

'The bedroom must be very damp,' James said, 'have you seen how low, it's underground?'

The young man admitted there was dampness in the house, but they were leaving because he had chance of a better job in another town.

In the car on the way back, Maria kept on saying that this one was the best of the lot. James contradicted her, saying that the humidity was no good for them. Definitely none of the three were any good, he said, and she must tell Mr Gill that they did not want them. He could send the gardener there; it was better to send the gardener away, not them, he concluded.

'James, I cannot tell this to Mr Gill. Don't you realise we have to choose one of them as soon as possible?'

'You tell him we do not want any of these three,' he insisted.

She had to do so. The following day she went to tell Mr Gill they had seen the accommodations and that none of them were convenient, as one was damp, the other had too many steps, and the other ugly quarters. Mr Gill had been listening and, when the girl could find nothing else to say, he raised his head and gave her a glance with just a flush of irritation, which she sensed. He still said nothing, but took his pen out and wrote a name on a piece of paper.

'Here, it is an agency, go and see if there is anything else.'

Maria took the paper and withdrew.

The agent wasn't very nice; he kept them waiting for a long time. Then he came out with some keys and wrote an address on more paper, made them sign another paper and said he wanted the keys back that same day. As it was in the evening they had to do the same as before, but luckily it was not raining.

When they found the house they did not know which district it was. They opened the door and a sudden blow of air greeted them. It was dark, and although finding the switch was easy, no light came. The floor was bare, and the street light dabbled through the window on to the dusty boards. There were no shutters, and no curtains. James took out a torch and searched the dusty walls. They were a dirty yellow, and there were cold, dead ashes in the fire place. The torch met a door which James opened, and when he went up the wooden steps they cracked and squeaked. A shiver passed up Maria's spine, but she followed him. The room was a replica of that downstairs, except the fireplace was small and narrow.

'And from what or where can we get furniture for it?' asked Maria.

That problem struck the couple just now, as they had no furniture, and how could they live in an empty house?

'James, we have no money saved, can you realise now that all our earnings go on the car?'

'And you do not realise that the car is indispensable,' replied James as they descended the steps, 'let's go.'

'What do we say to the agent?'

'That we do not want it,' James stated, 'haven't you seen how the plaster is peeling from the ceiling? And the amount of paint needed for the doors!'

'We could do it ourselves, decorate it nicely,' suggested Maria with little conviction.

The keys were returned to the agent. That same evening, over supper, James began to blame the gardener and Mr Gill once more, with his words thickly and continuously dropping out of his mouth like a ruttle of rust rugs. Later in bed, his chanting would not stop, and Maria moved close to him, longing for the warmth of his body.

'Come on darling, come, shut up. Let them alone now.'

'Oh, yes. And you still think that we should not have bought the car, what would we do now? Walking up and down looking for a house. Walking, oh, no!'

'Others go walking. Besides, perhaps we would not find ourselves in this situation otherwise.'

'You are silly, what do you know?'

He kept still, not responding to her caresses. Then she turned her back on him, her head low on the pillow, and the tears began to fill her eyes. She felt again the terrible, pungent disappointment of the day he bought that car without consulting her. Now she was waiting, with all her being wanting his love to compensate her sorrow, yet the minutes ticked away empty of him, deepening her unhappiness until tears fell down her cheeks. She had to search for a hanky, but she was not going to make any approaching gesture. He must move to her, as he was the one to blame and all of this was happening because of him. She had told him so many times and now she would not move; he must. She fell asleep.

The next morning found her in his arms. No one knew who made the reconciliatory move. It didn't matter, and they kissed and Maria got up refreshed and happy, and ready to face the new day.

The day, however, brought no joy but another worry. Before setting off to work Maria had to hurry James. He always waited until the last minute to get up. Mr Ross had called on the interior telephone saying Mr Gill was already having his breakfast; he often did that so that James had sufficient time to be with the car at the door. Today, Paul Ross's voice sounded impatient, and he insisted in hurrying James up.

'He is coming straight away,' Maria assured him, and she was impatient too.

She always felt uneasy until she could see the car pass by, but it had only been few minutes, and she knew that Mr Gill had come out and waited at the door for his chauffeur to drive up to him. In spite of Paul Ross's warning and

Maria's urging, the car had been late more than once.

That morning, Maria went to her work in deep thought, considering if anything could be gained by talking to Mr Gill. She would like to speak to him, as she could speak English well enough, she was sure, to be able to explain their problems, and she would ask him for advice. She felt anxious to clear up any misunderstanding, and to reassess what was expected of them. She would beg him to be patient with her husband, as he was learning, and of course it would take time. She could say their contract stated 'domestic resident' so, why not let them remain in the premises? They would promise to make as little noise as possible and never again upset the gardener. Did the gardener's wife prefer the top flat with the pink bathroom? Well, they could move below, of course they could do that!

Maria was thinking about all this while cleaning Penelope's room, and, folding her clothes, she realised how little they were seeing her lately. James wasn't taking her to Harrogate any more for music lessons, had she given up playing? The Hebrew teacher still came up to the house to teach her, but Penelope did not go up to Maria and tell her how boring it was to learn Hebrew and that she would rather be taught Spanish. Neither did she go to James for little things to be done on her bike, as his hands were not magic any more. What had happened? Had the novelty wore off? Yes, it was bound to, but something else had happened, too. Certainly, they were no longer regarded as 'very nice'.

At midday, Maria was going towards her flat, and was so preoccupied that she nearly bumped into the gardener, who, ignoring her, continued on his way, walking like a telephone pole bent by the windy gales of March. She stopped to recall the first day of their arrival, and a lump went to her throat. They had now broken all the plates of the new service, and none remained.

She went up to the flat, but James was not there. She began to prepare dinner, slowly, so she would not make any noise. Her ears stretched to hear the first sound of him arriving, and she was suffering from anxiety. Where could he be? Neither the Ford nor the Rover were to be seen anywhere.

Then she heard the sound of the door, and she ran out of the kitchen and called, 'Where have you been until now?' in the same instant.

'I have been in the Flamenco talking to Julio.'

'So long!'

'He says they cannot do that to us, this of taking us to live elsewhere. According to our working contract they can't.'

'I was thinking about that too, our Permits say 'resident', and that means we have to live where we work.'

'Julio says he has been living in this country some time and he knows the English are a rotten lot. He says we better go to the police, to the aliens department and explain to them.'

'Do you think there is need for that?' she said, 'I have been considering speaking to Mr Gill.'

'What for? When the masters turn against the workers they are vicious, they tread on us with both their feet. See what happened to Valencianeta, her mistress left her in the street, locked out without her luggage, and the police had to go in and get it for her. And the girl did do nothing but forget to feed the dog a couple of times; these people love more their animals than a foreigner.'

'Well, I don't know. That girl always exaggerates, and, besides, she does not speak a word of English, and I believe she was shouting at her mistress as it were making herself understood. Our problem is not the same, and we will not solve it by going to the café bar to spend time complaining and listening to the other Spaniards complaining about their employers. I will speak to Mr Gill, I will, he'll listen to me,' Maria concluded decidedly.

'You'll get nothing out of it, let's go to the police.'

'To lodge an accusation of what? We are still living here. You let me talk to Mr Gill first, and please, James, do whatever Mr Ross tells you to. Do your work properly.'

'No one can complain of me. The cars are better looked after than ever before.'

'It is not that alone what they want.'

She could repeat this a hundred times to no avail. To him the other things were not important; the shining cars had to shun all the flowers and vegetables of the earth. The polishing of the windows, the punctuality, the language barrier, nothing was worth a thought in comparison to his ability as a chauffeur or mechanic.

'You know that gardener ignores me?' she commented.

'He is an imbecile, and his wife.'

'I never see her, as she is always inside the house. I think she reads romances all day long!'

That afternoon, Maria was fretting, and Anne Ross's little eyes rested on her many times, yet the woman's lips let nothing out. Evening was closing in when Mr Gill arrived, and Maria waited for an opportunity to speak with him. Then it happened, upstairs. She was going to descend the service steps when he came out of Penelope's study.

'Sir, would you have a moment? I'd like to speak to you.'

'Yes Maria,' he stopped to listen.

'I would like to...I would like to say if...' she hesitated, all her determination evaporated. He did not go forward to help her, but instead he remained silent, head slightly bent.

'If we go to live away from here,' she continued, 'how can we keep working on the same conditions of the contract?' She paused – she had said it – and she breathed deeply, wishing he would say something. 'If the gardener and my husband do not quarrel any more... the accommodations we have seen are so... not very convenient,' she paused again, feeling that she was doing no good. Suddenly, she raised her head to look straight into his eyes, 'what can we do?' she concluded, more firmly.

Then came his answer.

'Look, I have given my advice once, and if you do not want to follow it, do not come to me for more.' The last word was uttered when he was already in motion towards the large staircase. He left the girl there, rooted in the middle of the landing.

'But...Mr Gill.'

He was down the stairs, and never turned around or heard her. Maria painfully moved herself back to the narrow staircase, and, cheeks burning, she went out through the garage door. She immediately told James about it.

'You see? I told you. What we have to do is go to a solicitor.'

'A solicitor!' she replied, alarmed, 'Isn't better that we say to Mr Gill we want that house, the one with the garden?'

'No, we go to a solicitor to defend our rights.'

'Even if we have the right to stay here, can't you see? We can not stay in a place where we are not wanted.'

'They will want us, the solicitor will tell them. I have spoken to Mr Ross and he has given me an address, he is a good man.'

'Paul Ross will tell Mr Gill and there will be a real upheaval. The Rosses are stuck to the masters like sheep ticks. They are the perfect example of servilism, and if they see the masters displeased with us will not speak in our favour. Certainly not, they agree with the master always, they are good servants. There we are, we should do the same,' Maria concluded.

'You are mistaken, Mr Ross says he is tired of working for Mrs Gill, that she is impossible. We are going tomorrow to see the solicitor, and you'll see, everything is going to be all right.'

Maria did not want to go but there was little alternative. It was too late to say to Mr Gill that they would take one of the houses. Besides, his manner had cut off all Maria's hope of approaching him again. That night she could not sleep, turning her body one way, then the other, as with her mind. Thinking and thinking, her thoughts found only that emptiness which needs to be filled with answers. Any question is a cell of thought in the brain, a double cell like an open sea shell, then the answer fills the twin leaf and the cell, thus completed, closes up. But there were no answers for Maria, and the emptiness repeatedly echoed the questions. What should she do? James was asleep, although his last words still floated on, 'go to a solicitor, we have to go straight away!' so persistently that they covered her thoughts, filled the empty cell and closed it. Then Maria fell asleep.

The next morning, James returned from taking Mr Gill to the factory. It seemed five minutes since he'd left.

To Maria's surprise he said, 'I did a short cut, and there was no traffic this morning. Are you ready?'

They went out, saw nobody about and, believing they were not seen, rushed quietly away. Soon, they were sitting in a waiting room. A little while later, a door opened, and a gentleman dressed in black led them into an office. The man wore thick black rimmed glasses over a prominent nose. Maria noticed its sharpness, and began to feel uneasy. The man was asking questions and scribbling notes.

Maria told their tale, but soon realised how futile such an exercise was. James's words, urging her to say this and that or the other, became empty of meaning, even to her. The solicitor stopped writing.

'Well, madam, when your job has been changed, or when your wages have been reduced, come and see me and I'll see what I can do for you.'

He was dismissing them, and, stretching out his hand, he gave her a paper. She had to look at it for a few seconds before understanding what it was.

Then, turning to James, she said, 'that's a receipt for a guinea, pay, we have to go.'

A few minutes later, sitting in the car, James was telling her she did not do it right, that she should have explained better how stupid the gardener was, and did she not mention everything?

'Why didn't you tell the solicitor that the gardener is to blame for everything that is happening?' he demanded.

Maria's vision was blocked by the black suited, large nosed gentleman and James's grumbles made her cry back at him.

'Oh, shut up, will you, shut up man! Yes, I told him all you said! Can you see we spend a guinea for nothing?'

Closing her eyes she took a deep breath to clear out her mind. When she opened them again to see where they were the car had turned down Almondley Lane.

'What time is it?' she asked.

'Half past ten.'

'What's Mrs Gill going to say? I am so late today!'

She rushed up to the flat, put the white overall on, took her coat and rushed back out. James could do what he pleased, but she had to comply with her work. On arriving at the house she went straight upstairs, aiming to do the beds very quickly. Going to Penelope's bedroom, she bumped into Anne Ross coming out.

'It is done,' the woman told her.

'I'll make Mrs Gill's.'

'It is also done.'

'Ah,' Maria stood, vaguely waiting for something worse. Anne Ross was not smiling; there were no creases forming around her eyes, yet she looked older. It was strange how she had seemed to Maria to have a baby face before now. She must be nearly sixty!

'Mrs Gill wants to speak to you, follow me,' said Anne, and both went downstairs, using the big staircase. The cook left Maria in the luxurious entrance hall. A few seconds later, she returned, saying, 'go to the drawing room, madam is waiting for you.'

Maria had been in the drawing room when the family sat by the fireplace. It was a very large space with three grand windows, framed with thick velvet curtains which were gathered at each side with golden cords. The tassels hung one foot above the floor, and there were satin and gold antique armchairs. Maria used to think they were museum pieces, too precious for anyone to sit on. But today Mrs Gill was sitting in one of them, with her knees together and her hands quietly folded on her lap, like a painting. She had at one side of her the jar containing the gardener's flowers, and her background was the crimson velvet. She only needed a crown on her head and a cushion under her feet to look like the portrait of Queen Elizabeth that Maria had seen in the Rosses room.

Maria stood in front of her with respect, waiting for her to speak.

'Your services are not required any more in this house,' Mrs Gill said in a cold voice, methodically, terminal.

'This morning I have come late, I am sorry, if you allow me to explain...'

'No,' interrupted Mrs Gill, 'there is no need to explain anything,' a short pause occurred, and then she added, 'and you know, you have been rude to me.'

This remark struck Maria, and her body stiffened. Was Mrs Gill going to humiliate or insult her? Was it not enough to sack her?

'Mrs Gill,' she replied, raising her eyes straight to the lady's level and, as she was no longer a servant, her voice came clear and firm, 'I have not ever been rude to you and you know it very well.'

Her steady gaze meant equality, and she would not return insults, nor be diminished. There was no need to prepare all this show, and her glance slightly ironically rolled over Mrs Gill's setting.

'Goodbye, Mrs Gill,' she said with great conviction, making a gesture of a dignified farewell and slowly, to give her time to answer, Maria moved to the door and opened it. Mrs Gill's answer did not come, and Maria went out and gently closed the door. Immediately, she let out a deep sigh of relief and walked to the kitchen, unbuttoning her overall.

'I am going, Mrs Ross. Here, the white overall I need no more.'

'What has happened? What she said to you?' the little woman asked, now wanting to talk.

'Nothing Mrs Ross, nothing. Mr Martines and I will look for another job and Mrs Gill for other servants.'

'Oh I am sorry, very sorry,' her eyes gleaming blue.

'No dear, don't be sorry,' said Maria, and at this moment she felt more sorry for Mr and Mr Ross, who would remain under Mrs Gill's authority, than for her and her husband who had nowhere to go. 'Goodbye, and thanks for everything, Mrs Ross.'

She went up to her flat, and James was still there, delayed from fetching coal.

'You're never eager to comply with your job, are you? Well then, no need to hurry any more. We are sacked.'

'WE SHALL BE all right here, won't we James?' asked Maria, opening the trunk and taking out some sheets. 'Are you helping me to make the bed?'

'First I'll light the fire,' he answered, 'did you say the mistress here pays for the coal? Yes? So you'll see how warm this house will be.'

This house was small. One door led into the kitchen, containing a ladder, a sink, a gas cooker, a shelf, a table and a bath covered by a wooden plank with a rail over it, from which hung a thin curtain. Then there was the windowless sitting room, and from there another door to the bedroom which was fitted with a good carpet. A semi-circular window was magnificently framed by thick double lined curtains that touched the floor.

'They are so thick,' explained the new mistress, 'because when a car enters the drive at night the lights focus on the bed. When I come back from wild parties I don't want to disturb you,' she said, quite casually.

Whilst making the bed, Maria wondered what kind of household they had come to. They had found this job through one of the Spaniards who frequented the Flamenco bar. On the day of the dismissal they had spent all afternoon there. James was talking, and Maria was quiet and alert to any piece of gossip which could be profitable for them. And someone did mention a widow that gave Spanish lessons, who knew of another widow looking for domestic help. She obtained the address of the first and from her the address of the second. The following day James and Maria went to see about the position.

The widow was a round woman, with a fresh and pretty complexion. Dressed in a dark skirt and white blouse half opened by the force of her generous breasts, she wore flat shoes and had unsophisticated manners, but did not look like a person given to orgies.

She and her three children lived in a Manor house outside Leeds surrounded by a large garden and a lodge by the drive, where James and Maria were settling in very happily. Everything was good. Maria had to do a lot of cooking in this house but they had their meals there. James looked after one car and was a gardener and handy man, and, thankfully, there was no other gardener. From the beginning, Maria had more work than James, who could finish at five o'clock in the afternoon, but she didn't mind. On the contrary, she was pleased about it, and it pleased her to see him free to work away on his pursuits around garages and workshops.

Maria and James wanted very much to get out of domestic service. By normal channels it would take four years for an alien to obtain residence and have a job of his own choice. Four years! After the experience with the Gills it was plain James could not stand this kind of work for that long. So Maria didn't worry about his going out looking for employment of his liking. Nevertheless, she made sure he was doing his duty for their new mistress, as it was necessary for him to take the children to and from school without a flight to the town.

The first week went without a hitch. One morning Maria was hanging the washing out and noticed the air. It felt warm, the grass was a tender green, and she breathed deeply, moving her eyes to the sky. How blue it was! It was like home, yes, the spring came to England too after all. She took the empty basket and, with a joyful elastic jump, went up the steps to the washing house. Suddenly winter was no more.

That evening, James came back from town very excited. He had actually been working in a garage workshop. Yes, it was only for two hours, but tomorrow was their day off so he would be able to work all day. They would pay him well and give him as much work as he liked, and he was so happy!

'Are you sure you have understood properly, James?' asked Maria, not giving her self too much hope, 'you know that without a permit...I don't know how?'

'Yes, they know,' he interrupted, 'if is only part time you know, just a few hours, is all right.'

'Well, anyhow, I think it is better if Mrs Munns knows nothing.'

James continued to chat about it, saying how well he would do the work, so well that they would ask him to do it again and again, and would be compelled to hire him, and they would pay him so much because no one was doing the things he could do. The place was very important, if Maria could see how many cars there were!

Maria sat by him quietly folding the washing, and, although she seemed to be listening, she stopped still, and, with one hand inside a sock, passed the other slowly across her forehead.

'What is the matter, have you a headache?'

'No, no. I was thinking what I shall do tomorrow while you are working.'

'Oh, you. What you ought to do is rest. After that you can go to Leeds on the bus and do the shopping. I am going to earn more and soon we won't notice that the wages are less here. Buy things to make a good supper, then you go to the Flamenco and wait there for me.'

Maria said yes, although it was not what she wanted to do. Where would the School of Music be? How is one to find out what is going on in a big town? Where should she ask? She hadn't the faintest idea. A stranger in a large city is like a person who has a car but has no key to drive it and is only able to look at its exterior, so that use and participation are beyond reach. Maria reflected that if James was doing his own thing she could certainly try to do hers. Why not? She would unfold the Mandolin, with a full day in front of her.

She smiled at him, and, taking her hand out of the sock, turned it out so that it was ready to wear.

They went to bed and, when the mistress's car passed their window, they were still awake. The headlights, two powerful beams, came through the thick curtains, chasing each other above their bedstead like two full moons.

'The man who is always round here is her lover. And they both get drunk. I have seen him today with a full box of bottles of gin.'

'No, James it cannot be, the children call him Uncle Albert. He must be a relation of hers.'

'You are telling me yourself how every morning you have to clean away empty bottles.'

'Yes and full ashtrays, and wine glasses, but that does not mean they get drunk.

' A car was heard, and then she continued, 'You see? He is going, he is not staying to sleep.'

'He's done.'

'Oh, shut up! And do not start getting into bother with him like the Gill's gardener, please.'

In the morning James went to work early. Maria remained in the house alone, as there was no need to go in the manor at all. She could do what she pleased. What a wonderful feeling! She began eagerly to tidy up her home. This bedroom, empty of furniture but for a double bed, needed a couple of stools. This would be the first thing they would buy; the kitchen chair had been placed there although it didn't fit. She took it and went back to the kitchen, where she considered the curtains, which were a faded crimson colour and very ugly. She would buy a piece of material, a gay red and white check, large enough for the curtains and the space beneath the sink. She went back to the sitting room humming a tune and proceeded to clean the fireplace and get it ready. James liked so much to see a lit fire every evening.

Still humming her song, it suddenly dawned on Maria how much she enjoyed the housework and was not in a hurry to take the mandolin out. This eagerness, which replaced the enthusiasm she had previously had for music, brought forward a feeling of slight resentment. She felt a sense of unfaithfulness, but why? During her years as a student she'd promised everything to her music; nothing, nothing was going to tear her apart from it. No matter what life would bring about, love, marriage or children, she had been firmly convinced that all this would compliment her music, not replace it. It was necessary to live and to experiment with the vital strings, life itself needed to tense these strings with the warmth of real living. What was happening to her? Was it that this new living would now fulfil her? A married life?

These reflections nevertheless led her towards the trunk to look for the mandolin. Then she sat on the floor checking the instrument, tensing the strings, looking at the papers, and decided she'd go to town to buy a new 'tooth'.

The road was not far away but the buses were far in between. Whilst waiting and seeing so many cars pass, Maria began to brood about James's reluctance to let her drive. Since they had bought the Ford, whenever she pointed out her wish he would invariably find an excuse, saying that the engine was not in tune yet, or it was raining, or the brakes were not so good. Another time it was foggy, or the road was icy, and it was always too dangerous for Maria to take to the wheel. The last time she'd asked it was the gears that were difficult to get in right. James was an expert and could manage very well but it would be madness to let Maria, who had no experience whatsoever, go on the road. If she thought that passing a test was sufficient she was mistaken. To drive well, he emphasised, 'One needs hours of practice like me. And besides, here you have to drive on the left. When the car is completed I'll let you practice a little'.

On her arrival in Leeds Maria went directly to a music shop, remembering having seen one near the Woolworth's store. There they sold records but, as Maria and James had no record player, it would be no use buying any. All the same, Maria searched excitedly through them. After a few minutes she stopped, holding in her hand Vivaldi's concert for flute and mandolin and, unable to resist the temptation to hear it, asked the attendant to put it on for her and locked herself in the listening cabin. As the first notes played she felt transported, and the cabin disappeared, with present forgotten. She was in the concert hall. Her dress grew longer and became silky, turning to apple green. As she played her first concert, she could hear the angels' wings beating above her, brushing white into the blue sky, up and down the steps of heaven. The clear waters of the brook fell over the slippery pebbles, and the fairies' daughters skipped over their ropes.

Little girls came in on tiptoe and brought flowers for her. White roses or red carnations? No – they were magnolias. Everyone was clapping. The floor was carpeted and soft, like the hall at the Gill's. No, no it was Mrs Munns's now, and James would be waiting for her.

Suddenly she felt a terrible oppression on her chest, and she needed air. The cabin was so small, what was she doing there? Maria turned the music off, and the silence brought her back to reality. She came out of the cabin, and the shop assistant glanced at her with cold incredulity. Maria did not buy the record; she went to look for another one. She eventually found it – Beethoven's five pieces for mandolin and piano. She kept it for a while in her hand, and the assistant continued watching and waiting. Reluctantly, slowly and carefully, she replaced the record on the stand, sighed deeply and moved to another counter to buy the plectrum.

Maria felt content as the time passed away unnoticed in the shop. She casually looked at her watch and was surprised to realise that it was almost time to meet James at the Flamenco. Nevertheless she didn't hurry, knowing full well her husband would not rush to leave his work in order to meet her at the set time. Even if this once he were to arrive before her, surely he would find someone to talk to and pass the time. She did her shopping with light spirits, happily looking forward to starting again with her music.

When she arrived at the Flamenco it was far past their meeting hour, yet James was not there.

She left her bags on a chair to approach the bar for some coffee. The wall behind the bar had a painted Manola, black, horrid and disjointed under a bolero skirt, and Maria turned her eyes away.

'A gentleman came asking for you,' the young man serving informed her.

'Ah, is my husband, where is he?'

'No he was not your husband.'

'No? And he was looking for me?' she laughed, 'why?'

'I don't know, but he was very impatient, and waited here few minutes and then said he was going to the market in search for you.'

Maria's smile vanished and she asked again, 'Are you sure he was not my husband?' 'Sure he wasn't,' Julio, who had appeared from behind, confirmed. Maria returned to her seat, puzzled at what the connection, if there was any, was between this person seeking her and her husband. She was drinking her coffee slowly when she became startled by a hand touching her shoulder.

'Mrs Martines?' she heard and turned quickly to see a worried looking middle aged man, saying, 'your husband sent me, he said I would find you here.'

'Why?'

'I am sorry to say, that...but that is...I am sorry,' he was saying awkwardly while Maria's heart began throbbing. 'Your husband has had an accident, no, don't panic, he is all right, but we have taken him to hospital, he has a broken leg.'

'*Mare de Deu Santissima!*' exclaimed Maria in Catalan, and, thinking she was going to faint, she stood up. Feeling short of breath, she opened her mouth for air, then, trying to close it, made a strange gurgling sound as if she was going to laugh.

The man took hold of her arm to steady her and said, 'Shall I accompany you to the hospital? My car is outside.'

He was already taking her bags and, when she recuperated her use of English she replied, 'Yes please, take me to him.'

Inside the car, through the town, and towards the hospital the man was explaining how the accident occurred. He was the owner of the garage where James had been working when he'd slipped, just a simple slip and fall, but they soon saw that he was seriously hurt and called for the ambulance. The owner himself went to the hospital and waited for the doctor to examine him. He said that James was asking for her all the time, telling him where she would be, so he went to the Flamenco twice and to the market looking for her. He had also informed Mrs Munns about the accident.

St. James's Hospital was enormous; it consisted of several buildings enclosed by a tall brick wall. The car went in through the big iron gate. The man knew where to go and they didn't waste any time, getting into a lift then walking down a long corridor to a wide door. The sign above the door said 'Ward 32', and a nurse was coming out of it.

'She is the wife of the Spaniard that broke his leg today,' said the man.

The nurse gestured and moved aside to let them in. Maria was instantly struck by the long rows of white beds. The invalids all turned their eyes on her, and she felt very embarrassed. She fixed her gaze on the black stockings of the nurse in front, thinking herself an intruder into the privacy of these men in their suffering. They stopped in front of a screen.

In all her life Maria had only entered a hospital ward once. In a flash she recalled the memory of that time and was seized by a terrible anguish. It had been a children's ward in Barcelona. A school companion was very ill, and she went to visit. There were two rows of white beds like these, but smaller, and the one behind the screen was hiding the body of the little girl she was too late to see alive. She could still remember the colour of that face, once full of freckles and laughter, turned ashen by cancer, as though a shake had slashed through her.

The nurse wheeled the screen open and Maria saw James's face. It was very white on the white pillows, and he had black patches for eyes and hair.

'Thank God they've found you! Where have you been?'

'Oh James, my darling! What has happened?' she cried, embracing him.

Then, at once conscious of the presence of the others, she straightened herself up again, but her legs felt very shaky. The nurse put a chair by the bed and made her sit down, saying she could stay as it was near visiting time and there was no point in going just to come back. The garage man wanted to leave.

'I am going,' he said, 'I'll take the Ford to Scarcroft Manor and, if you like Mrs Martines, your shopping bags too?'

'Oh yes, thank you, thank you very much, you are very kind, thanks.'

Left alone behind the screen she took James's hands and kissed him tenderly.

'Poor James, my darling! Does it hurt a lot?' she asked, noticing the apparatus hanging from the ceiling, holding his bandaged leg upward.

'They have to put a pot on it yet. I will mend well, here they know a lot about these things.'

'Do you know what the doctor said, did you understand him?'

'He said nothing.'

'I shall ask later. Yes, I'm certain you'll mend well, and they will give you painkillers. Does it hurt very much? Oh, how sorry I am,' and she went to kiss him repeatedly. Her heart felt full of anguish and sorrow to see him lying there suffering. She wished with all her might she could diminish his pain. 'Say what you want, what you need and I'll bring it for you.'

'I want you with me. Where did you put yourself this afternoon?' he reproached, 'I am here since two o'clock.'

She was thoroughly reproaching herself as well, how is it possible that Maria was transported into a place with heavenly illusions while James was suffering horrors in an ambulance and transported to hospital? How could it be? Her love was not great enough, she felt, as she should have had the foresight of deep revealing love.

'How could I imagine,' she said to him with conviction, 'what happened, it is true that I arrived late to the Flamenco and I am very, very sorry, besides even if I had been in the market with so many people the man would not be able to find me.'

'We have been given supper,' James said, speaking about another matter in too much self-pity to notice her avoiding saying where she had actually been, 'very early, before you came, but I ate nothing, it tasted like decomposed cabbage.'

'Of course you were not hungry after the accident. I may be able to bring you something to eat. Soup, the kind you like, eh?'

Meanwhile, the visitors had come and were now leaving. A nurse moved the screen away and asked Maria to call at the office for a visiting card.

'I shall write to you every day darling,' Maria promised, 'now try to sleep and the time and pain will pass.'

She went, feeling weak as though she was in a misty fog. The fog over her eyes blurred the person giving her the yellow card. Soon after, she found the street, but it was dark, and she did not know where to turn. She would have to ask the way, she must make an effort, and so she began to walk down the street until the fresh air cleared her eyes and stopped her voice from trembling.

When she arrived at the manor Mrs Munns was waiting for her. The mistress was full of commiseration and sympathy and almost embraced her.

'Get yourself a bed ready upstairs,' she said, 'you're staying here tonight, I don't want you to sleep on your own at the lodge.

'I don't mind being on my own,' she replied meekly.

'Well, tonight you'll remain here,' Mrs Munns added, 'I understand very well how you feel now. I know because when my husband...when I lost him. Oh, it seemed the world had ended. It was a terrible car accident. I only saw him once in hospital, terrible! After that everything was different for me.'

Maria stared in horror. *Only saw him once.* Those words stuck in her mind, increasing her desolation, yet she attempted to respond.

'But my husband...' Maria stopped short. How could she say your husband did die, but mine will not? She couldn't.

'Come,' said the mistress, taking her to the drawing room. There, she opened a cabinet, got out two glasses and filled them.

'Here, drink it. I think that will do you good.'

The young woman took the glass to her lips, and it tasted so strong she asked for more soda water, wondering if this would soothe the pain. One gets used to strong drinks or to strong strikes from life. That night, she slept badly. When light came it found her tired, but she got up and began her work. Wondering who would take the children to school, as the mistress hardly ever rose before nine o'clock, and if she did she wasn't lively enough to drive, Maria wished she had the confidence herself. Then one of the children came up to tell her that one of the neighbours, a very good friend, would take them.

Maria did not leave the house until she had cleared up after afternoon tea. Then Mrs Munns said that there was no need for her to come back that day unless she wanted to sleep there, which she was more than welcome to. Maria replied that she'd prefer to stay in her own home, but gave her thanks.

She had not been in her house since the previous day. Upon opening the door she saw the shopping bags on the kitchen floor. Slowly she unfolded the packets, and the two good lamb chops, which she would have to eat by herself. She placed the bottle of wine carefully on top of the larder, and then took the music things into the sitting room. The mandolin still lay quietly in its case. Maria looked at it for a few seconds, then, kneeling, she placed the papers, strings and nail into the case and reluctantly laid it down. Her hand went over it with a light touch, like a farewell to a child. Then she put the case in the bottom of the trunk, locked it and moved it out of sight.

After that she went into the bedroom, drew the curtains and stretched herself on the bed. She had half an hour before going to the hospital, which she used as time to think.

She began analysing her situation. It was very unfortunate that this should happen only a week after starting their new job. What would the mistress do? Would she wait for James to recover? The accident did not occur while working for her but somewhere else, and she could very well say it was not her responsibility. They had no working contract with her. The permit to work and stay in England was for a year and for Mr Gill. They had been to the police and declared their change of address and employment, and Mrs Munns confirmed she was giving them both, that was all.

What Mrs Munns wanted, reflected Maria, was to have no bother, and nothing to do. She liked to get up late, to eat well and to have people around her for drinks and conversations. The man whom the children called uncle seemed to save her any sort of work from replenishing her cellar to dispatching her correspondence. Maria had noticed that the letters sent to the manor were piling up, and lay unopened in the ladies bureau. One day, when she gave the mistress the afternoon mail she didn't bother to look at what they were and indicated for Maria to put them in the desk. When Maria opened the bureau, the pile of mail already there tumbled out and some fell on the floor.

Maria picked them up and Mrs Munns said, laughing, 'You know Maria, someday I'll be taken to prison for not paying those bills,' and, with a gesture of self forgiveness she added, 'I must ask Albert to look at them for me.'

It was not for lack of money that she disliked that work, because her husband had left her well off, and she was not mean – it was simply indolence. In spending she was careless; she had accounts everywhere, at the butchers, the bakers, with the coal man, and at the main stores so she could buy anything from a needle to a tennis net by simply picking up the phone.

Considering all this, Maria concluded that if James's accident gave no extra bother to her things could go well. Her mind cleared, and the holes in her thoughts became filled by this answer. She would do the work, she could look after the central heating and mow the lawn, she could do it all. It wouldn't be difficult, she assured herself, jumping out of bed. Today, as soon as I'm back from hospital, I'll talk to Mrs Munns, she thought.

The next day Maria got up early, and from then on every morning she was in the manor at half past seven, making the first tea of the day, having first passed through the boiler house, emptied the ashes and refilled the boiler. In the house she cleaned the fire grates, emptied ashtrays, dusted, vacuumed the carpets, made the beds and cleaned the bathroom. She then telephoned the grocer, washed the salad, cooked the dinner and scraped the pans. Later, she prepared the ice-cubes and even made the soda water having learned to manage the apparatus to convert water into carbonic gas. She washed and ironed clothes and did some sewing. In spite of the help from the daily woman she could not find enough time to include the gardening James was supposed to do. It was Uncle Albert who spent a long Saturday afternoon up and down the lawn pushing the mower.

The hour to go to hospital thus came quickly. Working until the last minute she had to run for the bus and, on returning, ran back eagerly to do her extra work. She served suppers to guests, or drinks, or coffee and then washed more dishes, more glasses, and cleaned the cooker or the fridge. Returning to the lodge at ten or eleven o'clock in the evening, exhausted with aching feet, legs and arms, Maria fell into bed and still made the effort to write a love letter every night to her husband, writing until the pen would fall out of her hand because her eyes had refused to remain open.

The days came, passed and were gone. The half hour visiting time was the shortest part of the day for James and Maria. The rest of the twenty-three and a half hours they had to live apart were longest and most unbearable for James. Everything around him was foreign – the way people spoke, the dull and monotonous meals and the absurdity of the timetable. That he should be awoken at six o'clock in the morning for a cup of tea was the limit! The pain in his leg was intense, and, so that the doctor could pull it regularly (causing him real agony) it had still not been plastered. All this drove him towards his wife, claiming her attention and wanting her love. The little time they were together didn't comfort him enough. He wanted her to be the first person to enter the ward and the last to leave it.

When the nurse would come in ringing the bell all the other visitors would go, but he would keep hold of Maria to kiss her more until the nurse stopped at the bottom of his bed with the bell raised in her hand and said, 'the time is up,' in light jest. Then Maria would walk along the two rows of the beds feeling very embarrassed, knowing that all the men on the ward were looking at her and laughing. She wished her husband's bed was next to the door.

Every morning Maria ran to the main road to post the letter she'd written the night before, so a distressed James could cheer up during the day. In the evening she'd run again to the road so as to not miss the bus, wishing to be the first to step into the ward, but the buses would not run faster for her and when she arrived at Beckett Street there was always a queue of silent people patiently waiting for the hospital gates to open.

'If I were to come by car,' she said to James, 'I might be the first in the queue.'

The desire to see her entering the ward must have been very deep because he consented in letting her use the Ford. 'Well yes, but you have to do as I tell you. First check the petrol, there must be enough, sufficient for a few days at least, you must be careful in changing gears, do not accelerate and press the clutch to the bottom. If you can't get the gear in, drive in first very slow, not to make water boil, you could burn the engine.'

Maria had not driven a car since she passed her test quite some time ago. Then, with the driving licence in her handbag she had felt very pleased with herself and very sure she knew how to drive a vehicle. Yet, since James had bought the Ford that confidence had been eroding away.

Coming back from hospital, thinking that at last she would use the car, she was seized by apprehension and decided she would practice before driving into town.

From the time James went into hospital she had been working non-stop. It had been ten days. She thought she might ask the mistress for a day off and then she could go to visit their friends, the Bentleys.

James and Maria had met these friends working in the Gill's house. Roy Bentley worked for the family on a farm they owned at Wyke. The place consisted of a few scattered fields, one or two manors and a row of cottages holding onto each other at the edge of an old lane. Dependent on the farm or manor, those dwellings possessed nothing but a handkerchief of rusty green land at the back. Roy and Andrea lived in one of the cottages with their two small children.

Andrea was a city girl, from Liverpool, where she'd lived and worked in an office until she married Roy, a young and restless printer, who was often changing jobs. At that time he was trying farming. Andrea, finding herself very much out of place, soon became friendly with Maria, who herself was feeling the strain of the new environment. They didn't lack for topics of conversation. The two men, although unable to carry on a conversation, could understand each other very well when bending over the Ford or the old Vauxhall Roy had.

As Mrs Munns thought it very appropriate that Maria should have a day off, she had soon made plans to spend the day in Wyke. The idea of driving didn't let her rest and she was up early to clean the house, as she hadn't had a minute in the past week.

When the house was tidy, she went to the car, which was still where the garage man had left it, by the wall behind the house. She sat in the driver's seat, and the first thing she noticed was that she could not reach the pedals. She stepped off and went to the lodge for a cushion. Stretching her legs, she thought, I'll manage now, and smiled. Then she turned the key whilst gathering around her memory all the things to be done. Gears – first, then the second once on the road. Ah, must remember to go on the left. She thought she would drive very near the kerb and slowly let the fast cars pass. Indicate when about to turn – yes, yes I haven't forgotten, she thought. At the third attempt the engine was ticking and she listened to it with joy, tried the gas and the noise accelerated. Now she had to turn the car facing the way out. Was there enough room? Yes, it seemed so. Maria easily put the car into first gear. James always exaggerates, she thought, with a sigh of relief. She lifted the brake and the clutch, and the car began moving. Her smile widened as she turned the steering wheel, and then she realised there was not sufficient space to turn the car in one go. Now she had to look for reverse gear. She lifted the clutch and the car went forward. She drove over the plants. She pressed the brakes, and the engine roared with an infernal noise. Panicking, she realised she was pressing hard with both feet. She quickly released the clutch and accelerator then the car stopped completely.

Sweating all over, and fearing someone from the house would come out to see what was happening, Maria tried to start the engine again and put it in gear. Not knowing which one would be in she lifted the clutch very slowly. Thankfully, the car moved backwards. Then, looking over her shoulder she saw it was going the wrong way, and she glanced at the steering wheel and turned it to the opposite direction, then looked back. *Stop, stop!* Now she was going much too fast. After a few seconds she looked forward and thought that this time she might be able to move out. She rested, and wiped her forehead, and her face was burning so much that she had to lower the window to get a gulp of fresh air. She pressed the clutch and changed gear then, moving very slowly, at last managed to get the car to face the way out.

When she arrived at the road she was smiling once again. Soon after, she was driving towards Wyke!

Their friends welcomed her warmly. She remained there all day, resting contently until the time for the hospital visit came. Then Roy turned the car on for her, giving her advice, but she had got over the first panic and decidedly started down the old lane. Up the hill she passed clattered cottages. Maria looked back and saw her friends waving good-bye, and she waved her hand and carried on driving, full of confidence. In those narrow lanes she felt sure that the only danger would be a large vehicle coming in the opposite direction, as there was no room for two.

That evening, she was the first to arrive at the hospital gates. The queue formed behind her as silently and patiently as always. Maria explained everything she had done that day to James, emphasising the excitement and contentment, and expecting his sympathy and for him to be glad for her, as was natural between two people who loved one another.

What she received was his reproach. She should not have gone to the Bentley's, as inexperienced as she was, and driving to the hospital and back home was sufficient. Besides, why go to see their friends on her own? And to invite them for tea on her next day off!

'It is not proper,' he stated firmly, 'not proper at all that while your husband is here suffering, you enjoy yourself.'

'It is not enjoyment, it is not a party,' she protested, 'it is just having company.'

'Think of me, think about me, my little darling,' he said, wanting to sweeten her.

'I do not cease to think of you, not for one minute all day and every day.'

'I love you more, do not make me suffer. Think about the day I shall be well. You'll see how I shall take you to nice places, we'll go out to dine where there is music, the kind of music you like. You shall see how well we'll enjoy ourselves when I am out of here. But now do not let me suffer. Today do ring me as soon as you get home, I like to know you have arrived. I do not want to be anxious thinking something could have gone wrong with your driving, you are so inexperienced!'

His tone and attitude, like that of a moaning, helpless child, made tears appear in Maria's eyes, and she readily admitted that she should sacrifice herself entirely. She would go from her work to hospital, from hospital to work. She would keep the freedom of her thoughts dedicated to her husband.

'Think about me at such a time of day,' he demanded of her, 'I will think about you at the same time and we will meet in thought, pray for me.'

She did as he asked, and she brought him soup she'd cooked especially for him, and fruits and sweets. One day she brought the bottle of wine but the nurse made her take it back, saying he could not have alcohol. James complained incessantly about the quantity of cups of tea he had to drink per day. Nevertheless, he was getting better.

Maria did not go to Wyke again, but she went to Mass every Sunday. One Saturday she went to Confession and, when she told him, he wasn't pleased about that either.

'Why have you to waste time like that? You are not committing any sin. Or are you? Is it so? Tell me, is it that you are sinning while your husband is here unable to move?'

'No, my darling no. It is only that it was a long time since I went and I wanted to go to Communion, that's all.'

Maria had the naivety of a bride who tells everything to her husband with the confidence that his responding would be in accord with her line of thought. It was as though her heart was upon her sleeve for him to peck at. The days of their courtship, when he did agree with what she said and what she believed, were not far away. But now her opinions were not valid, causing perplexity and somehow disgust to Maria. She had the feeling of being thwarted, yet she could not yet guess how to struggle against it.

One day she arrived at hospital more tired than usual, and the nervous tension of so many days broke her down in sobs. What was the matter? She could not explain, as she didn't exactly know, perhaps she was tired.

'If you are tired,' was his reaction, 'tired of your husband being in hospital. If you are so unhappy, why don't you go to your mother? You go to Barcelona, go there and wait for me, wait there until I'm better and I'll come and fetch you. Besides, why are you doing so much work? You mustn't sacrifice yourself for the others. You have to do all you can for us, only for me, not for the Munns, not for Uncle Albert or for anyone else...do you hear?'

As he spoke he grew cross, whilst Maria's tears were drying up on the heat of her growing irritation, provoked by the absurdity of his comments. It would have been enough for him to ease her tension and comfort her, and just to recognise that she too was suffering, even though she had not broken her leg. She was giving up many things as well.

The pleasure that driving was giving her soon ended. One evening on her way back from the hospital, she reached the crossroads at the end of

Beckett Street and the Ford stalled in the middle. She thought she had been too careful entering the crossing and hadn't given enough gas. Putting the handbrake on she tried to start the engine, but it did not work. The cars were passing left and right, and she tried again and again. The engine did not turn. Maria feared a policeman would come up and ask her to move and she did not know how. She glanced around and thought she could do nothing but try again, and she did until finally the battery went flat. Luckily, a young man approached and offered to push the car to the kerb and directed her to a garage further down the street. She was very relieved, and she went to fetch someone to have a look at the Ford.

The people from the garage had a look at the car, and found so many things wrong with it that she said she would have to consult her husband. There ended her driving, and she went home by bus. The following day, James said that he didn't want anyone to repair his car. Maria had to ask the garage to tow the car back to the Manor. Then once again she was running for buses, looking after the minutes and the hours with the added worry of having upset her husband after breaking his precious car.

TWO FULL MONTHS had passed. The children were on holiday, and played about the house and the garden all day. They always wanted teas and sandwiches for picnics, and it created a lot of work. It was the middle of summer, yet Maria would not have been able to tell if it was hot or cold, as she had no time to notice the weather. It could not have been very hot, however, because everyone was having a hot bath every day.

Maria was longing for James to come out of hospital. One day in late July she found him at home, his leg stretched inside a calliper and aiding himself with two sticks. She saw him, his eyes shining and, letting the sticks fall, he opened his arms, and she threw herself into them.

'Oh my God! What a joy!'

'I am home at last,' he said, pressing her tight against him.

They kissed each other rapturously, and one could not be untied from the other. The warmth of their lips melted together sweetly, and they shared a hug so tight that their bodies vibrated as one with the same current. The desire smarted her, as, unbuttoning her blouse, she let his hand cover her breast, whilst her hand caressed the skin of his back under his shirt. She pressed him close to her, wanting to feel the warm touch of his body that was so long yearned for.

Happy days followed. James had to go to the hospital regularly for treatment and Maria still worked hard, although now she could finish a bit earlier. Everyone was happy to see James back, and he was also happy, affirming that he would start working as soon as he was out of his calliper. Meanwhile, he would get up late, walk about the gardens, then to the house for his meals, where he would sit in the children's room watching television for hours. He cleaned his car and had a good look at it and another day he cleaned the Mistress's, still holding on to his crutches. Maria had given up the care of the boiler, for now James could look after it, but a few days later he let it die off.

'It does not matter,' he said, 'the weather is hot, they do not need heating.'

'No, but they want hot water.'

Soon, the taps in the house were running cold, and Mrs Munns complained. The boiler was by then very cold and not easy to get going again. James and Maria spent many hours trying to do so without succeeding and, in the end, Uncle Albert had to come and explain how these kind of boilers had to be lit. James, who had learned a lot of English during his stay in hospital, said that he already knew and that the blame was on the installation of the chimney. Uncle Albert replied that this was not so, and that the fault was theirs, as they shouldn't have let the fire go out. Maria left them and went back to the kitchen, uneasy, as she had noticed that the two men looked at each other with little liking.

On Sunday Mrs Munns, her children and Uncle Albert were having dinner, whilst, in the children's room, James and Maria were taking theirs. Maria had served at the table and, going from one dining room to the other, had already cleared the meat and served the dessert. As usual, there was a lot of meat left over. The size of the joint was always enormous as they were good meat eaters and fussy too; it had to be the best available and cooked in exactly the right way. What was left they ate later in salads.

Hot or cold, it tasted delicious, and Maria and James had never eaten meat so good and tender. That day James wanted some more so Maria went to cut a slice for him. She was putting it on the plate when Uncle Albert came in to fetch some more cream.

'What are you doing?' he shouted angrily at Maria, who looked at him with sudden fear, 'you are spoiling my joint!'

'No sir, I'm only cutting a little piece for my husband.'

'Is it that I haven't given him enough?' he shouted even louder.

He was the one who carved the joint and filled the plates whilst Maria, standing by him, would distribute them, taking the last two to the kitchen for her and James. Now the man seemed very angry with her, or maybe just with her husband. Maria wasn't sure.

'I do not want you to touch the meat again, understand?'

'I am very sorry,' mumbled Maria, feeling very ashamed. When she returned the plate to her husband she asked, 'Have you heard, James, what he said to me? He is cross because he says I have spoiled his meat.'

'Yes I have heard, he has no right to shout at you in this way. His beef joint, my foot! As if he is buying it. Believe me, he is very well paid for just to give pleasure to that woman.'

'Don't talk like that, please.'

The days were longer and dusk came very late. After supper, Maria and James usually went out. He had repaired the car and she was driving.

Leg stretched, he sat at her side directing her constantly: 'accelerate', 'don't accelerate', 'change gear', 'look behind', 'don't overtake', 'hold your foot' and so on, getting on her nerves and shattering her confidence as if she was a mechanical puppet.

'Leave me alone, please!' she protested, 'stop treating me as if were a learner. You behave as if I've never driven alone before.'

Nevertheless, he persisted in his pestering so much that later, when he was able to bend his leg and took the steering wheel, she was ready to give it up completely and swallowed her frustration the best she could. With his much improved English, he was eager to make himself understood by everyone, or at least it seemed so because whoever was facing him would invariably reply, 'Yes, yes'. If it were the English person talking to James he would say, 'Yes, yes'. Maria was not sure how much he understood, and worried about the danger of a misunderstanding. It was a difficult task, even in Catalan, to explain the rules of English to James, because he always understood the concepts of his own imagination better than what was said to him in any language.

They visited the garage where he had had his accident and visited others too. They went to see the Bentleys, who then came to have tea with them at the lodge. Andrea, who was always wishing for company, liked to converse with Maria while Roy would sit with a child on his knee, patiently saying 'yes' to James and waiting for his wife to finish talking.

And James was not working yet. One morning, after taking tea up to her mistress, which she did as usual before starting her work downstairs, Maria went to drink hers when, suddenly, she left it untouched. She was sick of that incessant English tea drinking! When Maria had served and cleared the children's breakfast, she picked up the tray and placed upon it a plate of cornflakes, a large cup of coffee, three pieces of toast and two boiled eggs. She checked with satisfaction that it was a good breakfast and moved towards the door when Mrs Munns stepped into the kitchen.

'Where are you going Maria?'

'To take breakfast to my husband.'

'Don't you think he could come for it?' and glancing at the tray added, 'why two eggs?'

'Is...it is...' the girl felt troubled because she saw the mistress was not pleased, 'no I do not give him two eggs everyday, one is mine, I was not hungry today.'

With the tray in her hands, and unsure whether to leave it in the kitchen, she made a gesture to retract when the mistress said, 'Go now, go, I do not mind that he eats well, but here in the house, you understand?'

And she opened the door so that Maria could leave the room.

'Thank you,' Maria said, wondering if Mrs Munns believed her about the two eggs, because it was true. She'd always brought his breakfast to the lodge without anyone objecting. It was unfortunate that today Mrs Munns had noticed it.

On arriving at the lodge she explained everything to James, and she expressed her suspicions that they may be getting tired of him not being able to work yet.

'Well, if they think I am going to work before getting my leg right they are mistaken.'

'But James darling, you could do something. You have been able to repair your car and they've seen it. So you can try to do a bit for them. Consider that we have to stay here until you get a permit to work in a garage.'

He ate his eggs, drunk his coffee and remained in bed. He did not like to get up early, nor did he think he had a duty to perform. His wish was to work as a mechanic. When he was just back from hospital, he wandered about the house and garden asking what he could do to help and was told that he should rest his leg. Then, as he became stronger and better, his interest in work gradually diminished. His outings became more frequent and his determination to obtain other kinds of work firmer. He decided to visit all the garages in the area until he could find someone interested in his work, and would consequently write to the Home Office for a special permit.

One day, Maria returned home from work later than usual as there had been guests at the house, and, stepping in, she called out, but a strange silence replied. She rushed to the bedroom and, there on the floor, she saw the empty calliper.

'He is gone without me!' she exclaimed with regret.

Slowly, she turned to the sitting room where she dropped herself into an armchair, pulling a face. Feeling nauseous but not knowing why, she then recalled the green sauce she'd made and later ate, and thought that now she was going to be sick. Stretching her stomach carefully she remained very still, looking at the fire burning in August. In her country no-one needed a fire in summer!

Her body was still, but her mind began to work, and she became aware of the emptiness and the need for answers. Was it because the attitude of Mrs Munns was changing? Had she not been taking care in doing things right? Maybe she was tired? Yes, that was it! But it should not be so now that she wasn't running back and forth to the hospital everyday. She was falling into a heavy sleep, into the emptiness, her mind trudging forward to nothing.

When James returned, he showed so much happiness at being able to walk unaided and feeling no pain that Maria forgot that she had been left alone. Saying nothing, she gave him a sweet smile and they went to bed. Maria was blind to what Mrs Munns had seen that morning with the two eggs. Her vision was still concealed by the opaque veil of romance.

The next morning, when Maria was hanging out the washing, a sheet rubbed the floor and became muddy. She didn't feel like washing it again, so she had a look and shook it off and thought it would pass. However, when Mrs Munns put the sheets away she noticed and complained to Maria, adding that last week she did not leave the clothes very clean either.

The clouds were gathering and every day Maria was becoming more sick of food, and, in particular, tea, which she could not drink. On Sunday some guests came for lunch, and all that morning she was busy in the kitchen. Uncle Albert had come a few times to look at his joint of meat, which today was exceptionally large and had to be perfectly cooked. Maria hadn't had breakfast that morning and was feeling a bit faint, but everything went well until she began to serve. Uncle Albert was carving the meat, and Maria was at his side with a plate in each hand. Once the plate was filled she moved to the table where the eldest of the children sat, as she always served first.

'No, that is for Mrs Willis, the guest,' he said.

Maria, ashamed of doing something incorrect, withdrew the plate so quickly that the jolt made the plate in the other hand tilt and all its contents went on the floor over the carpet. The meat, the peas and the gravy all splashed Mrs Munns's stockings.

'Oh my God!'

Terror struck Maria and she stood, with the two plates in her hands, one empty and the other full, like a desolate statue of justice. Someone took the full plate from her, the children started to laugh and Mrs Munns, who was drying her legs, was saying, 'Don't worry Maria, pick it up.'

Whilst Uncle Albert looked as though he was going to slap her, the guests carried on conversing as if nothing had happened.

Maria crouched and began picking up the peas one by one, not wanting to ever get up, and not wishing to show her face, which was ablaze with embarrassment. She never would have were it not for the daily woman who came to help and began cleaning the floor with a wet rag.

Later, when the two women were doing the washing up, Maria must have looked very ill because the woman said she would finish on her own and sent her home. She was feeling bad and very miserable, and needed the rest of the day to get over the mishap.

The next Monday all the family went to Scarborough for a week's holiday. The young couple were left to look after the Manor; to water the garden, to pick potatoes and to wash a pile of blankets. Maria was looking forward to this almost free time as she thought her sickness was due to excess work and tension. Staying in bed longer would cure it but she soon found herself feeling worse than ever.

Nevertheless, she went to the washhouse and began to put blankets into the machine, when suddenly her heart jumped so strongly that it reached her throat, almost choking her; she felt dizzy, and let herself drop on top of the pile of blankets.

It was then that the thought dawned upon her. Will it be? Will it be that I am? She got up faster than she'd fallen, so quickly that she felt dizzy again, and for a moment very weak and faint. Like a falling leaf, she had to hold on to the door.

'James...James!' she shouted, 'where are you?'

She wished to tell him immediately, and started out towards the plot where he should be picking potatoes. He was there and she approached him, her pace slow. The fresh air had cleared her faintness and she felt perfectly well.

She stopped short, suddenly overcome by a strange sense of shyness and simply asked, 'What are you doing?'

'These potatoes are no good,' he said showing her a small one, 'look at them, too little, the famous English potato,' he sneered and then asked, 'What are you doing?'

'The blankets,' she replied, 'will you help me to hang them up please, they are so heavy.'

'After I have finished this row I shall not pick any more.'

Maria went back to the washhouse. Her look had slightly changed, as though a reflection of light had travelled through her.

'When I am sure I'll tell him,' she decided.

Before the Munns family came back she went to the doctor. They'd known Dr Hyman since their

days at the Gill's; he was a Jew and a friend of
the family. He was a stout, rather short man with
a round face, round nose and large eyes that
protruded but were softened by his look of
sympathy and understanding. He had a sweet
smile like Maria.

He had always shown interest in her and when
she had told him her troubles he began to laugh.

'You've got yourself stung by a bumble bee,
haven't you?'

She did not understand what he meant and
blushed, then laughed too.

'To be certain, come back in two weeks time
and then I'll tell you what to do.'

Those two weeks passed very slowly, and the
house went back to normal. The work would not
diminish, although Maria's energy did. She felt
bad all the time, as the feeling of sickness was
continuous and she hardly ate. By now she knew
she was pregnant and although this knowledge
gave her profound joy she could not dwell on it.
All her mental energy was concentrated on supp-
orting her body's strength. She had to keep on
working, so she hid her nausea and did her jobs
well. She had to get up in the morning when all
the cells of her body were calling out for stillness
and rest. Her eyes would not willingly open nor
would her legs sustain her upright, and her hands
would not move. A great struggle went on every
morning, which ended with the victory of her spirit,
when her body would obey and get in motion.

As the weather was still good and meals could
be taken outside, Mrs Munns decided to have
the dining room spring-cleaned. Maria promised

to do it thoroughly and began to clean the carpet, which was the worst. With her knees on the floor, and a brush, shampoo and water she started work, but halfway through the task her strength failed. Stopping frequently to look through the open window, she could see James at the bottom of the garden with a hoe in his hands. He seemed to be working. The mistress was sitting on a deckchair near the house with a tray of drinks at her side, perhaps observing him. Maria sighed deeply, then went back to her bucket.

Her day off came and the carpet was still not finished. That day she went to the doctor. The visit was long, and Dr. Hyman seemed to have plenty of time for her. He asked about her husband and what plans they had for the future, he asked about Mrs Munns and what she was like, what work Maria was doing, and how many hours she worked each week. Sitting on a chair by her side, his mannerisms were like those of a friend, and Maria felt unwary telling him everything.

Then the doctor, pressing her hands lightly as they rested on her lap said, 'Today, when you go home, see Mrs Munns and tell her you are expecting, will you? As soon as you arrive,' he urged. 'Come back and see me in a month, or before if you feel the need,' he got up and gave her a prescription, then he continued, 'take the pills, as they will help diminish the feeling of sickness. I'll write to the hospital and book you in for when the time comes.' Maria stood up, and the doctor put his arm over her shoulder and saw her to the door. 'Look after yourself,' he recommended with a smile.

'Thanks,' she answered with the same soft smile. Her eyes were wet and sparkled as she left the room.

James, who had driven her there and sat in the waiting room, jumped off his seat when he saw her. 'What? What he said? You've been a long time in!'

'Yes,' she nodded.

Outside on the street, he embraced her in a demonstration of joy, saying how happy he was.

'Stop, James, stop!' she said, untangling herself.

He helped her to get in the car, solicitously and fussily. 'Carefully darling,' he said, starting the car, 'you shall not drive any more. God forbid you never know what could happen, an accident or a shock, no, we are lucky my leg is so much better.'

'Where are we going?' she asked, seeing he'd took the wrong turn.

'To the town centre, it is very early.'

'No, please, I want to go home. I don't feel well to go shopping or anything.'

'You won't get tired, we'll go slowly.'

'I want to get home,' she insisted 'I have to talk to Mrs Munns.'

'No need to tell her so soon.'

'Turn please, take me home. You go if you wish but leave me at home first.'

This time he gave in and brought her back to Scarcroft, but his consideration for her of a few minutes ago had vanished and he just left her in front of the road gates, not even taking his hands off the steering wheel.

'I am sure he has something on his mind,' she thought, walking straight to the Manor and past her lodge. There, she met the widow on the corridor between the kitchen door and the children's room.

'I have to talk to you, Mrs Munns.'

'Yes, what do you want to tell me?'

The place was obviously inconvenient, but Mrs Munns did not move, and stood adjusting her blouse and tucking it into her skirt as she repeated, 'What is it you want to tell me?'

'I have been to the doctor,' Maria began indecisively, 'this afternoon, I've just come back,' she paused for a second, 'I am going to have a baby.'

'I know, Maria, it's written on your face. It is very nice to have a baby,' she continued, 'when I had my first I felt the most unique and happy woman in the world. I had three and I would have had more but for losing my husband.' Then, changing her tone of voice, she asked, 'What is your husband going to do now?'

'Oh, yes, now his leg is better.'

'Yes, of course, because you cannot work any more. Have you seen how you look? And the weight you have lost these past weeks! Your husband is not going to do for you what you have done for him,' she assured curtly, 'I think you'd better look for another place.'

'Perhaps he will do it,' Maria replied trying to put some conviction in her voice.

Uncle Albert had come in and, standing by the widow, gazed at the young woman and said with much callousness, 'That man will never do anything, and I'll tell you Maria, send him back to Spain, he is no good for this country.'

Maria, unable to sustain herself any longer, leaned against the wall, totally overwhelmed.

'I am sorry for you Maria,' Mrs Munns continued, 'think about what you must do, but in your state you must not work.'

'I'll think about it,' she uttered, dragging herself to the door that was so near but seemed so far away from her.

Not knowing how, she found herself in the lodge, and she languished on the bed with anguish. She did not know how long she stayed wishing only for the return of James with the medicine, and her mind centred on the means to alleviate her physical affliction. If she could eat it may pass, but she had nothing in her stomach. What if I get up and try something? she thought, but the sole idea of food revolted her stomach and throat. After a long while, after which she thought she had slept, it was dark. Then James came in, joyfully calling her name from the door.

'Are you bringing my medicine?' she whimpered, still in bed and wishing intensely that someone would take care of her. She longed for a return to the past when her mother would bring aromatic infusions to make her stomach better. But her family and her country were so far away! And how helpless she felt.

She took the tablets from James's hand. He sat on the bed and began to open a parcel. When Maria saw it she sprung up, staring at the parcel incredulously.

'No, don't tell me you have bought it!'

'Why not? It is very nice. We'll be able to take photos of our baby.'

'He is not born yet!' she screamed, 'we need many more things before!'

'We need a good camera, the other one is rubbish, this will make such good pictures.'

'Whatever it can do doesn't matter. You mustn't spend the money! Besides, with what have you paid it? Tell me, with whose money? With the money I have earned? I, slaving away being everyone's servant!' Her voice became harsh and thick and she stopped.

'We'll pay for it by instalments,' he continued calmly.

'James!' she cried, losing her patience completely, 'take it back, take it back tomorrow! We are sacked!'

James stopped, and looked at her in disbelief.

'Yes, sacked, because I am pregnant and you are not capable of doing the work they want! You are capable of nothing! You are incapable of understanding that we cannot spend money on a camera! You are useless, you are stupid, very stupid, stupid *and* useless!' In her desperation she threw the words at him furiously, and her frustration at her powerlessness to make him understand the situation as she saw it forced an angry tear down her cheek.

'Am I not capable? Who says that? Full well capable of making you a baby, and you'll see what a baby it shall be,' he said, and taking hold of her he tried to caress and kiss her.

Maria tore away from him and, with a rapid jerk, jumped out of bed saying, 'Uncle Albert says you are good for nothing. He says I should send you back to Spain because you'll do nothing in this country. He is right, you do not even understand we need a cradle before a camera!'

James, still trying to calm her down, tried to embrace her again whilst saying, 'He is the one who is good for nothing more than a drone sucking the widow!'

Maria pushed him back, screaming, 'Leave me alone! Leave me alone! Go away and leave me alone! Why don't you get lost?' then, breaking down into sobs, she put her shoes on and, before he could retain her, ran out of the room.

Without stopping she went outside, walking fast and straight in front of her as if she were following a line that lead where she knew. It was dark but it didn't matter, and she passed the potato plot and carried on until she bumped into the surrounding wall of the property. It was low with uneven protruding stones and, without hesitation, she climbed it and slipped down the other side. The ground became rough and thick with trees, and she slowed her pace and turned to see if James had followed her, hoping he had not. Walking further until she felt her legs going wobbly, she then sat at the foot of a tree, leaning against its bark. It was a quiet night, the sky was clear. She raised her eyes to the stars shining above her. How bright they were! She stayed there, quietly gazing at the wonder of the still, clear, and far away starry sky. Nothing in between, not even a leaf to interfere, only the mysterious distance. She waited until its calm had descended upon her, involving her and moving into her.

After a while, she noticed the freshness of the night and seemed to hear the echo of Dr. Hyman's voice, saying, 'Look after yourself'. She got up, the feeling of sickness gone. She was well and began to walk. She would solve all her problems, she thought, and she would find the answers to fill the emptiness of her mind. She must think, think and act. She reached the main road, and her step was firm and steady as she walked towards her home.

James was outside looking for her, but she had made her mind up not to quarrel. He seemed to have done the same, saying that he was suffering and they must love each other. She made no reply and let him kiss her. He made supper, which she was able to eat, then he did the washing up, and when he went to bed Maria was already sleeping.

The next morning she woke up feeling sick again, but she headed out for work, and took the first cup of tea to the mistress. She made breakfast as usual and everything seemed to be as it always was. Later, she entered the dining room thinking she must finish the cleaning of the carpet. She was looking at it in wonder when the daily woman told her that Mrs Munns had asked her to finish it. Maria glanced at the woman and then at the carpet, where, in the far corner, there were marks from the brush, which were almost dry. She left the room without a word, and walked upstairs, expecting that the beds might be done too, but they were not and she proceeded to tidy the rooms.

At about mid afternoon one of the children came running in to Maria and said, 'Quick, go and see your husband!' The boy was very excited.

Maria went out quickly, thinking that James might have hurt himself, and headed to the lodge. He was not there. She was moving back out again when she saw him coming, using the stick again but swiftly and in a strange trot as if in flight.

'What has happened?' she enquired, going towards him.

He entered the lodge.

'What's happened James?' she persisted. But, in answer, the kitchen darkened and the big figure of Uncle Albert, just fitting into the doorframe, covered the light of the afternoon.

'Do you understand me well?' he said in a curt, authoritative voice. 'I do not want to see you about any more. I'll tell Mrs Munns to serve your notice immediately and you go at once, get out of this place fast, you understand?' Seeing Maria, he addressed her. 'Yes, *you* understand me, don't you? Well, I do not want to see him any more.'

He corroborated his last words with a look of contempt towards James, who, at that moment, appeared to be very angry.

'You go, imbecile, or I'll give one to you!' James shouted in Catalan and rising his stick.

'James, for the love of God!' cried Maria.

But Mr Albert didn't understand Catalan, nor did he see the risen stick as he turned his back and headed towards the house at great speed.

'James, why have you quarrelled? Tell me what has happened!'

'That I am good for nothing. He shall see that I am not. I'll find work straight away.'

'Calm down, James and tell me what he said.'

He kept repeating the same thing, that he was deeply offended by Uncle Albert's scorn. He, who always found someone ready to admire the things he did, at least would imagine he was admired only by the way he was gazed at. Be it a man or a woman, if they were to listen to him without interruption he was sure they were admiring him or amazed at what he'd made. And now Uncle Albert was so blatantly showing his scorn, and was making him mad. It didn't occur to James that Albert could be right, as he did not have a shadow of a doubt about himself. If anybody was lazy it was Albert, if anyone was superficial and out of place in England it was certainly not James, as he had a lot of things to show these people yet.

'I am going to see Roy, he knows someone who works in a very important garage in Leeds, you see if don't find work immediately,' he concluded, and left the house.

Maria, who was still standing in the middle of the room, heard him start the engine of the Ford and pull out in second gear. She let the minute pass, then she went back to the house, thinking she would speak to Mrs Munns.

At the Manor, Uncle Albert was coming out of the sitting room, and passed her without turning his head. In the room, Mrs Munns got up from her desk with a paper in her hand.

'Mrs Munns,' Maria began, at the same time taking the paper being stretched out to her, 'Mr

Albert says we must go immediately,' and she paused, as the widow looked uneasy, 'I do not know what has happened between Mr Albert and my husband. I am afraid they quarrelled.'

'Oh he has already told you to go? Why did he ask me to write a letter then?'

'I don't know,' Maria replied, as she unfolded the paper and read, *This is a final notice. You are dismissed, and requested to leave the premises in seven days time.* Maria raised her eyes and gazed at Mrs Munns. 'Do you want me to work those seven days?'

'No, Maria, it's better if not,' she replied, then, as if she had to look for a better reason to sack her, added in a dry tone, 'you know, you are very slow in your work.'

Maria instantly recalled that Mrs Gill had also tried to offend her. Why did they have to sting like wasps? At that time, Maria had defended herself with dignity, but now, although she felt deeply hurt, she didn't reply. She thought about the quantity of plates she had washed in this house, really washed, not like the English women who never rinsed off the detergent. The carpet she had spent two days cleaning, when the daily woman finished the other half in just half an hour. It was obviously less well done, but did it matter? Now she had been told that she was slow. She had no strength to contradict her mistress.

Mrs Munns, giving her the last of her wages, four pounds for her and nothing for James, added, as if needing another reason to sack Maria, 'You have used a lot of coal, too much indeed. Even when the weather was hot and fires were not needed we could see your chimney smoking.'

Maria's lips remained tightly closed. It was James's fault; she had known they were using coal unnecessarily. At last she mumbled, 'I am very sorry.'

Mrs Munns, who was not, after all, a woman without feeling, said quietly as Maria's back turned, 'Take care of yourself, you do not look well at all.'

Maria arrived at the lodge full of nausea and dropped into a chair, bending over her stomach. She was alone, and there was no one to give her a glass of water or her tablets. After a while she got up, took her medicine and curled again into the armchair. Her head began to throb with questions. What were they going to do? Where could they go to live? How would they get money for food? There were no answers, only emptiness. From now on they couldn't go to the house for their meals. What could they do? In her state, Maria would not find work, and even if she were well, how could they do domestic work? James was definitely useless at it.

'What shall we do?' she asked aloud, but got no answer. The emptiness persisted, then deepened, like a bottomless precipice.

CHAPTER SEVEN

LATE SEPTEMBER AND rain. For a few days, water fell non-stop. From where she was sitting, Maria could see a plucked field, green and soggy, with some cows gnawing despite the rain, constantly, calmly, patiently, like a strange replica of the country people.

'This field and these cows belong to Mr Gill, don't they? Are they also from the farm where Roy works?' she asked Andrea, who sat nearby with little Simon on her lap.

'Yes, and all that field behind too,' she said, getting up, while Maria stretched her arms and received the child from her.

'Let's see if you can walk, hey.'

She steadied him on the floor but the infant remained still, propping his little arms onto Maria's knees and gazing intently at her.

The mother turned the clothes on the fire-guard, nappies and more nappies, folding some and leaving others to dry, then removed the protection and threw coal into the fire. Maria was attentively following all her moves, looking for something she could do to help, eager to show her affection and gratitude. Her eyes shone with emotion as she recalled the previous days.

James had been accepted, provisionally, in to a Leeds garage workshop to work as a mechanic. They would have slept inside the Ford or under a bridge if it had not been for Roy and Andrea. They offered them shelter in their home. They had a room with a double bed to spare, they said, and James and Maria were welcome to use it until better accommodation could be found. However, Maria thought it would be trouble for them, but it was the only alternative they could see, floating as they were in a sea of uncertainty, like bodies from a shipwreck holding onto a drifting log. Maria felt a profound admiration for their friends' generosity.

The house, with just two rooms upstairs, was too small for four adults and two children. The bed occupied all the space in James and Maria's room and the ceiling was so low and slanting that James could not stand without bumping his head. He would grumble and complain about the people who made the houses so small, the houses for the poor. Until now they had been frequenting the houses of the rich with large rooms and tall ceilings. Even the little lodge had all the modern conveniences they needed, but this cottage, a forlorn place, had no bathroom and toilet except for a hole in a hut a few yards away. James felt annoyed at having to wash and shave in a one tap kitchen sink and walk outside for his necessities. It was not that he had lived in luxury all his life – on the contrary – but he said he had come to this country to find better living conditions. Britain was a modern, advanced country, so why then, were there all these old fashioned standards of living?

In spite of his complaints, he wrote letters to his family in the same enthusiastic manner, telling them how well he was doing in England and that they wanted for nothing. To his last remark Maria was indignant, simply because a few minutes before he'd been grumbling about the poor and dull supper Andrea had given them. She tried to make him understand the difference between having everything and wanting for nothing and being in want of everything for having nothing.

'We are now in the nothing, we have absolutely nothing, no home, no job, no money.'

'Yes, but what you want me to say to my parents? Things to make them worry?'

'The truth or nothing,' she answered categorically, incapable of telling a lie even to make her own folk happy.

'But what is truth?'

What truth was to Maria, what she saw as reality, James didn't see in the same way. For her, the difference between fact and fantasy, false and faithful were separated with a straight and clear thin line. But not for James; his border line was wide, sinuous, intricate, where his mind flowed and very often got lost.

Andrea was taking the child back in to her arms.

'How do you feel now Maria? You don't feel so sick do you? Shall we have some coffee?'

The two women went in to the kitchen entrance and wash place where, by the gas cooker, there was a cabinet like a writing desk where Maria sat two mugs.

'When I was expecting my first I felt very sick too,' Andrea continued whilst placing the kettle onto the gas ring, 'it goes you know, after the third month you begin to feel better. For the second baby I was very unwell but only in that I had a constant urge to go to the toilet. It was very embarrassing; I couldn't go far from home.'

Maria looked out of the window at the low stone outbuildings shining grey under the rain.

'Why do you have two out there?'

'For when it's full before the council comes to empty it. The other houses only have one.'

'So this is a reserve one?' Maria asked, and they both laughed.

'However,' Andrea continued, 'I would not like to have another baby here, not until we are in a better house.'

Maria put a spoonful of coffee in each cup.

'You don't want sugar do you?'

'No, no sugar for me thank you.'

'Do we give something to the children?'

'We'll give them a biscuit until tea time.'

Andrea filled the mugs with boiling water, then added a drop of cold milk and they went to sit back by the fire.

'Does Roy like to work on the farm? I mean, does he like to be a farmer?'

'For now he is interested, but I can see that it's not his future.'

'James was asking me the other day, why is he not going to work at Rowland Winn like him? Do you think he would like the change?'

'He likes cars very much, yet he lacks the training; cars are his hobby, he has no other entertainment or vice, he does not smoke,' Andrea answered, glancing at the cigarette she was holding, 'nor does he drink. And James, is he happy? I hope he gets the permit. I believe he'll get it, as he is already working and that means they are interested in what he can do.'

'I pray to God he gets it! In the meantime having to wait so many weeks is very worrying. Now they are advertising for the job he is doing and if any Englishman applies for it they'll have to give it to him in preference to a non-residential foreigner. Then James will have to go and if he cannot find another job quickly, as our permit has expired, we will be sent back to Spain. Can you see what a failure it would be? Terrible, we don't want to go, we can't, we have nothing there either. He says he'd rather go to Canada, I don't know...'

'Don't worry, here everyone specialises in one thing and they will not easily find a British person to do what James can do as a mechanic and electrician.'

'Well yes, you may be right. Then, suppose Rowland Winn wants him, but will the Ministry grant permission? Will that take long? What shall we do in the meantime?'

She finished her drink and once again gazed at the wet fields. It was still raining but the cows had gone.

'For the moment you are all right here aren't you?'

'We are an inconvenience to you.'

'Not at all.'

'I am very comfortable here. Only James was complaining last night because he had to get up and go to the toilet and he got wet. It's his fault, he forgot to go before,' she laughed, 'besides, you know they went somewhere for a drink last night?'

'Yes, Roy told me, although he doesn't much like to drink.' Then, lowering her voice, Andrea continued, 'shall I lend you a potty?'

'No, of course not, let him go out!' Maria did not want to talk about it any more.

The afternoon slowly slipped by, but conversing with Andrea and entertaining the children wasn't much to keep the hours occupied. Maria was physically resting and she would have been feeling well, except her body was engaged in the process of reproducing which caused an unbalance of functions. Her mind, however, was working continuously, trying to stabilise her situation. If they had temporarily solved one problem, a lot remained to give her a feeling of unease. They had already spent four days at Andrea's house and the question of paying board had not been mentioned yet.

However little cash Maria had, she had to give some to James for petrol and dinners at work, whilst at the same time begging him to take the camera back, although he argued that it was not worth it for the three pounds deposit, and that by the time they had to pay the instalments he would have the money. It was no use trying to make him understand that then they would have other things to pay for, things more necessary than the camera. He would not listen and she got cross and vexed, firstly for the waste of money and, secondly, because he was taking no notice of her opinion or her wishes. She was not sure what was hurting her the most, but whatever it was it began to eat away at her inner happiness and self. She knew she must protect herself. We all have deep inside us an impulse to safeguard our own happiness. Nobody else would do it for her, but perhaps the new being growing inside her would help Maria to feel less attached to James and less vulnerable to his careless actions.

The rain still fell outside. The drops of water rushed down the window panes, running in rows. Some fell individually, hesitating until another joined in and together they followed their course more quickly, travelling down the square piece of glass before blending into anonymity as they hit the ground.

'The rain is beautiful,' Maria commented.

'You like the rain?' exclaimed Andrea with surprise, 'I am fed up of it, I wish it'd stop. We could go for a walk as far as the Co-op. What can we do for tea today?'

'Baked beans on toast!' burst in the little girl.

'You like them so much,' said Maria looking at the child that she had believed was completely absorbed in her play, 'we ate them yesterday!'

Then she stopped short, seeing that it was better for the mother not to do anything more complicated, as that kind of meal took less than fifteen minutes to prepare.

That evening they all sat at the table. Roy ate his two slices of toast topped with pinkish beans soaked in tomato juice, and he skilfully cut little squares and, without dropping a single bean, put them into his mouth whilst also cutting small pieces of his daughter's portion. Andrea fed the little boy. Maria ate her meal indifferently, commenting on the weather and trying not to look at James's attitude and manners. He was sat with one elbow on the table, his hand holding his cheek and his fingers above his eyes in order to see better, or perhaps not to see what was on his plate.

'These meals are more miserable than the ones we had in hospital,' he grumbled in Catalan.

'Roy, the cows, are they left out all night even if it rains?' asked Maria, ignoring James's remark.

He cast her a glance of annoyance.

'Oh yes, it is nothing to the cows, sometimes they shelter under a tree,' Roy answered.

'Haven't you heard me?' insisted James in his own language.

Andrea looked at him and politely asked him, 'Aren't you hungry James?'

'James shut up, please, eat and pretend you like it,' replied Maria in the same tongue.

'A cup of tea?' Roy addressed him with the tea pot in his hand and proceeded to pour the yellowish, weak liquid.

Maria turned her eyes away, feeling the return of her sickness. Then she said to Andrea, 'Yes, he likes tea much more than the baked beans I'm afraid,' and gave her a smile.

'If you could see the meals we had at Mrs Munns's!'

Now James began explaining his feelings in English that was sufficiently good for Maria to feel uneasy, as he proceeded to describe the good food in that household, rendering more obvious the stinginess in this one.

'If the cows eat so much wet grass the milk...?' she tried to divert attention in vain.

'Some pieces of meat roasted beautifully, big like that!' James carried on and, to make his point, made a gesture with his hands, covering the full length of the Bentley's table.

'Can I eat a biscuit?' begged the little girl.

Andrea got up and returned with a tin of biscuits, which she left on the table. James, moving away his plate, was the first to put his hand into it. His words and actions were becoming so uncouth that everyone was suffering from them except himself and the children. Maria tried once again to bring up the subject of the good milk produced in England. Andrea, irritated, smacked the little boy's hand because he let his biscuit fall to the floor, cloaking her real intention. Then James got up and declared he was going out, rushing Maria to get ready.

'Wait until I clear the table,' she said, going to the kitchen with the dirty plates.

Roy followed her, 'Don't Maria, I'll do it, you go with him, do go.'

She did not resist thinking that James needed some air, and she took her coat.

They drove along the old lanes. After a while they came up to a group of houses with the inevitable fish and chip shop.

'We'll get some, as you do not want to make nice soup for your husband, naughty!' James said, stopping the car and hugging her.

'Look James, I've told you,' she said with patient countenance, trying to explain how one has to behave in somebody else's house. She explained how very fussy the English were in certain things, that she and James were foreigners and had to adapt to the English way of life or be patient if they didn't like their ways.

'I will not do anything that can upset Andrea, have you noticed she is excitable? She has none of the so called English *flema*. Roy, yes, he seems to be never disturbed but she...'

People were coming in and out of the little shop. Big breaths of burning fat came out, disappearing into the humid air. They bought fish and chips and sat in the car. They were cooked without salt.

'How insipid the English are.'

'They do not eat them saltless, have you not seen the salt and vinegar on the counter? It is we who don't know *their* ways.'

'Come on then, you go and put salt on,' he said, sending her off.

Later, they stopped in front of a public house. James went in, but Maria preferred to stay outside. The night was serene, the rain had ceased and she looked up at the sky. It was black, with only one or two shining stars.

It might rain again later, she thought, and the English cows are always outside. No, in the winter they have shelter, a roof over their heads, warm stables. We need our shelter too, a home for the baby. She sighed deeply. My God, when?

Observing how many men went in to the building, she waited for her husband to come out. These English bars really were a nuisance. Why was there so much secrecy? With their glazed windows and closed doors, no one could see what was going on inside, and she wished they were transparent like the bars in Spain. At least then James could see her waiting; otherwise, he might forget that she was there.

That night they found a chamber pot under their bed.

'Don't use it James, it nauseates me, please!' Then, seeing he wasn't taking any notice of her, Maria repeated, 'Don't James! Look, I will not empty it. I am telling you, I won't.'

He remained unmoved and deaf to her pleas.

The following night he filled it up and Maria, in tears, turned her back on him, then, in contact with the cold wall, sobbed for a while. The next morning she anxiously waited for a chance to be alone in the house. At last, Andrea went next door and she took the pot from under the bed. It was filled to the rim, and she was careful not to spill any of the disgusting deep yellow liquid. Holding her breath so the smell would not pass through her nose she went down step by step, crossed the sitting room, then the kitchen and then the yard, looking right then left for any chance of a passerby. She opened the door and, as fast as she could, walked the few yards to the hut, raised the wooden lid inside and emptied the contents of the pot. A shiver shook her from head to heels, then she closed the door behind her.

She shut her lips firmly and her grievance took a resolute turn. She moved to the road, leaning over the stone wall, looking over the wavy green fields. The romance there was in her love ended there; cleaned out like the wind drives the mist, like the leaves drop out of trees, like flowers wither out of water.

Out of my hopes, she thought, this is my lot.

She was perplexed that she didn't despair. Love wants so much and renders so little. What is it? Her look, hardening deeper, became lost in the infinite horizon beyond the soft rolling hills of England.

Andrea was pushing the pram with Simon in it, Maria walked next to her and Annette sometimes ran in front, and lagged behind at other times. Going along the old lanes traced time out of mind, and conjured up images of cavaliers and serfs going to and from their dwellings, skipping past the thicker parts of the woods in fear of wild beasts. Gradually the woods became fields and later they were enclosed by dry stone walls; amazing low lines of flat, rough, grey-blue stones emerging clear cut over the tender evergreen. Later, the car and tractor arrived, and the lanes were asphalted, yet their twisted trail never altered. Perhaps it was in respect for the walls that the course of time had given so much work.

Perhaps it was in order to keep the fields wholesome. The walls were often pulled down by animals or angry weather, then rebuilt stone by stone, with expert hands searching for the exact sized one to fit neatly in, never using cement, but keeping the art of dry stone masonry alive. The continuity of the English landscape had been preserved, where the rush of the modern world had no business to interfere, nor the diabolic motorways which did not respect the primitive paths, the slopes, the hills or the ditches of nature.

After a long time spent walking between these walls, the group could see the row of new buildings along the plain. Annette was not running any more and was holding onto Maria's hand.

'You are tired Annette aren't you? I think we are getting there.'

'Yes,' affirmed Andrea, 'it is one of these houses.'

Soon they saw its blue sign, the only distinction among the semi-detached red brick buildings. They approached the door and knocked. A man in blue uniform opened it.

'My friend who is a foreigner,' Andrea began, 'we came to declare her new residence, she lives in my house now.'

'Come in please.'

Andrea left the pram in the hall and was going to leave Simon in it but the child moaned so she hooked him on to her side.

The policeman was already looking at the documents Maria had handed him.

'Mrs Munns gave us notice three weeks ago,' she began, 'now my husband provisionally works for Rowland Winn of Leeds, as we do not have the Ministry's permit yet. But they are taking the necessary steps. Meanwhile, we have no fixed residence, though we think we had to let you know.'

'Yes, yes, very well. Tell me why were you sacked?'

'She is expecting,' interrupted Andrea.

The man with the blue suit glanced at Maria and nodded.

'I would work if I could find a job,' she said.

'This permit for your husband, when he gets it, exempts you from taking a job. However, not if,' he paused, looking intently at the document, 'your permission to stay in this country has expired.' He raised his eyes and, seeing the fright in the young woman's face said quickly, 'That is, unless where he works has already applied for an extension,' then, taking a pen, he began to write.

'I believe so, but they have advertised his job in order to give preference to an English worker.'

'Yes, I know the procedure,' then he stopped thoughtfully, staring for a few minutes, 'look madam, what you can do is the following. Can you write English?' he addressed Andrea, and not Maria.

'Oh yes,' both women replied.

'Well,' he proceeded, 'you can write a letter to the Home Office, explaining your case, saying how much you need this job for your husband because it's all he can do. Add that you cannot work as a domestic because you are pregnant

156

and state that you need a residence. You explain properly and you'll have an answer, I am sure. I'll give you the address and you can write directly to London.' He scribbled the address and handed the piece of paper to her. 'Here it is.'

'Thanks very much. May we tell the firm concerned?'

'Yes, naturally. And they can send the application at the same time if they haven't done it yet. Remember, there are two things you'll need; the extension of your staying and the special permit. Also remember that nothing exempts you from declaring your residence to the police wherever you go.'

'Yes, thank you, you are very kind. I'll do what you advise straight away.'

They got up and the policeman, seeing them to the door, added more details of his recommendation.

'Thank you very much,' the two ladies repeated.

'Not to mention it, I'm at your service.'

Yes, Maria thought with admiration, a perfect subject of her Majesty the Queen.

Later, they went to the Co-op to buy provisions and Maria found the opportunity to ask, 'Andrea, how much shall we give you for our board?'

Andrea was looking at a lamb shoulder but ended up buying a piece of leg. 'Oh yes, we shall count what I spend extra. Shall we have enough with this piece?' she asked, studying the leg. 'I suppose it depends if it shrinks a lot.'

'No, you tell me what you think and it'll be all right.'

'I do spend a lot for the children. I like to give them something nourishing to eat. Have you seen our neighbour's children? They are fat and podgy, as all she gives them are starchy things like corn flakes, biscuits, bread and potatoes. I prefer to give mine cheese and meat; it is more expensive, however it is better for them, ah, and fish.'

Moving away from the meat counter they went to the fish counter and bought some fish to boil.

On their way home the children were tired and Maria pushed the pram whilst Andrea carried Annette.

'She is very heavy isn't she?'

'Yes, although not so heavy to me as she is to you; one gets used to it, it is like training for any sport.'

That evening they ate boiled fish and tinned peas. As they talked about the letter Maria was going to write to the Home Office, James was distracted from his fish and ate it all with out any remarks. Besides, he had his first wages and was very pleased. He gave five pounds to Maria and convinced the unwilling Roy to go for a drink. The women were pleased to be left alone, and one went to draft her letter whilst the other proceeded to warm the water for the children's bath. Maria gave the five pounds to Andrea.

CHAPTER EIGHT

IT WAS SUNDAY, and Maria and Andrea made
dinner. The meat, cooked in the old fashioned
fire place oven, was quite good and there was
harmony amongst everyone at the table, until
James placed a bottle of wine in their midst.

'We'll celebrate with Spanish wine!' he
declared.

Andrea, who at that moment was bringing in
the dessert, gave the bottle an unhappy look.

'We have nothing to celebrate yet James,'
Maria said.

'Oh, how nice,' commented Roy politely.

The wine on the table wasn't causing any
excitement; on the contrary, it seemed as if
the Bentleys had recollected their proper
English reserve. The bottle, next to the teapot,
appeared an odd contradiction, as it stood there
contravening an established order of abstinence.
In this family the father was allowed the luxury
of a car, the mother a packet of cigarettes and a
lipstick, and the rest of their things were simple
and sparse. This was a Puritan tradition that
they had adopted. Even the children looked at
the bottle with reluctance. James, being a man of

little subtlety, thought their glances meant they wished to drink it. He did not ask for glasses, but got up to get them himself and then proceeded to fill them.

'I do not want any,' said Andrea watching him carefully.

But he didn't take any notice.

'Yes, it is good,' he said.

'No stop, please stop,' she insisted and he stopped at half a glass, then carried on filling more glasses.

'No, not for the children, not a drop. Please, James, you may not know that alcohol is no good for children.'

'Yes it is, Spanish children drink wine and they are healthy and strong.'

'Anyway, it's illegal here!'

'James, do not give them any, they wouldn't like it, they are not used to strong drinks,' said Maria in a conciliatory way.

'It is not strong at all, this is mild,' and he continued in Catalan, 'they are silly – they do not know what is good.'

Then he filled his glass and drank it all in a gulp leaving the empty glass on the table with a gesture of satisfaction, as if having provoked the admiration of young and old. Everyone was looking at him, then he refilled his glass and drank again. Roy was drinking from his glass too.

'Water is for *granotas*, how you say *granota* in English Maria?'

'Frog.'

'Ah, water is for frocs, frocs.'

'No froggg....froggg,' corrected little Annette.

'*Granota* is Spanish? Look, I can say it better than you, frog, *granota*,' said Roy.

'No, *granota* is Catalan, it is not Spanish,' explained Maria, 'Catalan is the language we speak, as we are from Catalonia. It is a part of Spain, but we are not exactly Spanish.'

After a while, concord restored, they finished the pudding and the tea, and the bottle of wine was apparently forgotten. That Sunday afternoon they went to visit the grocer, a man who drove his shop to homes throughout the countryside. Once a week he passed through Wyke, and he was friendly with Andrea because she made coffee for him. He never came out of his mobile van shop, although, whilst sipping his coffee, he would spend time talking with her. Andrea, her eyes walking all over the stands, would sip hers and ask for what she wanted. She had told him about James's skills with cars and he wanted him to have a look at his vehicle, so he invited them to his house.

He lived just outside Leeds in a new estate surrounded by woodland, which had beautiful detached houses with neat gardens in straight rows, each house a replica of the next. To honour the visitors the family had prepared a good tea with a great variety of vegetables, especially salads. James soon remarked how the English meals were nothing compared with the Spanish food, and, just in case they didn't understand what he meant, he implied, with a gesture of his arms, that he meant all the food that filled the table. He refused the lettuce because he said it tasted of nothing without olive oil. He did, however, drink tea and eat cake, and after that he left the table without a word of excuse or thanks and went to look at the cars. Andrea was busy with her children's good manners and apparently took no notice, whilst Maria was engaged in conversation with the daughter, who was studying music. As soon as James finished repairing the vehicle they returned to Wyke.

It was late in the evening when Andrea finished putting the children to bed and went to sit by the fire. She took some clothing off the fireguard and then moved her seat closer to the grate to make room for Maria.

'The Bishops are a very nice family,' commented Maria, 'the place they live is beautiful; to us it seems a place for rich people, or gentry, not a small businessman.'

'Yes, he says he went to live there for his child's health, because of the clean air. They are very fond of their daughter; the mother does everything for her. I think they are spoiling her. The father works and works, and at six in the morning he is already out in his van shop.'

The two men sat at the table, engrossed in a piece of a radio.

'Where did you get it from, James?' asked Maria.

'From the garage.'

'Look Andrea,' said Roy to his wife, holding it up, 'it had been thrown out for scrap.'

'We'll put it in your car shall we?' asked James in a teasing tone. 'As soon as it plays, so you'll be entertained while Roy drives.'

'I have enough entertainment with the kids.'

'To your kids you have to give some wine sometimes. This law you English have is ridiculous.'

Maria was looking at the fire, where the orange and yellow flames were silently diminishing.

'It is not!' Andrea's tone startled Maria, and, lifting her gaze, she saw that the flames were suddenly in Andrea's eyes, moving and menacing. 'James,' Andrea continued, 'you mustn't say that our laws are ridiculous. I'll tell you that spirits are dangerous, they are to adults and even more so to children. If you encourage them and the children become accustomed to them, they can become alcoholics and that is an illness.'

'Oh, that is nonsense. Besides, I have seen more drunkards here than in Spain!'

'I do not mean drunkards, I mean alcoholics, and it's not the same thing. Don't you understand? Alcoholic drinks are not good for your health.'

'Yes they are, wine is good for everybody,' he insisted.

'It is not! It is not, it is not!!' She jerked up towards James as though she was going to strike him, and screamed the last 'it is not' hysterically. Everyone looked at her in sudden alarm and the pause that followed carried a strange silence which was impregnated with the echo of her shrill voice. She then curtly uttered, 'Goodnight,' and quickly left the room.

'Of course it is no good,' affirmed Maria, 'why don't you shut up James?' she asked in a restrained tone.

Roy, looking somewhat troubled, said, 'Don't worry, she sometimes does that. She is very nervous.'

'Oh, women!' exclaimed James as if he was used to that kind of hysterical behaviour.

Maria was going to contradict him, but stopped short when she saw the two men, full of indulgent superiority, smirking amongst themselves. She turned her back on them.

She gazed at the fire again. The flames had consumed themselves, the bright ember had almost swallowed all the black of the coal. Will the ember alone have enough strength to change all that into grey fine ashes of tomorrow? wondered Maria. Her look fastened on the grate. Upon her dawned the emptiness of the hour, the dreary emptiness of unsolved problems. Then her mind began to work and worked incessantly, searching for the idea that fulfils, for the knowledge that knows what to do and how to do it, for the thought giving impulse to the action. She would search until she found it.

James was touching her shoulder, 'Let's go to bed.'

She shrugged off his touch, 'No, I am all right here, leave me alone. You go. I'll come later,' she concluded in a softer tone. Then she said to Roy, 'Goodnight Roy, I'll lock the door when I have been outside and I shall put all the lights off, don't worry.'

Alone, she continued her reflection. Why had Andrea been so irritated with James? It was not just because of the drinking customs in England. Was it because she found it difficult to make him understand her point? Was it his lack of good manners? Because he wasn't saying please and thank you and continually? She took the poker and turned the embers, breaking them, and the yellow and orange became an intense red. A notion began to emerge in her mind; it was not convenient to continue staying with the Bentley's, as their friendship, which Maria valued, was now in peril. Andrea didn't complain about anything and would not in future, and surely by now she was sorry that she had let herself get carried away by anger.

At that point Maria decided that they must immediately look for a place of their own to live, before their relationship with the Bentleys suffered more. What would Andrea's attitude be tomorrow? It was obvious that the environment she was in didn't satisfy her. No doubt her children gave her satisfaction, as she loved them very much, and not only did she do everything necessary for their care but she also gave them plenty of her spare time, sometimes just for cuddles. It was the place where she was living, the countryside she did not like; she didn't even know how to look at it and never noticed its changing beauty. She didn't see the leaves' colour, the clouds shaping or any of its natural inhabitants.

Andrea could, however, see the house very well and now and again had spasms of cleaning and decorating, but the big grey flagstones remained barely covered by pieces of carpet and the mean construction of her dwelling depressed her. She would return to sitting by the fire with a child on her knees and a cigarette in her mouth.

It was difficult to guess if Roy gave her satisfaction, as they seemed to be quite content with each other although the romance, if they'd had it, was gone. Perhaps they believed that demonstrations of love were not polite. If that was the case, the way that James constantly fondled Maria was probably another source of irritation to Andrea. Yes, they must find a place to go, she concluded, resolute. When she got up and went outside to run across the yard, it was cold and dark.

The next morning Maria finished her letter to the Home Office. Later she walked through the fields along the lane to the main road. There, under the giant trees, she stopped to wait for the bus to Leeds. The walk had tired her and she glanced around for a seat. There was nothing but dried leaves slowly dying. Cars passed continuously, zooming quickly by, indifferent to the solitary human figure standing by the roadside.

At last the bus came and she stepped on, grateful to have a seat and half an hour more to think about what to say to her husband's boss. She went straight to the Rowland Winn building, and to Mr Todd's office.

'Good afternoon, Mr Todd, I am Mrs Martines,' said Maria.

The man sitting behind the desk raised up quickly, stretching out his hand.

'How are you, madam?'

'How are you, sir?'

'Sit down, please, tell me, shall we call your husband?'

'No, it isn't necessary,' she smiled, 'how do you understand each other? Is he speaking better English?'

'Yes, at first he couldn't understand the job cards but now he's made friends with the other mechanics and they help him. He told me this morning that you would call, although I didn't quite get what he said about the Home Office.'

'The policeman in the district has advised us to write a letter to the secretary,' she took the letter from her handbag, 'would you like to read it?'

Whilst Mr Todd read it she moved her eyes around the room. There were no windows, only a partition of half glazed glass panes. Pointed nails protruded through sheets of paper hanging on the walls, and a calendar with a picture of a naked woman rested above the man in grey overalls, who now was bending his bald, pink head. A hot mug of tea sat on his desk. Maria decided this office was not to her taste and that she would soon go.

'Do you think the permit will be granted?'

The man put the letter down, leaned back in his chair, gazed at the young woman and, lifting the letter, said, 'This letter is very good, I think they will take notice of it. We'll also send a petition.'

'When? How long do you have to wait for a response to the letter?' she asked and her tone, although appealing, revealed her anxiety. 'We are living with some friends now,' she added, 'and we are all right there but it is a bit inconvenient, also it is very far even if he comes by car. With this insecurity, we haven't looked for more suitable accommodation.'

'I think you could look at a furnished room here in Leeds, as it is easier than finding a flat or house.'

'Do you know of any?'

'No, but if you look in the *Yorkshire Evening Post* it's better than going to an agency. There are a lot of advertisements.'

'You drink your tea Mr Todd, I am going to post the letter straight away,' she smiled at him, as she got up to leave, 'you'll send the petition today, won't you?'

'Yes, I shall, don't worry.'

'The policeman told me we also need to extend the staying permit. I don't know if they have to be applied for together.'

Mr Todd had also left his seat. 'You mean both things don't go automatically? I'm sure you are not going to be kicked out of the country!'

'Are you sure?'

'Yes, as the steps to keep you here have already been taken. We are giving Mr Martines work here as long as he wants it.'

They were out of the office and crossing the workshop.

'Fred, where is James, the Spanish man?'

'Down there,' a man answered, pointing to a car that James was emerging from underneath.

'Your wife and I have been talking,' Mr Todd said, with a pat on James's back. 'It has been very nice to meet you,' he said to Maria, and without another word he bolted away as if in a sudden hurry. James led her to the door whilst she explained how the interview went.

'Do you drink this tea as well?'

'Yes, all the time.'

'Go, then, or it will get cold.'

'You wait for me at the Flamenco and we'll go home together. What you have to do these two hours is...'

'Let me go, James, I am a bit sick,' she interrupted him, 'bye bye.'

They kissed each other and she left.

Why hadn't she taken her tablets? Now she was feeling ill and it was nobody's fault but hers, and why did James always tell her what to do?

I'll do what I like, she thought. After walking towards the Headrow, she reached the Town Hall. There were some benches and it was sunny so, after posting her letter, she sat facing the stone lions. She felt depressed when she thought she should feel happy. The visit with Mr Todd had gone well, the permit would be obtained and they would not be thrown out of England. James was in his element, but Maria was not. Staring at the enormous lions, she thought how stupid they were. What were they doing there? They were out of place, and out of their own environment, like her.

My music has been laid aside, my country is so far away, all these people are strangers to me, she thought.

They were walking up and down the busy street, some briskly, others slower, some crossing lights. People, essentially alike but all different, in groups, in families, in one country.

How does God look at us? wondered Maria. Like the whole ocean? Or does he look at every drop separately?

She continued sitting below the stone lions for some time, pondering. Two young women stopped by her, one pushing a pram. She was fussing the baby's covers. 'He is fast asleep,' she said to her companion, and they walked away.

Maria suddenly started. What about her baby? She had done nothing yet! At last, she left her seat. She would go shopping; she would look for wool, baby wool. She remembered a book she had once read about China, where the babies were dressed in bright colours. What if I dress mine in red? I like that colour, she thought. She walked up the street and arrived at the John Lewis department store. However, finding that they were closed on Mondays she bought the paper instead. Whilst paying for it she realised that all the money she had was half a crown, which was not enough for wool, but she could have a coffee while waiting for James. At the Flamenco she met the Valencianete girl.

'Hello Conxita, what are you doing here today? It is not your day off.'

'My missus is on holiday. This is Carmen,' she said, pointing to a girl on the same table, 'she is from Badalona. She has left her job in a house and now she is working at the hospital with me.'

'Ah yes, how long have you been here?'

The young woman had black hair and a yellowish face with wide open eyes that, every now and then, had a frightened look. She explained that it was only a month ago that she had come from Spain to a farmhouse, where she was given only eggs to eat, but that she grew tired of them and could stand it no longer.

Bringing both hands to her face she asked, 'Can you see how pale I am?

Maria was drinking her coffee and answering Conxita's questions. No, they hadn't got the permit yet, but would like to come and live in Leeds, as soon as they found a place, and yes, she *was* feeling better.

Carmen, opening her eyes wide exclaimed, 'Oh, what a joy it is to have a baby! Me, you know? It is many years I am married, but my husband...no, nothing, you know, nothing!' The pause that followed was uneasy and painful, with a world of tragedies to guess at. 'He went to America not long ago; I didn't want to follow him.'

'*Xiqueta*, my husband not even with a rocket on his bottom would he go, stuck to my skirts and my purse strings. But I have come here, I am so peaceful now and he can look after himself, he must, he is not a baby.'

Maria was listening, not understanding those failed hopes and broken lives. She still had hopes for her future, but she felt a wave of compassion for the two women and the others who also came to the Flamenco to pour out their sorrows. There was that girl from Extremadura who came to England to start a new life, yet, like many others who think they can leave their burdens behind them, was deceived. Her tragedy left such a deep mark on her soul that it overpowered her. She could not get over it. One day she told Maria her story, how her boyfriend had died of typhoid fever and she had his baby and, as she was not married, her father disowned her and the people in her village stoned her. Later, her son died, just a few days after he was born. She ran away from her people and her country and in England she served in a big house, and was trying to save money. But, uprooted, her inability to understand the language and communicate with anyone made her miserable.

That evening, at the Bentley's house, James and Maria felt hopeful. Maria indicated that, following the advice of Mr Todd, they would look for accommodation near the garage works. Andrea was in a good mood, as if the incident of the night before was forgotten. James was nice too, and even his manners had improved, as he praised the fishcakes he was eating and told Andrea that her tea tasted better than the tea at work.

In the *Evening Post* there were a few adverts, and Maria replied to three of them. When the answers came one was situated on the other side of Leeds, another was too expensive at four pounds per week and the other one, with no price, was situated near Rowland Winn. James and Maria went to see it the same day. The district was like the ones they'd seen when still working at the Gill's. It was a poor area, with short streets, cul-de-sacs and rows of identically built dark, terraced houses.

They knocked at the door, but there was no answer.

'What shall we do? It is strange nobody is in, isn't it?'

James pushed the door. 'It is open,' he said.

They stepped into a dimly lit corridor, and the smell of frying fat greeted them. Suddenly, a man came out of a door at their left. Maria, startled, hung onto James's arm, and the man began to speak. He said that they had to go downstairs, where the caretaker lived. He wore a white shirt, with a pretty flowered apron tied around his waist. 'You'll forgive me, but I'm cooking my supper,' he said.

His eyes were so clear that they seemed to give light to the corridor. He bowed at them and retreated to his room, whilst Maria restrained her urge to laugh and said 'thank you,' then rushed downstairs.

'How funny! Have you seen his curls, James? He seemed bald facing us, he is like a snooker ball!' and she laughed.

'But where are we going?' asked James, following her.

'The caretaker lives downstairs.'

At the door they heard a child's cry. A few seconds later, a young woman opened the door. She was carrying a child in her arms, with its face covered in tears and snot, and another in her belly. Her skin and her hair were both extremely pale.

She asked what they wanted and said that her husband was out, but that if they didn't mind waiting he wouldn't be long. No, they didn't mind, Maria told her, and remained standing in the middle of the room whilst the woman silently watched the opposite door. She placed the child into a cot by the fire place and the infant gazed at the strangers. His tears dried up on his red cheeks but his nose was still running. Maria, glancing at the mother, wondered why she wasn't wiping him clean. Poor thing! Her heart sunk, seeing those four walls and their contents, evidently all the possessions and living space of the family.

James was getting impatient when the door opened and a young man appeared. He was thin and fair, and could not have been older than twenty. He looked Maria up and down.

'I will show you the room,' he said, taking them out and upstairs, 'the rent is two pounds per week in advance. The bathroom is on the upper landing with a gas heater, goes with shillings everyone pays their own. Look, it is a very nice room, the best in the house,' pointing at a sofa he continued, 'this is the double bed – it opens, the wardrobe is large, there is another one for the kitchen things, the fireplace is big, the gas ring goes with shillings as well, here the sink, all complete a very nice room.'

After seeing the cluttering of the room downstairs, this one had the appearance of being clean and tidy. The couple looked at each other.

'What do you think, Maria?'

'I think we should take it.'

'Somebody else has been to see it and they'll come back, but if you pay now, it's yours,' the young man said.

James took his wallet out, 'Please make a receipt, Martines is the name.'

'I am Paul,' he replied, searching his pockets and taking out a piece of crumpled paper where he wrote, 'Martines'. 'No need for a receipt – I'll give you the keys now and you can come when you like.' He put the paper and the two pounds in his pocket, then handed them the keys. 'This one is for the outside door,' he said, and concluded the transaction with a long look at the couple, appearing pleased with his new lodgers.

BOOK
TWO

WHERE THE COUPLE went to live was in fact a miserable place. Maria would have preferred to remain in the country, as the countryside was more healthy and more open, with more space above to raise one's spirits. The only window in their new room overlooked brick walls, darkish roofs and darker chimneys, all coloured crimson grey, with not a piece of blue sky anywhere. In the streets there were no trees and no flowers that could be recognised. The low privet bushes that separated every front door could not be distinguished from the walls or the soil, as they all bore the same crimson grey dust cover.

Seen by daylight, the room looked dirtier and more worn than it had when Maria and James previewed it by electric light. Under the scrutinising eyes of Maria, big grey marks were appearing all over the place – on the fireside rug, on the arms and backs of chairs and on the linoleum by the stove. When the sofa was opened the mattress showed a large ring of dried urine.

'Oh, I'm not sleeping there!' exclaimed Maria, nauseated.

James was looking at it hesitantly. 'What are we doing then?' he asked.

'I don't know,' she replied, making an effort to look at it again.

Both were prepared to look on the bright side. After all, for the first time in their marriage they were going to live in their own place, completely independent of other people. That in itself was a source of satisfaction and they had taken the room with enthusiasm.

'You'll see,' said James, folding the mattress, 'I'll take it down to Paul, I'm sure they have been sleeping on it themselves. They'd better have a clean one.'

After a while, James came back without a mattress. 'They say that there isn't another one, but I've told them that we will not sleep on that.'

'Without a mattress we cannot sleep!'

'I am going to fetch one, from the Bentley's perhaps. You don't worry, I shall solve this problem. Leave it to me and I'll come back with a mattress for tonight.'

'Well, I wish you good luck,' she said and proceeded with her scrubbing and tidying. Not until the room had been cleaned throughout was she satisfied and sat down. It was very late, past midnight, but James had not yet come back and Maria was anxious. Then he arrived carrying a double mattress that was not new, but was clean. From the Bentleys he had gone to Andrea's aunt and the lady had given James her spare mattress.

It was November, a cold afternoon, and Maria walked down the street, pulling up the collar of her red coat. She had bought it the last winter and luckily it was wide, wide enough to wear all this winter, she thought, but her skirt would have to be let out. Very soon she'd have to buy a loose top, a wide one, as soon as she earned some money. She turned the corner of Woodhouse Lane, walking towards the hospital buildings.

James gives me so little money, of course his wages are small, but it's not enough. I don't have enough, she thought.

When Conxita and Carmen asked her if she would teach English to them she had agreed at once. She was on her way there, happily carrying a couple of books under her arm. It was a long time since she had been able to buy anything for herself because James and his car needed so much. She said that now they lived near his work he could walk and save petrol, but he complained about his poor leg.

'It still hurts,' he said, 'and I walk up and down the garage all day long'.

She was saving as much as she could, buying the cheapest food and throwing nothing away, while he did the contrary. When he wanted continental food he went and bought what he liked.

She entered the hospital and turned left towards the nurses' accommodation. Conxita worked as a maid to the matron and she had a nice room to herself. Because they spoke Catalan, which was different from the Castillian of the other group of Spaniards, the two girls had become very close friends, and in their spare time met in this room. They bought an electric ring to cook little meals of *Escudella de pages* or *Paella a la valenciana*, trying to console their deep longing for the motherland! The meals at the hospital were dull and monotonous, yet extraordinarily abundant, so much so that food was thrown away. The girls, amazed at the sight of such squander, picked things up from the kitchen waste. Sometimes there were plates full of cold meat, whole half-pound packets of butter and always lots of bread. They often gave some to Maria, which helped her need. Even when the butter had gone rancid, the three girls, who had experienced near starvation in their country during the Civil war, could not bear to see it wasted and would rather use than see it thrown away.

Two hours later Maria came out of the building, feeling very pleased with the addition of ten shillings in her purse. When she entered the house at Wellclose Terrace the door of the first room opened. The bald man was coming out, this time with no flowered apron, wearing a perfectly tailored suit. Taking his hat off, he waved down to Maria.

'My name is Komskinett, I hope you like it here.'

'Yes, thank you,' she answered, smiling gently.

'It is cold today, there is a lot of fog isn't there?'

'Yes, very,' she went towards her door but the man followed her. He was carrying some books.

'You like reading?'

She stopped, surprised, then her eyes met the man's clear grey eyes, almost transparent, like mirrors. As they reflected her image she felt desirable and beautiful, and her gaze moved away in confusion.

'I work in a book shop,' the man continued, 'look, this is *Kipps* by H.G.Wells – have you read it? It's very interesting. And this is Graham Greene's *The Power and the Glory*.'

'No, I haven't read this one.'

'Here, take it.'

'Oh, no, no.'

'Please, you'll like it,' he insisted, 'you being Spanish, you must be Catholic! Read it, you can give it back to me when you've finished.'

She took the book and, as she had her key out, unlocked the door, thanking him at the same time. She quickly slipped into her room, closing the door carefully so that he could not say anything else to her. She heaved a sigh.

'Well, how funny it is! I have been in England for over a year and no man has looked at me. I have come here to this scruffy place for foolish Paul to come in with some excuse or other and look at my legs. And this other man, strange type! It is funny, it makes me laugh!'

Then her laughter stopped suddenly, as it wasn't funny at all. It wasn't funny living here and it was not funny that men looked at her.

Later, when she went to the bathroom, she carefully observed herself in the mirror. The pallor which Mrs Munns had noticed had now completely disappeared. Her cheeks had some colour in them and her mass of black hair, tied up in a crowning knot, gave her a distinguished air. She got up on the edge of the bath to look at her waist. I hope nobody has noticed anything yet, she thought, and her baby, whom she could now feel independently moving, brought to her eyes a sparkle of emotion.

It often did, amidst the anxiety of waiting for the Home Office reply, money shortages and the difficulties of living in such a reduced space. A sudden pang of the purest emotion seized her and rolled her heart towards the most profound corner of her inside, where a new life was forming. A life that did not seem be wanting to take hers and was not sickening her any more, but giving her sparks of health and vigour, and filling her eyes with a beautiful light.

Other times, however, when her hopes would suddenly vanish, and the great emptiness would prostrate her. There were so many unsolved problems and unanswered questions. Since their arrival in England and the situation at the Gills's they had been going downhill, before finally ending up in this scruffy place with squalid accommodation and strange people. The place was unfit for a baby, her baby could not be born there and he must not be born there. She would not have him there, quite definitely not there. The permit would come – why not? Maria hoped that, when it did, James would earn more money. They would move to a better place; from here they would not descend any lower. But how?

The emptiness overwhelmed her again and her strength of will vanished. She could not understand why it was running away from her so easily. She needed to try harder to keep up her spirits. She still responded to the instinct of going to her husband for support, an atavism remnant from the days of male dominance. When was she going to learn? When would she realise that James was not a source of strength? Suddenly, a ray of enlightenment downed her. She would begin by not telling her husband how Paul molested her or how the bald man lent her books to read. If James were to have a quarrel with any of them now, surely they would have to go somewhere else, somewhere even worse. Might the rosy clouds Maria had been folded in since her youth be clearing away? The ideal love, truthfulness, complete loyalty and confidence were all illusions, like dreams that waking dispels.

The days went by and James, pleased with his work, got up early every morning. At midday he came home for dinner and at five o'clock he returned for tea. He went out again many times to do some work or other for private customers. He was working hard and was eager to do well. Maria, left alone for so many hours in that place, could hardly endure to look at the walls that enclosed her. She often went out to wander about the streets, and would stop by the baby shops and look in the windows until her sight became clouded with tears, then move on aimlessly and finally find herself back in their miserable room.

One evening she went downstairs to fetch some coal, as it was kept in a vault there. She was filling the bucket when Paul opened his door and invited her in. Refusing to listen to her excuses for not wanting to do so, he made her enter the room. His wife sat by the fire, the days of her pregnancy clearly coming to an end.

'I know you are expecting too,' the young man declared carelessly with a glance at Maria's waist, 'we have some books you'll be interested in. Look, look,' he urged, opening a large, illustrated one.

The first picture was of a bag containing a foetus. Paul was turning the pages with delight. Next was a foetus, almost fully grown, but with two heads, then another with huge genitals hanging flaccid to its turned-in feet. Maria moved her sight away; she didn't wish to see any more.

'They are things of nature, these things happen,' Paul said.

'No, they are monsters, they are mistakes of nature.'

'Yes, they happen, look at this – he has turned-back legs.'

'No, please I don't want to see!' she protested, frightened for what he wanted her to see or realise.

His glance often flicked to his wife's bulky stomach.

'It is good to know about these things,' and with intense morbidity he turned the pages and pointed at women giving birth to monsters.

Maria, resisting looking at the book, rested her eyes on the figure sitting by the grate. The young woman was still in her teens, yet was expecting her second child. Maria saw her pallid, indifferent, cold face, her eyes like empty glass, motionless like stones, and shivered. She spun around and went out in a flash, wanting to run upstairs, but her heart had sunk heavily to her feet and hindered her step.

She did tell James about this episode, adding, almost in tears, her desire to leave the house. She made him understand that to quit the room was the most important and urgent thing they should do.

By the end of November, after many monotonous grey and cold days, the sky cleared and a few rays of sunshine brightened the outlook of the immigrant couple, who, despite longing for their homeland, did not want to go back to it. The letter they had been waiting for came at last. The Sub-secretary of State had granted James Martines permission to stay in the country working as a motor mechanic for Rowland Winn Ltd.

What joy they felt! Immediately after, James and Maria started to look for a house. They went to several agencies without any success. Maria had the feeling the agents did not want to give them anything because they were foreigners. They always asked the same questions: what nationality are you? How long have you been living in England? How long are you going to stay?

Once, there was a little flat they liked very much and, when they said so, the agent asked for a full year's payment in advance, something that wouldn't have been asked of a British couple. They had to let it go. Others, looking at Maria, would point out that no children were allowed in the flats. It was all very discouraging, as they'd seen all the newspaper adverts and there were plenty to buy but only a few to rent, and they would not go near a bed-sit.

James not too shy to ask everybody he met if they knew somewhere for rent, but the days came and went. The coloured lights and Christmas decorations were already out, and Maria was sad, thinking it was not possible to cook a Christmas dinner with only one gas ring.

Yet another day came and the sky was greyer than ever. Maria took a bundle of clothes and went to the laundrette. White soft flakes began to fall from the cloudy grey sky. Let them fall, Maria thought, let them cover all this slum, gentle clean snowflakes.

She felt the joy of approaching change. That evening, James came home with the address for a house that a workmate had given him. They decided to go and see it straight away and left their tea uneaten. They did not worry about the snow that, by now, was thick on the ground. The scrap of paper said Harehill Avenue, a name Maria liked. In her imagination, she saw hills and hares running wild over Leeds.

Number fifty-two was at the end of a row with a front garden. The avenue was lined with trees and the back door led to a quiet street. The house seemed nicely situated. A young couple lived there and both were tall, fair and extremely nice. They reached an understanding very soon, as the young man offered to speak to the proprietor and was prepared to lie about the fact that they were foreigners. The young woman offered to leave the curtains hanging and the gas cooker for very little money. They discussed moving in and moving out for the same day so the house would not cease to be lived in.

James and Maria left, happy and grateful. Outside, the shadows of branches drew thickly in dark and geographical shapes over the snow and made everything seem new and different. How the snow shone! Sat in the car, they gave each other a prolonged kiss.

'Here we'll be all right, you'll see.'

'I am sure we will, I like the place very much James.'

To have two big problems solved left them with no worries at all, and that night neither clouds nor emptiness perturbed their minds.

It was only in the morning when Maria began to think about smaller problems, now getting larger to occupy the place of the ones not long gone. She started making an inventory of their belongings, including clothing, kitchen equipment and furniture. Then she made a list of things they urgently needed. A bed, a table, chairs, a wardrobe...she stopped with her pen mid air, her other hand pressing her forehead, then she wrote MONEY in big letters and carried on pencilling over and over it and underlining unconsciously, enlarging the words at the same time as it was growing in to the biggest problem yet.

They had no money, so how would they manage to buy what they needed? For a while she repeated the question and again no answer came. Presently she got up, took her coat and went out. Before she reached the outside door the bald man came out of his room. This time he offered Maria a book of poetry.

'Do you like Wordsworth, Blake?'

'Never read them. I don't like poetry – I prefer music.'

'Don't you feel well today?' The searching light in his eyes went all over her and a shadow of concern set in his brow.

'I am all right thank you, Mr Komskinett,' she smiled, 'I'll give you your books back. We have found a new house and we shall move soon.'

She had read *The Power and Glory*, finding it very disturbing, as her religious stability could not understand the problems of the priest meddling with the landscape and the Mexican revolution.

'Oh, how much I shall miss you; your smile illuminates my existence. How sad you'll leave me.'

'I am sorry,' she moved from the door. She was in no hurry now. Poor man! How miserable his existence must be when he needed the occasional smile of a foreigner to brighten it. Of course, he did live alone in the ugly house.

'How long have you lived here?'

'A year, I don't come from Leeds.'

'Aren't you English, either?'

'Yes, but my father was Polish. He died in a concentration camp. Then my mother, who was English, and I came to England. She was killed in the last bombing of London.'

'What a pity, I am sorry, very sorry. Do you read a lot?'

'I want to write my memoirs, you know? But I do not have much talent,' he added, lowering his head with a gesture of resignation.

'Are you sure? I would think you have, just try to start writing and see how it goes.'

They conversed for a while and, when Maria thought he was comforted, she said she had to go shopping and left him.

She went to the John Lewis store to look at furniture. As soon as she saw the abundance there she rushed back to the lifts. She was wasting her time, as James would be coming home soon for his dinner. She descended straight to the basement and bought a packet of sausages.

She was just turning the corner of her street when James's Ford turned too.

'Where are you going? Jump in.'

'Just to cross the street? Don't make me laugh!' Laughing was the thing she felt least ready to do. It took the same time for her to cross the street as for James to park the car in front of the door. He wanted to kiss her, but she skipped him. She was definitely in a bad mood.

'What is the matter? Come on, I'll help you make dinner. I must go back to work straight away,' he opened a packet of soup while she put the sausages in a pan.

'I have been to see furniture. Do you think we can buy what we need?' she asked, then thought about what a stupid question it was. He would answer 'yes' even if the reality was quite obviously different.

'Yes, darling, of course we can. The job I'm doing for Mr Biggs will cost him quite a lot and I will make a lot of profit out of it.'

'When shall you finish it? Will he pay soon?'

'This weekend, if he has bought the new parts for it.'

'How much money do you have apart from that?'

'Tomorrow, we'll have the wages.'

'And nothing else? You must have some more!' Her tone of voice was becoming more alarmed.

'But what do you think? I have paid the instalments for the car and for the camera, those were in arrears.'

'The camera, the flipping camera!' she cried with sudden fury, remembering how very upset she was when he bought it. 'Why haven't you taken it back? I told you, I asked you! We do not need a photographic camera for anything! We do not even need the car; we could sell them and furnish the house with the money and live decently, and use the trolley bus like so many others. Harehill is not far from the centre!' What had she said? My goodness! She was so absurd.

'You don't know what you are saying,' James said, and looked at her with an exasperating air of superiority, 'we'll have more money than we'll need.'

'You are the one who doesn't know, your feet are never on the ground! Would you like to count the money we have now? Count it, come on, you count it now.' She got up to fetch her purse and emptied its contents onto the table, 'Look, that's all I have, one pound, two shillings and four pennies!'

'Don't shout, silly, eat your soup,' he replied, showing no intention of counting his money or telling her what he had.

'Have you enough to buy a bed?' she insisted tearfully.

'We'll buy it on H.P.'

'And the deposit?' she asked, with her hand to her side as if in pain.

'Haven't I told you I'll get paid from the Biggs job? Well then, shut up, you shout too much,' he concluded harshly, serving himself a glass of beer.

'But you should save a bit more, tea is cheaper to drink.'

'I am fed up with tea!' he said, and, dumping his empty glass on the table added, 'you drink it,' and quit the room at once.

Maria burst into tears, one hand pressing her side and the other over her eyes, feeling awfully unwell. Perhaps that was why she was so excitable and tactless, she thought. Why had she insisted on selling the car? It was James's most precious thing! She knew very well than they would sleep in it rather than sell it to buy a bed. She looked for a hanky and dried her tears, as she was due for English lessons at the hospital. She must rest, then she would feel better.

A week had passed, and there were only ten days until Christmas. All was settled for the move to Harehill Avenue on Saturday. Maria felt full of enthusiasm, as she liked the ground floor flat.

'Now I will leave you,' said James, 'I am going directly to see if Mr Biggs has the new parts and I'll do the repairs. Don't you worry if I come home late. But I'll bring the money we need to buy the bed tomorrow. You go to sleep and rest; tomorrow we'll be busy.'

She did, and lay in bed, not sleeping but waiting for her husband. The uncertain light of the fire was giving the room a warm glow.

It is not so terribly bad here, she thought.

Now that she was feeling better, she was predisposed to see things at their best angle. James was working, he'd bring in some money and it did not matter if last week he'd promised the same, as it wasn't his fault. Besides, he had done another small job and his wages had been increased by ten shillings a week. They had been to a second hand shop and bought two chairs with this half a pound. They were very ugly, with patterned holes on the wooden seats and black paint that was all peeling off. James would have bought a double bed with the other half a pound, but it was so old and sore and cracking that Maria said it would be impossible to sleep on, adding that she wished very much to have a new bed.

She used her usual tact of pleading for a new bed without mentioning the camera or the car, and all went well. Her thoughts were of happy expectations, and there was no emptiness in her mind. She was dozing and half asleep when James came in, and faintly heard the door, but didn't open her eyes. A few minutes later she opened her arms and felt the body of her husband close to her.

Caressing him gently she murmured, 'You are tired, my darling,' and fell sweetly asleep.

The rain had cleared out the last corners of snow, and now the sun, coming obliquely into one's eyes, was so low and feeble that it didn't blind or warm anything. Nevertheless, it was a pleasure to see it shining. Maria had been up and about for some time when James got up.

He went to kiss her and said, 'Mr Biggs was not at home, he had the new parts but was out.'

She was not surprised, and she looked at him and said, 'That means we'll have to sleep on the floor, doesn't it?' and laughed. 'Do you think they'll take the lino covering the floor or leave it?'

He gazed at her in surprise. He had thought she would start crying, but no, she had laughed instead. Who could understand women?

'If we do not go to John Lewis's for furniture we have more time, so get cracking, help me move the trunk while I fill it up.'

That first night they slept on the mattress on the bare floor. After going to Mass on Sunday they ate dinner using the trunk as a table, and in the afternoon James went to see Mr Biggs. Maria remained at home and went from one room to another making plans and combining imaginary furniture. Then, when sorting out real things, she brought out the bundle of baby clothes Andrea had given her. There were little cardigans and tiny socks, and looking at them she felt grateful and sad too. It was pitiful that her first baby, new to the world, would have to be clothed with second hand stuff. I'll have time to make something new, I'll buy material in the market for some shirts, she said to herself, smiling her sweetest smile, and closing her eyes as if she wanted the light of her look to go inward, very deep, to the bottom of her womb where her infant lay.

On Tuesday, James dropped Maria off outside John Lewis's on his way to work. Once inside she looked at the bedroom suites. The simplest ones consisted of three pieces and the bed. If she bought one she'd hardly have enough money for the deposit, and, besides, she needed to fill in some papers and get her husband's signature and references. The process would take too long, and they'd have to sleep on the floor for some time. A very attentive shop assistant explained and showed her everything, then he said there was just a bed, in very plain, light wood, with no mattress, for only six pounds, and asked, would she like it? She bought it at once and arranged for delivery the same day.

In the evening, when James came back, both of them assembled the double bed and made it. Later, they would buy a new mattress and, next week, with his wages they would pay a deposit on a wardrobe and dressing table. After that they would buy a carpet, then easy chairs for the sitting room. How nice it was to think about all the things they were going to buy. This state of expectation had its special pleasure, a pleasure which Maria was now living fully. She had left behind the anxious state of questioning, abandoned 'how can we?' for 'when will we?' and it was much more satisfactory.

Another Catalan joined Maria, Carmen and Conxita's group. Pere Serra was from Barcelona,

and had come to work as a waiter in a Leeds
hotel to earn money and learn English, then
return home and use his experiences to earn
more money. He left a wife and two children
waiting for him, and in his wallet he carried a
photograph of them. He showed it to everyone,
saying how clever his son was and how he would
not have to be a waiter, but something much
better, like a doctor, perhaps. It was heartbreaking
to see how much he missed his family and his
home. A family man alone in a strange city,
feeling terribly lonely, would seek the company
of other people like himself, so the Catalans met
in every spare hour they had.

Without knowing exactly whose idea it was
they all agreed on spending Christmas together
in Maria's house. The girls would make Christmas
dinner and expenses would be shared. James
went around the second hand shops and bought
a table and four chairs, ugly but wide and solid,
for one pound ten shillings, which was cheap
enough, so that the kitchen-diner was furnished.

On Christmas Eve, James was sitting in front
of the fire, his legs stretched and resting on the
hearth. Maria entered the room dressed, ready to
go out.

'James, don't fall asleep!' she exclaimed,
shaking him gently, 'don't you want to have a
bath? It is almost quarter to eleven, Mass starts
in an hour or so.' He didn't move. 'Come on, the
water is hot. Are you listening?' She approached
the fire, warming her cold hands. 'James!' she
repeated, 'Come on, move.'

'Be quiet Maria, let me alone. I don't feel like a bath now.'

'You see, you should've gone before me, as soon as you arrived. Now indolence has taken you over, hasn't it?'

The clock was moving, but James wasn't. Maria waited, her mind going over the preparations for tomorrow, thinking about what was done and what else needed to be done, and sat quietly by him for a while.

'The bath has refreshed me, I was also tired. If you have a bath you'll feel better too,' she glanced at the clock and continued in an alarmed voice, 'it's eleven already James, quick!'

'I do not feel like going,' he said, his position unchanged as if he was glued to his chair, 'why do you want to go to Mass?'

'Because it is Christmas and we have always gone to midnight Mass.'

'For once, we can very well leave it.' Obviously, he was terribly averse to moving.

'Oh, we must go, we agreed to go and I'm ready!' The passing minutes were getting on Maria's nerves. 'James, come on, get ready.'

She was making an effort to speak calmly, but he had closed his eyes and his attitude was definitely not active. Watching him, Maria's irritation raised up like waves on a stormy sea, as though tongs of fire were burning on her cheeks, then she seized his arm with both her hands and began to shake him violently. 'Get up, get up, get up *now*!'

He loosened himself with a jerk, 'Do not pester me any more, *you* go to the flipping Mass!

What do you want *me* to do there? To see a bunch of hypocrites?'

'No, no, I do not want to go alone, you have to go too,' she was weeping, 'you promised me you would go.'

The tears were running fast and hot down her face. She let herself go, like a rug on water. Her head bent over the back of the chair, she cried loudly, sobs of fury and sobs of despair rising from her chest. She wrenched her hands, drinking her tears and biting her lip.

James folded his legs, resting his elbows on his knees, holding his head in his hands giving no sign or making any gesture to soothe his wife. His indifference was the most irritating thing. As the minutes passed, Maria's sobs and attitude of desperation seemed to diminish. Then James gave a kick to the burning embers, a cascade of sparks went up and suddenly a wave of fury seized Maria completely. She got up and, stretching her arms out, threw herself over James. She would have scratched, stroked or bitten him, but at last he got up and pushed her away.

'You are stupid, a very stupid fool!' he shouted, moving away towards the door.

She had fallen on the chair and was crying loudly, 'I do not want to go alone, you have to come, you *promised* me!' She stood up to follow him and began to pull at the back of his cardigan, 'No, you are not going to bed, you are not, we must go!'

This time Maria's determination to get her way was formidable. Her tears of frustration and grief were caused by the realisation that her husband did not care for Mass, and that her illusions of converting him had just failed. Nevertheless, she would not give in. The pressure of time propelled her to use all her might. She kept holding on to his cardigan, her mind focussed, and she could see nothing but the desperate need to make him go out with her, as nothing else mattered.

After some struggle, and some following him from side to side to get him to put his coat on, she found herself in the car without knowing at what time he had given in. She was blowing her nose and drying her eyes while he started the engine swearing non-stop, cursing the priest, the Mass and the Catholic customs which, to him, were far worse than those of Protestants.

When they arrived the church was already full, and someone stood to let Maria sit, so she must have looked terrible with her red nose and swollen eyes. Now and again a repressed sob would shake her shoulders. Watching the lights, she could see a goldish circle moving. Sometimes it was bright, others dim, and she thought fog had entered the church. Either the sound of singing was coming and going or she had noises in her ears. Communion finished and she was going to sit down when she noticed the floor coming towards her. She clutched the pew; was she going to faint?

Somebody took her out on the porch, where she was given water, and she drank it slowly, then breathed deeply the fresh night air. She looked at the stars and thought about peace,

peace and goodwill to man, a peace that was so unobtainable, as were the stars high above in the sky. She was overcome by an infinite sorrow. Mass had finished and James came out.

'What are you doing here?'

'I fainted a little.'

'It is your fault,' he replied, taking her by the arm and going to the car. She was silent, and he said nothing else. No words of comfort or repentance were uttered, and they arrived at their home and quickly went to bed.

The following day Maria's eyelids were swollen and her smile was very scarce.

'You do not feel well today, do you?' asked Conxita as soon as she stepped in.

'No.'

'How big you are getting, dear girl!' exclaimed Carmen, looking at Maria's tummy with envy, yet with feminine generosity she added, 'you sit down, we'll do the work.'

Out of their bag they took a big bird, already dressed for the oven, and proceeded to work busily in the kitchen.

Later, Pere Serra arrived, bringing drinks and forced joy. James didn't get out of bed until the table was already laid. They ate and drank profusely; joy was becoming less forced and more real as their bellies were filled. Everyone was missing their homeland and their own families. Maria was missing hers with double the intensity after the terrible upset she'd had. Her fallen spirits searched for relief in thoughts of her family, yet only sorrow sank her deeper.

The days went by. The couple had never enjoyed much of an intellectual relationship, and now there was no communication on this level. However, the acquired habit of sleeping together made them love each other again. Maria was preparing herself for the coming of her baby. Dr. Hyman said she must go to the hospital regularly for pre-natal examinations. The thoroughness of the tests surprised her, as her health was watched carefully, and she was told what to do and what not to do, and given calcium, iron and vitamins as if she was incapable of knowing any health care.

She spent hours in hospitals with the ritual of undressing, waiting in a cubicle and then dressing again. She often came out filled with strange anxieties, as if the baby she was carrying was not hers. Why was so much care being taken of her? After all, she was a foreigner, and her baby a foreigner, too. Or was it? Was the baby going to be taken from her? A baby born in England would be English; it was going to be different from her nationality. Therefore, it would be a perfect baby for the state! She remembered the book Paul had shown her. Good God! I do wish my baby to be perfect, Maria said to herself, and she willingly submitted her body to the care of the state. The welfare fathers!

The preparations for the baby were underway. James was making a cradle with new sticks of wood and Maria had bought a piece of cloth, which she stuck and stitched to make a little mattress, then dressed the cradle with nylon frills. It was so pretty.

Conxita and Carmen were busy sewing the Christening robe. By that time the English lessons had come to an end, due to a lack of time, which was used on other matters, like their friendship with Pere. The two girls wasted no effort in making his stay in England more bearable. They had the idea of renting a flat where they could live together, and cook meals *a la catalana* to give each other company and comfort.

When James heard about it he commented, 'it must be Carmen's idea, haven't you seen the way she looks at Pere? There is something going on with those two.'

'Well, no, it can't be. He is very fond of his wife.'

'Yes, let him be…Conxita is as silly as you are, she sees nothing.'

CHAPTER TWO

SUDDENLY, MARIA FOUND herself awake. The light, filtering through the curtains, was so soft that she knew it was not morning yet. What has woken me? she wondered, listening intently to her own being. Lately she had not slept well at all, her bulk hindering a comfortable position, her heartburn causing her uneasy rest. Sometimes, it was a kick from the baby which roused her from sleep, but now it was none of these, as she felt well, and was completely awake and alert. Then she perceived a wet trickle down her legs, moved a little and noticed the dampness of the sheet.

The time has come! she thought, in a troubled state, her heart beating faster. At first she felt breathless then, realising she was frightened, made an effort to calm down. She let a few minutes pass, keeping very still, then stretched out her arm to touch her husband.

'James, James, wake up.'

'What?'

'It is time,' she said quietly.

'What?' he sprung up.

'No need to hurry, we have time yet.'

'What time is it?' he put the light on to see his watch, 'it is six o'clock, what do you want me to do?'

'Nothing, nothing. I think we can wait another hour, sleep if you like and I'll wake you up again. Put the light off.'

Outside, the light was increasing. As the thin flowered curtains let it through, she could see all the objects in the room; the cradle covered with a dust sheet, the tiny garments, carefully folded. After so many months of expectancy, at last the time had come. Now she needed to get ready for the delivery. She had heard a lot about the importance of relaxation, but trying to practice it now was useless as all the nerves in her body were tensly waiting for the first contraction. She decided to get up, and she dressed slowly. Then she began to put into her case what the hospital had stated; no more, no less.

'James, will you get up now, you have time to leave me in the hospital without being late for work.'

Soon after, they were in the middle of the hall at the maternity unit of St. James's Hospital. Maria folded her coat over her voluminous tummy and James, close to her, holding the case, seemed undecided and shy but nevertheless very conscious of the transcendence of the hour.

A nurse came up to them and, taking the case from James, said, 'You can go now, when you come and see her this evening you can take the case back.'

Her other hand pushed Maria gently away. Maria turned to look at her husband, who stood still in the middle of the hall, dismissed from interference in what was going to happen. When she thought how little a part he would take in the birth of his child, she felt sorry for him and wished to go back and embrace him and tell him not to worry. But the nurse pressed her forward. They went into a ward, where the nurse drew some curtains around a spotlessly bleached bed, then told Maria to undress and lay in it.

'Put this on,' she said, handing her a rough nightie, 'the midwife will come to examine you in a minute.'

Left alone, Maria began to wonder if the feminine instinct to give birth existed or had disappeared from lack of use, as she seemed to be at the mercy of this institution. She had to follow instructions step by step, which were so efficiently given that no-one would dare to take any initiative.

'Any pains?' the midwife asked, whilst pressing Maria's stomach, feeling for the position of the baby's head.

'When did your waters break? Did you lose a lot? No, well it's going to be long...' she concluded, glancing at Maria with sympathy.

Another nurse came later with a bowl of water and shaving things. Maria felt uneasy, but she resigned herself to it, and was given a purge. Later, she was taken to the bathroom and told to wash properly, with the door kept unlocked. All privacy had disappeared.

When she went back to bed she felt very tired, and was told to relax. Surprisingly she could, as her pains, which were light and sparse, did not disturb her much. The screen was drawn back and she became aware of the other patients on the ward. On her left a fair young girl was wringing her hands, and got out of bed, claiming she could not lie down, only for a nurse to make her lie again, examine her and, with a 'not ready yet,' leave her. This was repeated three or four times. The girl lost control, whining continuously and intercalating a shrieking cry, then calling out for the nurse. Maria, watching her, was wondering if she would be reduced to the same state of desperation. Presently the young girl was taken to the delivery room.

Sat on the bed facing Maria was an older woman, apparently calm, who commented, 'it's the first child and she is very frightened,' her hand closed tight on the bed covers, her knuckles as white as the sheets, she added, 'mine is the sixth, I am used to it.'

Further down the ward there was someone crying quietly. Another woman was out of bed and paced the ward up and down, clip, clap, with her slippers. Every one was grotesquely deformed, reduced under gripping pain, exulted by the expectation, and all were draped up in the great mystery of life. The hours dragged on, and the ward was not quiet. If it were not the suppressed cries causing a din, it was the panting or the sighs, or, worse, the atmosphere well charged with so much silent pain in that reduced space, straining the stillness.

Maria was ordered to sleep; if the pain came more frequently she was told to press the bell near at hand. She did not think she would be able to sleep as the pains were coming every twenty minutes. But she did not know she had been given a soporific. She was told what she had to do, yet not what they were doing to her. She fell asleep.

The contractions came and the pain was distant, almost like in a dream from which Maria wished to wake and could not. She did not know if her eyes were open or closed, if she was in a nightmare or reality. She continued to hear confusing noises, which sounded far away yet, at the same time, near, as if they were coming from inside her. Maria feared the baby would come and she would not be able to wake, and felt anguish and anxiety at the thought of not being able to help out because she could not wake. Deep sleep blackened everything, then another sharp pain half wakened her. She fought with her dimness, moving her head from side to side, her arms out of the sheets, her mind wanting to alert her body, sweating, wishing the nurse would come and waken her.

Suddenly, her eyes opened completely and a nurse was leaning over her asking, 'Are you all right?'

'No, no, of course I am not all right.'

The nurse applied the instrument she was carrying to her stomach, then watched, waiting for the next contraction. 'Don't tense yourself up, let go, let yourself into the pain, do not be afraid,' she said, looking at her watch.

'I can't! It's terrible,' Maria said, as soon as the spasm had passed.

'Well, it won't be long now, check the frequency,' and she turned to go.

'Please, don't leave me,' begged Maria weakly.

'I'll come back,' answered the nurse calmly, without stopping.

Maria decided to pray to pass the time. The clock on the wall marked four o'clock. She began with 'Our Father,' but the panting of the woman in the next bed distracted her. After a while she began again, but in the middle of 'Our Lady,' a piercing pain seized her to hell and back for a few seconds and she was covered in sweat. Did our Lady have Jesus without pain? She thought about her mother with a feeling of gratitude and reverence she'd never felt before, and she thought about the six women around her, all suffering, and her mind spread all over the world too, where so many women would be bringing a new life forth. A profound sentiment of sympathy, understanding and sorrow overflowed from her heart. Endless minutes passed, then the midwife arrived to have a look between Maria's legs for any sign of the baby's crown, but shook her head thoughtfully and went away.

The woman next to Maria, who was reduced to a screaming bulk, was taken away to the delivery room. Then a new arrival was heard, as a wailing voice went on for a while, mixing with sharp peremptory sounds until footsteps faded away, followed by heartbreaking sobs from a woman who was being deprived from the company and comfort of her husband.

Maria, in spite of her efforts and goodwill, was fast losing her calm. She let some loud cries escape from her mouth. It came to the moment when she believed she would not be able to stand another contraction. She shouted for the nurse, who came, gave her an injection and left her alone again. It didn't soothe the pain, or accelerate labour. She thought once more that she would not be able to stand much more. It was eight o'clock, and she could not have breakfast.

At last the midwife came and Maria looked at her, imploring her help.

'We'll take you to the delivery ward, shall we?' asked the midwife.

They put her in a trolley while she, gathering strength, reinforced her spirit for the great moment of her baby's birth.

'Thank God!' she exclaimed, stretched on the tall, narrow table while the nurses around it watched her, waiting, observing the working of pain in her face and body.

She was given a gas mask and shown how to use it. She felt the refreshing smell was scant relief, yet used it with frantic hope. More minutes passed and a doctor came. Maria's feet were covered with some thick socks and her legs held up through some rings descending from the ceiling.

'When we tell you to push, do it with all your might!' a nurse said.

By her side someone was holding her hand, a reassuring, sympathetic touch. It was not her mother's, nor her husband's, but she needed any human being at that moment. She pushed so hard she thought her lips would burst, and still the head of the baby did not come through. The doctor made an incision to enlarge the opening;

she didn't feel the cut of the surgical knife, but the warm bleeding. More minutes passed.

'We are going to operate,' decided the doctor.

Immediately, a surge of movement went on around her. Some nurses proceeded to empty her stomach by placing a rubber tube into her nose, and she felt a terrible disgust and violently moved her head to the side.

'We must empty your stomach for the anaesthetic,' the midwife said.

Then Maria sneezed the tube out of her nose and at the same time the pain became so pungent that she pushed with more than all her strength, thinking it didn't matter if all her body burst and took her life with it as long as her baby came out. And come out it did, and from all those present a sigh of relief came out, too. Maria felt a splash, and saw the white overall of the doctor being covered with red spots, then closed her eyes, exhausted.

Two nurses, one at either side of her, were pressing her hands, crying, 'Come on, another push! Another push for the baby's shoulders!'

This time, it was easier and the infant slipped out completely, held by the doctor's hands, who showed the baby to Maria with great satisfaction, telling her, 'It's a girl.'

Cutting the cord completed the separation of mother and baby, then the tiny being made her first independent sounds, crying quite loudly. A nurse wrapped her in a blanket and presented her to Maria, calm joy on her face. There was a strange anxiety still in Maria's.

'Is she all right, healthy?'

'Very healthy indeed!' she was immediately assured.

How marvellous! She felt the hot blood coming out of her, and the midwife pressing on her now fluffy stomach. The afterbirth slipped out, viscous, like a slug. The doctor was stitching her. She felt no pain at all, only an infinite restfulness, and the strange new dimension of her feeling of love towards the direction where the baby was put into a cradle.

When Dr. Hyman entered she smiled happily, pleased he had come. He pressed her hand, congratulating her, and said how well she had managed to have her daughter.

Maria was washed and given an injection, whilst her blood and sweat soaked shirt was changed. All this was done with much care and consideration, and she was helped to some tea, then transported to a new ward and into a clean bed.

'Please telephone to my husband,' she asked before falling asleep.

At twelve o'clock she was woken for dinner, and a nurse told her to sit up. Maria was surprised at the order, as she was so stiff, and she said she couldn't, but the girl didn't take any notice and simply propped her up and filled the space behind with a pile of pillows, then put a tea tray over her knees.

The ward was very large, with two rows of beds, and in each one a woman was trying, with more or less difficulty, to get into a position to eat. Plates of food were being placed in front of them. Maria looked at hers in great disappointment; it was so English! The little pyramids of mashed potatoes next to the pile of peas near the meat, a few carrots, all on a base of brown gravy. How foreign she felt in that moment, longing for home. If she had been at home someone would have made a special broth, a piece of chicken, perhaps, and a glass of wine to bring her strength back. Above all she would have been left lying down very still, as still she wished to stay. Tears came to her eyes.

The woman next to her asked, 'What have you had?'

Turning her head, Maria recognised the fair girl, the one she had seen wringing her hands in desperation, who was now calmly eating her mashed potatoes. She was as pale as the sheets, with deep violet lines under her eyes.

'A girl, she was not born until this morning,' Maria replied, wondering if her own colour was washed out, too. She immediately began to eat.

When a nurse passed by, Maria asked where her baby was and if she was well.

'She's in the babies ward with all the others, of course she is all right! Now, ladies, get to sleep, all of you face down on your tummies,' she commanded in a loud voice, walking along the rows of beds checking each occupant. All the mothers abided and any new arrival soon followed the rules of the ward, with a kind of fear and a feeling of 'must do or else'.

After carrying the baby for so long inside herself, the harsh separation was unbearable. Maria longed to have her baby near. The feeling of loss was evident and the desire to stretch her arms for the weight of the baby on them, the desire to retain that weight, was strong. Why, oh why, was the baby being kept away from her?

The ward became very quiet, and there were no nurses to be seen. The babies must have been far away because no cries could be heard, and Maria fell into a slumber like the other women. She was woken up by the noise of women moving and some getting up, then the door of the ward opened wide and the cries of babies, like waves of wailing wind, invaded the place. All eyes were fastened on that opening, and after a few seconds a nurse appeared, wearing into the curve of each arm a bundle crowned by a tiny head. She approached a bed where a mother with outstretched arms and bare breasts received her baby with great delight. The nurse addressed another mother, giving her the second bundle. More nurses came in and started distributing the precious little ones.

Maria's eyes followed them avidly, and each time a nurse went towards her she felt a punch of anticipated joy, only to see her pass by. Her eyes then looked back to the door with renewed anxiety, until no one else came in.

'They won't bring yours yet,' the woman on the other side of Maria said, looking at her with sympathy whilst accommodating a pink little head on her breast.

Maria felt a lump in her throat and could not answer. She turned her head, only to see another mother gazing lovingly at another tiny bald head. She was sobbing, unable to stand the distance from her baby and so much intimacy of love in the open.

'What is the matter?' asked a nurse, leaning over her.

'I am in pain,' she said, finding this answer easier than the real cause of her sorrows, 'as if I am going to have another baby.'

'Ah, those are after pains, it happens sometimes, I'll give you something for it,' she said, then went away and came back with a glass of water and some pills.

The water cleared Maria's throat and she asked, 'Why can't I see my baby?' Her voice was breaking again.

'Don't worry, your baby is all right, she does not need feeding yet.'

Maria couldn't hold her tears any longer, and, bearing her face on the pillow, she let them overflow. The desire to have the infant near was overpowering, yet her body, battered and bounded, could do nothing towards the fulfilment of her impelling need. She bravely tried to console herself, thinking that they would bring her baby as soon as the ruling hours had passed. The comfort was slow and scarce in reaching her.

Time was moving on. The nurses were taking away the well-fed babies. Maria, calculating how many more feeds there would be, repeated to herself the need to adapt into the routine of the hospital. Suddenly, she saw a smiling nurse, the same one who gave her the pills, coming straight to her with a swathed bundle.

'Look dear, here is your baby,' she said, opening the bundle, 'she is very small.'

'Ah!' Maria gasped with delight and stretched out her arms. What a soft, sweet weight! Behind the screen of tears the happiest smile ever seen in that ward blossomed through, and even the nurse felt moved.

'Have her a little while,' she said quietly, as though she was breaking a rule, 'I'll come back.'

That evening, at visiting time, she waited for James with emotion. She saw him coming, his eyes shining; he too was moved and he embraced her tenderly.

'Have you seen her?'

'Yes, I came at midday, the Sister showed her to me, but through a glass door. They didn't let me hold her, they didn't let me come here and see you because you were sleeping. Did you get my flowers? It's the biggest bunch on the ward isn't it?'

'Yes, thank you, she is pretty isn't she?'

'Yes, very pretty, she is like you.'

'Like me? No, she is like a Spanish Pea, sigronet brownish and all,' she was smiling, yet closed her eyes, still feeling the exhaustion of the past struggle.

'Have you suffered a lot?'

'She took so long to come...'

'We shall call her Elizabeth after the Queen. She must be named like the queen of England.'

The half hour was soon over and, as the last visitor went out, the first baby was brought in. The baby's cries were gradually replaced by suckling noises and loving hushed voices. Maria closed her eyes and remained quietly still.

At six o'clock in the morning everyone was awakened for their first cup of tea. Bowls of

water were given to the women who were unable
to go to the bathroom to wash and change. Once
the rituals were finished the wailing babies were
brought in. Now it was Maria's turn. Her eyes
fastened to the entrance. The nurse gave the baby
to her and remained at her side, ready to help.

'She won't find anything, but if she sucks the
milk will come sooner, put her head like that...'

Why would she not know how to place the
baby on her breast? She had played with dolls as
a little girl, hadn't she? Was she not supposed to
have knowledge of these things naturally? Of
course she had! She dismissed the nurse with a
turn of her head. Now the tiny baby, using her
instincts, was sucking with pleasure. Maria's
pleasure was new too, a strange mixture of sexual
sensation and spiritual fulfilment: the fullness of
giving, of pure, undemanding tenderness. Later, the
rush of milk came. Her breasts became so full,
they were like two millstones, her temperature
rose and she felt a very oppressive pain.

In the evening, James, making fun of her said,
'You look like a milking cow!' but she could not
laugh, as she felt depressed, and was ready to cry
after seeing her husband's glances towards the
other women on the ward. The majority of them
were well made up, with pretty bed-jackets.

'This one on your right – she does not have her
husband today?'

'Come, James don't look at the others, tell me,
how do you manage? What are you doing? Do
you eat well?'

The half hour fled away. Afterwards, they had
to give Maria some pills and bathed her balloon-like

breasts with hot water, then used an apparatus to extract some milk, which was a very painful experience. During the night she could not sleep for discomfort and real pain. In the end the night nurse decided to bring the baby from the nursery, where she was yelling her little might off. Then mother and daughter comforted each other the best they could.

The next morning everyone was woken at six o'clock. No wash bowl was brought to Maria and she was told to go to the bathroom. No-one ever asked her how she felt; they just counted the days, and decided what should be done by counting the hours since delivery. She was convinced that she could not walk two steps away from her bed, and she said so. But the nurse had no time or patience for Maria. She felt forsaken and was really scared, as she was losing a lot of blood and could have a haemorrhage, or lose her balance and fall on the floor. The day before she had seen the woman a few beds further down, blanched like the ward walls, being helped by a companion less weaker than her to the bathroom, pace by pace. Poor girl, Maria had thought.

Now she felt sorry for herself. She would be fine without the wash but not without the bedpan, so she had to get up. When she put her feet on the floor, she felt a rush of blood pour down and stopped still. Frightened, she did not know what to do. At that moment no nurse was in sight and everyone else seemed occupied in their routines. Tightening her lips, she went one step forwards. If I drain myself it's their fault, because they made me move, she thought, and she continued, with determination, carefully on. When she finally reached the bathroom, pale and shaky, the blood was trickling down her ankles. She did what she needed to without stopping any longer to wash. How long it was to her bed! She was there before her own legs had taken her. How wretched she was!

She lay down flat, closed her eyes and remained perfectly still until her baby was brought to her. The nurse had been right, she was able to move. But was it necessary to impose so much on the poor women, after they had already suffered so much during labour? On the same day, she was ordered to have a bath. A nurse with more human kindness filled the bath for her, checked the temperature and added disinfecting salts to it. This one did not assume she was well enough but asked kindly how she felt and even offered to help her in. Then she waited until Maria had finished and helped her back to her bed, which had been made with a new clean sheet.

The doctor was doing his rounds. He inspected the newborns, then the new mothers. When Maria saw him enter the ward, she realised how important a person he was at the hospital. His train was made up of several people, all attentive to his suggestions and gestures. The Matron, with her black dress, neck and cuffs of white lace; the Sister midwife, the ward Sister and the nurses. All wore the cleanest of uniforms and did not have a hair out of place. The doctor, very conscious of his bright feathers, like a cock, was going by, stopping for a few seconds at the foot of each bed to read the chart the Sister held up for him and, after a short glance at the woman, continuing down the row of beds.

Maria watched him from her bed. The imposing group inspired fear in the mothers, and no-one dared to open their mouth. Since their entrance she had made the resolution to speak, and ask him a question. He was approaching, and her resolution weakened. She was worried that her English would be bad and he might not understand. But the question was important. The doctor was near, and her heart was throbbing. He was already looking at her chart. It was now or never.

'Doctor, is my baby all right?' she audibly articulated.

Sister gave her a glance of surprised reproach. Yet the doctor's eyes lifted and he made a gesture of listening.

'Why?'

'She is yellow.'

The doctor then looked at the Sister as if asking, 'which is the baby of this woman?' He had no need to say a word, as the Sister was efficiently telling him about little baby Martines, that he had seen a short time ago.

'Oh don't worry, it is not important, because she is so small her red blood cells need to adapt. Otherwise, she is very healthy.'

'Thank you,' said Maria, and she smiled, 'my breasts hurt an awful lot,' she continued, her courage fully back.

The doctor checked the hardness and immediately moved away, saying to the Sister, 'She must feed the baby more often.'

Seconds later, he was at the foot of another bed. Maria's daring was loosening the knot of the other women and, following her example, they began to clear up uncertainties and worries which had too often been smothered, or, if stated, dismissed with that very English horror of fuss.

The transit in the ward was continuous; every day new people were brought in on a trolley. Deranged women, unrecognisable, were left on beds. Every day women went out transformed, happy, excited, trying to get dressed into a last season dress with the illusion of being fit again.

Those whose delivery had been normal, or even those with a few stitches, were anxious to go home after the fifth day, as was Maria. It was not so nice now that somebody else looked after her baby, and not so agreeable to follow all the rules and routines of the hospital. There were women who found Sister so-and-so quite daunting, or nurse so-and-so quite bad-tempered. They passed information on, saying 'if you do that, this Sister doesn't like it,' or 'don't do that! Nurse so-and-so disapproves,' and so on.

One woman had the radio on all day because she had forgotten the day she came in, and everyone wished, above all else, for quiet and rest. The midday rest was respected by everyone, but only for one hour, and Maria found the wakening vexing as no babies were brought in but some exercise had to be done on top of the bed to help regain their figures. The majority of women did this with a complete lack of conviction or liking.

In the ward there was no boredom but a lot of longing. One afternoon when Maria could get about, she approached a group of mothers. One was crying, and Maria had seen her before, but now her blue eyes were veiled with sadness. Maria asked her what the matter was.

'She is crying for her son,' answered one of the group.

'Is he not well? I thought she had a girl.'

'Yes, but it's for the one she has at home, a two year old boy,' added her friend and, to the afflicted mother she said, 'Come, do not cry any more. How many more days to go? Two?'

'Three,' the young woman answered between sobs, 'only because yesterday I had a temperature, so now I have to stay for one more day.'

Maria moved away, unable to understand this split direction in sentiment. She found the mother of five she had seen on the first day, who was knitting, with the same careworn face.

'How are you? How are your children doing?'

'Ah, very well thank you,' she replied, without stopping her knitting.

'Do you miss the others very much?'

'Oh no, my husband looks after them, he does not go to work when I am here, he stays at home. I am coming every year you know?'

'Really?'

'Yes, I like having babies.'

'But don't you feel ill?'

'No, during pregnancy I feel better than ever,' she replied, her needles moving at the same steady pace while Maria gazed incredulously.

'And the labour pains?'

'Those soon pass...one gets used to it.'

'Unbelievable!' muttered Maria, turning slowly towards her bed.

It was visiting time. A nurse with her back to the closed door shouted, 'Are you all ready ladies?'

At the end of the ward a mother was still out of bed, so the nurse waited for a few seconds before opening the door. The men began to enter and spread about the beds. They came smiling, some bashful, others with decided airs, all well groomed or trying to be so. They brought sweets, flowers, drinks, clothes and news from home, all received with joy.

Maria fixed her eyes on the door, waiting for James. Was he coming? The minutes passed by. On her right the girl who had no husband was tearfully talking to the woman sat by her.

'No, no, no. I don't want to give him up. He is mine.'

'But dear, it is all settled.'

'I can't let him go.'

'Neither can we keep him at home...'

James's figure appeared in front of her, stopping to kiss her.

'I am sorry to be so late, it's because I had to come by bus.'

'Why?'

'Do you remember when I told you about some lads on business with smashed cars? Well, I have sold the Ford to them in exchange for a Vauxhall.'

'That is not running?' exclaimed Maria.

'No. It had an accident, but I will repair it immediately and it will be much better than the Ford. You'll see how well. We are going to make a lot of money and will be able to go to Spain for a holiday, to visit our families and show them our little girl. You'll see how happy they will be to see us. When I have this one repaired I will sell it again for more than four hundred pounds, and then we shall buy another one. One even better, I am sure. You don't know what a good business it is and how much money can be made buying smashed cars. These lads buy them from insurance companies for nothing. Cars that had only slight bumps and are written off. They have piles of them, some are fantastic!'

'What have you got for the Ford?'

'The Vauxhall is a lot better, the roof is smashed in but the inside is perfect, and the engine too.'

'Tell me how much you got.'

'Didn't I tell you it's worth more than the Ford?'

'Yes, but it's not running. I'm sure you'll have to buy new parts for it.'

'I believe I have done a good deal, swapping it!'

In that vein he carried on talking enthusiastically about his new enterprise until everyone had gone. Even knowing how easily he exaggerated, Maria let herself get rolled in by the illusion. Maybe, she thought, they would earn a lot of money and would be able to go to Barcelona and buy new things for the baby.

It was eight days since she'd entered the hospital when James was told to bring her clothes and the baby's. Her eyes shining, she entreated him not to be late, and she passed the time dreaming of the important day they would bring their daughter home. She would be so happy at home with her husband, having little Elizabeth with them all the time. In her imagination she was treated like the queen of her home and was waited on and looked after, with all the attention due to her delicate state, because it was very important what she had done; to have a baby was not a small thing. Even though she had spent nine days with women who had done just the same, for James she must be unique, as his wife and his little daughter were like no one else in the world. She was sure he had prepared a nice welcome for them. She would be very happy; they would be extremely happy together!

The day before, the unmarried girl went away. She went without joy, looking down and preoccupied, and told no-one where she was going, but everyone knew she had no home of her own and no loving husband to rely on. Yet she left with the baby in her arms. Did she change her mind? Did she give her own, painfully delivered, child to someone else? So many lives pass by, and we are unaware of their destinations.

At last the morning came for Maria. She bathed and got dressed and, although she did not find her waist as thin as she would have liked, it was not important. She put on her red coat, and the baby was well-wrapped in a shawl. Her cap went over her black round eyes. Mother and daughter rested on the top of the bed, waiting.

The minutes were very long. Ten o'clock came and James was not there yet. More minutes passed. Then a nurse came to say he was downstairs waiting. Thank God! With a careless goodbye to the ward, she went without looking back and the Sister followed, carrying her case. James was by the lift, looking very impatient, and said he was in a hurry.

'Have you hired a taxi?'

'No, a client brought me here in his car, he is waiting.'

'We have to register the baby; the office is there by the entrance.'

'Can we do it another day?'

'Where is the car?' asked the Sister.

James took the case and Maria said goodbye to the Sister, thanking her, rather moved but without knowing why. The Sister held the baby while Maria stepped into the car.

'Look after yourself,' she recommended.

James did not sit by her but in the front next to the driver, a man who, half turning his head, asked, 'How are you, Mrs Martines?'

'I am well, thank you,' her reply came out dry and short. Her joy had disappeared, like the morning sun, now behind a clouded sky. It began to rain.

When they arrived at the house, the car stopped right in front of the back door.

'Wait a minute, while I open the door.' James, descending, said, 'I don't want you to get wet.' They went into the kitchen and immediately he said, 'I am going to put a cover over the Vauxhall,' and left.

Maria sat in front of the fireplace, looking in disbelief at the grey cold ashes. She felt a shiver and pressed the baby closer to her.

'I am happy to be home, I am happy to be home,' she repeated to herself, opening her eyes as wide as she could, otherwise tears would have dropped over the baby. 'Now, your father will come this minute and he will light the fire and we shall be warm,' she whispered.

But father was not coming, and, although men's voices could be heard outside, the minutes passed. The rain had ceased.

Then Maria thought if it was possible that James had forgotten they were there.

CHAPTER THREE

JAMES CAME IN, eyes sparkling.

'Well! what is my little daughter doing?' he asked, leaning over to hold her.

Maria shielded the baby with both arms.

'We are cold.'

'We'll have a good fire in no time,' he answered, turning to the grate and scratching it vigorously. He began talking about his business idea.

'That man who took us here said it is fantastic what I am doing; you shall see the money we'll make. I have been able to open the windows of the cellar, remember it was stuck? I have fitted some plugs for a portable light. The window will do as a door to come in and out; I have the car just in front of it. The cellar is tidy now. I'll show you all the things I've done while you were lying in hospital. There is plenty of room. You'll be surprised at how many tools I already have. That Vauxhall will not be long in running. The engine needs only....'

'Have you bought anything for dinner?' she interrupted.

'Carmen and Conxita will come tomorrow, they will bring everything. They are very anxious to see the baby. My darling Elizabeth, how pretty she is. Is she not?' He looked at her with great delight.

'Wash your hands and you can hold her,' granted Maria, when the warmth of the fire was getting to her heart. She gradually felt stronger. The important thing was not to let her spirits fall, and not let the first unpleasant circumstance down her; she must try to be as happy as she intended to be.

'The bedroom will be as cold,' she said, then, softening her tone, added, 'we feel it more because the hospital atmosphere was so hot. Will you bring me the cradle in here please James?'

He finished drying his hands, then went to fetch it. Maria handed the infant to him. He took her with care, watching in ecstasy until the baby began to cry.

'It's time for her feed,' observed the mother, putting the kettle on the gas. 'I'll put a hot water bottle in her bed. Yes, you can take her cap off now.'

She put her coat aside and began to open her dress, accommodating herself by the fire. Both looked on in wonder as the tiny creature sucked energetically for her life. Presently James made a gesture to go, so to retain him she said, 'Fill the bottle, please. Where do you want to go?'

'I must work on the car if I want it to be ready for the baptism.'

'It will be next week. Put it into the cradle.'

'There is no need to baptise so early either. We must celebrate properly. I need a new windscreen; luckily only the front one is broken.'

'Work this afternoon, stay with us now, please.'

But he was already by the door.

'What do we have for a meal now?' Maria continued, in a further attempt to keep him, 'I must have my rest after dinner, I think...we were woken at six o'clock you know. Perhaps we should have our meal early. Why don't you begin to prepare it while...'

'It is not twelve o'clock yet. I have time to work a little, now that it is not raining. I bought two nice steaks.' He pointed to the larder and, with his other hand, turned the door knob and swung away, not seeing the begging look of his wife. He did not even hear her plight.

'Please don't, you'll forget.'

A good piece of sky could be seen through the window; the clouds tearing themselves apart to show the intense blue in the light of spring.

Spring, thought Maria, passing the baby to her other breast. 'It is good to be born in spring, isn't it little one?' She kissed her tenderly. 'You'll have all summer in front of you, before the winter cold comes back, to grow big and strong.'

After changing Elizabeth's nappy she wrapped her tight, brought her wind up and put her into the warm cradle, whispering gently all the time until the infant was asleep. Then she went into the bedroom. The bed was unmade, the sheets dirty. She wondered if James had been sleeping in his working clothes.

I think he has passed all these days without changing or even washing, she thought.

She began to pull the blankets. How little strength she had! She left the bed to approach the window, so she could call James to come and help her, and she saw the car.

'Oh, good God!'

She could not refrain from her horrified exclamation. Was that the car to take the baby to her baptism? It had no wheels, no roof! It was a half-dead monster, lying on its belly over the grass as if it never again could get up and run.

James was leaning over it attentively, absorbed in its care, and did not hear Maria knock at the window, or see her gestures. She gave up and went back to try pulling the sheets off on her own. It took some time to make the bed. Several times she went to the window, yet her husband did not once lift his head from the mass of scrap he was working on. She stooped to pick up the dirty sheets and took them to the bathroom. She felt her arms and legs were rather shaky, and decided to have a rest.

As she sat by the fire her temper began to alter. She was hungry. Why wasn't James coming to prepare their dinner? It was past one o'clock! The baby, now peacefully asleep, would wake before she had her rest, and she needed a proper, laid-down rest.

Maria could not wait any longer and got up and went out, turned the corner of the house and shouted, 'James...James! Why aren't you coming?'

He twisted his head.

'I am busy, you have your lunch,' he didn't move an inch from his broken car.

She moved back to the kitchen in trembling anger. Of course she would have her meal. She made some thick soup and fried the meat. She was very hungry, and would have enjoyed eating if she had the company of her husband, which she was convinced was due to her. No matter how impossible it seemed, she was left alone to care for herself on the day of her return home with their baby daughter. To think there that there could be anything more important than that for James. Where was the homecoming welcome she had so looked forward to? Her tears, falling on her plate, turned the meat bitter. That was the homecoming she had so much looked forward to!

Maria woke up because the baby was crying. At that moment James entered the bedroom.

'You have left the baby alone and she is crying!'

'Alone? Aren't you in the kitchen?' and, with a glance at her watch, Maria said, 'three o'clock! Of course, it is past her time.'

'Come on, she is crying so much!' he urged impatiently.

'Well, bring her here to me then,' she turned her back, still feeling anger towards him.

'How?'

'As you please, she is your daughter,' she replied, dryly. However, she got up and was ready to feed her when he came in carrying the cradle.

'I could not leave the work I was doing. Now I have straightened it.' He seemed to be willing to excuse himself.

It was, however, too late, and Maria did not answer, nor even look at him. All her attention was directed towards the pleasure of feeding her baby, and she did not want any interference. She detached herself from her husband, and her will and mind rejected any inclination of feeling towards him. Her mental attitude was reflected in her gesture of deep concentration in feeding the baby. Nevertheless, that did not affect her husband at all; he stood by the window watching his invalid car, talking about his work, and glancing at his wife only at intervals. There was little doubt which sight attracted him most – the pile of scrap or the maternal group. Maria kept her head down, not caring to know.

Maria, perfectly healthy, only needed to recuperate her strength and steady her mental equilibrium. In order to regain the latter she repeated to herself that James, because he loved them and cared, was working hard non-stop, as he was so eager to get money in order to provide for their needs. And they had so many! On the first day she realised that the most urgent was a baby's bath, as it was difficult to use the kitchen sink, and even dangerous, because of the taps. However, she got used to it, taking extreme care not to bump the baby's head on them. She also needed a low chair to feed comfortably, so James shortened the legs and sandpapered one of the ugly ones, and that was better. She needed a pram to take the baby outdoors, and to take her shopping or to the launderette.

That first Sunday the girls came and did all the washing and drying for her. How would she later manage to carry the infant and the washing up to the launderette? Some shops were near. However, the first time she had to go out and leave the baby alone, the worry she felt was terrible. She rushed to the grocers across the street, where she waited in a queue whilst, in her mind, counting all the things that could happen to her baby. Then she made her purchases with trembling anxiety and rushed back. The instant she opened the door, hearing the baby scream, she flushed, and, scared, picked her up panting, worrying, blaming herself for the abandonment and damage she'd caused. The infant only had a bit of wind, which came out as soon as she was lifted. Nothing after all. But the young mother could not stop reproaching herself for the rest of the day.

The baby had not been registered yet. It had to be done. Maria told James every day, but he could not find the time to do it.

At last he said, 'You go, I'll finish work early tomorrow and you go. You'll do it better than me; I'll look after the baby in the meantime.'

She preferred not to because of the walk up the hill to the hospital, as she was still feeling rather weak. She recalled how eight days ago she had to rise from her bed thinking she would not be able to reach the bathroom, and how now she thought the register office was too far away. But she went. When she arrived there, the man behind the desk stood up and gave her a chair. She was very pale, and sat down and smiled.

'I came to register my baby daughter, she was born here.'

The man returned to his chart and was writing and asking questions. 'Very well, very well, just wait and I'll give you a copy, you'll need it for the Maternity Grant.'

'Do I have a Maternity Grant? I am a foreigner, you know?' she asked in surprise, adding, 'how much do I owe you?'

'Nothing; about the grant, yes madam, everyone resident in this country has the right to it. You fill in this form, and send it together with the certificate to the Department of Social Security, and you'll get the cheque in due time.'

'Oh, thank you very much!'

Outside, the colour returned to her cheeks. She felt a lot better, quite strong really. She could now go to the church and register the baby in the Parish. She passed the church on her way back home, and for the priest told her that, on the next Sunday at three o'clock, there would be administered the sacrament of baptism. She felt so light hearted after accomplishing these two duties that she decided to walk home instead of taking the bus. The sky was pink, giving a warm tone to the streets, the chimneys throwing smoke up, straining to reach and fuse with the clouds above.

Maria walked on. After turning down a few streets, she walked down Harehill Avenue, then glanced at her watch, startled. It was so late, Elizabeth would be crying with hunger! Feeling that she should have taken the bus after all, she quickened her pace.

On entering the house she found James with the baby in his arms, pacing up and down the kitchen in a frenzy. 'It is hours since she is crying. Where have you been so long?'

She flung her coat off, dropping it on to the chair, short of breath and sweating. 'Give her to me,' she said and placed the infant immediately to her breast.

'I have lost a lot of time, I could have been working on the car,' he complained.

'Well, go, then go, I shall manage now.'

It rained in the morning, and was still raining when James came back from work. Before entering the house he went into the garden to check if the car was well covered. Maria saw him pass by the kitchen window and hastily put his slippers by the fire. 'Is it wet?' she asked, as soon as he stepped into the room.

'No, but I had better raise it a bit because the humidity of the soil gets into the chassis. Where is Elizabeth?'

'In the bedroom, I have been washing nappies, I must get them dry. If we had one of those hangers, you know – one of those that go up and down from the ceiling – it would be very convenient,' she said, then, reflecting, added, 'maybe tomorrow will be sunny.'

'We must talk, Maria,' he said in the same thoughtful manner, frowning his eyebrows, forming a deep pleat over his nose. Observing his look, she realised that it wasn't the problem of wet nappies that clouded his thoughts.

'We need money,' he concluded.

'Well, I know that; you should have a rise. Do the other mechanics get the same wages as you?'

'I don't know, they never show their packets. Only the black man does, and he gets the same as me.'

'The black man? The one who makes the tea? Is he as skilled as you? I think we'll have to ask Mr Todd to pay you more.'

'I have told him. But, it's not that. It is that we need money to buy replacement parts to finish the Vauxhall; we want it for the baptism, don't we?'

'No James, I wanted to tell you yesterday but you worked so late...I went to the church on the way back from hospital, there will be baptisms next Sunday, we can take our baby...'

'This Sunday? No dear, no! We must celebrate well!'

'With the car finished?'

'With the car and champagne. I want a great feast for my little queen Elizabeth.'

'But if we do not have the money we can't, can we? So we won't celebrate. The important thing is to baptise her soon.'

'The first thing and the most important is to finish the car. We must find the money wherever we can.'

'No James, the most important thing is the baptism; the church is not so far, I walked to it yesterday.'

'Yes, while your daughter was killing herself crying!'

'Look James, let's not quarrel when we have so many problems to solve; it is better to talk calmly. There is a lot of work to do on the car, is there not? Well, if we have no money it can not be finished until we have some. It may be a long time, too long for a baby to wait to be baptised.'

'In this country many people don't christen their children until they are quite old, the time is not important.'

'I would like to keep our country's custom in this respect.'

However, James's brow was still dipped. He was cross at having to choose between his daughter and his car, and wanted to be able to show them both off.

'We could ask for money from a bank, to borrow and repay when the car is sold.'

'We might. The car cannot be left stuck like that,' she stated, 'we must look for someone to lend us money. Do you want your supper now before Elizabeth wakens?'

That Sunday in late April the afternoon weather was magnificent and some very white and thin clouds were running about the sky, but swiftly, without disturbing nor darkening the sun's brightness. Conxita came early, bringing the Christening robes, all lace and ribbon on embroidered nylon. The women dressed the baby with much joy and care as if they were little girls playing with dolls. The cap and mittens that Maria had knitted were set aside to be put on later.

James came into the bedroom to get ready, and put on his only suit. 'I have bought a bottle of champagne,' he said.

'Yes,' Maria replied in a complaining tone, 'and I have nothing to wear, look, my get-away dress is the only decent thing I have and I can't get into it, I can not fit in!'

She had to wear her everyday clothes with her red coat, but she did her hair nicely and put the mantellima on.

Pere and Carmen came later, and Carmen immediately took charge of Elizabeth, and carried her all the way to the church. It was a collective ceremony. Several babies received the holy waters in the simplest way and with minimum fuss. There was no music but the wailing of the babies, no show of emotion, sentiment or joy. The church received five new Christians and the bells did not toll for them. It was the English way of doing things. The Catalan group walked back home, missing very much the festivities of their own country. They walked down the quiet streets on the quiet Sunday afternoon in that quiet quarter of Leeds, in quiet old England!

The manner in which Carmen held and fussed over the baby was rather strange, and worried Maria a bit. Conxita busied herself chatting away in her gracious Valencian tongue, while Pere and James emptied the bottles of champagne. They were all in a good mood. James joked about having seen Pere and Carmen going about the dark streets arm in arm the night before, something they denied vigorously, and no-one else thought funny.

A week later, James declared it was impossible to continue work on the Vauxhall without the new parts he needed. It had become imperative that they find some money. He addressed Maria in distress, so insistently that she could not ignore his plight, and agreed to accompany him to see the manager of a bank.

At midday on Monday James came to the house in his lunch hour, and Maria and little Elizabeth were ready to go to the bank.

'Change your shirt, James, and put a tie on, quick, it is ready on top of the bed.'

'No need to, better they see I am a worker.'

'Yes, there is need, you can be a worker and still wear a clean shirt at the same time.'

They left the house, and walked up Harehill Avenue, with James carrying Elizabeth in his arms, seeming pleased.

At the third corner, however, he passed her to Maria saying, 'Nobody carries babies in their arms in this country.'

'Absolutely no one, your daughter must be the poorest child in England!' she said mockingly.

He didn't think it funny and asked in an emphatic voice, 'What do you mean by that? With the money borrowed from the bank we will immediately buy her a pram, like that one.' He pointed to a passing lady pushing a magnificent pram. 'Our daughter is going to have the best pram of all.'

'Well, not like that one. Don't you see I shall stumble, I won't see what is in front of me.' Maria stopped, feeling rather breathless, as the baby was quite heavy.

They reached Roundhay Road and on the corner was a branch of Yorkshire Bank. When they entered, in its reduced space there was a counter with a clerk behind it, and a door on the right with a plaque saying 'Manager'. There was a bench on the other side where Maria dropped herself at once.

'Don't you think we should have asked for an appointment before? What if he is not in?' she wondered anxiously, looking at the closed door.

'Go and ask, come on,' James urged.

'No, you go James; you know how to do that.'

The clerk, indifferent but well-mannered, asked them to be seated while he went in. James sat by his wife. 'We can ask them for one hundred pounds instead of fifty pounds, we'll pay them back all the same, you shall see.'

Out of the door on the right came a man with well-groomed grey hair, who signalled them to follow him. As they sat in front of his desk, Maria began to speak.

'We would like to ask for a loan.'

'Ah, yes, you have an account with us?' affirmed the man, rather than asking.

'No, no sir,' answered Maria a little awkwardly, 'but we can open one, of course.'

'How much do you want to ask for?'

'Fifty pounds or more.'

'We have thought of one hundred pounds,' interrupted James.

'Well, it is like this,' explained Maria, 'we are going to start a car business, we are going to repair smashed cars, but we need the money to buy spare parts. We'll pay it back as soon as we sell the first car.' She smiled, yet the manager wasn't impressed, and continued to be cold and quiet.

Addressing James, he asked, 'Where you work?'

'Rowland Winn of Leeds. I have a job.'

'And do you think of leaving that job?'

'No,' said Maria, 'he works on the cars at weekends.'

'I see, how many cars you have?'

'One to start with, but more to come,' Maria said, 'but later...'

'There is a lot of work, a lot of business to do,' interposed James eagerly, 'thousands of pounds of profits can be made, and quickly, too, a car with a little bump can be bought for fifty pounds, once done can be sold for five hundred pounds.'

The manager, after listening for a few minutes asked, 'The house you live in, do you own it?'

Maria stood up to quieten the baby and, rocking her rather impatiently, answered, 'No, it is not ours, we are renting it.'

'Well then, I am very sorry but we can not help you.' He got up, but James was still sitting, not wanting to give up his hope.

'I assure you...' he said, but, unable to find the words in English, turned to Maria in Catalan, '*diga-li Maria que li pagarem qualsevol interes ques ens demani.*'

'We shall pay whatever interest you ask for,' translated Maria.

'Naturally madam, but that is the least thing.'

The Manager was already by the door, and had to turn to address them. James still sat in front of the desk. 'Look,' he added with a gesture of impatience, 'if you don't have any guarantee, that is, some property for the value of the loan, no bank will lend you the money.'

By now Elizabeth was really noisy and Maria went out quickly, feeling rather ashamed. She did not stop until James caught up with her at the corner of the street.

'Here, take the baby, see if she quietens down. There is nothing we can do with the bank. That is plain, if one has money, one can have some more, yet if one has no money at all, it is not permitted that one should have some. We shall have to think about something else.'

They walked, heads down, to Harehill Avenue. Maria was deep in thought, and the more she recalled the face and attitude of the Manager with his hands folded perfectly still over his desk, the more vexed she felt. Then she began to wish the obstacle removed; the forces that give impulse to struggle growing inside her. Until now her mind had been fully occupied with recent events, and she was still busied with the emotion, joy and pain of looking after her new baby. The little being was the axis of her existence, around which a profusion of problems revolved. She had been employed day and night, sorting out and adapting herself.

Back in the house, alone and feeding the baby, her mind was engaged. How are we going to manage it? How can we obtain the money we need? What can we do? she asked herself, her questions like piano keys, each lifting up a little to show the vacuum, the emptiness of no answers. Presently the baby finished her feeding. Maria lifted her up to her shoulder.

'I think you'll have to stay without a pram for a while yet,' she told her, gently rubbing her back. The baby pulled a face and let out a mouthful of milk. 'Well, you've had too much, haven't you?' Maria wiped her, changed the nappy, took it to the bathroom, then rinsed it, routine like, as her mind began enlarging awareness for other matters. In the evening, when James came home, he said he had thought about their friends, the Bentleys.

'When are they coming to see our baby?' he asked.

'No, James! We cannot ask them for money, they are buying a house, remember! Since they have moved to Holbeck and Roy got the new printing job they have come only once to see us. Andrea was even saving on cigarettes! Don't even *think* about asking!'

'But they must have some money they could lend us. Tell me, when are they coming, do you know?'

'In her last letter Andrea said she'd very much like to see me, but they did ask us to go and see them.'

'They would understand, with you expecting... write to her,' he insisted, 'invite them to come this week, to come for tea.'

'Look, I do not want to ask them for money. Not when I know they are trying to save every penny. We will be fine if we do not buy anything but the basic necessities and you get a rise. When you are not working on the Vauxhall you could do some repairs, and soon you will be able to buy the window and the other parts.'

'Tomorrow after work I'll go see the lads who sold it to me. They may give me credit for some parts.'

'Do you want me to speak to Mr Todd? Tell me,' she insisted, when he did not reply, 'I think they are abusing you for being a foreigner, or is it that...' she stopped suddenly, and a shadow of suspicion passed over her brow, 'is it that they are not pleased with you?'

'Not pleased with me! Of course they are pleased; no one does as complete a repair than me!'

She did not doubt it. But she also felt that James might use some of his working time for his own pursuits. Though she said nothing, inwardly she made the decision to see Mr Todd at the first opportunity. That same evening she wrote to Andrea, as she certainly did wish to see her dear friend.

On Thursday afternoon the two Catalan girls came to visit Maria. When she saw them, she had an idea, and she put it forward.

'I want to go into town, would you look after little Elizabeth please?'

'Yes, of course, we will!' replied Conxita, as Carmen instantly took the baby in her arms. Maria went to do her hair, put some lipstick on and her red coat.

'Her feed is at three o'clock; if I am not here or if she cries give her some boiled water and sugar. It is ready, look, here.'

Going to town was not the same as going from Wyke. After a five minute walk and four minutes on the bus she was on the Headrow, and from there she walked to Woodhouse Lane. Rowland Winn was on the next corner.

Mr Todd looked rather surprised to see her. Nonetheless he was very polite, and offered her a seat and began to enquire about her health and that of her daughter. He spoke about the weather, saying that surely it would rain before nightfall, or the next day, as it was spring time, it was expected...

'Are you pleased with my husband? Is his work all right?' interrupted Maria.

'Oh! Yes. He is a good mechanic and a good electrician.'

Maria flashed her reply at once, 'Why, then, do you pay him like an apprentice?'

She did not know what an apprentice was earning, nor did she know how much skilled mechanics should earn, but surely eight pounds and ten shillings wasn't much. If it was the same as the black man earned for making tea and cleaning the floors, then her husband was not paid according to his job. It was a suspicion, but she risked as much that it was a sure thing.

Mr Todd stared at her for a few seconds, his mind perhaps recalling his letter to the Home Office.

Maria took a breath, smiled and continued, 'you see Mr Todd, he's been earning the same for some time. Now he is speaking good English. We thought that maybe he could have a rise, it'll be very convenient... you know, with the new baby, we have a lot of expenses.'

'Yes...yes, of course.'

'Do you have any children yourself?'

'Yes, a daughter, she goes to school.'

'How nice.'

'Yes, well then. I'll see what I can do for you. I'll have to speak to the management first, you understand.'

'I am sure you'll put a good word in for him, won't you?' she gave him her best smile, got up and stretched her hand out to him, 'thank you very much.'

He said his thanks and ushered her to the door. As she passed through the workshop she was told that James had gone out to test a car.

Half an hour later, and very pleased with what she had done, Maria sat at home feeding the baby. The three women indulged in small chatter about the little problems of other people.

On Sunday the Bentleys came for tea. The two friends had many things to tell each other and it gave them great satisfaction to do it leisurely, while Roy and James were outside with the cars and the children were all well fed and not crying. Later, the darkness outside brought the men inside.

'Andrea,' Roy addressed his wife, 'you should see what James is doing, it really is extraordinary. It is a pity he needs some money to finish. I wonder if we could lend him some. What do you think?'

James had used his time well, thought Maria, looking at her friend uneasily.

'Well, I don't know Roy, we borrowed money from my mother to pay the deposit on our house, she said she doesn't want it back but...I don't know.'

'We need it truly desperately,' Maria agreed, 'I was thinking of using the Maternity Grant when it comes, although I'd rather buy a pram for the baby. I don't know how to manage without it.'

'Well, we'll think about what we can do,' promised Andrea. Soon after that they had to part, and she kissed Maria, promising to write soon.

Monday was always a good day for Maria, as she liked working days better than Sundays; work of any kind was always better than rest. Sunday quietness brought longing memories. This Monday morning she woke up feeling more energetic and lighter; perhaps because she had to get up and feed the baby only once, perhaps because the early sun came into the room, or perhaps because James was getting up too and wouldn't be late for work. To see letters on the floor by the front door was also a sign of joy. That day, there was the expected one from her mother, along with a brown envelope. She opened it hastily.

'James, the grant money!' she shouted happily, 'Look, twelve pounds, isn't it un-believable what this country gives away. It is fantastic! On top of getting free medical treatment, free medicines, free vitamins and staying in hospital for nine days, paying nothing, on top of that they give you money! What a country England is! Now I am going to buy a pram for my daughter and put her outdoors to sleep just as all the English mothers do.'

'Do you think the Bentleys will lend us the money to finish the Vauxhall?' was James's only reply to his wife's excitement.

'I think so, they are so good people! Well, if you want, we can wait before spending this twelve pounds. Now, you go to work, come on, and work well; do not distract yourself with your own problems. Everything will be all right, bye,' she kissed him lovingly.

Thursday's post brought Andrea's letter, which contained a cheque for twenty-five pounds and her apologies at not being able to lend more, but her wish that they make good use of it. Maria, shaking with emotion, showed James.

'How good they are! They always get us out of our worries. I'm sure they are the best friends you or I have ever had.'

On Friday, James received his wages, with an increase of one pound. So, on Saturday, in a state of exhilarated happiness, they went shopping. James would have spent all the twelve pounds on a pram. But for Maria's sense of priorities they bought a cheap one, a grey one without any beauty in it. The rest was spent on a baby bath and other urgent necessities.

The same afternoon Maria put Elizabeth out in the garden, in spite of it not being a sunny day, covered her well and went into the house. She was making another step towards the long process of the baby's independence from the mother's womb. Yet she did not rest easy, and worried all the time. She looked through the window often and went out several times to check that the unusual quietness was not a frightening death or something else as dreadful. In fact, the baby slept longer than ever, proving the English treatment of children very reliable.

James bought the spare parts he needed to continue his work on the Vauxhall, which completed a good week. On Sunday morning at Mass Maria reminded James to be grateful to God for their improved situation. He, without complaining, kneeled beside her.

CHAPTER FOUR

IT WAS SUMMER. A real summer. It was hot, it was dry. It was unusual for England, which was always soaked in water, falling from the clouded sky. The ground was surprised by the constant clear sky and blazing sun drying up its core, which soon began to crack with worry. The people, for no other reason but habit, planned ahead for the future with the circumstances of the present, and busied themselves with measures, dispositions or prohibitions quite out of proportion, and, it could be said, as fantastic as if the country's meteorological disposition had turned around for good.

That summer people saved water. There was no watering of gardens and no washing of cars. The Englishman who cleaned his car on Sunday morning and tended to his garden didn't know what to do, so sat in the sun and got as red as a shrimp while watching his yellow lawn wither. But Maria was happy. She liked the heat, and felt nearer home. She liked to see little Elizabeth kicking off her blanket, showing bare legs. She didn't need to run and cover her, as the infant was thriving under the hot sun and warm air.

Maria lived not on memories and longings, but rather on idealistic hopes. The happiness of the present filled the hours with peace, and without anxiety. The good weather and the settling of her body contributed to her great physical well-being. To see her daughter sleep, eat, smile and to watch how the small being was stabilising herself into the game of living, gave her a joyful satisfaction.

Rowland Winn sent James to the Batley workshop and he was away all day, coming home at six o'clock to eat his meal before going out again to other jobs. He had sold the Vauxhall, not for four hundred pounds as he had assumed but for two hundred and fifty pounds. That was quite good. The money was well administered in buying another car, which he soon mended and was now running; plus another car which at present was lying in the garden looking very poorly. James gave his wife a regular amount of ten pounds per week for housekeeping, and he kept for himself the extra money from the other jobs. They now earned same amount they had when they were first employed by Mr Gill. Maria had to pay the rent, the gas, the electricity, the coal, the furniture instalments, food and clothing for the family of three, and it was very little. Nevertheless, she did not feel economically oppressed; she looked after every penny and had a good sense of her priorities.

She was so well accommodated with her present situation that James's ambition to become rich, his pompous talk of grandeur and his plans to visit Spain did not alter her humour. She played her music during the long hours of his absence. One day James said he had met a gentleman who had just come from a holiday in Spain, and was so enthusiastic about the country that he wished to learn the language.

'He says he would like to meet you, I think you could teach him Spanish! He'll come tomorrow with his wife.'

'Ah, very well!'

It would be good to teach again, for the extra cash and the mental exercise. But Maria worried about where to receive them, as the front room was bare. Well, she could move the table from the kitchen. The next day, she did so, bringing the chairs, too. The room looked terribly inadequate. She stood, contemplating the emptiness, when the bell rang. The couple came in, well dressed, sun tanned and smiling.

'My name is Graham Abley, and this is Sybil, my wife.' The young man spoke in a very nice manner.

Maria stretched her hand, 'How are you? My husband tells me you just came back from Barcelona, and I can see it.'

'From Mallorca, we liked it very much!'

He had a pleasant, light air, and scarce hair over a wide forehead. He was not tall besides his wife because she was taller, slender and moved gracefully. She bore an elaborate hairdo and her make-up was skilfully applied. Sybil was beautiful. It was a kind of beauty Maria could appreciate: dark eyes, dark hair, and not English at all.

One can feel uncomfortable when confronted with human ugliness or deformity. After the first gaze it is difficult to find where to put one's sight again. Maria thought it could happen with the super beauty. The elegance of Sybil, her styled shoes did not fit the uncarpeted floor, nor her fashionable clothes the kitchen chairs. The shabby surroundings were so unsuitable that Maria, feeling very self-conscious, moved her eyes uneasily, not knowing what to say. Then James came to join the group and immediately began to explain his business scheme. They followed him outside to admire his work on the smashed car. On his ground he found it easy to talk and there was no need, nor was there opportunity, for others to speak.

The following day the lessons started. Sybil learnt fast, as she had a good memory, could pronounce the Spanish words well and always did her homework. Soon she was moving forward, and her husband, being not as quick, or less interested, was lagging behind. He would sooner go to chat with James in the garden than see his wife learning more Spanish than him.

Very soon Maria began to wonder how long the lessons would last when, one day, the couple asked if she would be willing to help them in a matter concerning a businessman in Mallorca. They asked her if she would be so kind as to go to their home and talk about it, on any evening. They said it was fine to bring James and Elizabeth.

When the family went to the house, they were received with the most courteous manners. Sybil took Maria upstairs, and they put the baby in the middle of the double bed between cushions. She said Maria should not worry, because if Elizabeth awoke they would hear her from downstairs, as they would be right below her. Downstairs, in the beautifully furnished sitting room, Graham was passing drinks. Maria was scared of getting lost into the luxurious chair, and sat on the edge awkwardly, fully conscious of the contrast between her barren sitting room and this one.

Graham was explaining, 'For some time we have wanted to start a business in Mallorca. Last summer we left some money deposited there, while the solicitors prepared the contract with the gentleman who is going to be my partner in running a restaurant. How the matter is now we don't know, as we have written twice and had no reply.'

'The Spaniards are not very quick at answering letters. You'll get a reply sometime,' Maria commented.

'Yes, but we would like to know if this man is going ahead or not, I think if we telephone him it would be effective, at least more than writing again. I have his telephone number. Could you talk to him for me, Maria?'

'Today?' she exclaimed, placing the empty glass on the glass top of the side table. 'Well, yes. Why not? If you tell me what to say.'

Whilst waiting for the trunk call they ate sandwiches, cakes and drank the inevitable tea. James talked in eagerness about his business scheme.

'The question is,' he continued, 'to have capital. Now, nobody gives me credit. But if I get five hundred pounds clean out of this Cresta I am now repairing, I shall laugh at the bank and all the managers!'

Thank goodness the Yorkshire Bank Manager is English, Maria thought, otherwise he would have laughed at us the day we went.

'We went to the bank to ask for a loan,' he explained to the others, 'but we were refused because...'

The telephone rang. Maria somehow nervously picked up the paper where what to say was jotted down. Graham gave her the receiver.

'Senyor Canals? Senyor Canals, escolti parlo de part del senyor Abley d'Anglaterra.' The person at the other end didn't know what she was talking about. Maria had to explain and repeat the name, as Sr. Canals had forgotten and needed reminding. Maria turned to Graham: 'He remembers. What else shall I say?'

'Tell him to write stating clearly what his intentions are.'

'Escolti...' proceeded Maria over the receiver, explaining what was required. Sr. Canals said he would think about it, and she put the telephone down, looking at the people watching her.

'It hasn't been successful,' she commented, 'first, he didn't know...I had the impression Sr. Canals had not given it another thought since last summer.'

'I do not think he is interested,' said Sybil, looking at her husband, 'he gave me the impression he was an opportunist.'

'But he was more eager than we were! He persuaded us to put some money in to the scheme.'

'By now he will have found another tourist,' interposed James.

'Maybe now he'll write,' said Maria, 'the telephone call would have been of some use.'

'If he does not write straight away, it is finished,' concluded Graham. 'I could buy accident damaged cars with you, James, couldn't I?'

'There is a great business in them!' said James, jumping up, with his bright eyes, ready to explain about the fabulous profits again, but Maria got up swiftly.

'We must go, Elizabeth will waken soon and cry for her feed.'

'You could feed her here,' offered Sybil nicely.

'Yes, thank you, however I think it is better that we go.'

When they were in the car James, glancing at the baby, still sleeping in her mothers arms, said, 'I do not know why you are in such a hurry, we could have stayed longer, and we could have ended up borrowing money from them.'

'That is precisely why I am in such a hurry, James. It is better to leave those two to talk about it first. You know she would like very much to live in Mallorca? Let him convince her of the contrary first.'

'They must have plenty of money, don't you think? With that magnificent house so well furnished!'

'I don't know...he works in the furniture business, Cavendish, I think.'

'She must earn a lot of money as well, being a model.'

'Yes, I suppose so. She is so beautiful!'

Maria had not seen the Catalan girls for some time. They had not visited lately, even though their flat was not far from Harehill. She wondered why and decided to go and visit them.

It was one of those quiet afternoons when the leaves on the trees lose their vigour, and let themselves fall aimlessly, branches down. She walked to the flat, pushing the pram. Conxita received them with demonstrations of pleasure.

Taking the baby into her arms she exclaimed, 'Oh, how pretty you are growing! Ah, look how she laughs, xiqueta, how the time passes!'

Then she sat on a stool, putting Elizabeth on the rug, and let her arms drop into unusual stillness while a dark shadow went over her face, her look passing over the baby's head and deepening into something beyond the room. It was a harrowing look.

'What is the matter?' asked Maria in alarm.

'Don't you know?' swinging her head she said, 'Xiqueta, you wouldn't believe it.' She kept moving her head from side to side.

'Say what it is, tell me, what has happened?'

'They don't want me any more,' she hesitated 'Pere and Carmen. They make my living here impossible, and, I could not believe this, she is pregnant!

'*Reina Santissima!*' cried Maria, greatly shocked, 'how terrible! James told me they were carrying on, but I would not believe it!'

'Nor would I, and I had it in front of my eyes all the time. How silly I am. I am going back to Valencia, I am going home.'

'For a holiday?'

'No dear, I am sick and tired of everything, of everything. But at least if I'm back in my homeland...' Her voice was breaking like glass.

'Poor Conxita!'

Maria remained with her friend for a little while. There was no way out of her sorrow; no comfort for the rejected woman, treated treacherously by the people she had put her entire confidence in and loved. The breakage was too big a smash. They said farewell in a moving embrace, and both knew without saying that they would see each other no more.

Well, Carmen certainly had a maternal instinct, and with a strong and demanding intensity. Remembering the possessive way she held the baby at the baptism, Maria thought about Carmen's desire to become a mother, that had for so many years been unsatisfied. The sight of another woman's fulfilment had stirred the waters of desire, like a diving duck on a pond, making the waters trickle and ripple. It is growing waves of desire, not the simple desire for sex, deeper and more complex, twined and tangled up, maternally inclined, which throws a woman into the arms of a man. And men, strange beings, what reason do they have for their sexual desires? They may have none. No scruples or consciousness. What impelled Pere, a married man and father? The loneliness? Maria could not understand. As she walked down the street, pushing the pram, she was unaware of the fog spreading all over that, descending silently, had changed the afternoon to the evening, and was turning autumn into winter. Five days afterwards, autumn was no more.

One morning Maria woke up early, and the wind and rain were battering the window, persistently, like myriads of tiny knuckles knocking the glass panel. Something more than the rain wanted to get into the bedroom. Maria watched how the wind threw the water against the window. She listened to the sound of the rain pushing furiously, only to bump into the glass barrier where it broke into shrieks of impotence then slid down to the ground, unable to enter the room. What was it? With awe she raised her head, her senses abnormally whetted by a strange presence outside her window shouting to come in.

It is only winter coming back, she said to herself. But why doesn't it want to come in to the house?

The way the wind pushed against her window as like a carrier of a message that must be hurled. She left her bed and went to the window, thinking how wet the cars laid on the garden would get. This was the problem of the moment: to find shelter for the cars and room for James to repair them. They had already had a warning from the landlord, as he didn't like the look of what was supposed to be a garden, not a scrap yard.

She looked out at the dim light of dawn. A street lamp, still lit, swung at the push of the wind; in spite of which, it all seemed very quiet. She observed the stillness of human life around her for few minutes, then let the curtains she was holding up drop and went slowly back to bed. Slowly, too, the message she had to know was dawning on her. It wasn't outside; it wasn't the wind carrying it. It was inside her, and, as the tender light of the morning opened up, growing towards brightness, the notion flew up to her mind: she was with child.

She got into bed, lying with her head on the pillow with a sigh. A soft smile floated on her lips, and her eyes were wide open, thinking. She had been very happy that summer, but it had come to an end. Tomorrow she would put the mandolin back into the trunk.

James's enthusiasm for going to Spain was increasing every day, and he said how pleased their families would be to see them, to see how well were doing, and how much money one could make in England. He worked really hard, and was often outside in complete disregard for comfort or appropriate tools. Not rain, nor cold, nothing deterred him from continuing his work. He did not take notice of other things around him, and Maria was sure he hadn't noticed how much more little Elizabeth was crying during the night, as he came to bed and slept soundly. He had only eyes for his 'beauties' lying in the garden. He did not see the pallor of his wife, nor how scarce her smile had become, as the claw of nausea seized her. She waited to tell him. First, she went to the baby clinic. She had been going regularly for the baby's immunisations and weight checks, to the place where the welfare state tells mothers what to do and what not to do, for the good health of its new subjects.

That afternoon, with the confidence the National Health Service provides, she went to consult the doctor. The doctor was female, and wore a white coat over a full figure. She had fair hair with little curls all over her forehead, and Maria thought she was very nice and had great admiration for her being a doctor. She told her how sick and depressed she was feeling, hoping for some comfort. However, this time, the blue eyes of the doctor went to Maria's face like two piercing nails, then directed them, no less hard, to little Elizabeth. Under her soft curls her brow thickened. The infant was still incapable of doing anything by herself, and she needed all her mother's attention. The doctor's eyes went back to Maria.

'You should have taken more care. If you feel ill it is your own fault.'

Maria, taken aback, blushed deeply, and did not know what to say.

'Do you want some pills?' the doctor asked curtly. Her tone of voice was hurting Maria's sensibility, and she stood up.

'No, no thank you,' she answered and went swiftly to the door. While she was in the cubicle dressing the baby, she had to make an effort not to sob. Why had she been told off? She could not find any blame, there was no one to blame. The doctor's rebuke had not been deserved, and she felt very miserable.

She passed a few days in the same decayed spirit, hesitating between telling her husband or not. She feared going to Dr. Hyman in case his reaction was like the doctor at the clinic. She decided in the end to go, and just after he arrived, Dr. Hyman gave her one of his most generous smiles. He told her to give up breast feeding completely, as Elizabeth could not find milk there, and that's why she cried so much. He said it was better to give her more Farex and as many bottles of milk as she could take. He also gave Maria some tablets to ease her sickness and a tonic. She left the surgery as if she had already taken it.

In the evening, she told James. He took her in his arms readily, and looked happy.

'This time will be the boy, you'll see.'

But, after a few seconds he asked worryingly, 'Do you think we will be able to go to Spain?'

'I think so, yes if we go for Christmas, the worst of the sickness will have gone. I'll feel better then,' she finished with increasing animation.

'If Graham decides to buy the Cresta we could go by plane. That will be better for you and Elizabeth.'

'Do you think we shall have enough money to buy all we need?'

The question was directed more at herself than at him. She knew that the answer had to come from her own common sense.

CHAPTER FIVE

SINCE RETURNING FROM Spain James complained about having to work at the Batley workshop. There was not enough repair work to do, and they made him sweep the floors.

Did that mean that Rowland Winn had lost interest in James's work? Or was it James who was not so keen on working for them? He had always had the inclination to go his own way; and more so now that he had discovered a kind of work where each car was a challenge and, once finished, a show piece to use in furthering his pursuits. How routine the client repair jobs at the garage workshop would appear to him! All the spare time he had was employed in his new venture. The second hand car trade was booming in those years, and there were so many accidents on the roads that the insurance companies paid their clients handsomely; often the full value of the car for just a scratch. The companies then sold the cars for scrap and the scrap yard men, seizing their gain, resold them to motor mechanics, who were able to cure the scratch or bump. The men who bought the second hand cars with low mileage, paying a reasonable sum, didn't need to know they had been in accidents. (The ministry of Transport test disposition came much later.) Meanwhile, it was a good opportunity for a skilled man to make money; even more for the unscrupulous.

The three brothers who called themselves 'Auto Enterprises' had a field on the outskirts of Leeds. It was one of those old green fields encircled by dry stone walls. In a corner stood an enormous corrugated half moon shaped shelter, reminiscent of a past war. Cars, like wounded beasts, mutilated, were silently lying down, scattered over the field. It was like a strange deaf war, against anybody, with each driver a potential enemy, let on the road with all the necessary power in his hand to kill. The cars lying there had left lives broken without repair. However, many would be put back on to four wheels to run like mad over the motorway, the stage for so many tragic accidents. But the men looking over the scrap yards thought nothing of this. What mattered was to have a car, make it run, sell it for money, reshape more cars, make them run and make more money, then make more run. To where? But no-one wondered about that, either.

James wished to have a garage and a field for himself, so that he could purchase directly from the insurance companies. It was his dream. To Maria it was a paramount necessity, not a dream. They had a third letter from the landlord, not only asking them to remove the things from the garden, but threatening them with eviction if they failed to do so. She composed a letter of apology and asked for more time, promising to clear up as soon as possible. Then she wrote to Rowland Winn, asking how long James would be at Batley and how he worked. She addressed it to Mr Todd, as James said it was he who provisionally sent him there in the first place. If he had forgotten about moving James back to Leeds, the letter might be effective, thought Maria. After posting the letter, while on her way home she thought she was not sure of the consequences it would bring. What was she asking for? It was better for her husband to work in Leeds, yes, but what else? Her husband was complaining, but why? Because he was made to do other jobs he didn't like doing? Whatever Mr Todd's answer was, would it satisfy her? Perhaps not.

Meanwhile, one evening the Ableys came to visit, but not for Spanish lessons, as these had finished some time ago. James said they wanted to talk about business, as he had seen a convenient place, with plenty of space for cars. They all went to see if it could be bought. James, at the wheel, was talking.

'It's the ideal house, you'll see. The man who lives there has a transport business, with heavy lorries. The outbuildings could be made into a workshop, as there is plenty of land, and the house stands alone. It is quiet, and nobody will complain about me making noise in the evenings. I could work there very well. Turn cars over faster than anybody else.'

They passed Batley, then Dewsbury and continued on. They were running alongside a river, one of those English rivers of limited perspective, the unknown deep of green water, sliding almost still in a sneaking kind of manner. Past Battyeford there was flat land and a bridge on the left, and they went over its planks noisily with trepidation, then came to a narrow bridge over the canal. A few yards on the left rose a big, solid, square building in dark grey stone. The car stopped in front of it.

'This is the house,' stated James, as proudly as if it was already his own. Everyone stepped out of the car. Maria, with Elizabeth in her arms, felt a bit sick, and looked at the house. The front of it was darkened by the fading evening light, and it seemed to fall over her.

'Look at the chimney leaning – it'll drop.'

The house was very old, and the roof was slightly sunken in on the chimney side.

'That is nothing!' assured James, who could find no fault with it.

Inside the house there was a woman wearing an apron with a child in her arms. The room was spacious and disorderly, and there were other children playing about. She uttered few words, obviously resenting being unprepared for the visit. Then a stout man in a dirty shirt came out of another room, picked up a jacket from a pile of clothing in the corner, put it on hurriedly and asked them to follow him outside.

Between the house and the road there were the roofs of other buildings. One wall was in ruins, and the windows in the others had no frames, like eyes without pupils. The building had been a pigsty, and remains of dry excrement were still visible. Sybil and Maria made an instinctive retreat.

'Of this I can make a workshop,' James was saying, with his amazing optimism.

The silhouettes of the lorries stood dark against the pink sky.

'What a beautiful stretch of sky!' exclaimed Maria.

'Yes well, I am going back to the car,' replied Sybil carefully finding her way through old tyres, oilcans, greasy rugs and other undefined bulks.

'I am too,' Maria followed her into the car, and they waited there silently for a while. Then Sybil asked Maria if she liked the place.

'Well, it is...' hesitating, she continued, 'a bit depressing. If I had to come here to live I think it would depress me. Look, there is not a single tree around, only those walls rise solitary over the plain.' The three men were coming back and stopped by the car, talking.

'James, we must go, Elizabeth is restless.'

'Yes we will go. What do you think girls?' he asked, slightly turning his neck and, without waiting for an answer, he continued, 'here is plenty of room for lots of cars, the place is good, he wants one thousand, five hundred and fifty pounds.'

'That is too much for the state it is in,' interposed Graham.

'Oh, he will come down, I am sure, he wants to go, he *has* to go. He has had complaints from the water authorities.'

They crossed the two bridges and took the road back to Leeds. James's talk continued in the same enthusiastic vein. He could see nothing better than this house. His wishful talk, or the distance, was improving his companions' view of the place. It began to seem less depressing, and even less inconvenient or expensive. Maria arrived home in an ill state, and, feeling unable to put the baby to bed, stretched out on her own.

'You, James put her to sleep, give her a bottle, please.'

James, with the child in his arms, paced up and down the length of the bedroom, intending to quieten her without further ado.

'She is hungry, she won't stop crying!' pleaded Maria feeling her stomach and her head in complete revolt.

Presently, she got up and ran to the bathroom. This time, with great effort and much pain, she vomited. After a while, trembling and wet with perspiration, she returned to bed. The cries of the child, in the background of her own suffering, seemed distant. James had gone to the kitchen with the baby to prepare a bottle. Maria was cold, and she was shaking like a leaf with no branch to hold on to.

Cold, how unhappy it is to be cold! She made a move to cover herself and crouched under the blankets. She wanted warmth and rest, and not to think. She covered her head in a hopeless gesture, as if it was possible to avert the problems towering above her.

Every day she went to the front door to pick up the post with a tight heart, as if she knew what was coming. And it came. Graham was the first to come. James was not in, and he spoke to

Maria. He began to say he had some news to communicate – that he had been offered a promotion as head of the sales department at the Liverpool shop.

Maria's mind darted fast like an arrow: now Graham Abley would decide to join them on the car business, he would put in some capital and, instead of selling furniture, sell the cars James built. Because naturally, he would not go far away. He was not going to accept this job, of course!

'I am going there tomorrow,' he continued.

'Where?' asked Maria, her head still up in the clouds.

'To Liverpool, of course. To look for a house. I do not have to start until next month, but I don't know how long will take to find accommodation.'

Flap! Inside her head, the penny dropped.

'Ha!' she said meekly, 'so then you'll leave Leeds.' And us, she thought. The confidence Graham had shown in James's ability had been like a stake of support, and she had been holding on that hope. Now what were they going to do?

'Will you tell James? When I am back from Liverpool I'll come see him and we will talk about what we will do.'

And then he said goodbye.

In the evening, when James came home and was told, he did not appear to be worried. His reaction was, 'We shall buy the house at Battyeford.'

'But James, where we find one thousand five hundred pounds?'

'Graham will lend it to us. He said so, he has promised,' he replied, with some uncertainty in his tone, frowning his eyebrows in that manner which could foretell the confusion between reality and imagination. Maria was watching him with growing concern as he continued, 'tomorrow I'll go to see if that man has put his price down.'

Then she asked, 'How is your work going? Have you seen Mr Todd lately? He must have my letter by now. Tell me.'

'I don't know,' he replied curtly and went out. Maria thought it strange that he didn't use the opportunity to complain about Rowland Winn.

A few days later the letter came. Maria opened and began to read it. As she was reading her blood was getting cold, and she felt as if a rock had fallen on her neck and the head rolled senseless over her body. It was impossible to finish reading, and she had to hold her head and recline her body on the wall. She made an effort to breath and began to read again.

Mr Todd told her how displeased they were with her husband, how unhelpful he was, the many times he did not present himself for work, the many, many times he was late; the lack of interest he had for the firm. Mr Todd suggested that he would be better working for himself, and that he had no intention of taking him back into the Leeds workshop. She could read between the lines the consideration given to her, and that if they had not sacked him it wasn't for lack of wanting.

The blood suddenly came back to her face, hot; she felt it burning her cheeks and covered them with her hands. Good Lord! she thought, Another failure! Luckily he has left early today. But where to? To work? How easy it is to believe what one most desires! Maria had attributed his previous lack of willingness to the kind of work he was doing as a domestic servant. When it was finished and he worked in his own trade she had been fairly tranquil.

Now the same had happened. What caused it? Why? The letter bewildered her: was it a warning, advice, or was it to be taken as a dismissal? She was at a loss as to how James would take it. She decided to say nothing and wait for developments. The day passed heavily with all these anxieties.

In the evening she was clearing the table, unusually silent.

'Don't you feel well today?' asked James, seeing her thus.

'As always. There is a letter from the hospital. I have to go again for X-rays, they are so keen on making sure I do not have tuberculosis!' she said.

Well, she shouldn't have spoken about the letter. Soon he was inquiring.

'Mr Todd has not written, has he?'

She did not answer, and put the plates in the sink, her back on him.

'Neither will he, he is a two-faced man. And I repaired his car radio for nothing, you know? Now when he comes to Batley he doesn't even say hello to me.'

She wheeled round swiftly, her good intentions drained away like washing up water, and spat out imperiously, 'Where have you been today? Tell me. Have you been wandering about or have you been working as is your duty?'

'What you mean?' he replied, stung by her tone, 'my duty...my foot, they must do theirs first and pay me better and...'

'You should be the first to oblige in your work. It is you who can't work well for anybody!' she accused him furiously, with rage, with all the upset she had carried through the day now spilling out of her system uncontrollably. 'First it was the domestic service, then your leg...what now? What stops you from working properly? Look, look at the letter, won't you look?' and she took the cramped letter out of her pocket.

'Now I want to work for myself!' He protested.

'Well then, you must have patience until four years pass. You know we are not residents of this country yet.' He was eyeing the letter somehow pale and shaky. 'You understand it? It says they are fed up of you.'

She noticed his hand holding the paper quivering. His long hands were never clean. Yet his were hands that knew tenderness and she still loved them. Appeased, she took the paper from him and began to translate in a soothing voice that lifted away the bitterness.

'What do we do now?' asked James.

'It is better you continue working,' she suggested, 'at least finish this week. Then we'll tell Graham and see what happens.'

However, Graham was not coming. The days were passing, grey days, all equal; grey was the sky, grey was the land – as grey as old ashes. A cold February stretched out, melancholic, with sunless days, where morning and afternoon looked the same.

One morning another letter came, this time from a solicitor acting for the landlord. He was reminding them of the terms of the contract, and. ended the letter giving them fourteen days to clear the garden or an eviction order would be issued. The law would put them on the street.

Maria was not surprised. For some time the menace had been dangling over their heads and now at last it had struck them, her anguish had disappeared. It was no longer an undefined problem; it was real, urgent, unavoidable and calling for immediate action. James did not go to Rowland Winn again. As for the manner in which he managed his final dismissal, Maria was not sure because his explanations were a mixture of twisted vagueness, complaints and intentions. She let it be and looked forward, feeling that it was more important to solve the present problem. As Graham was not coming to see them they decided to go and see him. They found the house closed. As it was a Saturday, they decided that the Ableys could be out shopping and went away.

The following morning they called in on their way back from church, and their disappointment was great when they found the house still locked. To cheer themselves up, they took the road to Harrogate. Their faithful friends the Bentley's would be in and would welcome them.

The Bentley's had problems too. Andrea was expecting another child, she was more excitable than usual and their house had become too small for them. They were anxiously looking for a larger one. Nevertheless, the unexpected visitors were received with great kindness, and the interchange of mutual problems kept them in eager conversation for the rest of the day.

Graham arrived at James and Maria's house on Monday evening to let them know how happy he was and how lucky he was to have found a house near Liverpool. He told them that they would move there by the end of the week. Maria marvelled at the speed he had found a house, and only wished James could find something as quickly.

She wanted to make clear the situation about Graham's intention to help them. James had said that Graham wanted to put money in the business, to help in the purchase of a convenient place. It had seemed so when visiting Battyeford. However, it had only come from James's lips. Maria had not heard anything as clear from Graham. What had been his intention before now, she wondered, how could he buy a house for himself and help them? Would he? It was all very clouded for Maria.

Graham advised James to continue looking for a place, because he said the house at Battyeford was no good, and assured James that he would sell his cars better in Liverpool than in

Leeds. He spoke as if the distance between both cities was nothing, nothing at all. Maria listened helplessly, realising that the urgency of clearing the garden was not taken into account.

More days passed by. James was still using the garden as a workshop now all day long, coming in and out, and flattening the little green grass left. The Ableys had gone. Maria's worry increased, her nerves on edge, and she felt sick and ill all day. James's last wages had lasted as long as possible, and now she had no money left. The thought of having no further income anguished her. There was electricity to pay for, the gas was already due, the instalments for the furniture, and they needed to buy food for the baby.

Talking to James was no consolation; he refused to worry about it. They had a few pounds in the bank that would last until the car was sold. Besides, Graham would lend them money, insisted James, so why worry? But Maria's worry persisted, like a grub set on the mouth of the stomach. At the same time the emptiness in her mind was whirling around in search of answers for their problems. It didn't leave her in peace. At night she could not get to sleep. In her slumber she was startled up by the cries of Elizabeth, and she would have to get up, prepare a bottle, give it to her, then slumber, only to be awakened again by more baby cries. Then she would have to rub the baby's gums with syrup to soothe her pain. Again, she would try to go to sleep, until the child cried once more.

One night James lost his patience, rose from his bed, took the child up, shook her violently, shouted at her and, seeing the infant crying even more loudly, went with her to the kitchen and left her there alone. Then he went back to bed.

'But, James, why have you left her, poor thing!'

'She is a pest. Let her burst.' he replied, turning his back.

Maria got up and went for her daughter, embraced her, comforted her, then sat by the dying fire. They both fell asleep crumpled on the armchair, uncomfortable and getting cold, just because the father wanted his rest in comfort. The father who, after all, would wake the following morning at his own pleasure, while Maria would be up early and go about the housework as usual, only a little more pale.

CHAPTER SIX

'JAMES, WHAT TIME is the lorry coming?' Maria asked as soon as she woke up, hoping it would be late, as she felt tired, and would rather remain in bed longer.

All day yesterday she had been on the move, gathering things, filling boxes and cases and trying to reduce the bulk of things in order to minimise the space used and facilitate the transport.

'We are not in a hurry, it won't come until after lunch.'

'Nevertheless, get up, we have a lot to do.'

She began to ask for help, but, seeing him accommodating himself under the sheets, she got herself up and began to dress while considering whether to bath Elizabeth in the morning or later that evening. As there might not be time later due to having to set up in a new place, she decided to bath the baby, give her a good breakfast and put her in the pram, where she would sleep for at least a couple of hours, and allow Maria to carry on with the packing.

Presently James left the bedroom and went out to tidy the garden. He trailed his half re-shaped car, his tools and spares to the other side of Leeds at the Auto Enterprises place where they would keep his goods until a better site could be found. For some time they had been looking for a garage and, apart from the house at Battyeford, nothing was available or suitable. Graham had convinced them that Liverpool was a big place for big business. Why not go there too? They would make so much money! Troubled by the pressure from the solicitor, who threatened them with immediate eviction, to Liverpool they were moving.

The lorry was to take their belongings to the Ableys' new house, which had enough room for them to stay until a place could be found. Maria had her reservations. She didn't like to take shelter, again, in a friend's house. They were very good friends, but living under the same roof, in intimate crowdedness, could cause unpleasant frictions. They all assured her that it was no inconvenience at all, and the Ableys were going to Switzerland for their winter holidays, so the house would be just for themselves for two weeks. That also made Maria uneasy, as she would not be capable of leaving her home, with all her belongings, to another family, however good friends they might be.

'You, because you are Catalan, would not do that, but the English are very generous, as you can see,' said James, and without any misgivings disposed himself to use the Ableys' home, leaving his own with no remorse.

But not for Maria, who felt like the house she was leaving was the first one she could call her own home. It had been furnished by them with their own things bought one by one, now piled up, and dreams of things, now left around the corners, like torn cobwebs. And that home, empty of palpable objects, full of illusionary longings, was hurriedly left behind for another that was not their own. She was not happy to move to Liverpool.

But they got into the car to follow the lorry without looking back, engulfed in the forward way. Only the little child sobbed her unknown sorry to her sleep. The sky hung low like a dusty sheet, and they tried to hurry before darkness and fog could fall over them on the Pennines. When they arrived in the city the sky of light grey had become dark grey and was now pitch black.

They crossed Liverpool and, under the tunnel to the other side of the Mersey river, they took a solitary road to Birkenhead. It was a long stretch of road, so long that it seemed the end would never be met. At last they arrived. Maria saw nothing but welcoming light coming out of the open door of the house. She went straight in, carrying in her arms the sleeping infant, the other throbbing inside her womb. The lorry had not arrived yet, but all assured each other it wouldn't be late.

While they ate supper they talked about James's permit for his own employment, which had been denied so that he had to look for the alternative of finding a sponsor. The solution came from Graham, who would officially employ him. Sybil was full of her skiing project. After the meal she went to show Maria her gear; every garment was dashing new and very elegant. How beautiful she would look with these bright colours over the white snow!

'Do you know how to ski?' Maria asked.

'No,' she answered, 'never been!'

She was going to take lessons. A fantastic holiday indeed! James planned to take them to the airport the next morning. Meanwhile, the lorry had not arrived and Maria was very tired. She could not pretend to smile any more, as every effort tightened the skin of her face in pain. Elizabeth, waiting for her cot, slept peacefully on the sofa.

Then the lorry arrived at last. A grisly rain was falling. The driver had lost his way, he said, and crossing the river by ferry to regain the proper route took a long time. As the man had to go back to Leeds on the same night everyone was helping to unload. The furniture went into a hut in the back garden, the cot and the cases upstairs in the guest room.

The following day, Maria found herself alone in a beautiful house, surrounded by furniture, curtains, ornaments and carpets all over. She moved about in a sense of unreality, like a dream had materialised, which was only marred by her fear of braking or spoiling what was not hers.

Then the Martines once again began their pilgrimage through an unknown city looking for accommodation, viewing houses, flats, garages, apartments and workshops in the first week. In the meantime, as the return of the Ableys approached, their worry increased. Only one place had been capable of fulfilling their needs.

Maria could already imagine them there. It was a little house at the edge of a wood, with a piece of land and a large outbuilding that was easily convertible into a garage workshop. A wide path united these to the main Birkenhead to Liverpool road. Inside the house there were all the necessary fittings, such as a bathroom and a good kitchen.

Meanwhile, James was not working, only spending the little money they had. The Abley's house was situated in a residential area, and the few shops there seemed exclusively for rich people. When Maria, pushing the ugly grey pram, bought the cheapest food, rejecting the more expensive, she had the feeling of being oddly misplaced and looked down on.

So the grey pram toned well with the grey landscape, the most desolate Maria had yet seen in England. The stretched thin land flat like a board, colourless, pulled out to the end where the water met it without emotion. Sea and land blended together in undefined gainless colour. Further still the line of the horizon could be seen or not seen, as it melted away with the whitish sky. It was very flat, with no rocks, trees, or anything, like a grey shroud, cold and wrapping the rows of luxury dwellings, so new no flower or tree blossomed there yet.

Maria was very depressed in those surr-oundings. Inside, the comfort of the house oppressed her with longing, because it was not hers. Outside, the cold landscape saddened her. On not one day had she seen the sun. It did not rain – the grey changed its shade from white to black and that was all.

'Look James,' she said by the end of the second week. 'You keep on looking around but I am very tired. I think we have seen enough places, besides we can't decide for ourselves, can we? So let's see what can be decided when they come back. Do you think you could work on the car and finish it soon, even though it is at Auto Enterprises?'

'It is very far...too far to go and come,' he hesitated.

'But we need money very soon. Listen, if you do not give me some I cannot do the shopping this Saturday. We cannot eat the provisions Sybil has in the larder. We cannot.'

The next day was Friday and James went to Leeds to see what could be done, and to get the last money they had in the bank. So Maria set up to dedicate the day to her babies. Elizabeth was very restless and was eager to put her feet on the floor, and that day she made her first step. The young mother, down on her knees, received the unsteady child into her outstretched arms. To the other child, still so much a part of herself, she would give her sweetest smile, her senses, to hear its growing life. Poor infant – how few thoughts I give him, my mind so engrossed with other problems, she thought. Then she proceeded with renewed energy to knit a little wool garment.

James arrived in the evening, very tired and in a bad mood, and anxious about his tools and things being at the mercy of the elements with no one caring about them. He had come with the last of their money, and gave three pounds to Maria, saying she needed less than him, as he had to buy petrol.

'And when the three pounds are finished, what will you buy? I'll give petrol to Elizabeth instead of milk, shall I?' she replied in a very irritated tone.

'Don't be silly, the Ableys will be back.'

'Yes, you seem very sure of their help. But I'm not.'

'They have let us stay in their home, haven't they? Well, they will let us money too.'

'Even if that is so, we must not abuse it,' she replied, 'what if happens to them what happened to us when we went to Spain?'

'What? What do you mean? What happened to us?'

'Nothing! Don't you remember? We spent more money than we should, and we still suffer for it.'

'Oh, but they are rich!'

'Well, we shall see.'

She could not sleep easily. She strolled among the debris of uncertainty, navigating in the deep fog, and nothing was clear to her. James was relying too much on supposition. Graham had not stated, at least never in front of her, how much money he intended to put into the business. He seemed to be pushing them forward, but where? They needed to have a path; one cannot walk on air. They had come to Liverpool looking for a house to live in and a place to work, not knowing who was going to pay for it. Graham? James and Maria had nothing, didn't he know?

She would speak to Graham very clearly. On Saturday the whitish sky was melting over the flat land as it meant to flatten it more, swathing everything and everybody in a humid sticky mantle. Not even the cars on the road could run from it, and yellow headlights could not disperse the fog.

Maria fastened a scarf round her head and went out alone. James was still in bed but would look after Elizabeth while she did the shopping. Walking her way across the thick fog, she was more decided than the cars, as last night the determination to clear the situation had come to her mind. She bought a chicken and the necessary trimmings to cook a good meal for everyone, so that the Ableys, when well received, would be well disposed to attack the difficulties.

On her way back the basket began to feel its weight, and she had to stop to rest. She felt less spirited, musing about the money spent, perhaps too much, as there were only fifty shillings left out of the three pounds. She stooped to pick up the basket. She felt too big already for someone who was six months pregnant. Before she reached the house her mood had changed, and she felt very silly.

James in bed, the car in the garage and me walking all that way in the fog loaded like a donkey, indeed! she thought.

The following day James went to the airport to fetch the Ableys. By midday they were in the house, with happy, newly tanned faces, and an air of light cosmopolitanism somehow distancing them from the Catalan couple. They ate the chicken casserole Maria made and drank the wine James had bought then, when they were sat comfortably in the sitting room, Maria thought it was the time to begin her questions.

'I have told him!' interrupted James and addressing Graham continued, 'we could go and see it today.'

'We must decide soon,' continued Maria seeing that Graham did not reply, 'for this is three thousand pounds.'

Graham twisted his mouth, and Maria quickly added, 'the truth is that we do not know exactly what we can spend.'

'It has a lot of land,' James added, 'and it is in a good position.'

'I think it is a lot of money!' Graham said and, after a pause, 'yes, we can go and see it this afternoon.' His conceding tone promised nothing. His attitude was not enthusiastic. 'Haven't you found anything else?'

Maria detected a veiled reproach and immediately proceeded to explain all the rounds they had done through the town, and the many places they had viewed adding, 'this house they asked three thousand pounds for would also rent for five pounds per week.'

'Five pounds is still a lot if one does not make a good weekly wage,' said Graham and, looking intently at James, he asked, ' are you sure you can make it? You need at least twenty pounds net.'

'If I can work comfortably with the right tools, I can finish a car in one week with a net profit of one hundred pounds. You can see,' he addressed everyone, 'it is important to have a place where...'

'Without the risk of being thrown out,' added Maria.

'Let's go then,' conceded Graham.

'I am not coming,' said Sybil, 'I'll look after Elizabeth.'

James was driving, and Maria sat on the back seat. The afternoon was nice, as the fog had been lifted by a warm air pushing towards the sea, and the sun could be seen like a giant orange, orbiting solitarily over the land.

Graham did not like the place. The out-buildings were sufficient, yes, but the heating needed would take another five pounds a week. It was too far from the road, and one had to pass through somebody else's estate. Maria became very quiet, as less and less she understood what was expected from them.

'Tomorrow I'll begin to help you to look for the right thing. I know an agency dealing with this kind of property, a house-garage-workshop. Tomorrow it will be the first thing I'll do. Don't you worry now,' he concluded, once they were back at the house.

The rest of the day passed nicely. Only Maria made a couple of attempts to bring the conversation back to her problems. Yet someone or other skewed the conversation away to other topics. Soon they retired to their respective rooms. James and Maria admitted deception to each other; both had the illusion of obtaining the little house near the woods.

The two women had eaten their meal. The men being out, Sybil was ready to go too.

They had been talking to each other in polite conversation, which says nothing.

'Can you lend me some money, Maria?'

The sudden question shocked her, and, opening her eyes wide she put her head down quickly in embarrassment, as if she had made the request herself.

'Yes, I think so,' she stumbled, looking for her purse. She opened it, and the lonely half-pound was there. She took it and handed it to Sybil. 'Do you have enough?' she asked uncertainly, seeing Sybil's unsatisfied look. 'Sorry, I have no more.'

'Well, I think so. Thanks, bye bye.'

Maria was left cold, with the purse in her hand still open, empty. She was ready to give in to desperation but the wailing of her daughter, holding onto her legs, brought her back to reality. There were nappies to change and wash. She knew now what she feared before; they had come back from Switzerland skint, and, if their purses were as empty as hers, worse consequences were to come soon.

The next couple of days passed in a tense atmosphere. The two men went out together, and spent their time talking and making false schemes. Sybil, well dressed, went out modelling or looking for more work. Maria stayed alone in the house cleaning, washing and cooking for everyone. Everyone behaved very amicably towards each other. However Maria, who preferred to clear ambiguities, lost no opportunity for a hint or a straight word.

'We are disturbing you, we are causing annoyances here, we must decide one thing or another.'

'Oh no, not at all, you are not in our way, never!' Sybil assured her, with exquisite politeness.

'Today we have seen a flat, haven't we James?' Graham said one evening, 'it's not bad.'

'It needs rewiring entirely,' James replied, somehow complaining.

'Oh, but you can do that yourself easily, it will cost you nothing.' After a pause he continued, 'we have to go out tonight, you do not mind being on your own, do you?' He had changed the conversation again.

Maria's smile was becoming less sweet by the hour, and only her mouth made the gesture, as her eyes acquired the stillness of a cross mind.

Why? Why they don't tell us straight they have no money to help us? she thought. 'We cannot continue like this much longer,' she insisted. She could not add that she did not have any money to buy the next tin of baby food.

'Today we have been to see a garage,' James said, when the Ableys had gone upstairs. 'If I can work there, we will have more money.'

'You mean for a job like at Rowland Winn?'

'Yes but this is a smaller place.'

'But...?' she gazed at him in astonishment, as she could not believe what she had heard.

'In that way I could earn some wages until we find a better place for working the smashed cars.'

'But James, that is impossible...that is not a solution!' She bit her lips a she felt she was losing control of her manners. The Ableys came in the room.

'We have to lead a social life. We need a big house to entertain as we have many friends. We have many expenses. But you don't, you are not in the same position,' Sybil explained in a matter of fact tone.

Hearing the last sentence, Maria felt gall coming to her mouth, and her lips twisted slightly, yet she swallowed, faking a smile and said, 'Enjoy yourselves, then.'

The gall was making havoc inside her. As soon as the sound of the car was extinguished, she burst into a low cry. 'James, I cannot stand this any more! I wish we never had come to Liverpool!'

James stared at her with his deep frowned brow, and his lost look only exasperated her more.

'You are a credulous fool, you believed so easily that he would lend us all the money we needed, didn't you? Even that they would buy a house for us, with their richness, a house like this one didn't you?' She looked from ceiling to floor in painful mockery. 'They don't have any money, only pretences, they may even be in debt for what we know, this new house and their holiday in Switzerland, as good as the Joneses! Haven't you heard? They have to entertain in the upper society, but we do not, who are we? Nobody. Tell me now, how is the flat you have seen today? Good enough for the poor falling class like us? Tell me. How is it?'

'*Es una merda*,' he admitted between his teeth, 'has no electricity.'

'You see? You see? What do you think? We have to put ourselves there, then you go to work at a garage, only to be sacked like everywhere else. No! Not that again! We must do something of our own account,' she paused, 'something,' and paused again, her fire gone, 'but what?' Her voice was wet and thin, and sobs, smothering her, had passed quickly from rage to the most harrowing affliction. She left the room and ran upstairs, dropping over the bed in a fit of sobbing.

A while later James came up, his head bent.

'Do you realise our situation?' Her composure regained, she asked, 'do you see how desperate it is?'

He sat on the bed besides her. He was without words, and felt completely downhearted.

'Let's think James,' she said in a more resolute voice, blowing her nose with a soaked handkerchief, 'we must think what we can do, let's consider carefully.'

An interval followed in silence, then Maria continued thinking in a loud voice.

'If we went back to Leeds? Liverpool is terrible...it is inhospitable, and everything is much more expensive. The buildings are so black, and everything and everybody is so grey.'

'In Leeds I know a lot of people of my trade,' he interposed.

'Do go,' she said in a sudden animation, 'without delay, go and find a place. Any place. I'll follow down. My state is advancing and without knowing where the baby is going to be born. I am so anxious and nervous that I don't feel well at all.'

'I'll go tomorrow.'

They got into bed, more reassured. If Maria could see the direction they were going in her energy would double and her courage take her forward. There is nothing more exasperating than the emptiness of not knowing where to turn.

'Lets pray James, we need God's help,' she said, but in the middle of *Pare nostre*, she was asleep.

Sybil arrived from town. She was emptying her bag over the kitchen table. Maria stood by the gas ring watching Elizabeth's supper, and could see that the variety of fish she had bought were quite expensive. She thought Sybil must have been either been paid from her modelling, or that she may have borrowed money from someone else. Maria wondered if she would return the money she had lent her, but realised that Sybil had forgotten.

'Today I shall make dinner myself,' said Sybil, taking a tomato and onions from the vegetable basket. 'In the hotel we stayed at in Switzerland, we had a fish dish we liked so much I asked for the recipe. Look, it is here.'

Maria glanced at the *Zuppa di Pesce*.

'You know Maria,' continued Sybil, 'to keep one's husband happy one has to be a good cook. Graham likes continental food, so when I have more time I think I'll go to evening cookery classes. Don't you think that men's stomachs are very sensitive?'

'I don't know,' hesitated Maria, wondering why a woman as beautiful as she was needed to worry about making complicated meals to retain her husband's love, 'yes, maybe, I have not thought about that.'

While conversing they had nearly finished the dinner, and Maria fed Elizabeth. Her mind was full of other words she wished to utter and did not dare. The cold amiability of Sybil interposed like an iron rail, invisible to touch, although so near, as if it were her who put it up. She could not understand why. If they were not friends it was not Sybil's fault, as she was always so nice! Was it Maria's? Her answers to Sybil's questions were often dull, monosyllabic and uncertain. Well, of course all the other words were stuck up in her mind. Suddenly, she decided to get them out.

'Do you know what Graham wants us to do Sybil?'

The beautiful woman stopped, straightened up and looked at her in surprise.

'I mean, does he want James to work on accident cars or to work in another garage?'

'Oh! I don't know...I think he wants him to do the cars.'

'But, do you think we will find a convenient place here? And for you also.'

'It does not need to be convenient for us.'

Now Maria looked up in wonder. 'I do not mean here exactly, in Birkenhead or Liverpool,' and after hesitating she said what she really wanted, 'or in Leeds if it is so expensive here. What do you think your husband wants or what he proposes to do for us exactly?'

'I do not know, Maria, I think that for the moment he proposed to come here...'

'Yes,' she interrupted the other's hesitation, 'that was nearly two months ago, now the time has passed, he might think of something else. James and I...we think, we don't know for sure what to do. The thing is, James has gone to Leeds today to look again.' It was obvious that to Sybil the matter was not more important than what her husband would eat, as she was more attentive to the fish in the pot.

'Yes, they smell delicious,' admitted Maria, giving up the talk and going upstairs to put Elizabeth to sleep, and delaying her return downstairs for Graham to come home and his wife to explain the conversation the two had just had. James planned to be late home, as on leaving that morning they had agreed that he would not come back without some sort of solution. At last, with nothing else to do upstairs, she came down. Graham was in the sitting room reading the papers. Sybil was putting the last touches to her pot.

'Can I help you lay the table?'

'Yes, please, shall we wait for James?' she offered politely.

'No, no need I am sure, he will be back late.'

They were already sitting at the table when Graham asked where James was. Maria, refraining to answer, glanced at Sybil. She had said nothing to her husband, and said nothing now.

'He has gone to Leeds, Graham, we think that it may be easier, after all, to find something there than here.'

'Is it good Graham? Do you like it?' his wife was anxiously asking.

'Delicious,' he replied, filling his mouth. 'Well, today I went to see the garage, and they said he can start work next Monday. Maria, I think he should accept this job.'

'Yes, of course, but,' she could not tell Graham, how could she? How could she tell him how disastrous her own husband was at working for others? 'what do we do about the good prospects of working with the cars?'

'Oh, he can carry on working on them.'

'But, where? And where do we live?'

For the moment you could rent the flat at Walelsey until a better one comes up.'

'James says it's not suitable for children,' she replied, although James had not mentioned that.

'You could stay here for a few days more,' offered Sybil. She got up to take the plates away, and Maria followed her to the kitchen.

'Thanks very much Sybil, but I must know where my baby is going to be born, I must be prepared by the seventh month. Besides, the doctor must see me again, I haven't been for two months.'

Now she could see clearly what kind of help the Ableys were prepared to give, and it was not precisely what she desired. There was now a need for a decision on their own account. Not knowing what could happen the next day was maddening for Maria, and unbearable, yet no one else around her seemed to think so. The Ableys gave no signs of being inconvenienced. Why was she not content? Why not enjoy the comforts: the central heating, the carpeted bathroom, the television? Even the good meals, as she bought no more food, having no money left, and James would not spend his. However, she could not reach this state of compliance. She was finding it more difficult to master polite conversation with smiling, and her face, tense with the effort of trying to do so, would drop as soon as she was alone, like a mask. Her troubled eyes were lost into the emptiness of unanswered questions.

The majority of questions were not answered because she did not have the courage to ask them. She could have said, 'Graham, how much money will you put into the business?' She could not tackle people face to face for fear of losing face, or fear of the answer. And she was very, very silly to believe what James said. She knew well his way of turning things to suit his own desire. She knew by experience that he could see pink for red, even white for black, and still she considered his opinion.

Which of the two men, James or Graham, was more at fault over the Liverpool business was not clear. She had the feeling that James was not alone in stretching his arm further than his sleeve, nor in coating bare objects with the green leaves of fantasy.

After the Ableys went out, she sat on the edge of the sofa, alone, her face towards the television yet her mind and ears tense and away from it. When the interfering sounds annoyed her she switched it off. The silence was heavy, worse. She put it on again. It was after ten o'clock and James was not back. The telephone was soundless. She went to the window to look out.

Cars passed, but not one stopped. She went back to the edge of the sofa. When the telephone rang, she was startled.

'Hello...yes, James it's me, where are you?'

'I am at Navigation House.'

'Where?'

'In the big house by the canal, at Battyeford, remember? It is still for sale, he is asking one thousand pounds now. Listen, what do you think if I tell him we'll have it?'

'It depends on what we can do while looking for the money.'

She was not keen on the house, yet it was better than the uncertainty there.

'Listen,' James continued, 'do you know that part of it was made into a separate dwelling, that was let to an old couple, but is now empty? Well, they say we can go there in the meantime if we want. You say, Maria, what you think?'

She soon realised he was giving her the full responsibility of a decision. Reacting quickly, and without any hesitation she said, 'Tell them yes, James.'

Through the apparatus his breath came faster, then she heard him moving away, before his faint voice came back, 'I'm staying here tonight, tomorrow I'll fetch my things from Auto Enterprises and I will arrange something to move our furniture back here. I'll come tomorrow; don't know what time though, how is Elizabeth? Tell the Ableys goodbye!'

And the click was heard.

'Please to God we shall not regret this!' she exclaimed, joining her hands, 'and thank God that I know what I am going to do tomorrow!'

The following morning, when the Ableys were having breakfast, Maria, choosing her words carefully, explained James's call from Leeds, and the accommodation in the house at Battyeford, omitting the compromise entitled to buy the property. She couldn't tell how would they take it, as it was a sort of slight to them, having relied so much on their council, to turn and do the opposite of what they had advised.

'We thought we should go,' she said and waited for the effect of her explanation.

However, the good manners of the English couple let nothing pass through the surface. Graham was buttering his toast, and perhaps his knife slipped faster and his eyes lost some of their morning gloom, but otherwise Maria did not know if it annoyed him or took a load off his shoulders. As for Sybil, her radiant beauty shone in the gloom, and her smile did not alter.

'When will you leave?' she asked, filling her second cup of tea with a steady hand.

'James will be able to restart work in his car immediately and finish it...'

'I shall sell it here straight away,' interrupted Graham, and he rose from the table, kissed his wife and left the house.

That means, reflected Maria, he still wants to do something with us, to get some profit from James's work. Of course, as things were officially he was responsible for James's employment in the country.

'Yes, Sybil you can go too, I'll clear up, I feel better today,' she said, and Sybil left the house too.

March was well on the way. The wind pushed big lumps of seawater over the land towards the unsheltered new houses. Maria was busy about the house, and now and then glanced out of the window. The colours were gradually changing, and the moving grey snatched reflections of the blue sky. Well now, she thought, the sun at last shows his bright face after hiding it so much. I won't be here to see it.

She closed the case with determination. Her mind went straight like a jet towards the big house she had seen only once in the twilight, hovering over her. James was happy. He had already installed his scraps in the half ruined pigsty, deterred by nothing. She, likewise meant to install herself in the house, in whatever state it was in. Yes, tonight they would sleep there.

CHAPTER SEVEN

MR ROMMEY, THE owner of Navigation House, went to Liverpool in one of his lorries to fetch their belongings. The Martines family followed in their car. The journey was heavy going for Maria, with the restless Elizabeth jumping in her arms. It was dark when they crossed the canal. At Navigation House the freezing darkness overpowered all. Maria shivered as she felt the cold stone floor through her soles, until James found a bulb and the light came on. The whole downstairs was one spacious room. Mr Rommey and James began to pile up the furniture in the middle of it.

The fireplace was one of those old-fashioned black iron grates. Between it and the next wall there was the sink, with only one cold tap, a gas ring and some shelves, and they were all very clean.

As soon as the armchair came in Maria put the infant in it and proceeded to build a fire in the fireplace. There was a bucket of coal and a few faggots that James had left the previous day, and she only needed paper and matches. But the fire didn't pull; the smoke was backing into the room.

'What are you doing?' protested James, 'don't you know how to make a fire?'

'It does not pull, it must be that the chimney is too old,' she replied mournfully.

The two men had left everything as if it was ready for a bonfire, and it was impossible to find the kitchen things. The smoke didn't help. Elizabeth was wailing because her supper was late and she was hungry. The baby things were under a mattress that Maria had to move herself because James had gone to help the man park his lorry. James should be helping me, she thought. Couldn't the man do it for himself?

On her knees, feeling the cold creeping up her tights, she searched for a tin of Gerber baby food, then for the milk, which she could not find. Her strength was failing. The heaviness of her body raised a sense of sorrow for the unborn child. She believed that she had to satisfy the call of her body for rest and food, otherwise the sufferer was the child who grew in it. Her sadness was mixed up with visions of rickety babies that filled her mind with anguish. It turned into rage against the objects and people around her.

'Shut up, shut up!' she shouted at her daughter, 'stop crying, will you? It is your father who should be here!'

The poor thing stopped instantly and looked at her mother with enormous bewildered eyes. The child's gaze melted the anger of the mother in an instant. She took her over her shoulder, then proceeded to light the gas with her free hand. Her sorrow for the other child now increased.

Silent tears were running down her face when James came in.

'What is the matter? Why are you crying?'

'It is the smoke in the room...I am hungry...'

He gave a surprised look at the dead fire. A few half burned sticks let go of a streak of smoke, which went directly up the chimney.

'The smoke? But it is all gone! Do you want me to cut some wood and make it better?'

'No, better fetch some milk, we don't have any,' she said, and seeing him disposed to go out added, 'and please come back quick, I can't put up Elizabeth's cot on my own, and I have not seen the room upstairs, is there any light? Do we have more bulbs?'

'I'll come back immediately,' he said, and he was gone.

Maria sat with the baby on her lap, and, using a chair as a table to feed her, blessing the manufacturers of baby foods that shortened a mother's work. Elizabeth, who never ate much, was soon satisfied. The mother finished the few spoonfuls left and that little warm nourishment gave her the comfort to bear her tiredness further.

James came back with milk and eggs. After the beds were put up she asked where the bathroom was, only to learn with dismay that there wasn't one, and that the outside toilet was far from the house, at the end of the garden. It was very late when at last she laid her painful body on the bed. She tried to sleep, but was too tired. She could hear trains pass, the noise faintly increasing as if they were crossing through the house, although she had seen the railway line far over the mound. The noise was followed by a stressed silence. Then the unborn child kicked and her anguish rose again.

If the baby was not all right it would be her fault. It was her preoccupation, and the high pitch she took her problems with. Why could she not rest, and keep still when she was tired? Why did she expect James to notice how much she needed things doing for her? How she wished intensely to be pampered! Instead of sulking and waiting, she should tell him to do this or that and sit back. But no, she was carrying on getting knotted inside, waiting for him to grant her wishes. Why was she still in her dreamland? He would not see her state, he did not caress and look after her. His mind was full of other things. Why was her spirit so miserable? Again the tears filled her eyes, wetting the pillow, and sleep did not come to comfort her, while her husband at her side had it all.

Mrs Rommey came to see her. She was still a young woman and might have been pretty at some time. She carried a child in her arms. Her hair was untidy and her countenance careworn, yet she offered herself to help. Maria let her in and asked if she could give her the name and address of a local doctor, because she didn't feel very well.

'You have tired yourself out,' the woman answered, looking around the room.

A fair part of the stone floor was already covered with a carpet, the old fireplace crackling with flames, the table by the window, the chairs well placed and the sofa arranged for comfort. The only reminder of the previous night's disorder was a pile of empty boxes in a corner.

'There are so many things to do,' she smiled at her, 'how many children you have?'

'Six.'

'*Mare de Deu!*'

'Four go to school, Andrew will start after Easter, he'll be five, and this one is only three years old,' she said, letting her descend to the floor by Elizabeth, where the two little girls stared at each other intently.

'There is a Doctor in Mirfield,' she continued, 'it is not far from here, he is very good with children.'

Maria jotted down the address, and said that James would take her in the afternoon.

'You can leave the little girl with me, I'll look after her.'

'Oh! Thank you very much indeed, that would be a great help.'

The doctor's waiting room was square, small and bare, but for two wooden benches and a table crumpled with dated magazines. James and Maria sat for exactly two minutes, then James got up, saying h would go round the village to see was it was like, leaving Maria with her thoughts. Dr. Hyman had been so good to her; it was a pity they had to leave him. Maria wondered how the new doctor would treat her. She looked at the door in expectation. At that moment a woman came out with a crying child.

'Stop moaning, he didn't hurt you!' she said.

Now a man went in, hesitated, then turned back to leave his hat and stick over the bench.

Then the door closed. Next it was Maria's turn, and she felt nervous.

The doctor's surgery was installed on the corridor, it seemed, as it was so narrow, the couch at the end of it just fitted in head to foot. Any patient could feel submerged in such a small space, and more afflicted, thought Maria. She was, however, mistaken. As soon as the doctor began to speak she felt better, as he had a soft agreeable voice that was reassuring. It filled the space and pushed the walls back, and soothed the troubled spirit of the poor pregnant woman.

'Do not worry, I'll find a bed for you in the nearest hospital. It is rather late, but if there is no room you can deliver at home.'

'Doctor, in this house there is no bathroom, no hot water and the toilet is far away.'

'Even with that we could manage: we have units of emergencies provided with everything needed. The district midwife lives in Battyeford, you see. I'll tell her to come and see you.'

He made her lie on the couch and examined her.

'Yes, I think it is well placed. And do not worry about the health of the baby more than your own. You know, the infant takes from the mother what he needs for his growth and is not much affected by what you do. Unborn babies have quite an independent life of their own.'

She came out of this visit very much liberated from the anguish that had been oppressing her. James was outside.

'What did he say?'

'He told me not to worry, and to rest.'

'You see? I told you!'

'What do you know? You have no idea of what I am going through.'

Contemptuously, she got into the car. James had a manner of always knowing it all, and nothing was ever his fault. It irritated her ever so.

She intended to make him participate in her pregnancy, in part because she wished for sympathy and care, but also because she believed that as the father it was his duty to be concerned with the formation of the new being for which he was responsible. But she bumped into the absurd barrier raised by generations of savage men, men with hunting instincts, men with passion and lust. They were completely ignorant of all that concerns women. She tried to pass the barrier with her hand on her heart and her soul on her eyes, only to feel rejected by the other side. However, she still would persist and hope that the barriers would one day crumple down.

In June the second child was born. Maria had had the first experience, so was confident that she knew it all. That morning she had risen with a pain she recognised at once. At nine o'clock they were on the way to Dewsbury Hospital, and she was anticipating the pleasure of a warm bath after so long suffering the lack of one, and with the inconvenience of washing with a bowl of water in front of the fireplace.

She left Elizabeth in her father's arms and entered the hospital rather quickly as the pains were coming faster and stronger. Once she was in bed and the preliminary examination had finished she was left alone. The minutes passed. She asked the woman in the bed next to her where the bathroom was.

'There is no bathroom on this ward,' the woman replied.

And then Maria regretted very much having left home without a wash. She felt embarrassed when a nurse arrived to shave her dry skin.

Time was ticking on. Women groaned, cried and called for assistance but nurses seemed to be scarce. To Maria the pains were increasingly strong, and she was full of perspiration, so held onto the bars of the bedstead, biting her pillow rather than scream. Suddenly, like a tap burst open, a flush of water flooded her bed. She called for the nurses, and two girls in uniform came and changed the bed, then without a word left her alone again. The pain was terrible and she couldn't believe it could be so bad. She began to pull her own hair, then panicked and shouted for the nurses to come, before losing her senses and screaming at the top of her voice. The midwife came to her, a tall, dark woman with a large face. Maria thought she looked like a horse.

'It is terrible, I can't stand any longer,' she said imploring.

'Come on, don't fuss lassie, it's not your first baby,' she replied looking curtly at her.

'I don't fuss, it is really terrible!' cried Maria, and pulled the iron bars over her head, shaking them from side to side in utter desperation. As soon as the stink of pain left her she saw the midwife move away. 'Precisely because it is the second I know it is coming!' she called with rage, which quickly turned into a sobbing moan. 'Please help me! It is coming, help!' she implored, seized again by the most piercing pain.

The woman in blue had her back to Maria, then decided reluctantly to lift the sheets over Maria's legs. She must have seen the crown of the baby showing, because, making a sign of displeasure, she drew the curtains around the bed and called for another nurse. The nurse arrived with a trolley stretcher, which the midwife refused. Then, crossing her arms over her chest, she fixed her gaze between Maria's legs. Maria, among so much pain and cold indifference, lost her serenity completely, and shouted in her Catalan tongue '*socors!*'

The midwife, unmoved and unmoving, waited for the head of the baby to come through, letting Maria tear herself pitifully. No one had cared to give her a laxative and upon her pain she had to bare the shame of dirtying herself. However, she made another great push and then she had the sensation that her bed was not touching the floor any more, and the noise of the ward faded away. Either the fog had got into the ward or she was floating outside! Oh yes, if she could let herself fly away there would be no more pain. But someone was calling her name. Who could be so far away?

'Mrs Martines! Mrs Martines! Come on, another push for the shoulders!' the voice said, coming nearer, 'another push!'

She obeyed, and instantly felt relieved. She closed her eyes, not wishing to see the hard and

long face of the midwife. She did not want the
midwife's eyes of cold glass to look at her baby.
Why was a person like her a midwife? Maria felt
sure she had never had a baby herself.

'Is it a boy?' she asked, with closed eyes.

'No, it's a girl,' a voice answered, while she
was moved to the trolley and wheeled away.

James would be disappointed, she thought,
being so sure it would be a boy. Although she
had already delivered she was taken to the
delivery ward and put in a hard bed, then given
an injection. The damp sweat was cold over her
skin, and she began to tremble. She was covered
with a blanket and left alone.

Still half numb, she began to look for her
daughter. Where had they put her? Then there
was a baby's cry, in the position she had left, but
she could not see in that direction. She tried to
move but her body was stiff, like a joint of wood.
Someone entered the room. On that sunny day in
June, mist was around her.

'*La meva nena?*' she inquired. No one
answered. She had spoken in Catalan. 'My baby?
I can't see her.'

There were two people in the room who,
although very attentive to the stitching of her
tear, were indifferent to her person. She wondered
if that was because she was foreign.

'Wash her legs,' one person said to the other.

Maria thought her legs must be bloody as well
as dirty. She could not feel them, and hoped the
brushing would revive them. She waited with
anticipated relief.

'I am thirsty...please!' she pleaded.

The young nurse nodded and went out of the room. The minutes passed by. Maria was reviving. She could clearly perceive the cries of the baby coming from a corner of the room, and they began to worry her. Noticing she could now move, she raised her head to see the baby for the first time. She was in the cot next to the wall, her legs uncovered and her arms up in the air, crying her little heart out for the loss of the sheltered, tight, warm, comforting womb of her mother.

Many, many minutes passed, perhaps hours, and nobody came; not the nurse to wash her legs, a comforting cup of tea or even a glass of water. Maria's thirst was great. She began to feel abandoned. Baby and mother had both been forgotten. She did not know whether to cry like the baby or shout in anger. Then she thought that there must be a bell about her reach. It had not been left handy for her, but she stretched herself up, got hold of it and moodily pressed it several times. Yet nobody came. Was the hospital deserted? She pressed the bell again and did not lift her finger until was tired of pressing it. At last a young woman came.

'What do you want, ringing so much?'

'I am dying of thirst!' she exclaimed, 'it is a long time since I asked for a drink. Where are the nurses?'

'It is their dinner time,' answered the girl, 'I'll bring you some water.' She left the room, and returned a few minutes later with a glass of water. Maria took it eagerly, only to push it away from her lips; it was tepid water that turned her stomach over.

'The baby has kicked her blanket, will you cover her please?' she asked the girl.

The girl went to the cot and the newborn stopped crying. Then she turned to Maria and smiled. Maria thanked her, smiling back. It was the first human gesture she had received since entering the hospital that morning, and she was grateful for it.

In the evening, when James came, she plunged into his arms, then burst into tears. He was very surprised, and did not understand what she was upset about.

'Do you think I am not happy because it is a girl? Well, no, it does not matter!'

'No, not that, it is that the midwife was telling me off instead of helping me!'

'Well, it is all over now, isn't it? Don't be silly and stop crying, everybody is looking at us.'

The ward was large, and each bed had a visitor. Each group had its own chatter, or its little sob, and no one was watching them. It seemed a place with more sadness than joy.

'This hospital is sad,' Maria was saying, 'I want to go home, James, this hospital is a disaster, not like the one in Leeds, I want to go home,' she repeated, without any common sense. 'Do you know that they gave me no dinner, because the baby was born at twelve, and all the nurses went for their meal, leaving me and the baby completely alone?'

Later, the nurses were bringing the babies in for their last feed of the day. Maria had not held hers yet and was pining for her. According to the hospital rules they would not bring the new baby to her until the next day. It was too long, thought Maria, and not fair. A sentiment of rebelliousness tickled inside her. She was not going to wait that long! She decided to pretend she was all right, as if it were the third day, so she could hold the baby.

A nurse left a baby on the arms of the woman next to her and raised her eyes to Maria, who caught her sight and said, 'My baby is the one with the name of Martines,' smiling invitingly and sweetly.

'I'll bring her next,' replied the nurse, going swiftly away.

Maria waited anxiously, hoping the nurse would not investigate how many hours since baby Martines had been born. Soon she saw the nurse coming back with a swaddling bundle and stretched her arms to receive it, feeling very emotional. She embraced her delicately with the unsteady watch of recognition, following with her fingers the line of the baby's face. Was she not perfect?

She bent her head over the face of the baby's, overwhelmed by a wave of infinite love. She uncovered her a bit more, searching with trembling fear for some imperfections, but then remembered seeing her arms and legs moving energetically in the delivery room. This calmed her, and she uncovered her breast and offered it to the infant, who took to it straight away, then mother and daughter, united again, comforted each other.

On the third day Maria was crying, as she longed to see her daughter Elizabeth. James assured her that all was well at home, and that he looked after her at all hours. He said that Mrs Rommey looked after her when he went to the hospital. However, he said it with a deep line on his brow, a sure sign of the lack of harmony between his words and the real facts.

Maria recalled the fair delicate girl crying for her son a year ago in the Leeds hospital. Now, only now, could she fully understand the sentiment, now that she was in the same position. She knew, so she understood.

However, she reflected, that is no virtue. If in order to sympathise and love each other we have to pass through the same experiences, how can we ever pass through them all? We'll never reach the state of perfect peace; we'll never be able to love our neighbours. And this world will keep on battling against hatred, indifference, disdain and misunderstandings. How sad it all is! Now she was sure the midwife had never experienced the pains of childbirth in her flesh, otherwise she would have shown sympathy. Also, whoever had dictated the rules for the maternity hospital must never had more than one child. The husbands, alienated so much from women's cares, were not ready to be more understanding and fatherly.

It was time for the doctor's round. The beds had been changed. To the more recuperated women, sheets had been given and they were told to make their own. It was shocking to see the poor mothers doing the job, as if they were in the barracks of the foreign legion. The matron came all in all starch and grey, shining like a pearl, then the doctor with his train of admirers.

On passing Maria's bed, she said, 'Doctor my baby is not normal,' and paused to reinforce her trembling voice, 'what can be done?'

The doctor glanced at her, rather surprised.

'Oh, doctor,' the matron quickly interposed, 'it is nothing of importance, that little one with the slightly flattened face.'

'The spine will not be twisted?' asked the mother anxiously.

'I'll examine her thoroughly,' he said, and addressing the head of the ward added, 'Later, sister.'

Maria watched them leave the ward. Now he'll have a look at my baby, poor thing! she thought. James had refused to admit any slight deformity in his second daughter, saying he had seen her as pretty as his first. But this was no comfort to Maria. James was saying that to console himself, she thought. Everyone else had seen it, she had argued, and the nurses and other mothers had all praised the others babies and not hers. What if the doctor found the baby twisted? What if the little girl were never to stand straight? What if she grew with a hunchback? Maria unconsciously prodded the thorn deeper. The sister came directly to her, and she panicked.

'Do not worry Mrs Martines,' she said calmly, 'the doctor had had a good look at your baby; you have nothing to worry about as she is perfectly straight. It is only her joint bone, and that happens sometimes when the baby rests too long in the same position in the mother's womb.

It will straighten itself out, and in time nothing will show, so you feed her well and she'll thrive.'

'Thank you!' cried Maria, relaxing over her pillows.

At visiting time she told James, only to regret it as his reply was, 'you see! I told you it was nothing!' which irritated her, and she moodily kept quiet for a while. In the meantime, he was passing his glance about the ward, inquisitively resting it on other women.

'Today I have come with Elizabeth,' he said, 'she is in the car.'

'James!' cried Maria, stretching up, 'Why didn't you tell me? Why? Was Mrs Rommey not there? What is she doing? How is she? Is she eating enough? Is she not too hot? I want to see her!' she pleaded.

'She does too; she calls you all day long.'

They exchanged a look, wondering what they could do.

'I was taking her up here but at the door I was told it is not permitted, so I had to take her back to the car and leave her there.'

'She will be crying...go then, go and see what she is doing.'

A flash of lightning and the idea came to her.

'Where is the car?' she asked, and glanced at the window, 'can it be seen from here?'

'I'll take it there. There is a yard under.'

'Well, go and wait there. I'll come down, there is a staircase there,' she was pointing to the opposite end of the ward.

'Do you mean? They'll see you!'

'I don't care, go,' she replied, resolutely.

She waited impatiently for the visitors to leave. Then she put on her slippers and dressing gown and, as if going to the bathroom, moved away from the ward, passed the toilets and stopped on the upper landing. It was hot, and all the doors were open. It was eight o'clock in June and the sun was still shining. She looked for the way James would be coming, and descended the steps to the next landing. When she heard them, her heart jumped.

'I am here...Elizabeth! My daughter!'

They were coming up. The father put the child down. The mother, unable to move another step, bent down, stretching both arms. The child darted towards her mother's arms and threw herself into them, her little hand clutching Maria's neck.

'Mummy...mummy!' she shouted with the joy of recuperating.

Maria could not, would not unfasten herself from the tender, loving hug, and tears ran down her cheeks. She laughed and talked, explaining everything to her daughter, whose eyes were open in wonder. Could she understand what mummy was saying?

No. She did not understand that she would have to leave after few minutes of having found Maria, and was inconsolable. Soon after, the mother walked up the fire escape steps, wiping her face, equally unable to understand.

Feeling as forsaken as her child, she made up her mind to leave hospital as soon as her stitches were off, as she had learned that if she wanted to go home early she could discharge herself.

315

The hospital, however, would relinquish further responsibility in case of any mishap. Nevertheless, on the sixth day she asked to be allowed to go home. Sister put forward a few objections, knowing that she had no bathroom at home, but Maria insisted, promising she would go next door to have her daily bath.

What softened the rigidity of the women was the either scarcity of beds, or the beseeching smile of Maria. The fact was that the next morning she was preparing herself to leave hospital. She had no illusions for a welcome homecoming this time. She just wanted to be at home with her two little daughters.

However, James did prepare a welcome. On the way there he was full of joy, saying she would have a surprise that she would be delighted with.

They entered the house. The first thing Maria laid her eyes on was a shining grey square box standing on four thin legs. James ran to touch the buttons.

'You like it?'

'Is this the surprise?' shaking her head, she asked, 'why is it so big?'

'It is the best, the last model.'

'Also the most expensive, I am sure,' she replied, 'and another thing to add to our H.P. commitments isn't it? Well, I am sorry that I am not pleased with a television set, when we have bare floors upstairs, and are still paying for the other furniture.'

With a sigh of fatigue she sat down, as she was not feeling as strong as she had believed. The noise coming from the set disturbed her. 'Put it off, please will you?' she asked. James turned the buttons and left the room like a disappointed child.

The days passed by, and Maria was not regaining her strength. She dragged her feet about the house. Her smile was scarce, except for her younger baby, who she loved with an unhealthy intensity. Maria had been going next door every day for a bath, taking her disinfectant salts. Mrs Rommey was a sympathetic woman who, in spite of always being very busy, would make her a cup of tea.

Soon James decided that it was unnecessary that she go next door every day. Her midday rest was cut short too, as James would find something more pressing to do than look after the two babies. She was feeling so unwell that she stopped going next door altogether. Her backache would not go. Sometimes the pain was so intense that she could not bend. At first she began to be frightened. She had left the hospital telling herself she would not put her feet in it ever again, now she had to recoil and ask James to take her.

There, the first thing the doctor asked after examining her was why she had not gone before. Her womb was out of place, which was causing her backache. Without any further explanation he inserted a ring to hold it into place and ordered her to come back at the appointed time. No more, no less. What else could she do but resign herself, like every other English subject, calmly and patiently gathered like sheep, under the mantel of the welfare state.

A month passed, then another. Maria's energy and spirit were down to the bare necessities. Her world of high and wide horizons had closed completely and was now down to her four nearest walls. She did not move out of the house, and did nothing but wash nappies, prepare bottles, warm water, bath the babies, dress them, undress them and feed them. Her milk soon dried out but she persevered in putting the baby to her breast, although the baby got nothing. Therefore, it wasn't thriving, and the little thing was always wailing for something. She vomited, or had diarrhoea, or had a cold, and her cries mingled with her mother's tears.

James was out all day out working in his car or the garage. He did Maria's shopping, but that was all his help. The matter of buying the house was stuck. They had gone to see a solicitor on their return from Liverpool; they paid a deposit of fifty pounds, with the other fifty pounds to be paid later. In the meantime, they paid rent to the Rommeys. Maria, striving with her back pain, was absorbed in the care of the two little girls, and let the other problems slip by.

One day the Health Visitor came in, and asked why Maria was not taking the babies to the clinic. She said it was in Mirfield, which was not so far away, and that it was a very nice clinic. The blue uniformed woman advised that her back would not be worse for a walk, and said that Maria looked very pale, and needed fresh air.

Maria required two days to gather enough strength to tackle the walk to Mirfield. She could fit the two children in the pram, with one lying and the other sitting. It was a good afternoon. She crossed the canal over the bridge, and a light warm wind came from the river. She turned to the right and the breeze helped to push the pram with its load. However, although the road was flat, she arrived very tired. The clinic was in the middle of a small, well-tended park. The place was welcoming and Maria rested a while under the trees. There were many, full of strength, tall, solid boughs. Maria, raising her eyes, saw what their house needed: trees, flowers and birds to sing, as her own music had been abandoned. Their huge house was surrounded by absolutely nothing of beauty.

The people at the clinic welcomed them, and the way they took care of baby Theresa was very reassuring. On her way back, Maria began to see how her little face would round up nicely. She thought about planting flowers along the sides of the path to the toilet. Perhaps they could even plant trees, then the house would not look so barren. She decided that she would return regularly to the baby clinic. In the park, she would rest under the big trees, letting Elizabeth run and tumble over the grass. Maria admired the fortitude of those gigantic trees, which always stood in the same place in all weather; gales, thunder, rain, snow, fury and calm. Yet they still had those movements of soft shaking leaves like smiles. Why? Because their roots are firm in the ground, in their native soil.

That was what Maria did not have, roots on the ground, to grow strong. Her native soil was so far away. How long would her longing last? Would she be able to root there in the darkish, soggy, green English soil?

BOOK
THREE

CHAPTER ONE

It was cold, piercing cold, penetrating everywhere like a sword, nothing to stop it. No thick walls, no soil, no wool; not even the fire seemed to have enough strength to overpower it. The mauvish purple flames licked the coals on one side only; the other remained black and cold.

Maria took the poker and broke the big shanks, then the flames, blasting, engulfed them, thus enlarging their domain of heat, which reached her legs and face, but her back still shivered. She turned her head to look at the door; were there any crevices left? Any cracks through which cold air would come in? That afternoon she had been round with gummed paper blocking up all the joints on windows and unused doors, blaming the stupid modern fashion that took away the window shutters. Those windows; even though they were on the outer wall, and the curtain at the inner, the space in between remained unnecessarily cold. So the diminutive 'Jack Frost' would come in through the slightest speck of hole. The elves from the realm of eternal Iceland were coming down to the English land, in great bands like an invisible army, compact and numerous and all armed with the spikes of seven fine needles. When people went outside these soldiers would attack furiously, leaving them white and blue, and not only the unprotected people's faces, but would throw themselves to their feet, pushing the piercing spikes through thick leather and wool to reach people's toes. They would look for the hands, pricking the finger tips even when hidden in gloves and coat pockets. Outside, there was no defence against this invasion, and people would go out on their business as quickly as possible.

Maria moved from the fireside to arrange the fold of the curtain to make sure no 'Jack' could come in, then she went upstairs into the little girls' room. Elizabeth in her big-girl bed, and yet she so small; she was curled under the blankets like a kitten. Theresa was in the cot, one hand hanging between its bars; a cold little hand that Maria gently placed under her covers, watched their peaceful sleep for a few seconds and left the room. She descended back to crouch by the fire.

James was out, like every evening, he had gone to the local pub; he seemed to have integrated with the society of the village. During the day he would come often to the house for his mug of tea. In the evening he went to meet other men to drink beer, and chat and joke and be admired. Maria didn't like the village folk much. Or his frequent going out. She often told him so. Today she had asked him not to go as it was so cold.

'Why are you not staying in today, the first day of the year? This special day.'

The first of January was a day like any other day in England, and she missed the holiday. But he went out, saying he had to see someone. Not his wife begging, nor the army of ten thousand Jack Frosts deterred him.

He always had to meet somebody to discuss a sale or a purchase. Many business transactions were conducted in the pub. However, Maria thought it could be conducted somewhere else than in a public ale house. The Pear Tree Inn was the first house in Battyeford across the river. It was a large building, with a porch, and rings to fasten the horses of the old post carriages could still be seen, as well as its watering stone tank, humid and mossy. A sign swinging over the door displayed a primitive drawing of a Pear tree. The inside was closed and welcoming, the air warm and thick. There was a room on each side of the bar. In one a piano could be seen; sometimes someone would play and others sing songs that folk knew from old times. In the other room over the chimney there was a black and white disc, and men passed their time throwing darts at it. Every night at ten-thirty the Publican would toll the bell, which hung from the arch of a door, clattering with other shining copper objects. Then the inflexible Englishmen would get the last drink of the day. That was the law of the country.

Maria was gazing at the smothering fire when she heard the door and looked in surprise at the time; it was only ten o'clock. She was not accustomed to see James back so early, not him fulfilling his promises. So many times he had said,

'I'll be back early,' and she had spent hours and hours waiting in vain. Inside the quietness of the big house her eyes fixed aimlessly, her ears on the outside for his step and upstairs for a child's cry or cough. Her imagination was filling her mind with worries and fears to drag the time low and slow.

When they first moved to the larger part of the house, she often feared the chimney would crash down on them, it was repaired later which cost a lot of money, but they were earning more. The ruined pigsty had been converted into a workshop. Once the Romneys had moved away the Martines couple spared no effort in getting the place workable.

It was Elizabeth's second spring and Theresa's first. Maria, in good health, full of energy, was decorating inside the house and planting a garden outside. She planted potatoes and cabbages, reared chickens. James planted apple trees. All they could do themselves, they did. No problem was too difficult to solve, no tiredness would slow their impetuosity to raise the house and the business. The new erect chimney, like a flag, was proclaiming miles around the transformation of the old Navigation Inn from the times of canal navigation, into an Inn-garage for automobiles. James had so much work that a mechanic was employed to help in the repairs.

James came in, his dark hair shining on his temples; his skin had lost that brownish colour of the Spanish country. Maria, looking at him, thought of the many years they had been away from it; nearly six.

'You are pale,' she said to him.

'Is terrible cold,' he answered, going near the fire. 'Tonight the canal will freeze, maybe the river also, you'll see.'

'I am pleased you have come early, James. I was beginning to think about what I was telling you yesterday and the wish to leave you is growing stronger in me...'

'Don't talk nonsense.'

'I am tired of spending the evenings alone just waiting for you, not knowing where you are or what you are doing from the time the pubs close until the time you arrive home. Like yesterday, that was nearly two o'clock in the morning.'

'I told you where I had been but you think wrong.'

'I do not think wrong. I so believe that the pub closes the door and you remain inside chatting. But I don't see the need for it, I don't understand the wish to remain so long there when you know I am here waiting and worrying. If you like better the company of your friends you will not miss me.'

'Don't talk nonsense,' he repeated trying to hold her hand, 'you cannot leave me.'

'Why not?' she responded, withdrawing her hand. 'You will miss me only for the work I do.' And she laughed ironically. 'For nothing else. Ah!! But then you shall have to remain at home and do your accounts, get Malcolm's wages ready, and make the invoices and write the cheques instead of staying in the bar drinking beer. And you'll have to wash your clothes and cook your meals, and make your bed and do the shopping and the cleaning. And feed the hens and the dog. And even more if I leave the girls to you; you'll have to dress them, and undress them, bath them, feed, wipe their noses and bottoms, look after them day and night. I repeat: seriously, James, do something for me, because when in the evening, when I get tired of waiting for you, here alone, I begin to think and miss my homeland, my family, my friends, my music; all my past life I seem to see wheeling round me, I see it all like a whirl flashing bright and beautiful, continuing its turning and I am at the margin of it, thrown out, excluded, alienated. You have entered into another world and you feel happy in it, but I am standing alone abandoned in between. And begin to feel like running.'

'Oh, forget about whirls, I'll make you a cup of coffee.' He got up to pass into the kitchen.

'You don't understand,' she murmured, fixing her look in desolation over the burning embers.

She had started saying she would leave him only to try and see if it would move him; perhaps it would be more effective than begging and crying. However, the words, said impulsively from her lips, now left an echo in her mind. An echo that resounded strangely in her consciousness. The Conscience will return faint arguments to fill the emptiness the question, like words, provoked. Yet no echoes, no arguments were comforting. There was the overwhelming desire that he would do something for her, only that wish to keep the light of hope burning. Hope was the supreme sense, like a steady pole to hold onto so as not to drift away in despair.

The next day she got up early, as usual before her husband. The window panes, thickly glazed, left no hint of what the outside looked like. Maria opened the door just enough to pick up the milk bottles.

'Look Elizabeth, here, like little men with long necks and a cap on.'

The frozen milk had sprang up a few inches under the bottle top. The little girl sat at the table waiting for her breakfast.

Then in came the mechanic and Maria gave him the garage keys.

'It is colder than yesterday, isn't it Malcolm?'

'Yes,' assured the lad, 'the river sides are frozen and the canal is thick like a skating ring.'

'What will the fishes do, Mummy?'

'In the canal there are only big rats, they will die, and it is better, do you remember when they killed all our chicks? Malcolm, have coffee. Will you finish the Vauxhall today? The spare parts have arrived.'

The young man was drinking his coffee, then, without enquiring about his boss, went out to his work.

When James came down carrying little Theresa, the fire was already crackling, moving bright specks up the chimney. He placed his shoes near it and moved on to eat his breakfast. Maria was also warming the garments she would dress the child with.

'You'll have to go to the bank, James, there is no cash to pay Malcolm's wages; unless Mr Rolt pays his account, it's more than two weeks since he should have paid.'

'Oh! he did pay, I forgot to tell you,' he answered while putting his shoes on.

'Well then, leave the money here,' she said, pointing to her writing desk.

'No, no, I'll go to the bank.'

'But wasn't it fifteen pounds? Then it is enough.'

'I have bought spare parts.'

'Spare parts by cash? Don't you think you may be buying too many parts? There is a pile of invoices from Galway's Smith. How many days is it since that Mr Rolt paid?'

'Last week.'

'Last week? And you have spent all those pounds, have you? Without writing it in the accounts book.'

'Put it now, dear woman, it is the same. Prepare the cheque and I'll go after dinner.' And he went out with the air of a man who always does right.

He was convinced everything was going on perfectly all right and, of course, thanks to him: his work, his sacrifice. Maria couldn't quite see what he was sacrificing, neither could he explain when she asked. But sacrifice it was, he assured, to work so hard, so much harder than any Englishman.

No, no, working is not a sacrifice, especially when one can work at his own pleasure, at his own trade, Maria would argue. What is a sacrifice is to live far from one's own land, and this we are both doing. Then she would soften, considering he must be missing his country too, as much as he would believe himself part of this English land and society.

The telephone rang. Someone asked for Navigation Garage, so Maria put the call through to the working shop and felt quite great for a moment. Yes, really everything was going on all right, as the changed name of the house was beginning to be well known.

It was their place, even if the Bank retained the deeds of the property; it was their own house, the business too. It was a year since they had finished doing sales through Graham Abley. By a Home Office ruling, they had become free residents in the UK. Really, we are all right, we are doing very well, Maria reflected, very well indeed, she repeated to herself to cover some corners of her mind, not fully aware of it.

She finished making the beds upstairs and came downstairs with frozen hands. She was warming up in front of the fire when her Elizabeth said,

'Mum, what are the rats doing under the ice?'

'I don't know, darling, they must have passed through the locks and gone to the river.'

'I want to go and see, Mummy.'

This child had a real fancy to every animal, wanting to see the rats of all things! Meanwhile, little Theresa, always indifferent to what was being said around her, was playing with her teddy bear conscientiously, wanting to put a cardigan on it but the sleeves didn't fit.

'Give it to me,' said Maria, 'Look, like that, see? Pull here, that's it. Now he will not be cold.'

The teddy bear had its neck loose and Maria straightened it, before giving it back to the child. The little girl took it with one hand and with the other hit its face, making it twist back, then she placed the toy in her arms, cuddling it sweetly. Maria's heart lost a beat. Good God. Was the infant conscious of her slight imperfection? Was she sharing it with her most loved toy? Was it a subconscious act of a sorry soul or was it the mother's imagination?

'We will go to see the rats; we will take the teddy bear for a walk,' she said valiantly.

As she needed some eggs, they would go as far as the farm. So, after dinner, she wrapped them up in their coats, fastened their bonnets, put on their scarves, the gloves, boots over their pants. They went out.

The lead-grey sky was menacing to drop over them. The road sides were as hard as the centre. The grass that had never before lost its green was spread upon the soil, searching for the moisture, petrified; was fast becoming black.

Elizabeth was pulling her mother to the edge of the canal, which was smooth like a plank of blanched green. The rats could not be seen, so Elizabeth insisted on going farther to the river.

Maria pulled the other way and into the farm as quickly as she could. The farmer's wife always went to the back room for the eggs, but that day she said she had none to sell as they all had frozen up.

'The eggs?' asked Maria, amazed.

'Yes, they are for throwing away, no good any more. I'll give you half a dozen of those I put in the fridge.'

On their way back home Maria hurried the children, as she was scared they could freeze and become stiff as statues.

James came back late from the bank. He said someone in trouble had detained him; the oil on the car had frozen too. The water pipes, twelve inches below the ground, had also frozen and many people had no water in their homes. It was the coldest winter people remembered in many years. In the evening James did not go out. Maria did not feel as cold. Even the fire was burning better. She sat at her writing desk to do the accounts, and he emptied his pockets, scraping everything out: invoices, cramped notes, keys, nails, washers, plugs, sweets, string; the load of a boy's pocket, together with a man's.

Maria was scraping his memory.

'What have you paid? What have you received?' And she was writing it carefully down until she felt satisfied. 'Take good notice James that there is nothing over, and we should buy a carpet for the steps, those stones are so cold!'

'Buy it. If you do not have what you want is because you do not want to,' he said, convinced that no one could be more generous than him.

'Yes, of course, you don't understand the priorities. You shall see how much the electricity will be after this winter with the heaters on all day long.'

'We will pay it all. Come on, let's finish and come and sit by me.'

She moved towards him, not knowing why or how she was again so softened to give in, a believer in his sweet words, forgetting the cold outside and her threats to leave him, thinking he did not go out just to stay in for her; yes, she believed because it was the deepest desire she had. It was the self-preserving instinct, because she had fallen to the edge, away from the trodden path.

The terrible cold weather lasted a few more days. When the temperature went up a little the sky began to drop its load. Flakes, small and greyish at first, that froze at the touch of the hard soil. When an isolating crust had been formed the white softness began to appear. It snowed all day and all night and the landscape became marvellous, very white and very quiet. Maria and the children watched in rapture; the canal had disappeared under the soft and clean cape, the steps in front of the house, the ugly bulks in the garage yard, they had all disappeared. Every sharp form and pointed corner was now rounded and smoothed, nature had done an act of pure beautifying. That morning the world could be seen as such. Elizabeth asked her mother if Heaven was like this.

'Yes,' her mother replied, although she added, 'thankfully, Heaven is a bit warmer.'

The snow remained outside longer than James inside his home. In spite of the promises to his wife, and the wish to retain her, no doubt something attracted him more powerfully outside than the company of Maria, who, all being said, had no admiration for him. At the pub there would be someone ready to laugh at his jokes, to awe at his schemes, to prize his person, and his ego would expand like a sponge under a tap.

The evenings at home were all right because Maria, more than anxious to make her company desirable, did her best to please him: she watched his favourite TV programmes with him, she cooked whatever he fancied, sat on his knees and caressed him the way he liked. But   perhaps she did not know how to flatter him, or because we are damned with this human greed that leaves no one satisfied, it craved on James like a grub eats cabbage.

He soon realised that if he went out and came back early, his wife received him amiably, smiling, so he could -and why not - have it all his way. That week he went out one evening, the next two, and then three. One evening he came later and the excuse given was accepted readily, as his wife believed in his good intentions. After that, it took him only one more to do as before.

One day an acquaintance told Maria that a lecturer at the Huddersfield Technical College was looking for someone to help him with Spanish conversation. Would she be able to do it? Of course she could. Anything meaning intellectual exercise attracted her very much. It could be the entrance to one of those whirls she had dropped off and missed so much.

As the classes were in the evenings, only one day per week, she forecast no problems in leaving the children in the care of James. However, she was mistaken; James wanted nothing of it; Maria insisted she wished to go.

'It is logical,' she tried to explain, 'very logical, that you go out and I stay in to look after the children; it is also fair that I go out and you stay to look after them. They are as much your daughters as mine. It is not fair that I help you in everything concerning the business and you do not help me in the house cares. Not only is it not logical; it is unjust. So you can very well stay at home one evening when I am out.'

'No. You look for a babysitter as the English do, and in that way we can both go out,' and the idea appeared brilliant to him, 'that will be very nice, you'll see. I shall come for you and we'll go for a meal together, to the cinema, or wherever you like.'

Maria gave in. She found a woman ready to come for few shillings, to sit by the fire attentive to the children's sleep. The mother would rush about all day in order to have everything done by six-thirty. The children had their supper, their bath and were already upstairs in bed. Then she would run out to catch the bus, always without a minute to spare, sometimes she had not yet crossed the second bridge when the red spot could be seen coming along the road. She would get on the bus, panting with fatigue and rage, at the thought of the many cars standing in the garage and the plain egotism of her husband not letting her drive one.

During the class she forgot everything. She was teaching with enthusiasm and pleasure and she was happy for a short time. Once the class had finished, to find her husband waiting for her would come as a surprise. His conversation and his friends would down on her, like aliens from another world. She would remain quiet and dull for a while.

One day, as she had just arrived at the College and was going up the stairs, she heard James's voice calling. Maria started.

'What happened?' she asked in alarm.

'What happened, you are thoughtless!'

He had the line between his brow and his eyes blazing with rancour. The hall was full of people, yet he saw no one, and seized Maria by her arm, pulling her towards the door. She, not knowing what was all about, resisted his pull.

'Let me go, please, what do you want?'

'You are a bad mother,' he spouted ruggedly, 'to leave your daughter ill. What do you think you are? You are coming home at once.'

'But James, for God's sake, is she worse?'

'You shouldn't leave her for anything,' and not letting her arm go he continued towards the entrance.

'But let me, let go please! I can't leave my class like that. Wait while I go and tell Mr Edson.' She shook herself free and went fast upstairs to find the professor.

'Mr Edson, I am sorry...' her voice unsteady, 'my little daughter is ill...' She stopped, suddenly wanting to cry, and covered her mouth with her hand while Mr Edson watched her with his grey eyes, slightly surprised. 'My husband just came for me...' She didn't know what else to say to make the matter reasonable, if she had come now, the class had not started yet, so why did she not telephone? 'We may have to take her to hospital,' she added, hesitating.

'I understand. You go. Go, I'll manage today without you.'

'Thank you!' and she disappeared down the steps.

Now she was feeling real alarm, in case her little one were more ill than when she left half an hour ago. She had given her a junior aspirin and left her quiet in her cot, recommending the babysitter to watch her often. Observing, there was nothing extraordinary happening. But only a small thing could disquiet Theresa.

James started the car in a jerk.

'It is unbelievable how you can leave your baby alone. How bad a mother you are!'

Maria, feeling hurt by this unjust attack, rebelled.

'No, I did not leave her alone.'

'The babysitter is good for nothing.'

'So are you good for nothing. Have you called the doctor?'

'No.'

'Why, if she is so ill?'

'It is you who ought to be with her.'

They arrived at the house, still arguing. Maria fled in, and found Theresa downstairs lying on the sofa, the babysitter by her.

'What happened, Mrs Jessop? How is she?' Maria asked, while observing the child attentively.

The little girl was still feverish, with bright eyes and a pale face; Maria, touching her forehead, arranging her cover, continued gently, 'Mummy has come back early, eh darling?'

'As soon as you went she started crying,' the woman explained, 'I was upstairs with her when your husband came up and took her down here.'

The husband, at this moment standing tall over them, ordered Maria: 'Go and ring for the doctor.'

'You can do it if you think is so necessary,' she retorted.

'But it is, you cannot see how ill she is,' he replied.

Maria did not see a desperate case, as the little girl, nearly three years old, had been in the same state before without ever developing real danger. She couldn't understand why James was so much alarmed now. However, she went and rang the doctor's number, but he was at the surgery. He said he would finish at eight o'clock, and would come soon after.

'I don't think is urgent, doctor,' Maria said in an apologetic manner, 'but she has a temperature.'

The doctor came, looked and prescribed. It was nothing to worry about, he assured them, if the temperature was not down the next day ring him and he would come back; and he went. That was all, rather a routine for Maria.

Nonetheless, James's behaviour had placed a sentiment of blame in Maria's conscience, a feeling she had never experienced before. She firmly believed she was as good a mother as the first, she loved her daughters and looked after them as well as possible. James saying that she was a bad mother was a stink in her soul. Thinking about a mother's duty, she wondered if, being a mother, one ought to be *that* and nothing else. Had to be the children's dependent day and night, never move from their circle, had to think about them at all times, had to love them constantly, and had to worry about them every minute they spent out of her sight. It was slavery, sweet maybe, but slavery after all, slavery of body and soul, from which her mind was in rebellion, moaning, squeezing, like vapour in a pressure cooker.

She pondered whether she was really a bad mother, because when she entered the College her children went out of her thoughts for two whole hours. Now, her conscience pained with remorse. Perhaps she ought to leave the classes. Well, no, her sense would reply, even a mother has to retain some individual personality. Two hours a week were not going to diminish her devotion, nor hinder her duty. Besides, children are, by God's will, the product of a man and a woman. It is logic then, she reflected over the matter; it is anachronistic that the mother alone should have the sole responsibility of looking after them. Why had she to be the one to get up every night? Since Elizabeth was born, she had never had a continuous eight hours sleep. Four years now, and not one single night without Maria having to get up for one thing or another. Sometimes she would say to her husband, 'Baby is crying again, you get up now, please James, I'm very tired.' He never would get up. It was either laziness, or the ill idea that it was not his duty, but his wife's.

She could not forget the night, not long after Theresa was born, when she was not in full strength yet, when she begged him to go and see what was the matter with Elizabeth. She had finished feeding the baby and sleep was over-powering her, but the husband, hearing the child still crying in the next room, and the mother paralysed at his side, got into a rage and brutally kicked the poor woman out of the bed. She fell on her hands and knees.

Her sobs mingled with her child's, she made a superhuman effort to seize herself from the floor, and move to her daughter's room. She was upset for some time after, and never again asked her husband to attend to the children at nights. However, she did not give up completely and would try to make him understand the unfair-ness in the distribution of responsibilities, the unbalance and injustice of it all. Vain hope. That man, as many others, had the male idea of privilege and superiority carved in his bones.

Once the doctor was gone James offered to take the babysitter home. He would come back straight away, he said. The woman lived at the other side of the river on a street leading right in front of the Pear Tree Inn. Too much of a temptation for James. He went in with the good intention of just having a drink. But, of course it happens: there were friends who asked him for a round, then he had to pay back his round, and so on.

While Maria watched Theresa's temperature, the ten minutes to take Mrs Jessop home passed, then another ten minutes, yet another ten; the child was getting sleepy and Maria annoyed. She began to go from one window to another, impatiently, glancing at the clock. Why did she want him back so much? To quarrel with him, surely. Her anger began to rise; she was feeling insulted, vexed, daunted and cornered. Closing her teeth tightly, feeling so furious that being able to shake her husband violently would only please her. It was eleven o'clock and he had not returned. When he appears, I will hit him with the first object at hand, she thought; looking around the room for what would be most crushing. She went to the kitchen and took a plate, as tales say couples throw crockery at each other's heads. But do they really? The weight of the plate in her hand alarmed her a bit; she could kill him. It was a pretty plate, one of the first things they had bought when working for the Gills. Too precious to break. She put it back. It would be better if she calmed down. As soon as he comes I'll speak to him, reason with him, patiently; to make him understand what he was doing wrong, she thought. Then she glanced at the clock; half past eleven. Immediately, a wave of fury drowned her intentions and she went resolutely to the door, locked and bolted it.

'I'll leave him out!' said to herself aloud, going upstairs.

Then she was busy moving the cot into her bedroom, so she could look after the child all night without much getting up. Maria began to undress, hesitating, not sure whether to get into bed or not, as she had always waited up for her husband. But, was it worth it? Why do I need him? Oh God! She pitied herself. Why do I want so much him to be here? Her mind was in turmoil. Suddenly, she heard a terrific noise. The door! It was the back door coming down.

It would be James. James wanting to get in. She took her dressing gown and went flying downstairs. The lock was jumping loose.

'Wait, wait!' she shouted.

'Open at once!' he roared.

'Why don't remain where you've been?'

'Don't be stupid and open up!'

He was forcing the lock again as if he had a tool in his hands. It was difficult to open that door facing the canal, as it was never used. At last it opened and he bolted in, flicking the screwdriver as if to hit the woman, but she raised her head in a defiant gesture and gathering all the menacing disdain she could put in her look, uttered, 'You are a bad father!' Posing for few seconds but seeing it did not do any impression on him, she threw herself furiously to attack. 'What have you done? Where have you been so many hours? Just to take the babysitter to the other side? Why didn't come back straight after? You think you can do what you please, do you? Why eh? Why? Tell me, why can you go drinking while your daughter is ill? And I cannot go teaching? I cannot leave her, no, but you, yes, you can do what you please. It is not right, it is not right. Do you hear me?'

She had been following him through the kitchen to the sitting room where he entered, ignoring her.

'Where is Theresa?'

She felt so intense a wish to hurt him that was ready to answer, *Dead and buried*. 'Had you been worried about her?' she replied instead. 'Poor you, all those hours! And now you are cross with whatever it was that detained you, isn't it? Or was it much more important than your little girl here and alone ill?'

'You don't understand anything, you were here.'

'Ah,' she interrupted, 'you were here when I went to the Tech and you came to fetch me.'

'It is different, you are the mother and that is your obligation, you are very silly if you do not understand this.'

'I do not understand because it is not just.'

It was pointless arguing, as to James injustice was nowhere, and the more his wife quarrelled , the more out of place her argument seemed to him. Neither at this hour would he care to descry. He went upstairs leaving her behind, still screaming. He didn't care a bit. He got into bed and when Maria, after being in the bath, had washed and calmed herself and went to lay beside him, he was fast asleep.

The next day, the constant attention to poorly Theresa, had to be added to the normal chores. Maria had washing to do. So, remembering the gypsies she had been scared of as a child, knocking at doors selling their wares and telling fortunes, always loaded with children, passing by in groups, in their carts, with donkeys and dogs, camping by the manure heaps. The women would carry their babies fastened in a bundle upon their backs, Maria took a blanket, wrapped Theresa, and passed a corner over one shoulder and the other through her waist, making a knot over her chest. The movement and the warmth suited the child while the mother bustled about the house. Her mind was wondering about the lives of the nomads, and the gypsies. Were the women free or slaves? How did they bear maternity? Travelling; with the open horizon in front of them. If she could be a nomad, just like that now, she would take Elizabeth by the hand and set off on their way. Walk through the open country to beg for a morsel if need be, sleep under the bridges. They would follow tracks and paths and roads through the villages and cities. Walking, always walking towards the South. Walking barefoot to the warm lands over hot soil. How long would it take to step upon the calid sands of the Mediterranean beaches?

Her rebellious mind made its way among debris, rising up like the flight of a woodcock on marsh land, always dropping and lifting. She was making dinner and mashing tea for the men outside, laying the table. A deep sigh dropped from her lips like petals of withered roses. Then she noticed the eyes of her eldest child, like two jewels of wonder.

'I am hungry, mum!'

Maria's soul came back and she sweetly smiled to the child.

CHAPTER TWO

IT WAS A beautiful September afternoon. The turquoise sky was deserted by the clouds, its expanse above the green and golden earth. The Public garden had still many flowers and also a large pond. The two children jumped eagerly from the car and ran towards it.

'Aih! wait for Mummy.'

The father stopped them as he was holding the door open to help his wife to descend. Maria heavily came out stretching herself up. It certainly was uncomfortable to sit in a low seat for so long. She didn't realise why James had decided to visit this park today. Because it was very nice and only a few minutes run, he had assured her. But it had been longer than half an hour. Being Sunday, they had been to Mass in the morning, she had made dinner, and going out again for tea in the park was more than what she wished.

Leaning on her husband's arm, they followed the children's runs to the bottle boats, red and white, navigating over the turned down sky. There were some ducks chasing crumbs of bread. The place was full of people enjoying peacefully the calm of the afternoon. The shining sun was giving warmth, and the warmth descended over people sitting on the benches, the ones lying on the grass, the ones strolling, the ones playing. Over the bough of trees, the bushes and flowers. It was a warmth that stayed, caressing everyone and everything as there was no wind to blow it away, Maria was smiling sweetly and contentedly.

'You see, darling, I told you you'd like it here,' he commented with satisfaction.

He was taking pictures of the little girls eating their sandwiches on the lawn, of them throwing the crumbs to the ducks, of them swinging on the swings. Then he took his jacket off and, lying on the grass, let his daughters trot over him pretending he was asleep, then, suddenly he got up and the children would roll down and all would laugh.

Maria, sitting on the bench while packing up the tea things, was lovingly watching them, until her smile turned inwards where the new life was soon to open up on the light of the world. She had everything ready. This pregnancy had been wearing rather well. The sickness, pains and discomforts had not been spared to her, but the mental worries now she was yes, living in the same home and with enough money to feed themselves, she had not suffered. The decoration and furnishing of the house was not completed. The stairs were still uncarpeted. It didn't matter too much. A cleaner was once a week coming to help, and would come every day as soon as needed.

Late in the afternoon, coming back from the gardens, the sun was colouring the sky an almost pale green, going away from the earth, which was now becoming dark brown. The silhouette of the huge house in this twilight rose strong and solid above the plane. It was their home, her home, and she felt happy. James stopped the car in front of the house door and helped everyone to descend. They were a family, as compact as the walls of their dwelling, for years to come thought Maria. The apple trees will grow taller and give fruit, the children too will have their roots here. Perhaps she herself was beginning to root...

People in Barcelona would be enjoying the festivities of 'La Mercè' the patron saint of the city. Here it was a day like any other, as monotonous as they all were, with no popular festivities. No saints' days to celebrate. Nothing to disturb the atmospheric calm of the people's environment, apart from the weather, of which there was nothing else worth talking about, as whatever was happening, locally or abroad, would pass unnoticed. Matters seemed to slide over the character of the English person and leave them unaffected. If there was emotion or sentiment it would be kept in; it would stay inside, not allowed to be externalised. Sometimes, Maria thought how regretful it was, as much controlling of emotion resolve itself in not having any, like the complicated rugosity of a walnut.

She was doing the washing up, automatically, her mind elsewhere wandering about the *Plaça de Sant Jaume*, hearing the music. Completely seized by a powerful longing for her people, she became immobilised for few seconds, the washing up water draining nicely. Slowly her spirit came back and she moved carefully, drying her hands, feeling a light shake of her body. She became still again, listening intensely inward. Yes, this day would be special for her even in England. A day with its own joy.

She went to sit by the fire for a little rest. Later she got up, walked to the telephone, rung the hospital then went to the garage.

'James, are you very busy? Could you take me to Mirfield?'

'Very busy,' he replied, 'can't you take the bus?'

'Sure not, not this time. I will remain there,' and she laughed. 'Malcolm, I'll leave your wages ready, if you do any overtime I'll pay when I come back, you don't mind?' The lad looked at her with a certain embarrassment, while James, visibly nervous, dropped his tools.

She calmly went out of the garage to the fenced garden where the children played.

'Girls,' she shouted, 'you want to come with Mummy?'

'Where?...Yes, yes!'

'Come on then, I'll wash your hands.'

And she washed them both and combed their hair, while explaining she would be away for a few days, that they must obey papa, and be good to Mrs Schofield, who would be coming every day to make their dinner. That she would come back with a tiny baby, and how they all would look after it. The little girls, very excited, ran to the car, yet Maria went upstairs to check that everything was in order: the cradle with baby's garments, plenty of clean clothes for the children, for her husband, the house clean and tidy...

This hospital in Mirfield was a wooden large hut for normal maternity cases only. It was raining. Maria, stretched over the delivery table, was counting the space of time between pains and lightning. The water was falling with great fury on the roof above her. As the flashes of lightning and the thunder were rolling ever so near and stronger, she tried to distract herself calculating what was longest - the pain or the thunder. The wild roaring outside gave the night a daunting ferocity. The two nurses at her side looked timorously at each other. The roof seemed to be giving in.

'It is raining cats and dogs,' commented one, raising a glance at the ceiling.

What strange coincidence, reflected Maria, what will my child be, coming to the world among this torrential rain?

One hour later the child was opening its eyes to that world. Another girl she was, and Maria, still lying on the table, could see the baby's shoulders, rounded and firm. She could hear her cry rising strong and constant in chorus with the rain. And she felt no worry for that cry. She thought how healthy and strong her lungs would grow, she would be able to fly into space...

She closed her eyes, all sounds fading away. The nurses left her there to rest for the night, saying they didn't want to disturb the other women by moving her into the ward. Perhaps they didn't wish to disturb themselves any more; they must be tired, as they had been at Maria's side all the time.

This birth went well and Maria regained her strength very quickly. During her stay at this Maternity hut, she could see her daughters. James would bring them through the grass lawn to the window near Maria's bed, holding one little girl in each arm, then only the glass separated them.

Once back home the routine was soon re-established. Maria was feeling capable of doing everything; by October she was going to the Tech, teaching Spanish again.

Time passed by. One good day when the cold weather was well in, and Christmas near, James came home with a new idea.

It was dinner time; he sat at the table and said, 'Today I have seen a petrol station that we could buy.'

Maria was serving the soup and stopped with the ladle in mid air.

'It is empty,' he added. 'It has been empty for some time, and I am sure we could buy it cheap.'

'James, we have not finished paying for this house yet. We can not involve ourselves in more debt.'

The family began to eat the soup but James's was getting cold on the plate, talking with enthusiasm about the money they could make in a petrol station. If they revive it, that they will.

Did they not revive and rebuild Navigation House? They would bring up the business there, however derelict the place was. The ESSO sign was still hanging there, which would have to be approved for the concession of selling petrol. There were so many things to do. He would go and see that person and the other, and he would obtain what he wanted, always, naturally...they were going to make so much money..!

Maria continued cutting the meat into little bits for Theresa, made Elizabeth to look at her plate and eat, passed one thing and took another, then sat down and ate hers too while thinking hard.

She loved that house now. All the work they had put in made so much her home. She had projects for more beauty and comfort in it. She lamented James's restfulness which was preventing him from rooting anywhere. The apple trees were doing well in that soil, their children were happy there, little Mercè will put her first steps in that surroundings. Why could not be so?

James refused the pudding, drank a cup of tea in a gulp and ordered: 'Get the children ready that we are going to see that place now. It is not far from here. I'll go down to see what Malcolm is doing and come back for you all.'

'Why in such a hurry? The baby has to feed.'

'It is a unique opportunity, you'll see...' and he was out.

When he came back the baby was still holding to her mother's breast. He was growing impatient.

'Can't you finish giving it to her in the car?'

'No. Of course not, there is no need for hurry. Put the coats on the girls meantime. Elizabeth give me, you can, one of those nappies, from that pile, look there, yes, thanks darling, here please. We'll change her as soon as she finishes. She is a greedy thing, isn't she? Does not want to let go. Don't get so impatient James, half an hour will not make much difference!'

They went towards the Valley past Brighouse, then took Manchester Road going up in the direction of the moorland. Between Elland and Huddersfield they went up a hill, a barren country. There, where the road changed to level, cut by the line of the horizon there could be seen the buildings, only the roof outline against the sky, and the silhouette of two rickety trees inclined pathetically towards the plane as if wishing to run down the hill.

A branch of the road took a dent of lane in front of the buildings. A flat drive of concrete and there stood four pumps. There they stopped, James jumped out of the car.

'That is it,' he declared spreading his arm, 'here is the garage, is enormous, there is the house.'

Maria stepped out with the baby in her arms. The cold wind furiously assaulted her. She recoiled to put Mercè into the car.

'How cold it is. This place is too much in the open air.'

'Of course it is here. But look, what a fantastic view,' he said taking them behind the building.

It certainly was a good panoramic view. Green fields, squared up by the lines of the dark grey walls. Here and there a farm spattered like octopus over the grass. Farther, villages and towns fading away into rolling hills. Above the great extension of the greyish sky, now menacing rain. The house: a bungalow of red brick and white painted windows, pretty but very small, surrounded by nothing else but grass, over-grown, flattened to the same direction as the clump of trees at the other side of the road. Everything had an air of desertion. Maria ran back to the car, the place was inhospitable. No...it would be foolish to buy whatever the price. She told James so as soon as he sat by her.

'Besides,' she added, 'here is colder than anywhere else.'

'The bungalow has radiators, can be seen from the outside.'

'Your customers will not come up here, so far from everything.'

'Yes, they will come, and others too, notice the quantity of cars passing this way.'

'I think we are all right where we are.'

'Here selling petrol on top of the repairs, we'll make a lot of money.'

'We'll have to spend a lot too.'

'We will sell Navigation Garage.'

'Well, we better consider it carefully. You soon get excited and all seems to you very easy ...but...'

'And you find everything difficult, if it were for you, we would get nowhere.'

'That is not true.'

'It is. Tell me if you liked to come to Battyeford.'

At the turn of the bridge Navigation House was showing its solid structure; it seemed enormous after viewing the bungalow, so small they couldn't fit there.

James left his family in front of the door and continued to the garage. Maria didn't see him until tea time when he ate and rushed out. No doubt he had gone to explain to his cronies his find and the quantity of money he was going to make. And that evening he was the one to pay for all the rounds. If his wife later complained of the amount of bills there were to pay, he would reply that she was the one to administer the money, so to worry was for her, not for him. He was earning the money, wasn't he? So, so, why had he to count the shillings he spent in the pub? There was no need, no need at all.

James, with his enthusiasm for the new venture, was never stopping for more than half an hour in the house or in the garage. Maria, as usual, went down the workshop every morning to see what was being done, always attentive to see the customers satisfied. Malcolm was a very good worker, and very seldom needed James's hand to finish a car.

It came the day when the young man gave his notice. He said there was for him a job in a large garage as a foreman, and he was taking it. He was sorry for her, he added. Maria's naivety didn't understand why precisely for her. However, she prepared his wages, his corresponding holidays, filled up his cards and the young man went.

A week had not passed yet, when Maria realised what Malcolm meant. No car was finished, no car went out. James went and came, was moving a lot, but of work, steady work, he did little; in fact, he had been letting Malcolm do everything. Now, if a customer waited for the vehicle back, and was not ready, the mechanic having left was a good excuse. But Maria was very soon tired of giving it. She told James to work more. The first time she said so, he looked at her as if she had insulted him.

'That I should work more?' he protested. Was she mad or blind? Couldn't she see how he did not stop all day long?

Precisely that was it, she wanted him stop and stay in the garage to finish the jobs lying about. There was a Rover with something to be done on the body; not much, but it was lying in a corner of the workshop gathering dust. What most worried Maria was that it was already sold; the client had paid a deposit and now wanted to complete the purchase and take the car. James had already fussed much about the profit on it, not taking any notice of Maria's argument that a car lying in the garage was not a profit whatsoever, and a one hundred and fifty pounds profit extended to several weeks was not the same than the one hundred and fifty pounds in a week. However, this kind of logic he would not, or could not, understand, to Maria's exasperation and rage when he would not change his attitude.

One morning she left the children well and safely provided, and decidedly went to the garage workshop; the Rover must be finished.

James was playing with some gadget or other. She glanced at the car on the same corner, untouched. Without a word she passed him by and went towards it, picked up a rug and began to dust the car. She had already learned a few things about car bodies, and could easily discern what was needed. Now she was observing the Rover with much interest. Then James left his toy and approached.

'What are you doing?'

'This little com that is missing, the new one arrived some days ago, didn't it? We can put it,' she said calmly as naturally as she could, pointing with her finger that part of the bodywork.

'That side has to be repainted first.'

'Oh, yes, of course. But doesn't it have to be polished, all that rugosity of the fibre glass?' She was already looking for the sandpaper, but he took it first.

'Let go, you do not know how it's done.'

'Yes, I do, you see,' she replied taking another piece and beginning eagerly to rub. Next to her he rubbed too. Maria closed her lips tight, not to let the sigh of relief escape from her chest.

She continued there, rubbing valiantly for some time, not reproaching nor pushing him or showing in any way how pleased she was.

When she saw him well engrossed in it, she exclaimed: 'Oh! the children, on their own, I must go and see what are they doing.' Then moved swiftly away; before disappearing completely she asked, 'Do you want tea or coffee? I'll bring down a cup shall I?'

'Tea please,' he replied without raising his head, now absorbed by his work.

The three children were peacefully engaged, two playing, the other sleeping in her cradle. 'I have more children than three,' she muttered, shaking her head and letting the sigh earlier retained escape out of her lips.

The car was finished and the customer pleased, thanks to Maria's change of tactics towards her husband, back handed ways, and control of her anger that she found more difficult. During all that time James did not stop thinking about the petrol station, and doing steps to buy the place. Wasting days on it. He could not get anything clear: one day he thought ESSO would lend him money. Another day it was BP, a good company, he said. Then, after speaking to the owner he thought could buy for near nothing because the proprietor had lost his wife there, was half mad and wanted to get rid of the place; had abandoned it, running away from it, wanted not to go near it. The place was desolated, indeed. No one went there, not even thieves or hooligans. Nevertheless, James insisted on wanting to bring his wife and children there.

He could work more than the English, he insisted. From that place of barren land he could make an oasis of beauty, it was like a well from which he'd extract buckets full of money. They would become fabulously rich. When someone told him it was a white elephant he would not listen, or wait for the explanation of the meaning of that.

For Maria, still in her basics, it was not buckets of gold she wanted but the necessities for everyday living. She could not run beside her husband on the truck of fantasy. She had to move the millstone, she had to buy the bread and pay the electricity, she watched the bank balance, paid the H.P. commitments. All that weight on her shoulders kept her feet on the floor, impeded her flying to the heights of James.

As the days went by the weight on her shoulders increased. Few entries in the books and many expenses worried her, especially in petrol alone; there was a standing order for fourteen pounds eighteen shillings for one month, only because James was constantly on the go. He had bought a Jaguar, a write off, he fancied, and got it for five hundred pounds. It was towed to the garage. Maria was horrified by its looks, like an accordion. Not that her confidence on James's ability was diminished, but in James's willingness to work hard it was somehow shaken. She knew that to buy the spare parts needed, they would have to ask for more credit. She advised him to do some repairs first to get money in; however James was very impatient, the first thing he did was to put an order for the parts. Well, the spare parts came; later the invoices, and the poor Jaguar remained lying on the floor.

In the evenings when the children were upstairs asleep, James was drinking in the pub. In the prevailing quietness, Maria pondered and wondered; anguish and emptiness returned to her mind. What to do? How to push James to work steadily? Was he tired? Had he worked too much these past few years? Would it be a solution to look for another mechanic like Malcolm? And leave James to waste his time and spend more than what he earned?

While thinking, she would be picking up the toys scattered on the floor, automatically tidying up, putting toys into the boxes each child had. Elizabeth's was full of all sorts of animals, Theresa's of bright rags, she always knew which were hers. Little Mercè had none yet. Elizabeth, just five years old, had started school, it would not be convenient to change so soon. She needed settling.

Maria was turning again the same question over and over: would it be that James was tired of Navigation Garage? Facts pointed to it. Then would it not be wise to accept this, and forget all the hopes and illusions put in the place as their home? And act accordingly or do something to revive his interest? What and how? No defined answer would come to fill the gap.

In that fashion more days and evenings passed. One morning as soon as James came downstairs, she said, 'You do not feel up to it, do you? The Jaguar I mean, it's too badly smashed. I told you was crazy to buy. I just been to look at it. Dust will finish with it.'

Contrary to her good intention, she was again attacking him frontally. Early on she had gone down to inspect the jobs to be done; the unproductive money lying there pained and angered her very much. She would address James with subtlety, yet her words were spattered in that disagreeable tone. Her patience was much too short. Him being late triggered them. Elizabeth had been ready for school waiting for her father, and as he came down at ten minutes to nine o'clock, the girl was going to be late. Maria's good resolutions had evaporated.

'Too much for me? You'll see,' he replied drinking his coffee in a gulp. 'When I get down to it I'll finish it in two days.' Seizing Elizabeth, he left the house.

'Well then, for God's sake get down to it,' she shouted running after them, 'now you will not come back till twelve o'clock, I know,' she added ironically.

He started the car and went, apparently unmoved. He would do whatever he pleased, while she wounded herself with pointless rage. But...and she lifted her head suddenly. If we had the sales of petrol, money will come in every day, something sure at least for the children's daily bread...

The idea had come to her and fast spread over her mind, rapidly covering every corner of it. She began at once to consider the possibilities in a new light. Why not buy the petrol station? After all, being abandoned and solitary could be an advantage. The more work there was and the more difficult to revive, the more spurred on would James feel.

She was certainly slower than James. It had been two months to arrive at the decision point. Now she began to attack and knock down all the doubts and difficulties, methodically one after another. In her mind she could not retain dark patches, insecurities or barriers. She would pull them down, to see the path clear. In this case it was for the way to the moorland garage.

Then she put all her mind on it. James, on seeing his wife thus disposed, blossomed up as dry land received by the rain. He remained in the workshop and let Maria to go and see and talk to the people concerned. After all, he said, you can speak and write English better than I. He, in the meantime rebuilt the Jaguar.

The owner of the petrol station was a strange man: tall, of colourless hair, pale face and dropping lips. When she met him, she said how sorry she was in sympathy for the death of his wife.

'Dead? Dead you say? I wish she were! She went down with the wind down hill. She dead?' he kept repeating, looking at Maria furiously.

She was embarrassed, not knowing how to put her feet out of the bucket and began to talk about the garage. But the man, by now too excited, was shouting that he would give the place to her, house, garage, pumps, poles and land. Whatever she wanted to pay he would sign the papers quickly, because he was sick and tired of it all. If they did not hurry, he was going to give it to the ESSO Company. Of the people involved in the transaction he was the only one Maria couldn't manage to understand. She felt sorry for him. She never found out what tragedy had perturbed his mind, or what force did take the woman away, the death called by illness or the stormy wind called by despair.

CHAPTER THREE

IN MAY THEY were there. On a bright sunny day. It had rained the day before, the clean grass was in the green of spring and looked new. The sunlight gives good humour. Everyone was joyfully transporting objects in, as ants carry their grain to their holes. Still busy in this, a car entered the drive, a Gazelle graciously stopped in front of a pump. They had to say, regretfully, the petrol was not in yet.

A few days before, Maria went to the Weights & Measures Offices for the permission to sell inflammables.

The clerk behind a desk filling the documents asked, 'Name please?'

'Maria Salvans,' she answered, unhesitatingly.

The man with the pen up raised his head and gazed at her with the slowness of thought, so peculiar of the English people, so exasperating to the Latins, when they pause before asking for what they don't understand.

'Maria Salvans de Martines,' she repeated, 'em, ie, ar, ai, ei.' She went on spelling, but the clerk remained with his pen still and his mouth closed.

Then Maria suspected whether his doubt was because she was a woman, or because she was a foreigner? She had the impulse to get cross; nevertheless, thinking better she smiled and carefully explained.

'The garage station is in both names, my husband and I. But I am the one who will sell the petrol. Put the licence in my name please!'

At last the man dropped his head and wrote, read it, stamped and delivered it, saying, 'As soon as the tanks are full let us know. You can not sell any liquid until we have checked the measures, understand?'

She left satisfied, pleased as if a battle had been won. She knew James wouldn't like it. Even though when they bought Navigation House and she asked it to be put in both names, he accepted and was pleased with himself because, he said, it was a progressive idea, not like many Spaniards, who had their women like slaves.

Though one thing is to accept equal terms on paper. Just her own on another was not the same. She almost thought herself disloyal. On the other hand, he may not take it in, was nothing but for her the responsibility of paying the annual fee. In that light she put it to him while he was looking at the paper with a cross brow. The petrol company TOTAL was new in the country, and anxious to get established offered many facilities to the Martines couple; a full loan with a minimum interest and a ten per cent deposit. They paid the seven hundred pounds straight from the sale of the Jaguar, and Lindley Moor Garage was theirs.

The house by the old Navigation canal was empty and for sale. They felt no regret; did not look back, and went up to the moors with too much work to do to stop for sentiment. The men from TOTAL came to put up the sign, tall as a poplar towering over the district. They put balloons on the pumps. James hung strings with red blue and white flags all over the place, as if celebrating the Queen's Coronation.

To find a school for Elizabeth was no problem; one school recommended the other. But the distances to take the child to school, go shopping, to the bank, to church and so many other things, were too far if using public transport (there was only one bus every four hours) or James taking her. It proved so inconvenient that now James could not find any more excuses for her not to drive, although, he said, her lack of experience would not grant her the use of a good car. The Jaguar had been sold to a farmer who not only paid handsomely, but gave them an old Land Rover, green like an army Jeep, which arrived stinking of cow's manure.

Then, one Sunday, James told Maria, 'Try this Land Rover, is a bit hard, but you'll get used to it.' He helped her to climb as it was high and had no step; he sat by and showed the gears management and left her alone to drive around the back and front by the garage and pumps. 'Do it until you have a bit more practice and tomorrow you can take Elizabeth to school. With this if you crash it doesn't matter.'

She thought it funny without realising how much more James cared about the well-being of his cars. The wife and children, if they had a bump in that Jeep, with no upholstery and metal bars, it could really hurt them, but that did not seem to worry him.

There were two ways to Greetland school: one cutting straight down the steep bendy hill, the other farther down the main road to Elland in much traffic. Both were quite dangerous, nevertheless Maria soon acquired the necessary skill; she fastened the children to their seats surrounding them with cushions. Never had a scratch or a bump.

When James had the compressor ready and the pumps in good repair the tanker came with its first delivery. Came roaring up the hill. White clean and new. From the cabin a man jumped out in white overalls ostenting the blue TOTAL across his chest. Maria, carrying baby Mercè in her arm, received him with a bright smile and went, indicating where she wanted the different grades of petrol. Later came Weights & Measures. Soon after drove in the first customer. James and Maria both ran to serve him, trepidating with emotion. He was pleased with such solicitude, and surely would come back. They didn't had to wait longer for the next; he went away very pleased too. Thus came others and Maria was taking money every day, keeping it carefully to pay for the first lot when the next had to be delivered, so she would never get behind payments. She learned to check the oil, the tyres, refill batteries, clean windscreens, nothing intimidated her.

The days were long and warm. When the light was fading slowly away, Maria checked the pumps' numbers, disconnected the electricity and locked up, going to the bungalow by the back of the garage to the edge of the boundary to enjoy a few seconds of contemplation, the last colours in the sky and the first lights on the land. That first June passed gloriously by.

Lindley Moor, so cold and solitary a few months ago, had undergone a complete transformation, equal now to a bee hive, and as if there was honey, all kinds of insects were attracted to it. James was surrounded by them. He had more helpers than he wanted with all sorts of products to sell. And he was easy prey.

One day Maria had been out, and when she came back, he showed her a few posters, some ready framed as a stand, depicting a man with a pointed beard. 'John Bloom Golden Trading Stamps' the writing boasted. Also, a few sheets of stamps for which James had paid ten pounds.

'We'll give one stamp for each gallon of petrol bought, people collect them, then they get presents. We will sell a lot more – you'll see how we double the takings.'

'Double the takings when you have given away ten pounds! No, I don't want that. I don't like this system. Who doubles the profits are they who sell the stamps. And do you think I'll put the picture of that man in front of the pumps? No, never. You give them back to him and we want the ten pounds back. You are very silly indeed. Is that you have no confidence in us selling without these kind of gimmicks?'

The day John Bloom called at the garage Maria gave him back the stamps and his ridiculous posters. The man refused bluntly to give back the ten pounds. Then she was vexed and cross with James. But he went back to his work and forgot about it. He was during that time working hard, not sparing himself, improving everything around the place, tirelessly.

Midway down the hill turning to a side road, there were a row of buildings, humble dwellings attached to a chapel of the Dissidents. All greyish blue, crouching low for shelter from the stormy winds of further up. One of these houses was a pub, half hiding between them. However, it didn't take long for James to discover it and soon to go there often. At first Maria said nothing, admitting to herself that after a full day's good work a drink of beer was good too.

Notwithstanding, she was the one to open the garage first thing in the morning, and close it last in the evening. She was at the watch of the pumps and the care of the house and children, sixteen hours a day non stop seven days a week, and nights too, if the children woke up. No one thought she could do with some rest. Not even herself. She was full of energy and feeling well. Too well, in fact. One day, while pulling weeds from the patch in front of the house, it came to her such an urge to clean it up, and plant some flowers and see them growing, that a strange suspicion dawned on her. Could she be pregnant again? With growing fear she waited for the first symptoms of sickness. Yet the days passed and she was feeling better than ever. Nevertheless, deep in her mind she could feel inbetween her activity that knock, light as a feather, the voice of subconsciousness was saying: must slow down, slow down...Please!...

By now James was back at his routine of drinking in the pub till late in the evening and naturally getting up late in the morning. Many mornings Maria went out taking the two children to school, leaving James still in bed with little Mercè. She would rush back, her foot on the accelerator up along those narrow lanes, to find, often, a customer waiting in front of a pump. Then she'd jump from the Jeep, she always had to jump from the tall hard seat. And when James, having heard the bell, came out of the house the customer was already going down the hill.

'Can you look after the pumps, James, while I give breakfast to Mercè, please?'

'Yes, but be quick because I have to go and fetch some parts...'

He would still stretch her further. And so Maria could not find the opportunity to speak to him. In the evening if he stays a bit with me, I'll tell him if he comes from the pub a bit earlier...I'll let him know, she thought.

The day she began losing blood, she was frightened. She asked James if he would let her drive his car. But he had recently bought a Spitfire, a two seater, soft top, bright red, beautiful.

'Certainly not,' he replied, 'you will not be able to control this car, is too fast for you.'

She, who was ready to tell him why didn't want to drive the Land Rover any more, recoiled with resentment and shut her mouth. After that, she proceeded to spare herself as much as she could. To get Mercè out of her cot and carry her was a weight to be avoided, she left her on the floor. Then she said to the older girls, in a high voice so James could hear from his bed, 'Papa is going to take you to school today.'

Mercè, crawling, had arrived at the legs of her tall chair. She lifted her up, she had to, and began to give her breakfast. Then the bell rang, a car in for petrol; she let a few seconds pass but seeing that James, too well accustomed, did not stir, she put the spoon down and went to serve the client. That was Maria's routine in and out of the house, her days were crowded her pace fast. How could she stop now?

Or perhaps there was no need, she doubted, she felt so well! In hesitation, with anxiety, she went to see a doctor. The doctor prescribed rest and some tablets. The visit lasted scarcely five minutes. She came out with the same anguish she went in with. Nevertheless, she took the medicine and tried to rest, let the crawling child get about all over the floor, show her how to climb to her chair and into her cot, went out to serve petrol without running. She also refused to drive the Land Rover. Yet all that was not enough, the woman should have stayed in bed or perhaps it was too late. She continued losing blood.

One morning she got up early as usual and went to the bathroom. Midway she felt a dislodgement that froze her soul. A few seconds after she was holding in the palm of her hand the little foetus, alive, with big head and small body, moving, defenceless. She was staring at it, horrified.

'James,' she cried, half fainting, 'James!'

She went to the bedroom. 'James, look,' she said with a veiled voice, as white as a sheet she was.

On seeing her thus he jumped out of bed.

'What's happened? What is this?'

'My baby...I lost it...Lost it...' Sobbing in despair she flung herself on the bed.

'Why didn't you tell me?' he exclaimed sincerely, sorry, not knowing what to do. Elizabeth came into the room.

'What happen to Mummy?'

'Nothing darling,' the mother answered, making an effort to be calm at the same time as hiding the swaddling under the sheets. 'Go and get dressed. James, help them please, and take them to school, breakfast first,' she still added.

Little Mercè had woken up and, shaking the bars of her cot, was claiming attention. Her soggy nappy was slipping off the plastic pants. Maria, feeling overwhelming despair, wished to drop into limbo, in the nothingness of nothing. Yet she got up and dragged herself to the telephone, rang and asked for the doctor.

'Doctor, I just lost my baby,' she said in a broken voice. It seemed the doctor was not understanding. Maria, standing by the telephone, losing blood in abundance, trembled violently. After a second the voice of the doctor arrived altered and urgent:

'Go to bed immediately and keep still. Don't move for anything. I'll come at once.'

James, with the children, had just gone that the doctor's car stopped in front of the door.

While the doctor was examining the foetus, Maria was sobbing. James came back when the doctor was ready to go; he put his scrutinising look on him, then his eyes on the woman lying down, down into a sea of fathomless sorrow, his sight passing then to the child waiting in her cot and went back to the husband. 'You look after your wife,' he said in a correct enough tone yet flared hardness. 'If she is not kept quiet in bed we'll have to take her to hospital, do you understand?'

James, with his brow knotted in great confusion, could not steady his eyes, the doctor seemed to summon him, he precisely who knew nothing. He saw the doctor out and then turned to Maria. 'Why didn't you tell me?'

How strange paternity is! Is it possible to ignore and to feel at the same time? Why it is possible for a father to ignore he is a father? It is not possible for a mother, of course not. Why is it so easy for a father to be indifferent, not to feel anything? Because by nature he is kept ignorant of his paternity. Why, if a father can be forgiven, why is it not forgiveable for a wife to keep the father ignorant? It is by nature. It is not by other reasons. Why? So she should have told him. Oh, her mean little vengeance, how absurd it had been! If people were behaving by impulses! If our feelings and sentiments were not rumpled up by social conveniences! Was marriage a sacred institution? Or the instinct of coupling for reproduction? So then, what is the father? Has sentiments for what? Or was a father forged by institutionalised ideas? All in all too complicated, too complicated for Maria, now feeling at her lowest ebb and in a strange confusion of remorse.

'Why didn't you tell me?' he repeated. 'What a pity. I am sure it was the boy this time.'

'I am sorry...I was hoping...I wished you would stay with me some evening...or if you would come early...I wanted to tell you.'

There was no reproach in her tone, only sadness and anguish and pain with great desolation. His attitude downhearted, he sat at the bottom of the bed, motionless unable to console his wife, as in shock.

After a while Maria said looking at her other child, 'Mercè's breakfasted. She must be changed ...if you go to the airing cupboard there are some nappies...warm some milk, also for me please.'

The doctor came back in the afternoon. He found her still sobbing. Her spirit had been more shaken than her body. He recommended her to make an effort.

'You must help yourself,' he assured her. 'The fortitude and strength you need you'll find it nowhere else but inwards yourself.'

And why was the doctor saying that to her? Why could she not lean her head on her husband's shoulder for comfort and uplifting? Why had she to be like a snail?

CHAPTER FOUR

IT TOOK SOME days for Maria to get better. Little by little the smile returned to her face. The first day she went outside her legs were trembling, the cold wind pushed, indifferent to her weakness. Throwing her against the first pump, its strength passed on to her; she, holding on the pylon proceeded to read the numbers, stretched up and went a bit more steadily to the next pump. She must check the petrol sold and count the money collected all those past days.

James was constructing a kiosk. Placed in the middle of the pumps, its iron frame dug on the solid concrete base, glass all round, its shape elegant, it was a good improvement and Maria said thanks for the shelter it provided. The cold weather was fast coming on. One could not go outside without a good coat. They were working hard so the winter would not find them unprepared. The central heating system for house and garage was almost finished. They had to do it all new, because the crazy owner, before handing them the keys, stripped off all the radiators and took them away. The Martines' consequent claim he heeded not. They also had to put a boiler as the

one there didn't function. The expenses were
very high. In the meantime, the house by the
Navigation canal was still for sale. There was a
man interested, a fireman, a short man, strange
enough. He would come up to the Lindley Moor
on his motorbike, his hands covered with
enormous black gloves, never taking them off,
and stop in front of Maria with no speech. He
wanted the house with dogged insistence and
they could not understand why, the man had no
money, and no Building Society was interested in
giving him a mortgage for such an old property.
The agency advised the Martines to wait for
another buyer, the solicitors the same. But Maria
would look at the man standing still in front of
her, thinking how the winter was advancing and
the closed house would deteriorate. Besides, James
was asking three thousand pounds; nobody
would pay that much if they waited too long.

'I shall ask the solicitor to make a contract as
if we were the Building Society,' she proposed.
'You could pay us through the bank in instalments, if you could pay now the three hundred
pounds deposit. What you think?'

The man hesitated for a while, then he said
he would come back with the money. James
complained because he wanted the bulk of the
money, they needed it badly, he said she was
being silly. What could happen if the fireman
didn't pay the instalments – more complications.

'I know well enough the things we have to pay
and how urgently we need the money,' she
replied, 'but is better to have the money now for
sure. With this we can pay the installation of the

three phase electricity supply you want, and the central heating and the rates. Don't you understand that is better?'

When the fireman came back Maria settled the sale of Navigation Garage and got a good smile from the quiet man.

Dark was coming early. The cold was intense. The wind brushing the grass, whistling, running down the hill. Maria was watching the sign pole rolling, fearing it would crash down. She was inside the kiosk with Theresa, always seeking her mum's company. Surrounded by large glass panels, it was funny to hear the wind as if outside without feeling the cold blast on you. A car pulled in and the mother went out to serve him, wrapped into a thick duffle coat. Filling the tank, she replaced the handle hose then addressed the driver for payment, when a sudden terrific crash startled them, and the noise of broken glass mingled with the screams of a child. Maria turned in fright; she saw Theresa still sat on the stool with her arms up covering her face and falling chunks of glass all over. James was running out of the garage followed by the mechanic, the customer slipped out of his car; everyone believing the little girl would be terribly wounded. James, cracking glass under his feet, entered the kiosk and took her in his arms; the child was screaming and a streak of blood running down her face. The excited father thought no better than reproaching Maria.

'You, stupid. Why had you her in there?' while taking her quickly to the bungalow.

Maria, hurt by the insult, was holding back the impulse to run to her daughter. She entered the kiosk, moved the broken glass from the till and gave the client his change, who was saying, 'I am sorry, I hope it won't be too bad.'

Soon after, going towards the house, her legs like rubber could not run as quickly as she wished. She found James wiping Theresa's face with a towel.

'Mummy, mummy...' the child called, stretching her arms and the mother took her up.

'Poor little Theresa, come, come; it is nothing that, isn't it? Let's see your face...'

She was taking the bonnet off, the coat, the gloves, realising how much all that clothing and some Saint from Heaven had saved her. She only had a small cut over her forehead.

A couple of hours later she was asleep. Mother had told the story of the little girl born with a star on her forehead, and her mother had to cover it with a bandage because it shone too much, and that she later became a princess. Maria remained a while in the dark room, her eyes fixed upon the white bandage on her daughter's curly hair. This child of hers was not strong as the others. Her heart ached with love, longing for the unattainable. A sentiment she experienced when putting the mandolin up in the attic. All the other things she'd never use. Her hot homeland, dry, golden. So unlike the soaked-green-windy moorland. And she thought about her youth with the ideals for love and perfection. How sad seeing flowers wither...all the flowers gone...where?

Up that moor the cold was really crude. One blanket more than down in the valley and fires burning day and night, people said, and it was true. The dwellers at the petrol station were defending themselves the best they could, if not so well as the naturals; they endeavoured to imitate them. A young lad who lived a bit further down near the pub and the Dissenters Chapel, was called Christopher, he was fifteen years old, still at school, and used to call at weekends and help in the forecourt. Maria, ready to go to church, waiting for him, would watch him coming up walking against the stormy wind, in sleet or snow battering his face, yet the boy, hands into his pockets steadily continued up the hill. On arriving he would shake off like a dog out of the sea.

'Aren't you cold Chris, would you rather stay at home?'

'Why? To be inside? If it is cold I am cold – if it very cold I put two jumpers on, if I am still cold, well, it doesn't matter.'

Maria was learning from these people, their steadiness and endurance she would admire. To the wind which always annoyed her, now she would stand facing it. To the snow she would go armed with a shovel and throw it out of her forecourt. The fog did not frighten. One morning it was very thick; when she stepped out of the house it seemed like passing into another room full of smoke. She opened the garage and put the electricity on. Couldn't have mattered – the lights could not be distinguished. However, the

English people did not recoil, she wouldn't either.

She got the little girls into the car – by now she was driving an old Hillman – and started for school. Sat on her seat she had a moment of doubt seeing a white sheet over the windscreen, which would not lift to let her see the front of the car. She hesitated, wondering whether to call James and make him get up and fight the fog. But the thought annoyed her. Perhaps she was beginning to be tired of having to call him to duty, or perhaps wanted to show herself capable. She took the brakes off and the car began to slip down. She knew the way well enough: past the pumps, then the entrance pylons and the road, when she thought the car was in it, got out and went to look for the kerb. She found it by the touch of her feet, yes, the car was right in the middle of the road, she must move it nearer the kerb, she did so gently bumping it, and once the car was straightened she let it go down. The tension was tremendous. She heard a car coming up roaring heavily, then fading away. They had crossed each other without seeing, and a shiver went down her spine.

At crawling pace she arrived at the village. Then she gave up. Taking the children by the hands she abandoned the car and walked the rest of the way. It was very late, the school was already full of children whose parents, beaten, or not beaten by the fog, at least had begun the journey early.

Maria, back at the car, stood by it not knowing what to do, not daring the drive up, nor wanting to leave the car. The fog was thick and silent around her as a shroud.

'What are you doing here?' a voice called.

'Ah, it's you,' recognising their near neighbour the farmer, 'I can see nothing. It is terribly foggy isn't it?'

'Don't worry, turn your car and follow the lights of my van.'

The woman did so, arriving at the garage at about eleven o'clock. James was waiting impatiently and reprimanded her as soon as she stepped off the Hillman.

'You shouldn't have gone. You do not have enough skill to drive into the fog.'

'I have managed very well,' she replied, 'while you were asleep.' And she went into the house to see what Mercè was doing. Her arms and eyes were aching. Indeed, one needs fortitude to live in this country. For the ones born here is their environment, they grow accordingly, but for others...it is worth it? she thought.

The days were becoming lighter and longer and the winter cold larger still. Sometimes the sun would shine, touching the yard, coming in the house promising the spring time, then would recoil, feeble yet as if in need of longer rest, to sleep tucked under the greyish sheet of the sky. Sometimes, one wondered why the wind persisted in pushing every object on the earth, bumping against walls that would not give, against trees that would not bend, against people who would resolutely keep their feet on the ground like needles in a magnet. Why would the wind not flow higher and send off the clouds covering the sun? It would disclose, now and again, such a magnificent spectacle of light over the whole panoramic view.

It had been a day like that and Maria was happy; the sunshine never failing to lift up her spirits. She had worked all day in preparation for the evening. She had been asked through the Tech by the Townswomen Guild to be in a panel of international representatives for women's organisations. She was very excited about it, she would have to say few sentences in public, answering questions. She was mentally preparing, tidying up her brains. Then she would have to tidy her appearance as well. What would the other ladies wear? A hat? Of course, she had one, luckily she had one dress too; it wouldn't do to wear just a shirt, no, it must be a good suit.

By seven o'clock she had the three children supped, bathed and in bed. At midday while at the table she had reminded James.

'Do you remember I am going to the TWG meeting this evening, is at seven thirty. I don't think will last more than two hours. I'll not be away too long.'

He had nodded.

Now she was getting ready, she had not a moment to waste. She put her hat on, looked at herself in the mirror, thought she'd do all right and, after a glance to the children, left the house.

Chris was at the forecourt taking care of the pumps.

'Where is the Hillman?' she asked, not seeing the car in its usual place.

'James got it into the workshop and is looking at it.'

From outside Maria could see her husband bending over the engine. She thought he was checking it for her safety. She smiled.

'Works alright, James? Ready?' She went towards the driver's seat saying, 'I don't want to be late. You look after the children will you?'

'No. Leave it...' he answered sharply, closing the bonnet, 'I need it myself.'

'Why?' she exclaimed in alarm.

'There is a client who wants to buy it...I am going to show it to him now.'

They were not alone in the garage; apart from Chris, there was the mechanic who worked part time, another man often there to nose about and a petrol customer checking the tyres.

'Move off,' James said, 'forget about silly meetings and look after your children as it is your obligation.'

'James!' she said, terribly worried. 'I must go, they are waiting for me. You can leave it for later...'

But he pushed her away, jumped in and with a quick start and expert acceleration had the car out of the garage; in a few seconds he was running down the road (a glorious exit, the tupping cock). Maria stood in the middle of the entrance, seized by all sorts of worries. With her hat, her stiletto shoes, her make up, she saw herself a ridiculous beggar girl: dirty with the mud thrown at her, tears tickling the back of her eyes. She bit her trembling lips. No one spoke. Chris was looking at her with his honey-soft eyes, startled. The mechanic went swiftly under a car. The parasite disappeared.

Then the client approached her and said, as if ashamed of it, 'I am going to Huddersfield; I can give you a lift wherever you go.'

'I am going to the Y.M.C.A. if is not too much trouble,' she said, making an effort to control herself.

'No, not at all, get in, please.'

'Chris, will you go to the house now and again in case the children cry?'

The lad said he would and she sat by the gentleman, who was a stranger, thanking him. Why did James have to treat her in that way? She couldn't understand. She glanced at her watch.

'Are you late?' the gentleman asked, concerned.

'Don't run, no, we'll be in time.'

She noticed her own voice strange in shaking waves. That would not do. She must calm down quickly. She must not think about this upsetting, the terrible vexation that she must put out of her mind. She must think now with her head, must not submit to the sentiment of despair pushing her tears up to her eyes. Must, must think forward about the ladies who would sit by her, the question the Chairwoman would ask her, what she was going to reply.

'Do you know where the Y.M.C.A. is? I do not want to put you out of your way.'

'I am going that way,' the stranger replied.

Whether it was on his way or not, that perfect gentleman left her right in front of the door.

Once alone in the lift she quickly dried her eyes, powdered her nose, straightened her hat, and looked into that fathomless well for the strength she needed. The meeting was a success. When it was over she found herself in the street and realised she did not know how to get back home. The Post Office was there and telephone boxes were at hand. She hesitated. Who would be at the garage? The mechanic finished at nine o'clock It was half past. Chris could drive but was not old enough to hold a licence. James, if by chance he had come back, how could she ask him to come for her? She felt so distanced from him! Impossible to think a way to address him. She opted for the Public transport and, changing direction, went for the bus stop. She knew some buses went to Lindley, the nearest village to the garage, then she would walk. There was no other way.

At this time the buses ran sparingly and almost empty. Maria folded herself into a seat, wishing the driver would go faster. She would be late, the distance was long. Chris would be impatient to leave. Would the children have been woken? Elizabeth suffered so often with earache. I hope tonight she doesn't wake up with it, Maria thought. She had taken her to the doctor many times. That winter she had a bad flu and too many antibiotics. It may be necessary to remove her tonsils. And she was so thin! The bus kept on his run and its stops. The mother mused about her problems. Little Mercè was very healthy, yet her legs, yes her legs were not straight, perhaps she began to walk too early, a fat strong baby she was. Must take her to the doctor.

The bus stopped and the three remaining passengers descended. The conductor stood by Maria looking at her, and the driver stopped the engine, wouldn't go any further. She got out and began to walk forward; lights behind entered the darkness of her way in good speed.

She could do it in less than half an hour. Nor did she walk many paces when her impetus failed, rather her feet, as those high heels would not carry her as long as to the garage. The wind, unsympathetic, would take her hat away, was battering her legs only covered with a thin mesh of stockings. My God, how long is the way! All was dark around, the stone walls at both sides of the lane pitch black, the fields beyond robbed of their green.

She stopped, ready to take her shoes off and continue barefoot, but, unsure if this would be better, decided not and continued forward, feeling a wave of toughness with a revival of the old rebellious spirit. It was not right, James treating her in that manner. Why was he doing it? It wasn't the first time he would slight her in front of the people in the garage. Months ago, when discussing the insurance with a broker, which Maria didn't think necessary to get involved with, he plainly sent her 'to do her washing up in the kitchen and let the men get on with the business.' She went away vexed, had no option. What can be done against men possessed by this narrow segregational view? That blunt persistence in thwarting themselves?

James was obviously resenting Maria's supervision over the business, resenting her effort to slow his bombast greatness, and her criticising his extraordinary faculty of accumulating bills. The other morning came in the post the one bill for the gun, and she went mad and shouted he was a whimsy capricious fool. Because they did not need a shooting gun, and so expensive at ninety-eight pounds! How were they to pay? It would be better if they paid the overdue rates. Could he see the good sense in Maria's moderation? No. Maria's slowness against his jumping ahead, he attributed to women's incapacity. He was making an effort to put her back into a woman's place: the kitchen sink, the child-bearing carer.

To hell with the Devil! She was tired of being a woman. Sick and tired to death. That is, if to be a woman meant only to be an irresponsible being, helpless, dependent on others like a child, incapable of having independent mind and of using it. James would treat her like that whenever he pleased, to show he was a man and master. Well then, if he thought treating her in this way she was going to be submissive and satisfy all his whims, he was mistaken. She could turn her back on him. Why not? She was very capable of earning her living and the children's. Ah, it would be better than to stand him with all his impositions and demands from her body and her soul.

She could not feel the ridiculous shoes hurting her feet, nor the cold, nor the wind. She entered the circle of light, her pupils enlarged by the dark and her rage burning in them blacker than the night. Chris, frightened by her look, said in haste that the children did not wake and James did not come back and he wanted to go.

'Help me to close up.'

'It is very late,' he excused himself, 'my mother...'

'Go then. And thanks very much. I'll see you tomorrow.'

The next minute the boy was running down the road. Maria passed the threshold of the house with her shoes in her hand, looked at the children, then put her boots on and went out. She took the numbers of the pumps, collected the money, then locked all up, still possessed by deep rebelliousness. She was wondering how James would like to do all this every evening instead of staying down at the pub, warm, chatting and drinking.

It was later than ten o'clock when she heard him coming back. Her first impulse was to shout at him, yet didn't, she pretended to be asleep and endeavoured to calm herself imagining how stunned he would be if one night he found the house empty. What would he do? Perhaps then he would realise what he was doing. It would be good to give him a fright. Yes, he might change, he could behave better, they could still be happy. There were so many possibilities...if he would curtail his expenses...they could live without worries.

'The Hillman is sold.'

'Many hours has taken you.'

They were having breakfast leisurely, it was Saturday.

'They'll fetch it this morning. With the profit there is in it we can go to Spain for Easter. You know it cost almost nothing, this Hillman. Don't you girls like to go for holidays to see the grandparents?' He glanced at his wife but she continued feeding Mercè, not taking any notice.

'You'll tell me how I am to go to the supermarket.'

'I'll take you in the Spitfire. That I'll sell after also. Do you know who wants it? Mr Roberts, do you know who I mean? Mrs Roberts is a friend of yours, they have a blue van.'

'Yes, I know. She'll have to drive the van, won't she? Surely a sports car is too fast for a woman.'

'I will buy a Jaguar for me. I shall buy a Vauxhall for you when we come back from Spain, eh?' and he stretched his hand to caress her, she jerked her face and went to the kitchen.

'You can do more than that,' she said, coming back, 'you can go to the supermarket, do all the shopping and pay for it, as you are earning so much money. You could also take your daughters with you, and you can buy some slippers for Theresa.'

'Look Daddy, look, what a big hole,' the little girl interrupted vivaciously, showing her father how her toe was popping out.

'Oh, dear, your mother lets you go like that? How cold your feet are!'

'Theresa! I have told you to put socks on. Don't you hear me?' the mother snapped at her.

The child, curling herself on her father's knees, felt quite happy and secured.

In the evening Theresa was wearing a new pair of slippers, which Maria thought too cheap for a daughter of a man dreaming to drive a Jaguar. However, this time she knew how to keep her mouth shut.

CHAPTER FIVE

MARIA WAS DOING the accounts sat at her desk in the garage's office. A folder thick with invoices lay opened.

'James,' she called her husband's attention, 'have a look. Do you think we can pay the oxygen? There are three invoices, all overdue, they say no more cylinders delivered until we pay.'

'They brought two full ones yesterday,' he interrupted. 'We'll pay when we come back from Spain.'

'But James, it is not only the oxygen, there is a regulator we got some time ago, it amounts to nineteen pounds and ten shillings; I'll pay that, shall I?'

'No, let them, they can wait.'

Maria moved her shoulders in a gesture of resignation and closed the folder.

'The rates we must pay. And we'll finish with this debt. Thank God! I have the fifty pounds ready for it.'

The safe was open.

'Have you counted with the petrol? We must fill the tanks before we go,' he advised.

'Yes, there is two hundred pounds,' she replied, holding a bundle of notes and placing them in the safe, 'enough to pay the last delivery with the oil included. When you go to Brighouse this afternoon take them to the bank. I shall go tomorrow to Huddersfield to the Rates Office and pay them in cash, they'll be pleased, after giving us so much time.'

Closing envelopes and gathering papers she felt quite satisfied, especially on being able to finish the matters of the rates, which had been bothering her for some time. The rates for this property were very high, almost two hundred pounds per year. She had been to the Rates Office to explain how they bought the place, how derelict it was, how much rebuilding they had to do, so many expenses that their money could not reach everything: could they pay by instalments? Yes, they could, and also there were allowances for first year business to be established. Now she was pleased to be able to complete the payment in their first year. She counted the notes again, left them in a corner of the safe and locked it.

In the evening the Roberts' came for petrol. Mr Roberts went into the garage to have another look at the Spitfire. James was telling him to try it. 'Why don't we go now for a ride?' he was saying, Mr Roberts standing still with bended head pondering.

Maria, seeing his indecision, said to his wife, 'Joyce, would you like to come in the house meanwhile?'

James, in the two seater car, was roaring the engine. Then Mr Roberts moved in to sit by him, and few minutes later they had disappeared behind the line of the summit. The two women, exchanging a look of comprehension, entered the house.

'Would you like anything to drink?'

'No, thank you.'

'Coffee, sherry?'

'No, really, no, we just had dinner.' After a pause she commented, 'Gary likes the car very much.'

'Yes? He does not seem very decided.'

'Oh, it is the price, my husband doesn't easily let his money go.'

'How lucky! My husband does it too easily.'

'I don't know what is worse,' and both laughed.

Joyce Roberts was a blonde; petite, smartly dressed - no one would say she was over thirty. The laugh ended in a note of dryness.

Maria said in a sympathetic tone, 'They'll be some time now,' the other woman nodded and both accommodated themselves on the settee.

'Are your children all right?'

'They are all right now, thanks.'

'My daughter's eldest had the 'flu also, they were coming for the weekend, but are not coming now.'

'It is difficult to realise you are a grand-mother,' Maria remarked, 'how do you manage to be so young? Will your husband let you drive the Spitfire? If he buys it, of course. Mine never let me.' Imagine what a beautiful picture this fine fair lady would make in the open sports car, running fast against the wind!

'Why not? There is no reason why I cannot drive it as well.'

'No, naturally, there isn't. No reason at all,' affirmed Maria earnestly, 'absolutely no reason for men to have the priority in the use of the vehicle. And for women loaded with children and shopping, going on foot or queuing for buses, no fairness. Or like me, using the worst car in the place,' she continued, 'and even less, when like you and I are working in the business as much as our husbands. Don't you think it is unfair? And there are so many! You see them smartly sat in a car, with spare room for three more people, going to work or to the football. Well, I can't make my husband understand this. And do you know? Now he says is going to buy another car, a faster one...for himself alone, of course!'

'It is us, Maria, who are to blame, we shrink too much and mould ourselves too readily to men's ways.'

'It's having babies that hinders us. One feels so anxious for love and attention, that we are ready to do anything in order to get some from the husbands.'

'We are silly, we can very well say so. When I had my first baby I had a terribly bad time, Gary doesn't like children; he had, and still has, an absolute ignorance about them. He made my life impossible. The baby was only weeks old and he couldn't stand her crying, used to smack her, the poor baby! We agreed we could not have any more children. But unfortunately, after a few years I became pregnant again, and because of him, I had an abortion, illegal, of course, that cost us a lot of money. I shall never forget as long as I live, the anguish I suffered those weeks: I was so ill too, the nurse had no sympathy for me, saying that I was the one to blame.'

Maria was listening very moved, remembering her unseeking abortion and ventured to say, 'The nurse might have seen your baby dying outside your womb, it's a harrowing spectacle.'

'Now they are going to legalise abortion, do you think that is better? If Parliament approves it will become legal.'

'Yes, I know. On Sunday at Church they were collecting signatures in protest against the project. I heard two women commenting, Catholic of course, probably weary of kids and one said, 'I think is a terrible dilemma; I do not know how a Government or any individual can condone killing. It must be avoided before.'

'Contraception you mean?'

'Of course, well, I mean I don't know, it is said that we have to accept what God sends us.'

'But it is not sent to us unless we look for it.'

'We? Or you mean the men who do not know what is all about? What can we do if we are married?'

At this point the two men came in. In spite of the run Mr Roberts was not ready to buy yet, he chose to think about it. Would James to put the price down?

Oh, no, James could not, he should ask even more, that car had many extras, the special steering wheel, very expensive. But as they were friends he was prepared to let it go. It was time to close and Maria got up, and all said goodnight.

After, she was saying to James, 'Why don't you reduce the price a little? He is right, the tyres are worn out almost.'

'No, let be, he'll pay, he has money.'

That evening he did not go out, and very obligingly did the washing up and left the kitchen completely clean. He used to do it sometimes, generally when Maria was cross about something or he was back very late. 'In that way you quieten your conscience you think,' she would point to him ironically. Now, hearing him busy by the sink, she was wondering what he might have done. Finding nothing, she concluded he was doing it just for her, and went peacefully to bed.

The next day everything was running normally. The weather was giving one of those promises of spring. In the afternoon Maria left the house with Mercè, ready to go to town.

She entered the office, then saw James leaving and called the mechanic, 'Do you know where is my husband going?'

'No, Mrs Martines.'

'Strange,' she murmured, 'he knew I was going...has someone called him?'

'He said nothing.'

'Well, doesn't matter. You look after the pumps. I shall come back before three-thirty and I'll pick up the children from school. Thank you, Allen.'

The man left the office and Maria proceeded to open the safe. Her hand went straight to the spot where the day before she had put the fifty pounds. It was not there. She groped to the bottom, stretched to see better. She may have put them on the other shelf. She looked for them with increasing fright, then frantically began to search all over the safe, removing papers and documents. She could not find the notes. Suddenly she stopped as touched by lightning. The vision of James's car running down the hill the moment she came out of the house. He had taken them. Could be no other explanation.

No one else had a key. For a few minutes she remained motionless, glancing out of the window with a strange look, empty and lifeless, a look of hopelessness. This time James had done a bit too much. Her mouth was set in a hard line, she turned to close the safe slowly, with an exaggerated calm as if in this manner she could placate the storm inside her. She took the little girl by the hand and returned to the bungalow, fetched the pushchair, fastened the child in it, locked the door, put her gloves on and started walking up in the opposite direction. A few paces and there was the crest of the hill. She walked without the purpose of going anywhere; it didn't matter where. She wanted the motion of her body to clear her feelings. No longer was there any need to go to town – in the Rates Office they could be waiting for the promised payment, she would not fulfil it. The line on her lips parted in a smile, a very unusual smile, devoid of beauty. Neither would they go to Spain, the family could be waiting too. Though this thought provoked tears, she rejected them with a gesture of hostility and left the road turning to the right, where a side track sinuously descended to the valley. She stopped there to look at the panoramic view. Somehow ragged, the ground was not soft but cut in rocky drifts. She walked down for a while, then thinking the walking up would be longer and colder, wheeled round and, letting the child walk, began to undo the course, still sullen. There was nothing to amuse them but weeds, rocks and cold wind.

Mother and daughter reached the road. Better to go back home and wait for James, see what he did with the fifty pounds. Soon she saw his car parked in front of the garage and knew he was back. However, she did not go to meet him. What she was feeling and fearing overflowed her measure; she had no desire to quarrel with him. She entered the house and took Mercè's coat off, telling her they had been for a long nice walk, now she could play quietly. Then Maria proceeded to do the ironing.

The clock had long since struck three and no stir from James. She began to lose her external calm, she better not. Then she left the iron and went to the telephone, calling the garage.

'Aren't you going for the children?'

'I thought you were going.'

'No, I am not going.'

'What happen?'

'Nothing,' and she put the telephone down.

She thought he would come and make further enquiries. But he didn't. After a few minutes saw him going down the hill.

Later, the children came into the house alone. 'Hello Mummy!'

'Hello darlings!' Maria kissed her daughters. 'Had a good day at school? You'll have a little to eat now.'

She was to be busy for a while. As James had no obvious wish to face her, it wouldn't be possible to speak to him till the children were in bed. Though he came to the house for his tea, the children being enough distraction, husband and wife did not talk to each other.

Two hours later Maria made for the garage, her attitude resolute, her look stormy, searching for James. She found him talking to a customer, who was always around like a sheep tick, he and his old van in want of something or other, forever offering fabulous deals, dubious gains which Maria never knew who was taking.

Today she would not listen to nonsense, went straight to interrupt them.

'James, I have to talk to you.'

'Don't you see I am engaged?'

'If you prefer I shall say it now and here.'

'I am going Martines. I'll tell you later more about it,' said the knave, noticing the determination of the lady.

James, visibly annoyed, followed her into the office.

She opened the safe and said, 'Today I could not pay the rates because I did not find the money here.' She pointed the empty space. 'Where are they?'

'Did you look properly?'

'What have you done with the money?' she insisted with growing impatience.

'And why do you think it is me who have done something?'

'Because no one else could have touched it,' she affirmed, 'Have you paid something that was more urgent than the rates, James?' she added in a low menacing tone, 'I repeat to you again, listen: if you and I do not work together in agreement, if you do not slow down in the expenses, all these things there are to pay will accumulate and smother us. We are not going to be rich but end up in disaster.'

'Don't talk nonsense. You women always think in small. One has to spend money to earn money. It is you who have to listen to me. People don't pay to us straight away do they? So we do not pay quick. Also, everybody waits. It is done like that.'

'No. One thing is the invoices for parts and material that is money to come back, but not the rates, the electricity, the loan interest, the telephone, all this must be paid at once.'

'Don't be ridiculous, nobody pays at once.'

'I am not ridiculous, I am not silly, do not say silly things,' now she was cross and began to raise her voice, 'for the rates we had a year to pay, what else we won't? And going back to the fifty pounds. I want them. We are not going to Spain unless we pay the rates first and that's that.'

'I have the tickets booked for Easter week.'

'Well, unbook them, if you have paid with that.'

'No, I'll pay them with the Anglia's repair profit. There are many things to receive, we'll have more money than we need.'

'Yes, sure. And don't you think that the people who owe money to us may not pay? What if they do as you say and make us wait? It has happened before, remember the Hemingways? Did not pay until we threatened them. And how long it took? Months and months. We tell the family we shall go for summer.'

'And upset them? When they are so much looking forward to see us?'

'Tell me, what have you done with the money?' she insisted, trying to keep calm.

'I needed them,' he admitted.

'Why? For what?'

'We shall sell the Spitfire, because, sure Mr Roberts will buy. I told you, in Appleyards there is a Jaguar they give it to me very cheap.'

'I don't see any need to push Mr Roberts. If you want another car more powerful, that is a fancy, not a need, you can very well wait a bit until we are more settled. Listen to me James, do not buy a more expensive car yet.'

'I have the opportunity now, I tell you, I can get this now for a very good price, this type of car costs more than one thousand pounds.'

'A thousand pounds! Are you mad? How do you imagine to pay?' she was staring at him in amazement, then her look took the light of knowledge: the destination of the fifty pounds, and the many more that would disappear through the same track. She must try to stop the crazy drain. She made a supreme effort to speak steadily and clear and, sat at the desk, took pencil and paper. 'Let's count carefully what money we have, to see if you can buy this Jaguar or not.'

He took a seat in front of her, his elbow on the table, holding his face with his hand; by the effort of his mind the brow twisted and lined his forehead. Maria looked straight into his eyes, but quickly looked aside, couldn't bear the struggle, the desolate confusion between reality and fantasy, between wish and duty; it was painful to see that intangible thing so turbid, so volatile, now and often clouding her husband's sight...to try and clear this mind was as difficult as catching the wind in one's bare hands.

Soon she realised the numbers she was making were not retaining his attention, nor deviating his sight from the mirage he looked on; this job I'll get so much, that car I'll sell for so much profit, the petrol sales will double, and so on...

'James, listen, look at what we have got today. Not what we will get tomorrow. The future is always uncertain. Think carefully, remember: you always have got less than what you had previously calculated. Take notice of what I said: we must spend for what we have earned not for what we will earn.'

'In this way we'll never do anything. We will have nothing in this way.'

'What is it then? You agree then; we don't earn enough to buy a Jaguar. Give me back the fifty pounds and forget about your fancy.'

'It is too late. I've already paid the deposit; they are keeping it for me.'

'Go and take it back. If not I shall go myself to Appleyards and ask for the fifty pounds,' she concluded impatiently.

'You better not,' he replied in a menacing tone.

'Well, you go then. I assure you that this time you are not going to get your way. The rates must be paid. If you get the car you and I have finished definitely.'

She made a resolute gesture and left the office, she walked up to the house but didn't get in, instead went round the back feeling terribly vexed, powerless and defeated in her effort to make him understand. She went to the open space to look at the stars, to listen to the wind; if she could gather fortitude and hope...

She had always felt very frustrated when her views were not attended. At the beginning of her married life, believing herself loved, this disconcerted her very much. Now was not for herself alone, they were a family, there was the children depending on their parents' stability.

Her emotions were tangled up in threats leading to the future, to the everyday bread and butter that was the business and the making or the unmaking. That terrible insecurity in the clouded look of her husband, his arguments, his words based on nothing solid...could her threatening shake him? Make him react in a positive manner? Perhaps, yes. He would understand that to buy the Jaguar meant to lose her. Hope is a very difficult light to put off, it burns in the hearts of people with very little. Just dim thoughts, far fetched, will revive its flame. James would not buy the car, would see there is no sense in expending so much money. There was no need for her to make plans to leave, they would not arrive at these extremes. She sighed at the beauty of the night and the invisible strength of the wind. (How vain is Hope).

403

One day passed away, and another. Work, continuous work, took the hours to the back of time, not to return. Now and then Maria had reminded James about the fifty pounds. She begged him to tell Appleyards he couldn't afford the E-Type Jaguar. Her words were taken away by the wind always running down the hill, passing through James's mind without stopping. He avoided to speak on this side of his projects. All his words concerned their forthcoming visit to Barcelona. It would be fantastic to see the family, to enjoy the good weather, especially after suffering so much up there; the bitter cold, the constant work, the winter was so long. Maria had to make great efforts not to be carried away with this enthusiasm. She continued affirming that if the rates were not paid she wouldn't go.

The day he came with the air tickets for her and the children, she was astonished.

'Is you then who is not going?' she exclaimed, uncertain of what to make of it.

'We cannot leave the garage long without you or me. The children will enjoy very much Palm Sunday. I shall come later.'

All Maria's resistance crumbled away.

'All right, I'll take the children to see the family, you meantime think about our situation. I want you to realise we cannot go to all that expense and buy the Jaguar on top. Even if you can't recuperate the money, don't buy it, is better to lose fifty pounds than our future happiness.' Those words she pronounced clearly when both were in the bedroom, so the wind will not take them away, she thought!

Later at the airport she repeated the same words, but as the plane was getting high James's figure, diminishing, appeared to Maria as a question mark, enlarging the emptiness and distress which would thwart the joy of revisiting home and family.

A happy stay was not to be. Pending all the time on how James was doing on his own at the garage, she could enjoy nothing much but the warmth of the sun. Then the blow came, fell strongly through her most inside. James arrived driving a fabulous E-Type Jaguar. He came into the village, roaring the powerful engine, as a conqueror. If he had not his hands on the steering wheel, he would throw up his arms as a symbolic embrace to all the admirers out to see him. Hiding her great disgust she had to smile and pretend pleasure to see him. Immediately she wanted to go back to England said the garage couldn't be left to Mr Fursden's care alone. Two days after James's arrival, she and the children were at the Prat Aeroport, saying goodbye to the family and leaving James alone to show off.

While suspended above the earth she pondered, her spirit suspended too between various contra-dictory sentiments. She felt her own cowardice, incapable of doing great things, for she had said that if James bought the car she would leave him. Well, he had bought it. And what she was doing now? Nothing but going back to the garage like a blind mole, running away, that returns to the known spot. Why couldn't she pass the garage by and go further? It would be good for James to come back with the 'fluming' sports car to find them nowhere. But it would not be so. The social barrier, the religion, the conventionalism were stronger than herself. She felt rage against it. Reflecting back saw James in his splendid attitude of satisfaction. Really, his arrival at Montcada, the village that had seen him the son of a labourer, watching him back from abroad driving one of the most expensive sports cars. It was a triumph. And she had intended to spoil it mentioning his fantasies, as the car was not paid for. Incapable of sharing his happiness in the pompous exhibition of possessions, she had fled from his side. Not to leave him completely, no, a coward she was. Just to return to the petrol station and follow the downhill into fraud and dubious deals, battling continuously, trying to safeguard some integrity, the moral values she believed to possess in good degree.

Because, what was it then, the extra petrol the tanker man brought in? Stolen; they accepted it to make the double gain. She was recalling the first time James went to tell her the driver who had delivered six hundred gallons, had twenty gallons left in the tank, and as this was his last call he did not know what to do with them, he could not go back to the depot with them. She came out to see what it was; someone had made a mistake in measuring, they would do the man a favour if they were to take it from him. They told him to drop it into their tanks.

'But we have to tip him,' James remarked.

'Of course,' Maria said, 'how much he wants?'

The driver asked for half the price. While Maria fetched the money the man emptied his tanker.

Then the man pocketed it and said, 'Don't tell anybody, please!'

Another time he came with fifty gallons, and Maria still believed those were left overs. Later, when she began to doubt the veracity of the driver, it was too late, she accepted and paid, and not just twenty or fifty but one hundred and two hundred, not one driver alone, these were several who robbed the company, as some other garages would be accomplices too of buying stolen goods. Moreover, would it not be stolen things that James and that 'sheep tick' were always messing about with? The things that drop from the back of a lorry. She was fast going down that slippery path. How could she stop and get out of this whirl, out of that crazy rat race for money which swallows up integrity and conscience. Every fabulous gain is immoral if someone in the line suffers or is deprived and abused. But then Maria could not reflect on it properly, her pre-eminent thought was to make the business run in a way to make enough to cover overheads; then surpass them, pay the mortgage and become the proprietors of that windy spot on the edge of the moors. Her dreams were to enlarge the bungalow and to plant a line of trees, tall poplars, for barrier and beauty.

When she, with the children, arrived at Lindley Moor Garage the Spitfire was there, quiet in a corner, elegant and petite, yet too small for James' illusions of grandeur. Gazing at it came to her the idea of what she would do. Yes, she said, it is not the solution but I shall do it. She paid Mr Fursden what was agreed with James for looking after the garage, thanked him and sent him away. She didn't like that man, his undefined age and his elusive look. Then she took all the takings and went out, not to Brighouse, where the bank was but to Huddersfield, to another bank. She entered decidedly and opened an account in her name only. She left a bit more reassured that she was safeguarding the drift. Of that petrol money James would not pay his car with. She had reached the conclusion there was no possible way to stop his craze for possessing and spending money.

James came back from Spain later than expected. It didn't worry Maria as she had more time to reflect on their situation. She telephoned the TOTAL petrol company and asked for the representative to call and see her. Then she waited.

James arrived, having had the prowess to cross France in record time. He was so full of it, talked to newspapers and all, like a balloon, ready to burst. Maria felt strangely seized by mixed sentiments, similar to when years ago she decided to marry him. A kind of pity, she was touched by his surrender to flattery, his vulnerability, his complete lack of responsibility, this kind of infantile behaviour mixed with strikes of the mature man, was rather pathetic if not tragic. Reaffirmed in her purpose, while he was playing with his expensive toy, she would keep her feet on the ground.

A family in a boat upon the sea, who shall steer at the helm? Who shall lead across rough waters? It couldn't be James. His magnetic needle moved at the impulse of his whims. When her compass showed a different direction, how could she follow his with the children on board? She must take the steering and do the best she could. Not her idea of a marriage, it was not. She always disliked to see wives as barges, neither a husband towed. Both like the double skipper, that was the ideal. They had done so when the weather was stormy. Now James seemed to be 'seeing his ears' and would disdain Maria's views. However, Maria was not made for a barge nor for towing, neither had she the temper to jump overboard. She had a good mixture of humanity in her soul, compassion, self-love, courage and cowardice, with the tendency to let things be equal to the impulse to challenge destiny.

When James finished his bombast on all his powers and those of the E-Type Jaguar, Maria told him about opening the account in another bank on her name only, for the petrol side of the business, which she intended to keep separate from the garage workshop. She would endeavour to pay the mortgage and feed the family. She said, 'If I do not ask you for money, it would be better, without asking you to pay bills we can be friends.' She was smiling, while his forehead twisted, unable to accept the notion of her separated account...her name... She added, 'Is it that you cannot manage the garage business alone and you need the WIFE to help you?'

'Of course I can, you'll see how much money I shall make this summer.'

'We agree then,' and murmured as she went, 'and much you need, too.'

The TOTAL rep called. Elegant as usual with his nice polished speech, he was talking to Maria standing at the side of the road, both observing the view of the forecourt and the kiosk, now with little panels of glass more resistant to the gales, under the bright morning sun, clean and pleasant.

'Yes,' confirmed Maria, 'the sales are up again; last week we sold seven hundred gallons, this summer we'll overpass the one thousand. And more oil too. Now, you see, I put the cans here and the customer can take the grade he wants,' after a pause she continued, 'now I want to ask the company to put all the forecourt deals in my name alone. My husband has brought himself a sports car and he has many expenses, we do not wish mixing up those expenses. You understand?'

'I don't know if that will be possible,' he replied hesitantly, not really understanding Maria's requirements.

'The licence to sell inflammables is in my name; I pay the cheques, I place the orders, in fact, whenever there is a problem I have to solve it. There is only the need for the company to make me a paper stating that I am the manager and is my only responsibility. That is all what I want.'

'I do not know...there is no woman as manager...I don't think the Head Office will do it.'

'No? Why not? You always come to talk to me. The office in Wakefield know they are dealing with a woman. I have been there to discuss policy.' Rage and vexation beginning to rise to her eyes, she looked up straight to this gentleman, then she saw him blushing, his head bent. Conscious of the poor validity of his argument. Maria moved her sight away.

'I'll try to speak to the management, I shall tell them what you want.'

'Do it please, it is necessary that. It would be better and more convenient for all of us. I am sure.'

CHAPTER SIX

THE ROOM WAS large, there were rows of chairs facing in one direction, looking like a cinema, yet it wasn't. Uniformed girls passed to and fro. A loudspeaker called names. The Martines family was there, all sat on their seats waiting, not quite so patiently as the other people there, for whom stillness seemed a natural way to pass the interlude.

'Elizabeth Martines!' resounded the voice.

Maria rushed to take her daughter through the door. The father remained behind with the other two daughters. While a nurse placed, very tenderly, the little girl by the table, Maria could feel her stomach up to her throat. A man in white overalls extracted some drops of blood out of Elizabeth's thumb. Watching it she felt dizzy and would have dropped on the floor but for another nurse holding her firmly and sitting her on a chair. Maria wished to lie down; instead the nurse pressed with both hands her head down to her knees.

'Let me,' sighed Maria wanting to stretch out. 'What stupid way to make me feel better.'

Nevertheless the blood was circulating again to her brain and the nurse let go and gave her a glass of water. When she was better she saw her daughter, quite composed, waiting for her, holding her bandaged thumb; Maria said how sorry she was and left quickly.

James and the other children, bored, had changed seats several times.

'What have they said?'

'Was only to analyse her blood. They'll let us know when to bring her back for the operation, before school term starts again. She will be all right. I have fainted like a silly girl. I don't know why and still feel sick.'

They went immediately to the car.

'I have done well to come,' James said.

Maria, still pale, reclined on the seat.

'Don't you be so sure. I continue believing there was no need for all of us to go to the Infirmary.'

He had insisted on taking them.

That summer they were very busy. Maria, always watching the forecourt, attentive to the bell ringing, never missed a client, counted every penny of the takings and knew exactly the margin of profit, and did not expend over it. She had enough to cover the housekeeping, never asked for money from James, neither enquired what he did or earned. She paid all the petrol expenses, even paid the overdue rates. In this way husband and wife got on very well. Only now and again would he take them for a ride in the car saying, 'Let's go here, let's go there.'

The children were always ready and happy, not Maria though, perhaps because it was not the place of her choice or because she really preferred to attend the pumps instead of paying

Chris to do it. And less did she like it on Sundays as Chris would bring his girlfriend and they would pass the time behind the garage, missing customers, surely.

Nevertheless, James would get his way. He had somehow imposed his authority of man over wife and children. That afternoon he did the same; after driving up towards Lindley Moor, he wanted to buy something and suddenly stopped the car.

'I'll buy you an ice cream,' he said, without waiting to see if any one fancied one and entered the shop.

Some minutes after he came out loaded with goods; it was an off licence so he bought wine, beer, sweets, packets of soup and the ice creams.

'You never buy this kind,' showing the packet to his wife.

'They don't sell it at the supermarket.'

Maybe they did or maybe did not. It was a more expensive brand. Maria would not spend more than she could afford, she was keeping all the family, while James did nothing but buy things when he pleased. In this way of course he could buy well and expensive stuff. Withal, since coming back from Spain Maria's behaviour was very tactful, criticising not what he did, not even complaining about the petrol he was using with the Jaguar, simply putting it down in her books as unprofitable expenses. Saying nothing.

It was August, summer declining. A summer which, in spite of the wind, the rain and its frequent backing to winter as all English summers do, had been very good. Long full days without time for regrets about the past and what could have been the present or the future. Maria went to sleep every night just with the thought of what had to be done the following day and that was plenty enough. That day she went to bed reproaching herself for letting few drops of her daughter's blood upset her.

On waking up the next morning she noticed in surprise that the feeling of sickness was groping the mouth of her stomach. In great alarm she looked for a calendar and began to count the previous weeks...months... Good Lord! I am done!...

A week later, all the family again took Elizabeth to hospital. Maria, in a small room began to help the child to undress and left her into the hospital nightgown, insecure, frightened, alone among strangers. Maria resigned like the other mothers were.

The nurse was urging them to go repeating, 'They'll be all right.'

That English 'All right,' good for everything.

'Yes,' James agreed, 'they do everything very well in this country.'

But Maria bitterly resented being separated from her child and replied, 'Yes, very well, like the slaughterhouse, they do everything on series as a conveyor belt.'

There was a ward with a row of spotless white beds ready to receive the children, boys and girls from six to eight years old. The nurses would sit them one by one in front of the doctor who would be cutting tonsils, scraping glands, one after another; he would splash himself with blood, but he would not move from his chair until the last child had been put in front of him. At his side the bucket was full of bloody particles of flesh. After, he would take his rubber gloves off and drink a cup of tea. Later perhaps, he would pass round the long line of beds where his victims lay in pain. Poor things, all yearning for their mums. Yet no mummies or daddies were permitted to enter the ward. Maria spent the night worrying about her eldest daughter.

The following morning she took the car and drove straight to the Infirmary, resolute to enter the ward. Her step was stopped.

Highly irregularly the matron said, 'Your daughter is perfectly all right, but it is much better if you don't see her.'

'Why?'

'Because if she sees you she will be wanting to come with you or she will be more restless, it is no good for them,' affirmed the uniformed lady.

Maria was not convinced, yet had to turn back without seeing her daughter.

The following day she went to fetch her. A weak, pale, crying child. The mother's eyes filled with tears. The father, wrapping her with a blanket took her straight to the car, not even saying goodbye or thanks. In fact, there was nothing to say, nothing to pay. How odd, just to do what you are told. In a country famous for its freedom with a democratic state breeds a health system of quasi-dictatorship.

Elizabeth soon got better, Maria didn't. That grappling in her stomach would not go. She told James, he seemed to be pleased about it.

'You must be careful now, we do not want to lose it again, besides this time will be the boy, sure will be,' and after a light caress he went towards the garage.

Maria was feeling worse every day. All her body was in turmoil, unbalanced, diminished, fluxed to a liquid state; the state of her mind beginning to follow that of her body, cramping down, crouching low, like fog upon the weeds.

She went to the doctor. Not the habitual but his partner, who interrupted her thus: 'Why do you complain? Didn't you know what you were doing?'

Maria became suddenly dry of words. No, the poor woman did not know. She looked at him with eyes that could have moved the stones. Perhaps the doctor regretted his harshness. He bent his head and began to write. Maria took the prescription still unable to utter a word and left the room.

Sat in front of the steering wheel she felt very much like crying, but could not drive in this state, hands and knees shaking. Better go walking to the chemist. Waiting for her medicine, calm was returning to her. People provided distraction, their coming and going, their indifference, their greeting to each other in the 'How are you?' with the inevitable, 'All right,' always given, whether the person was all right or cramped by rheumatism or gowned by a killer cancer. Those 'all rights' had their subtle nuances yet so light a note, that to a foreigner they were always the same. Why were these people so quiet and calm? She would never completely understand them. There, sitting, waiting, while the chemist handled medicines and talked of the weather. She felt very much a stranger among them, completely out of place and with the wish not to be there, not to be in England at all. She took her medicine, paid the two shillings everyone paid for any prescription and went out.

Eight years living amongst these northern people, and she could not yet define their characters. Sometime ago she bought a series of books; one was *The Island Race* by Churchill - then still alive - whom she admired. It was a magnificent volume she read while feeding baby Mercè who never wanted a bottle and Maria, to pass the time, used to put the open book on the bed in front of her while the baby sucked at her breast. History fascinated her. A hard, blood-thirsty, cruel race, the British. Not finding any similarity with the people of today, she pondered what a few centuries of civilisation could do. Now, to distract herself from the sickness and give herself a rest from the garage-house-children chores, she was reading it again in an endeavour to understand the people amongst whom she was living.

The terrible Vikings, the furious Saxons drunken with their own blood, their conquests. Later, the cruel crimes of kings and queens, chopping off each others heads for political power. Well, she believed they were far from it now. Though history needs a deeper study than she was given to, and how thoroughly civilisation works on the soul of humanity, requires wisdom and much reflection to understand.

It was October when one day James arrived from Manchester very excited, seeking Maria to tell her: 'Up on the moors is full of police, looking for the buried bodies of the children. They said one is found already.'

'What terrible thing are you talking about?'

'Don't you know? They've been digging for few days. They got the criminal, he is young, twenty-seven and a clerk in an office, would you believe? He and his girlfriend amused themselves torturing children, and when they were tired killed them and brought the bodies to bury in the Moors. The one the police found today had been interred for two years, only bones and bits of clothing...'

'Oh! Shut up, stop, it cannot be these retrogressions.'

'What do you mean? It is true.'

'You exaggerate. It cannot be so macabre.'

'Let's go and see, is not far...'

'Oh, no!' She felt so sick she couldn't hold upright and went quickly to lie down on her bed. But James followed her there.

'I am going up after, a lot of people go, they said there are some more bodies, and they will carry on digging till are found.'

'No, James don't go...let them alone.'

Nevertheless, he went to contemplate the ghastly scene and later pestered his wife with gruesome details of those horrifying Moors murders.

Maria's spirits dropped down to ground level, she couldn't stand anything. She didn't eat, she didn't sleep, the tears behind her eyes would drop at the least provocation, she was making life impossible for her and for the ones around her.

'Come on children get into the car,' said James, holding the door open, urging his daughters, 'are you not forgetting anything?'

'I have left my doll in my bed, papa, let her sleep all the time,' said Theresa.

'You, Mercè, leave the teddy bear here to sleep too,' he said, trying to take it from her; the child pressed it to her tummy and refused to let it go.

'You'll lose it.'

Elizabeth sat very serious, holding her bag of treasures.

'Let them take what they want, and let's go or we'll miss the plane.'

Maria was impatient to leave the Moors garage behind, with all the work and all its problems that had become as big as Mount Everest, unclimbable for her, to leave behind all these people with their strange goodness and these incomprehensible crimes. She could not get off her mind those children tortured to death so near from where her own children lived. She wanted to escape, to return to her people, however they were, they were more like her. To go; to walk backward, she wished. Get up to the aeroplane and descend to Barcelona. Return to her home, to her mother. As to undo the way already made. To extricate herself from all the anguishes of her body and the sorrows of her spirit.

James was earnestly assuring her how much he was going to miss them. But he was ready to sacrifice himself for their well being, as Maria needed rest to get well.

'Carol's mother will come to clean up for you, and wash your clothes. I have explained what she has to do, James, you will manage with the meals as you eat at any time, as you like doing. Mr Fursden has promised to look after the petrol, I hope he'll do it all right.'

Half an hour later Yeadon Airport was below them. Maria empty of any feeling of regret, the children surprised at having left their father inland.

However, no one returns to childhood, no one repossesses the past. Time carries its course forward, unconcerned. To be or not to be is not its question. Absence does not make the span stop. Maria found her mother getting old; tired hands no longer able to give comfort to the child reclining its head on her lap.

Not now, for a head of deeper anguish, no longer a child. She came to the full consciousness of what means to be a grown-up; an immense solitude, an independent person with no one to lean on, a dreary loneliness. How precious is infancy. 'Blessed be the meek'.

Maria spent hours in her mother's sitting room, knitting, quite alone, while her family followed the routine of their daily lives. Gradually, her health came back. At the same time her clouded spirit cleared up to consider her situation.

Why had she left Lindley Moor? How could she leave James alone at the garage? Yes, she was pregnant and she felt very sick. But yes, unable to do anything... But yes, she did something... Run away?... Or did James send her?

A pregnancy could turn a woman inside out or inside in, keeping her mind closed, shrivelled, incapable of thought and action. The letters coming from England began to alarm her. Each had a cause for anxiety. Soon it dawned on her that James was tired of the place. He wanted to sell the garage. He had put an advert, he had contacted an agency. 'It would be better to start a business in Barcelona,' he wrote. The sales of petrol were down. Mr Fursden was not taking good care of the forecourt. The bungalow painted would sell better, he had already engaged a decorator. He was going to Yeadon Air Club for flying lessons. That he might surprise everybody coming home in a private plane. That he was ill, his gums infected. The garage snowed up. Carol's mother too old to look after him. Patricia was a good girl, nothing of nothing; just looked after him. Had stopped all credit sales for petrol; better to get cash straight away. Sundays closed – no point in opening for one or two customers. He had quarrelled with the TOTAL rep. 'Some oil to pay that I have already paid.' She better clear it up. Feeling much better, she thought it was time she were back. She wrote a letter saying so. James immediately sent the tickets, pleased, he said, she could realise how much sacrifice it cost him to pay the expenses of keeping the family in Barcelona. Maria took the children from the school they were attending, packed and was ready when a telegram came telling her not to board the plane and wait. He was coming to spend Christmas at home and after the holiday they would all go back. Maria was annoyed at his change of mind yet could do nothing but unpack and wait.

Then came the telegram with his arriving time. That day Maria felt a wave of refreshment all over her as if wakened from a long lethargic sleep. She moved about preparing for the husband's coming. She dressed the children with care and smartened herself up. The little girls were very excited, specially Mercè, the one who had missed her father most. Earlier at the airport, up on the terraces, they were watching the planes come and go. Each one descending from the sky was father's.

'This, this is the one daddy's coming, look Mummy.'

'No, darling, that is not coming from England.'

The arrival time had passed.

'Another one coming, look that one...'

'Yes, this is it. Quick children, get down. Mercè come...' She lifted the child on her arms and all ran to the far end of the terrace to see the figure of daddy coming out of the plane.

Watching intently, their eyes fixed expectantly on the same spot, ready to lift their arms in joyous greeting, their look sharpening. Then there was no one else coming out of the plane. Their arms dropped.

'That is, we haven't been able to spot him among so many people. He'll be at the customs checkpoint. Children, hold hands, here quick, don't get lost, we'll find him there.'

Skipping people and trolleys, the mother and the three children looked anxiously for the father. He was nowhere to be seen. Maria went to ask if the plane from England had arrived. Yes. 'Where are the passengers?'

'All gone, madam.'

'Daddy, daddy come...Daddy come...' little Mercè was repeating, tugging her mother's skirt, wanting to be lifted up. Tears were running quietly down Elizabeth's cheeks. Theresa, with her enormous eyes, was restless, still looking for the figure of her father.

'Daddy come...Daddy come...'

'Shut up, will you shut up...' reprimanded Maria. 'Daddy does not come, don't you see? We can go back.'

Suddenly, she felt deadly tired and, instead of going towards the entrance, she sank into the first seat near by. There they remained a while, the four figures a sad bewilderment.

It was past midnight when a knock at the door startled Maria. It was James! Oh, how pleased she was! Hugged him tightly.

'And how is that you came so late?'

'It is because they had lost my luggage and I had to go to Paris for it.'

His absurd explanation bore not on Maria, glad as she was to see him. He was there and nothing else mattered. She was thirsty and he was her spring;

she could now quench her thirst. But if she had imagined their marriage could still bring forward some flush of love, she was mistaken. On getting near, the illusion disappeared like a mirage in the desert. James came not from a barren place (although the Moors were). He was not in want. Maria spent many bitter nights.

Her wish now was to return to England, there was her home, she should be there. She should not have left.

THE MARTINES FAMILY arrived at the British Isles in early January. From London to Yorkshire they went by car. The run of many miles was slowing the hours. Night came soon, the children fell asleep dreaming about the toys Father Christmas would have left for them.

'Mummy will also have a surprise,' emphasised the father while driving on and on.

Maria was worn out, and pleaded for a rest. 'We could continue the journey next morning.'

'No, it is not worth it, we soon will be there,' he replied.

After they left the motorway at Wakefield it was almost the end of the journey yet, through dark and solitary roads, another long hour had to be endured. At last the car left Brighouse and took the road up home. Looking for the silhouette of the bungalow or the landmarks for its welcome, there was nothing to be distinguished as the night was very dark.

Suddenly, the peculiar sound of gravel under wheels and: 'We are there!' exclaimed James and the engine stopped.

'Thank God!' corroborated Maria, the noise of the engine still in her ears, but happy and relieved. Moving her crumpled legs, she clumsily got out of the car. The frosty air made her shiver. James had opened the front door, the electric light dissipated the blackness. The girls awakened, rushed in. Maria, her brain quicker than her body, was arranging the things to do: Mercè's cot ready before anything...look for the bedding, the pyjamas, warm milk, and water for the hot water bottles...

James put all the lights on, the heater regulator up.

'What do you think?' he smiled with satisfaction. 'Look...the work Dad has done for you.'

Maria, glancing all round the sitting room, felt strange cold creeping down her spine, engulfing her heart. She did not recognise this room; it was not her home. Under her feet were no longer the bare planks of wood but a softness, she gave it a look: it was dark red, quite beautiful.

'Come, sit here.' James went to where she stood motionless, took her arm and pushed her gently into an easy chair she did not recognise. In front of her startled eyes there was a low table, on top of it a jar of plastic flowers. She had the impression of being in a furniture shop, lifted her eyes only to see the fireplace, but neither did she know that hearth. 'I have changed the old one for this, more modern.'

The children were making a lot of noise opening their parcels, but Maria could not hear them. James was not smiling any more. Why was his wife not happy with all the improvements he had done? Great things that he always made.

'Patricia made the blinds,' he continued, 'she said you would be pleased when back, she couldn't understand how you could live without a carpet, without easy chairs, without privacy; everyone passing by the road could see what we are doing in the house.'

Maria was too tired to reflect over the meaning of those words, and all these improvements; it was possible not even he realised what the implication was and not exactly why he did it. She got up.

'The beds for the children must be prepared, help me please.'

She entered the bedroom, noticing straight away that the cot had been used.

'James!' she cried in alarm. 'Who has slept here? It has been wet, it smells...look. Tell me, who has slept in Mercè's bed?' She touched the mattress – dry, but the mark was there.

'Patricia, she has a child, put the little girl to sleep while doing the work,' admitted James adding quickly, 'I am going to unload the car.'

Maria, full of rage and repugnance, turned the mattress and looked for clean bedding. After, she went to the girls' room and began to put clean sheets on the beds. She called James to help her, but he said must look in the garage and lock the car in.

The children were wide awake by now; there was no way of getting them sleep, excited as they were with all the new toys. Maria, half hysterical with weariness, summoned and shouted to no avail. She gave a smack to Elizabeth, then one to Mercè, and threw her into the cot, pulling the bars up in despairing rage. At that moment James came in.

'Why do you smack her, poor little one?' He took the child out of the cot. Mercè was in a tantrum, unable to stop.

'Put her back to bed, she has to sleep,' ordered Maria promptly taking the child from him. 'It is so late, can you see that is almost three o'clock in the morning? I must rest and you do not help me, not a bit.'

'I am tired, too.'

'It is your fault, we should have stayed in a hotel for the night and rested.'

'You know I do not have any more money.'

'Of course you have not! You've spent it all, buying settees and artificial flowers,' she replied with scorn.

Then she glanced at her bed, it was undone, the mattress covered with a blanket only. As if she could see something very horrible, she jerked and left the bedroom as if had been on fire. Hands round her protruding belly in a gesture of helpless protection, she rushed to the kitchen to sink into heartbreaking sobs, the bitterest ever. Where was her home? Her mother's home was not home any more. She came back to this, not her home either. Where was her home now? She cried a long time, lying over the sink, mopping her eyes and nose with the towel, completely abandoned to her despair.

When later she entered the bedroom her husband was lying on the bed without bothering to make it, he had covered himself with the blanket and was sleeping like a just man. She stretched by his side. God, my God, for the sake of my children give me some rest!

The following day everyone woke up late. For Maria five or six hours of semi-sleep did her good; she felt worn and achy with heavy eyelids, however, she got up and washed her eyes, noticing her spirit was, after the lapse of consciousness, cool and calmer. James was still asleep. She looked at him in the light of this refreshed spirit of indifference. She resolved to concentrate her attention solely on the children and the business.

First she gave the plastic flowers to Mercè to play with, thus soon be destroyed. Then she took down the window blinds. That mania the English had for privacy, she had not. Besides, she needed to be able to see the forecourt's comings and goings easily, without lifting a corner of the veil the other woman had put on, not to be seen. Moving about the new furniture, on the soft carpet, she could not take her mind from the thought that this Patricia, a stranger, had obtained from James so quick, what she, the wife, had not in many years. She lived in Navigation House wanting a carpet for the stairs, and in here nearly two years wanting a fitted carpet for the sitting room. Yet when the wife is away he, under the influence of another woman, goes and buys one, and not only this but a dining set, a three piece suite, kitchen pots and window blinds... Well, it could be funny if were not ironically cruel.

Carol's mother came up to see Maria. Yes, she was old, yet not unable to work. James should not have dismissed her. The woman was offended and told Maria so.

'The first day he told me not to come again. Ah! To bring that young woman, you know? No, I don't want to tell you, what carry on... They soon put the blinds up. It is not right, not right,' she kept musing, shaking her head, 'I am pleased you have come back.'

The TOTAL rep, the one Maria knew, well mannered and well spoken, did not come up to the garage again. James explained how he had thrown him out, saying he was the master there, not the TOTAL Company, and he disliked so much interference. Maria was worried for the seemingly broken relationship. She put in an order for more petrol. Then, before that was delivered came the new rep. This man was not so polite. He went straight to the point. He showed an invoice amounting to seven hundred pounds; she had already seen it.

'Before we send your order you must pay this overdue account.'

'I am sorry,' Maria replied calmly, 'all this is from when I was away. My husband did order that quantity. He sold it, he must pay it.'

'Your husband says the petrol is your concern.'

'Ah, yes? I have never ordered so many gallons at once. You can see for yourself,' and she showed him delivery notes, invoices, 'look, signed by me, three hundred, four hundred. Paid by me one hundred pounds, ninety-eight pounds. Now you come with an invoice for seven hundred pounds, well I am not responsible for it.'

'Your husband said you'd pay when you came back. Make me a cheque now and we will send the tanker this afternoon.'

'No, the cheque will bounce,' fixing her eyes on his face she continued with determination, 'sometime ago I asked TOTAL to give me the responsibility of the forecourt management. The direction took no notice because it is better to deal with men. They manage business better, don't they? When I was not here you dealt with my husband, a man. Continue the deal with him to receive these pounds.'

The rep was pacing the room, endeavouring to get out of a new situation, while Maria sat quietly waiting. Then he asked to use the telephone. Maria left him and went out to have a look at the children.

When she was back, the rep, who had spoken to his boss, said: 'We can send petrol if you pay cash on delivery.'

'Agreed, but it will have to be less of what is ordered, let me see,' calculating mentally how much money she had available.

'Cross out the Super, with the other cheaper grades I'll manage.'

'Right, we'll give instructions to the driver, you pay him cash and he'll drop what you pay for.'

Maria's smile extended over her face confidently. Then the man impulsively stretched his hand out to her.

'To a very unusual lady,' and left the place without ever asking for James.

The driver who came was new also, and made Maria pay before pouring a drop of liquid into the tanks. None of the drivers who sold stolen petrol ever came to the garage again, to Maria's great relief.

Winter was at its bitterest. The wind blew, pushing the little Jack Frosts in legions, sticking their forks everywhere. Few cars passed by, nevertheless

Maria kept the forecourt open with the lights on till eleven at night, the thick duffle coat and boots by the door attentive to the bell, watching through the window anxious to recuperate the lost customers. The few coming had to be well served, promptly attended to, she said, but James argued it was not necessary to bother for just one gallon or two. If a car stopped in front of the Regular pump, the cheap petrol, he would not stir out. Then Maria would rush out as quickly as her voluminous body permitted. She would give the customer her smile, equal for one gallon as for ten, then enter the garage, trying again to convince James of the necessity.

'What are you doing? Why didn't you move out to serve him?'

'Oh, I know this one, is a skinny. The other day came for half a gallon and he had to search all his pockets to pay for it.'

'It is better half than nothing. James, we are so much in arrears. Castrol wants to be paid, Galways Smith too. Have you seen their last letter? They are threatening now...'

'Don't take any notice, they will wait, and you stop bothering so much about the petrol. We shall sell the garage and go to Australia.'

'Australia? Didn't you said you wanted to go to Spain?'

'Where it be, but don't you see there is nothing to do here. That is Siberian country.'

'No. There is something to do here. I believe if we work we earn money, yes, but if you let the customers slip off we won't be able to sell the place even cheaper.'

It was to no avail. The enthusiasm for the garage in the Moors that made them leave Battyeford hardly two years ago had already disappeared from James's heart. Now, not even rebuilding smashed cars, only the quick gain on the buy and resale would satisfy him. What were they going to do? Weary, pressing her chin deep to her chest to avoid the attack of the frosty spears, she walked back to the house. Once thus returning she found little Mercè sat on the kitchen floor crying among the debris of broken eggs, the sticky sluggish whites and yolks slipping all over her.

'Oh! *Mare de Dèu* what have you done?'

Why had she left the eggs on the table? To rush out to earn four pence to lose a dozen eggs which cost thirty-three pence. If James came in now to see this disaster, he would still blame her. She engaged herself quickly to clear the mess. Nevertheless she would not be convinced, the petrol earnings was the only sure thing she had, however meagre it be, it was there and she doggedly held on to it.

The days passed on, dragged on. Her ankles began to swell, the veins on her legs ached. At the prenatal clinic they advised rest, as she had turned the seventh month. She worried for the little soul she was carrying, torn between her duty towards her body, and the need to provide the bread for it. If her husband would help her!

She tried again once more. 'The doctor said I must rest a bit more, you could stay longer at the garage and serve petrol in the evening. Instead of going out you could stay and close the garage,' she pleaded, with tears in her eyes.

'Close earlier, it is not worth for what you earn. I am told the transport business gives a lot of profit. Today I have been talking with someone who has lorries and he says...'

'You are not thinking of going in for lorry driving,' she interrupted him in alarm.

'Peter, you know him, from Leeds, is providing a Dodge that needs only a gear box, it will cost me almost nothing. Mr Kay is buying a Ford, he'll give up his present job, he says it is...'

The bell rang and a car stopped in front of a pump. James, excited with his new project, continued talking, not noticing his wife had left him to serve the customer. When she finished she walked slowly towards the bungalow, not wishing to listen any more.

That evening, when she had the children to bed, she called the garage and said to James, 'I am very tired, I am going to bed. Could you check the till and close at eleven please, not before!'

'Yes, I shall close,' he assured her.

It was only after nine o'clock that she heard him enter. He glanced at her lying down in bed.

'Are you all right there, aren't you?' he was taking his overalls off.

'Have you finished?'

'I have closed, nobody is coming.'

'What do you say? That you have closed? But...with the lights out, of course no one will come. Go and open again. Now that the cars have begun accustomed to seeing the garage open again regularly, you'll spoil it all.' He was putting his jacket on, Maria stretched up and said in altered tone, 'No, James, to the pub you are not going.' She had not undressed and now began to put her boots on. 'Do you hear me? For the love of your children stay in. Is it that you can't miss a single day of going?'

He went into the bathroom saying, 'Shut up silly, you are in hysterics again.'

Maria put her duffle coat on and went out into the dark night, into the garage and put all the lights on. As quickly as she could she returned to the house and, seeing James was still in the bathroom, slipped back in bed.

He came out from the bathroom and, seeing she had gone to open, became very angry.

'If you were so tired, you would not have got up and out. And now what? You want me to sacrifice myself for the bloody petrol! I am fed up with it, for the miserable profit it gives.'

'We earn our bread. Or is that it is more important your drink than the butter for your children? What on earth are you doing?' she exclaimed incredulously, on seeing him getting undressed. 'What are you doing?' she repeated in exasperation.

'You do not want me to go to the pub. So I am not going.'

He lifted the blankets and got under, covering himself up to his hair. Maria gazed unbelieving, almost in horror.

'James... But, James it is open... What if someone comes in now? Get up, for God's sake get up, it is me who has to rest.'

She was so stunned that on reacting, began to tremble. She sat up and felt sick. He didn't stir.

She began to imagine the bell ringing – in a moment it would. She looked at the bulk next to her, overcome with a strange contemptuous feeling, not felt before. Slowly she moved away from the bed, looked for some more warm clothing, put her boots on, she was hardly finished when the bell really rung, quickly fastened her coat and went out. She stayed in the kiosk until closing time. After eleven she walked to the house, bent like an old woman, sad and tired as death itself.

In the bedroom she did not enter. She had no wish to see the body of her husband resting, while hers was so fatigued, that she would willingly let her soul go. She spent the night on the sofa, turning her thoughts into her, where the infant lay.

The next morning James seemed to have forgotten. At breakfast he talked about the lorries and the money they could earn on transport. Maria asked him to take the girls to school because it was difficult to fit her bulk between the steering wheel and the seat.

'I'll put the seat backward.'

'Then my feet will not reach the pedals. It will be better if you do the driving.'

'I'll move the steering wheel,' he replied indifferently. He did do so. That afternoon he made her sit in the car and adjusted the wheel to the easiness of her belly.

'It is done, you see? It is easy. I put everything right. I have also looked for someone to help you. There is a girl who lives next to the pub. Chris's mother has told me. You can call and see her when passing.'

'So you want me to fetch the children from school?'

'I have arranged the steering wheel for you to drive comfortably, haven't I?' he replied in a patronising way, 'what you have to do now is drive with care.'

'Oh! I see. Thanks very much.'

But he did not notice the irony, and continued telling his wife how to drive and what not to do.

Maria engaged the girl. This girl, too young and not too clever, just left school, had to be trained and watched. Maria felt no relief and regretted the wages she had to pay. If only James were more willing to help! In fact, she was more tired every day and very ill at ease. James was completely taken up by the 'feverish rush for gold', had nothing in his mind but lorries and money. He had one already in the yard working earnestly on it. 'In four days will be running,' he repeated every day.

The weather was getting better. The stormy wind, whirling, whistling furiously around the place, would take away everything not holding tight to the earth. With dreary screams of triumph he would claim his own strength, frighten the clouds away, then the sun would shine, promising the joy of warmth and springtime. Yet Maria's soul was clouded and darkened.

She was preparing the cradle unmoved, she packed the few hospital requirements, instructed the girl. She waited in dumb humour but the signal, the call of the infant in readiness, was not coming. Each day was going weary, each morning more difficult to get up, to dress Mercè, to care for the little girls.

One Saturday she went to the bank, to the supermarket, drove back home, stopped in front of the garage and called James.

'Help us to get out,' she asked, stretching her arm, 'girls, get off, take the shopping to the house, please. James, you'll have to take me to hospital.'

'Now?' he asked in alarm.

'It depends if you help me to make dinner or not.'

He wiped his hands and followed her into the bungalow.

Two hours later they stopped in front of St. Luke's. Maria stepped out and went towards the entrance.

'Where are you going without saying goodbye? Don't you want your case?'

'Wait here, I don't know if they want me.'

When she found herself in front of the nurse she felt stuck for words.

'Are you in labour?'

'No, not yet... But I am so tired that... That...' her voice failed and her eyes filled with tears.

The nurse looked at her intently, knowingly. Took her arm.

'Come... Come... Where is your suitcase?'

'My husband is in the car waiting in case you don't want me.'

The nurse gave her another penetrating gaze then added, 'Even if you are not in labour, it is better you stay now, we'll see later.'

James, with the children, had left the car and they were entering.

'You can leave her in,' the uniformed woman told James, 'we shall let you know if to come for her tomorrow.'

Maria kissed the girls.

'Be good children, Janet will look after you.'

Then the nurse took the mother away down the corridor, separating the family once more.

While Maria was being examined the midwife said, 'Rest, rest now. If you don't start labour, you'll go back home but tomorrow, it will do you good to rest now.'

And so it would. At last she was given the rest her body and her soul desperately needed. She closed her eyes and remained stretched still, with no pain, no anguish, resting.

The pains came much later. The baby was born on Passion Sunday. It was a boy. A normal, healthy infant. Maria felt very satisfied. She had feared a girl would increase her husband's indifference. Now she was sure James would burst with joy. He might even be more attentive to her. It might improve the relationship of the marriage. She would try to be more patient, more understanding. She would not instigate him, so much nag at him, would let him be. He may learn common sense on his own.

Lying flat on the hospital bed, her body liberated from the burden of the baby, recuperating its normal functioning, predisposed her mind to see things in a less exalted condition. At the same time, she was feeling an intense desire to be a mother, just a mother. Ah! Like a gush of spring water born free out of the mountains, that will sink down and down to be piped for the needs of the town folk. So the establishment bore down on her. She was a wife, she would love the husband, respect him, obey him. He would earn the bread with the sweat of his brow as she was giving birth to his children with the pain of her body. So set up from time out of mind. Let it be. Let the illusion float dimly, softly through her mind. Let her be, just for a while.

Visiting time came. All the husbands arrived with flowers or parcels, many with anxiety pouring out of their eyes, eager to renew the bow with their wives, to understand the new situation. Poor men! How difficult it is to be a father. Nature will not help. No biological change prepares them. Their sexual function gives no kin of paternity, thus to feel fatherhood is an intellectual exercise.

James was approaching her bed radiating happiness, kissed her, asked how she was, handing his bouquet of flowers.

'It is a boy! Are you happy, aren't you? Have you been to see him?'

'No, I have just arrived. I have been to Wakefield this afternoon, gone with Kay, Peter has a magnificent Dodge, it can be loaded with so many tons as a wagon of a train, we are going to buy it together, he is very enthusiastic. We will start going to Ossett Colliery for coal to get used to it, to see how many journeys can we do in a day. If we earn three pounds for each trip and we can do three in the morning and three in the afternoon, it is nearly twenty pounds per day, don't you think it is fantastic? I am sure I can do more journeys than anybody else. Tony Kay says he can get cash to pay half of the Dodge.'

'Why are you not going to see your son, eh? I am sure you will find him prettier than this Dodge.'

'Yes, I will go in a minute...but listen, this Dodge cost eight hundred pounds only four hundred pounds each to pay.'

'Where are you going to get the money from?' she asked, at last roused from the new baby.

'I for the moment can't pay. I told him we can do some journeys first...but Peter will let us take it, because the licence has to be paid, but if I don't pay straight away but put the diesel free from our garage, Kay might pay all the deposit for the moment. The important thing is to make it run to start working as soon as possible.'

Maria was making an effort to listen to this, trying to feel his enthusiasm because, in spite of having produced a boy, she had failed.

'Go and see the baby,' she still insisted before the half hour ended, 'I like you to see him before you go. What are the girls doing? Tell me, are they well? Is Elizabeth eating enough?'

'Yes they all eat very well,' and without a pause he added, 'I have thought we'll have to order a lot more diesel, perhaps four hundred gallons.'

'We must pay cash, you know, unless you pay the arrears...maybe now you'll sell the Jaguar,' she mumbled, tired out, wishing visiting time was over and everyone gone, her husband the first. The nurse was ringing the bell, thank God! Closing her eyes she let herself be kissed, unresponsive, weary.

During the night she sobbed. The crying did not let her sleep. The night nurse, trying to reassure her, said it was the 'blues of after birth' and gave her some pills.

Every evening James came to see her and had nothing else to talk about but his lorries. If Maria wanted to know how the girls were doing, she had to be very insistent with her questions. His answers were short and lightly given. Maria wished to go home quick. It snowed during the night but now the sun, shining through the window, lay its rays on the bed, blanching it white like the snow outside.

Standing upright by the hospital entrance was James, holding Mercè in his arms. The two little girls darted at their mother as soon as she appeared downstairs.

'Oh Mummy, let's see the baby, oh, how small is he!' both wanting to carry and kiss him.

Maria embraced her daughters very tenderly, happy to see them, though she noticed at once how under the coats they were wearing summer dresses.

'Well, where are you going like this? Elizabeth, fasten your coat and you, Theresa.'

They got into the car.

'James, who has put these thin dresses on them?'

'What do I know!' he looked at the children as if he had not seen them yet, 'themselves, to be sure.'

'You shouldn't have taken them out girls. Can you see that is still very cold? Look at the snow, is all over.'

'It is sunny, mummy. Janet says it is already spring, I am not cold,' affirmed Theresa.

Elizabeth began to cough, a prolonged cough, that made the mother turn to look at her in alarm.

'You see, you have caught a cold, James can you see they are coughing?'

'Yesterday Janet washed their heads and they were running all over the place with wet hairs.'

'*Mare de Dèu!* Of course they have a cold!'

'As well as a good fire there was the central heating. The house was warm.'

'Too warm, I'm sure the regulator is at seventy per cent all the time. You never bother about saving anything.'

They arrived home. Maria found Janet full of make-up, lips and eyes heavily painted, wearing a mini skirt showing a good measure of thighs. She was, though, making dinner for them all.

After washing up was done the girl seemed tired. Maria said she could go.

'Have you been doing a lot of work? Haven't you? Did my husband help you enough, Janet?'

'No, he was going out all the time continuously,' the girl replied with a shadow of resentment. And you were elaborating your make-up to retain him here, Maria thought, nothing in the world will retain this man when he has another whim.

'I don't know how you manage Mrs Martines,' Without delay the girl put her coat on and went out, her countenance tired in spite of her youth and all the make-up.

The two older children continued coughing, the mother gave them syrup and dressed them with warmer clothes.

By mid afternoon a wave of weakness over-came her, the desire to be looked after grew in intensity.

'James, James,' she pleaded softly, 'Chris is watching the pumps, you can stay with us, is Sunday don't work, please! Look at your son, isn't he beautiful?'

She put the infant into his arms.

'Don't go out today. I am not strong yet, I need some rest, remember I was up at six o'clock this morning feeding the baby. You can look after your children. The four of them. What a big family we are.'

She put her arms around his neck and kissed him.

'Girls, mummy is going to lie down, you play but do not make too much noise.'

She left them all and retired to her chamber.

That night she had to get up several times because the two children were coughing out of breath. She did not know what else to give them, terribly worried for the other two, thinking Mercè would begin to cough the next minute and then the baby. She asked James how long they had been coughing like that. He did not know, he wasn't sure. She got cross.

'This is how you look after your daughters? It is unbelievable.'

Against all her good resolutions she was already quarrelling with him.

The next day Maria called the doctor. He said the girls had whooping cough and to keep them warm and quiet. The fears of the mother increased even more. The baby so tiny will catch it too, how could a nine day old baby stand it? she thought, he will die, and without any sense at all she was repeating, the baby will die...until James would get so nervous that instead of reassuring her would leave the house and not come back all day long.

When little Mercè began to cough Maria lost the serenity she had left. She sunk completely. She sat on the kitchen stool crying, her obfuscated mind seeing her children choke with that persistent cough, the sound of which had pierced her brain and she could not stop hearing. First Elizabeth, then poor Theresa, the gracious healthy Mercè would die too, and last the baby just born: to die.

Thus found her the Health Visitor. If she felt sorry for the disgruntled mother, it didn't matter, it was not her duty to feel, but to check on the health and the well-being of the new British subject. 'Pull yourself together.' The same she had been told after the miscarriage, this English philosophy capable of generating so much fortitude. 'Help yourself, gather and use all your resources, don't pamper yourself with those of others.'

Maria went to the bedroom to show the baby.

'When they are so small they very seldom catch anything, they are born with many reserves and defences. You keep feeding him, take those pills, will help with the abundance of your milk.' She gave her the pills, looked at her straight and added, 'you gain nothing to let yourself into this state of depression. I'll be back next week and I don't want to see you looking like this.'

Was it a command? That civil servant of the Estate, spotlessly dressed in navy blue, left the house carrying her small case and never turned her head, unsoftened, sure of her mission.

Gathering strength out of weakness as the Catalan saying goes, Maria managed to keep herself upright. Her mother would have said: 'Pray to God, confide in Him.'

God seemed to be as far away as her mother.

CHAPTER EIGHT

LINDLEY MOOR GARAGE was full of lorries –
enormous, noisy, smelly wagons. Men dressed in
overalls, coarse men, dirty men, shouting, swearing,
moved in and out of the garage, using tools, lying
them about greasy rugs and papers, entering the
kiosk to ask for cigarettes, for diesel, paying or
not paying. The arrival of the lorries coincided
with the children's bed time. Maria was considering
how to change the children's bath routine in order
to be at the forecourt when the lorries arrived,
and not leave James on his own.

The wagons left early in the morning. During
this period James woke up on his own and
was gone by seven o'clock. Then it was quiet in
the workshop. Maria, with Janet, managed the
forecourt very well, though she missed having
a mechanic available. When customers needed
repairs, she would make them come back Saturday
when James was not out with the lorry, but soon
had to desist as James complained and said if the
lorries needed something done, that was first. He
had no time for anything else.

Maria was helping Mercè put her pyjamas on,
could hear the noise from the yard reaching the

bathroom ever so loud that it worried her. She must finish with the children and go to help Janet. Suddenly, she heard the door opening and Janet's moaning voice calling her.

'What happen? Janet, I am here.'

'Oh, look Mrs Martines... Look what they have done to me,' the girl was in tears, with both hands trying to cover her backside, 'those silly men.'

Maria soon saw what it was all about, and flashed with rage. The girl's mini skirt was torn, showing her knickers with greasy finger marks.

'Who's done that? You must not give rein to them.'

'I was saying nothing to them... Roy and your husband...'

'You should put on longer skirts dear...come here, follow me.'

Maria went to the bedroom, put Mercè on her cot then gave a skirt of hers to the girl.

'Put that on and don't come out again, stay here, look after the baby, I still have to feed him.'

She went to the yard very angry and decidedly faced her husband.

'You are an indecent lot. What have you done to Janet?' she reprimanded in loud voice, to the men about: 'You, finish quick and get out, you Roy, what are you doing stuck there? If you have finish get out. This minute, OUT!' she shouted, stretching her arm towards the road.

'I have done nothing, James did.'

She went into the workshop. She had seen there a calendar she didn't like, now went straight to take it down. James followed and was going to snatch it from her.

'Let go, the men like it.'

'Well, I don't,' and *xis – xas* she tore up the bare ladies in four pieces. On coming out her sight bumped into the back of a lorry where a rude drawing of a penis was chalked on. Rage and contempt violently shook her. 'Wipe this off immediately,' she shouted furiously, 'or take away the lorry, or I shall!' and she turned to look at James. Her eye on fire meant exactly what she said. 'What do you think this garage is? You rogues, indecent, low creatures.'

Her disdain, in all its pitch, quashed the men sorry and they soon quit the place. She was more deeply hurt than disgusted, just to think of her husband at the same level as those knaves.

The next morning Janet came back with the skirt, saying that her mother didn't want her to work up there any more. Then Maria was alone with the children, the two eldest on school holidays, all day long. The weather was good, the road in full traffic, many cars called for petrol. For Maria, in and out of the house, it was too much for her. The children resented the lack of attention. She noticed but could not remedy; the customers' money was essential for them as nothing came from James's lorries.

When feeding the baby she would sit by the window, wishing with all her senses no car would come during these minutes. But they did, and she would snatch her son from her breast, fasten her bra, and run out, leaving the infant lying on the sofa crying. She would serve the customer swiftly and efficiently, with the smile on her face and her heart breaking into pieces.

That carry on was impossible. She must remedy it. On top of that Mercè was ill with jealousy. She had fits, she would stop breathing, her teeth clenched, becoming red and blue, really frightening her mother.

Meanwhile, James was skirting the garage completely and one could think his family too. He was earning a lot of money, he said, in transport there were a lot more opportunities than in repairs and petrol. If Maria had problems it was her own fault, she didn't need to because he had the solution: to go and live near the power station where the work was. To sell the garage or to rent it didn't matter but to go away from it.

Maria shrugged her shoulders.

'Well,' it seemed she had no wish to contradict him, 'it is the same to me. I have plenty of work with four kids.'

'Of course,' he earnestly agreed, 'you let me do. I always solve everything. In the meantime we can get a manager for the garage; you only have to write down the words for the advertisement, to go on the papers tomorrow.'

He would never put roots anywhere. No lasting friendships. The friends they made drifted off every time they moved. The true friends had been the Bentleys, very restless themselves, who had emigrated to Australia. This inhospitable hillside, she liked the place now, she would not willingly leave it. However, with resignation she would follow her husband.

The following Sunday she sat by James in the car, the baby on her lap, the girls on the back seat, the basket with sandwiches, the flasks of tea and of milk, the nappies and the cardigans in the boot. She had to lock the petrol because Chris had an accident and was unable to help.

James drove miles away past Yorkshire, where the land stretched flat in endless fields. Then at a distance could be seen the new atomic plant in construction. They entered a village to look at a house of white washed walls, no garden. Then at another one on the open land, without water or electricity. And still they drove to another dwelling among trees, it was very damp. The children and the father were enjoying themselves but the mother, with the baby, was wishing to be back home.

On arrival at the garage there was a man who had seen the advert waiting for them. He was young with light hair and a lively face, with an overall manner of cleverness. He assured them there was no need to see a solicitor to witness the agreement, which they could prepare themselves and sign over a stamp. It seemed all right. The couple engaged him.

Mr Lenem was living in Leeds, quite far to come every day, so he had the idea of offering to change his house for the bungalow. James thought this idea good and took the children with Maria to see the new manager's house in Leeds. Only to get into the district Maria began to feel a kind of anguish, recalling the time when they were looking for a house in order to leave Mr Gill's gardener in peace. Mr Lenem's house was one of so many alike in endless rows of undistinguished streets, bare of vegetation, narrow in view. Her soul sunk. Into the house her whole being felt shrouded. The children moved, restless, about the stuffy rooms. The baby began to cry. She went out, James following.

'Here you could be very well. Tranquillity, without the traffic of cars, without worries of any kind.'

She was silent, got into the car.

'Tell me, don't you think it is all right?' he insisted.

'For God's sake James! We couldn't manage in there, is too small.'

'Small? It is not bigger where we live now.'

'No, here I do not come,' her voice short and firm. 'Look, if you do not see the difference I don't care. But worse for worse. I rather go there, near Norton, the white washed house has no garden but at least the open fields are a few steps away.'

The matter was left at that for the moment.

Mr Lenem installed himself in the workshop with an air of being the boss all round. Maria could very well have turned her back and dedicated herself to the children and the house, as James was advising her to do. But she found herself unable to withdraw completely; each time a car entered the drive she was watching if Mr Lenem was quick enough and the client well attended. The man, probably noticing, suggested the bell should be disconnected from the house.

Then was the silence which worried Maria, thinking there was not enough petrol being sold as it was still her only income. James was not giving her anything from the lorries for house-keeping. Mr Lenem kept the profits from repairs but forecourt dealings were Maria's. The young manager did not inspire complete confidence to her.

During all this period James would go out not only every day to the nearest pub, but every Saturday had a bath, asked for clean shirt and pressed trousers, then in his E-Type Jaguar, roaring down the hill he would disappear, not saying where he was going, not even bothering to make the false statement that he would come back early. Because he didn't until well-nigh dawn.

On Sundays he was getting up when the dinner was at the table. Yet if he got up and the meal was not yet on the table, he would go for a drink; it didn't matter if his wife said 'dinner is ready in five minutes'. He would go and be back when he pleased, happy, with a bottle of wine in his hand, unconscious of the upsetting of his family having waited for him, not daring to eat a morsel because the mother wanted to inspire respect for the father and family life in the children. But Maria's life was getting more bitter every day. By now she had no illusions of reaching economical well-being. Yet, lack of money was not the biggest worry, she could work against it. What embittered her life, her cup full near the brims of gall, something less tangible, less easy to accept, what dishevelled her marriage, was the husband going out every night. Why? Where? With who? Why he comes back so late? What he does so many hours? Why? ... Why? she asked herself.

Into the quietness of the children's sleep and the darkness outside, the woman paced the floor of her house, twisting and untwisting those questions, exasperating herself with the outcome of no answers. And she would walk again up and down the length of the room, often looking out of the window, listening to the wailing wind pushing down hill. God knew what fancies, what lamentations were thrown out by desperate spirits when the wind that seizes them, shakes, drags and twists them, bears them down, down to the bottom of the land. Are they human, those shrieks of anguish, those howls of rage, those whistles of scorn? She would look at the clock, the perception of the time acting on her spirit like a thousand devils pressing her soul. And she would snatch any paper at hand, tearing it, for the need of controlling herself; she'd tear methodically piece by piece, each a little smaller, till no more papers were left in the room, only a pile of confetti.

Then she would look at the clock; again raising fury would make her pace the house to and fro, from window to window like a wild beast in a cage. At last a flush of common sense would clear her obfuscated mind, its little voice saying 'let him alone, your children are worth more than him, if you do not rest you'll not be able to stand them tomorrow, your children will suffer...' She had tried coaxing, she tried menacing and he was deaf and numb to all. He spoke of the lorries only, of the hard work he was doing, of the many problems they gave him. Maria, who had never been interested in lorries, was deaf too. Thus no dialogue between them, each one following their own arguments without listening one to the other; she had not even noticed how James's talk was now about the many problems the lorries caused, not about the money they earned. He had another fine for overloading them, an axle broke down, Tony Kay wanting more profit sharing than what was reasonable. All these would slide past Maria's mind, obsessed only by his outings and coldness for her. It was an obsession threatening her mental stability, she recognised she must overcome this malady. She thought of teaching Spanish again. Must deviate her thoughts, see other people.

She went to visit Carol's mother. The old lady lived in a small dwelling in a group of buildings in the middle of nowhere, between the valley and the hill top. She was pleased with Maria's visit and gave her a drink and a chair by the fire in a reduced room, more so for the quantity of cats, dogs, pot plants and tea pots all over the place. Little Mercè was leaning, very quiet, by her mother, baby Alexandre was left outside asleep in the pram. Maria listened to the small woman, her wrinkled face moving in tune with the cadence of her speech. She talked about her life, the many times she had been married, the many children she had, all dead now, only one left, Carol, and she was not hers but her husband's, she had adopted her, and she was lucky because Carol was a very good girl, she would be married soon.

'Oh, yes, she will go up to babysit for you, yes sure, I'll tell her. I hope she will be happy married, he seems a good lad, but of course, one never knows what destiny we are reserved for!'

In the old woman's eyes there shone the light of the spirit's endurance against all the storms of the weather and all the storms of life.

Going back home, Maria was pushing the pram with renewed energy. Mercè could hardly keep pace. She took her up and sat her over the edge of the pram, then kept on pushing up the hill. These English folk, they are amazing, she was musing to herself. Why do I have to pity my luck? There is no such thing as luck. As they say, 'you made your bed, you lay on it.' It could be applied to me.

It began to rain. She stopped for a second to pull the pram cover up and Mercè's hood, to herself was indifferent, she continued pushing, plodding up, steadily reflecting: 'Indeed, one is responsible for one's own action and its consequences, certainly must not blame the others.'

It rained all night and all next day. The lorries that went out in the morning came back midday. James was wandering about the place, restlessly. Maria went to point out to him that there were many letters needing his attention because, as the lorries were his business, she had not touched them.

After a while he was looking for her, his brow all in knots.

'Look, will you write a letter for me? You know how to write this kind of letter, tell them that I'll pay, that I had bad luck with the last lorry I bought. And if it doesn't stop raining even worse,' he added after a pause.

His wife was folding nappies, raised her head and said, 'To whom?'

'To Auto Enterprises, ask them to wait...'

'To Auto Enterprises?' she exclaimed glancing again at him in surprise. 'Write to them? But you always have dealt with them by telephone or calling there! Besides, what do you owe them? It is long time since you bought a car from them.'

'Yes, don't you remember? The last, the Simca.'

'Of that, it is more than a year, are you sure you did not pay for it? You sold the Simca before we went to Spain. James, why didn't you pay as soon as it was sold? Let's see, give me the letter.' She put a nappy, not quite dry, over the radiator, then took the letter. 'Is not from them,' she said immediately, 'they have given the matter to a solicitor. And you were so good friends!'

'They been waiting so long that I am sure they wouldn't mind to wait a bit longer.'

'You are mistaken. Here, they say, are giving you seven days.'

'That means nothing, you know many say seven days and it is fourteen or twenty-one. I think if you write a well written letter.'

'I write if you want but if we cannot state when we are paying, it will be nought, besides the letter is of the thirteenth. What day is today? The twentieth? It is too late. Perhaps you could telephone ...and believe me James, pay everything you can at once before the lorries swallow up all the profit gained this summer,' glancing outside to the steady falling rain added, 'that is already gone.'

The man remained there sitting by the dining table, looking at the scattered papers, trying to sort them out, often placing his hand, screening his eyes like a cart-horse unable to focus into a straight point in front. Though, unlike a horse, he could not plod on, reality never appeared clean in front of him, always roped like an oriental dancer with floating veils of fantasy.

Maria, changing the baby's nappy, wiping Mercè's nose, in and out of the kitchen, glancing at his pondering, was sorry to see his efforts in coordinating ideas and fact. In spite of his years and all his undertakings he was like a youngster in need of assistance. She felt moved, not for love, it was compassion, the strongest feeling she always had, but unknown, for him. She sat by him and took an interest in his papers, cleared a few concepts, made him see the urgent need to go to Brighouse to pay a fine. He agreed to sell one of the three lorries because, if the rain persisted like today, and he had to pay the driver, he would have loss instead of profit, and the licence too was very expensive if not working continuously.

The rain did some good to both. While he went to Brighouse and then for the children, Maria beheld the light of hope still burning. The wind that took the rain away, now dry and furious, was drinking the last drops of water left upon the grass between the crevices of rocks and hollows. The lorries were all out. Mr Lenem and his assistant were working in the garage. All seemed quite normal.

In the afternoon Maria put the infant in the car, fastened Mercè on the front seat and drove to school. The children were collected and she did some shopping in Elland, then took the way back to the garage. As soon as she reached the sight of it she had the impression of something unusual. A parked car was in front of the bungalow and a group of men were looking at James's Jaguar. A flash of lighting came to her that this car was not paid for either. With uneasy feeling she stepped out of her car, then she recognised one of the men, as he was from Auto Enterprises. She was already going towards them when Mercè began to scream, wanting to be unfastened. Elizabeth was knocking at the bungalow's closed door and the baby, noticing the rocking, had stopped starting to cry. Theresa was trying to take him in her arms. All at once, though habitual for Maria who, smiling at the men in an apologetic manner, turned her direction, went to the car, put the baby in Theresa's arms, ran to the door, unlocked it, went swiftly back to the car, unfastened Mercè, got her down and sent all them into the house. A few seconds after she faced the men.

'We want to see Mr Martines,' said the stranger.

'I am sorry but he is not in. He'll still be some time.'

'We shall wait.'

'Sometimes he does not come until seven. May I can help you?'

'No, No, we must see him.'

'He'll be late,' insisted Maria, 'If you tell me what is about I am sure I can...'

'No Madam, no,' interrupted the man, 'the matter concerns him.'

Then Maria turned to the Auto Enterprises man and said, 'I know he owes you money, I'll tell you what is there.'

He shook his head, this one of the brothers always was of few words and now he uttered none.

It was obvious that the men had no wish to deal with her, she shrugged her shoulders and said, 'Well. Here is very windy if you have to wait long. Would you care to come into the house? I'll make some tea.'

The men refused. Maria entered the house, somehow resentful of this so apparent hostility.

Busy with the children, moving about the house, she was glancing outside. The men continued, unperturbed by the passing of time. Maria's ear was attentive to the noise of the lorries coming back, uneasy with expectation. At last she heard them and ran to the window. The three men stepped out of their car and walked calmly towards James. She observed them talking, a few gestures, the silhouettes against the light of the garage appeared upright and quite still, without menace. She moved away from the watch point and continued attending to the children, somehow reassured. This evening she sent the two eldest to bed without a bath; that English custom of a daily bath was becoming too much for Maria's four children.

Soon after she went again to the window. James's Jaguar was gone, the Auto Enterprises car also. She went out to the door to scan the yard but James was not in sight. She turned back disappointed, thought today he had gone to the pub without even putting his feet in the house.

She was in the kitchen preparing milk for Mercè when he entered.

'Is supper ready? Where are the kids?'

'I thought you were gone.'

'No,' his voice normal, 'have you seen the Auto Enterprises people? I have given them the E-Type. So they will not pester me any more. Do you know? They have come with their solicitor.'

Maria wheeled round so suddenly that the milk spilled over, dripping through her fingers to the floor.

'Don't you see you are spilling all the milk?' He took the glass from her hand.

'But...you said you have given them the Jaguar? Given up your precious Jaguar?' She was automatically rinsing her fingers under the tap.

'I have enjoyed it for some time, they will finish paying for it,' he commented with a tone that sounded incredulously normal, 'I'll give Mercè her milk.'

Maria remained in the kitchen wiping her hands, unable to understand the calm attitude of her husband. He was only pretending, he must be very upset, it will show up later, she thought. It's impossible, he could not just give up his beloved sports car, just like that!

However strange to Maria it was so. In vain she searched for signals of sorrow or disappointment, careful not to provoke him in any way, fearing some anger would come out of his system against her or the children. His behaviour did not change. And she didn't know what to make of it. Was this enthusiasm for a fast car vanished? Had he been frightened by the determined attitude of the three men? Or was it that he had another caprice?

She, who had almost hated that car for being the cause of so many upsettings between them, could not feel any joy for the disappearance of it; on the contrary she was feeling sorry for her husband, absurd as it may be. Sports car or not, he didn't change his habits and would go out every Saturday smart and well dressed. Maria would look at him with a deep longing, she liked him cleanly shaved and changed, she wished to go with him arm in arm to feel the pleasant current the proximity of men provokes. But he would get into the car, her car, and without turning his face drive away. Completely forgetting the woman behind, the woman that had been his girlfriend, forgetting he had loitered the streets around her house waiting to go out with her. Perhaps too many years ago. Perhaps his desires were now for another woman. On reaching this point Maria's mind would slowly withdraw, entering other matters, never to entertain thoughts of jealousy: now Mr Lenem was beginning to give her serious misgivings.

Locking and bolting the door Maria thought this evening was going to be a perfectly peaceful one. The quiet hour when the children were in their first sleep. It would be for her of calm and repose. No uneasiness would disturb her, no wondering thought about James's late coming back. Tonight he would not come back. He had gone to Barcelona, to see what prospects were there for business. In England things were not going so well, not well at all; there was nothing else to do in England, he was ready to tell everyone. He was tired of striving for no results, not getting on, too many regulations, the lorries could not work properly. Now he had only one left, and that in halves with Tony Kay.

Mr Lenem was going to buy the garage, he was sure, then they would return to Spain where life was better. In the meantime Maria was sure of nothing. Mr Lenem had given instructions to his solicitor yes, but Mr Lenem was not going to pay for the garage. Almost from the beginning Maria noticed how he wished to make himself the master by other means, and she had him checked. She never allowed him to enter the sitting room. She would precede him and be in the office for the weekly accounts, which she demanded accurate to the halfpenny. She would spot any untidiness about the courtyard and point it out to him, she would reproach him for running out of petrol. She made him realise she was the mistress.

She put the television on and sat, comfortable. The time passed. When she retired to her bedroom the lights of the garage workshop were still on. The night was quiet, she could hear Mr L. working. What is he doing so late? she wondered. She didn't wish to be asleep while the garage was still open. It was one o'clock. She had the intention of going out to see what was going on, yet immediately thought not. No. That is probably what he wants. Precisely tonight that James is away. He never works so late. He wants me to go, and perhaps he'll convince me of something, she thought. She let out a scornful little laugh. Infatuated little fool... She remained still with the lights off until the man, tired of his unrewarded delay, closed and went. Then Maria fell asleep in peace.

James came back from Barcelona with no defined idea of what possibilities there were for them to live there. After all, nothing; he had spent a week's holiday. Full of words, that, yes, but of formal decisions none, this was for her to decide, he said. Precisely now, she saw only darkness around, the light of faith on him had been completely extinguished.

The garage under the Lenem management was not prospering. Since James came back, and because Tony was driving the lorry most of the time, he busied himself in the garage and then would go to Maria and complain about Mr Lenem, if he had lost one of his tools, if he had broken some concrete on the ramp, if he put stiff face at him.

Maria's answer was to let him alone. 'And me too! If he is the manager, naturally he doesn't like you to interfere with his work.'

'Well, look, it is better he buys the garage soon, and we go.'

'Where?'

'Wherever it be.'

'Wherever it be is nowhere, and nowhere is not a proper place to go with four children. If you do not understand, enliven yourself,' and she turned her back on him in bad humour.

Withal she decided to do something. She began putting some pressure on the manager for a deposit toward the place, and urged him to sign the contract of purchase and even more; she fixed a date in writing that if he could not pay by this date, he would accept the notice to terminate with their previous agreement. It worked. Mr Lenem quit the garage.

As soon as this problem was solved, Maria's efforts concentrated in reviving James's interest for the repair work; their future was there, she repeated, he would do better working on his own trade and leave transport aside. He argued that as soon as the new motorway was constructed it would cut the Lindley Moor Road to Manchester and kill the garage business. He was partly right. But Maria's contra argument was that in the meantime a new estate was being built on the top side of Lindley. The Moors were becoming fast peopled, houses growing like mushrooms. If they were clever, all the newcomers could be customers to the petrol station and his repair shop. She would have liked to clear up the mess he was in with the lorries, only if he were ready to cooperate, to speak clear. By herself she could not see the thread in the tangle.

Mr Fursden was again coming up to the garage. Sweetly offering his help, he would collect James's debts, as he was a debt collector and could be of great assistance, he said. He had been away from the garage for some time, in fact, since Maria had began to show her state, he had looked at her with some distaste. Neither had he been all the time James was busy with the lorries.

Now, every day, almost, he was in need of petrol or some other thing. The petrol he would serve himself, he had a credit book. Maria wasn't very pleased about that, many times after he left, she went to check the writings and the numbers on the pumps.

James would say, 'Don't you trust him? You don't like him?'

'No. Is not so, is he who does not like me.'

'He doesn't like women.'

'I do believe that, he lives for his dogs, doesn't he?'

'And for his friend,' he was laughing, 'one day we shall visit them.'

However, they did not go. It was them, invited by James, who came to the bungalow for supper.

Mr Fursden's friend, called Frank, was a tall man, very tall and thin, bent forward in his walk as if his eyes were too far from the floor and would miss what he might tread on. He was very attentive with Maria and moved her seat, was upright till she sat, thanking her graciously. Mr Fursden had mentioned him as an intellectual, if they could see the quantity of books he read, and he was a very wise man besides. Nevertheless, Maria could not maintain an intelligent conversation owing to her embarrassment. The two friends had sat together, unnecessarily near to each other. Fursden was waiting on him, touching his arm, lovingly holding his hand... Maria's face went through the tones of red, she did not know where to put her sight, while James was obviously enjoying himself. After the last serving she went to the kitchen and remained there till the men went out.

Later James said to her, 'I told you didn't I? That they live as man and wife and you did not believe me.'

'What I don't understand is why you bring queer people home to me, when they or others are rough or ignorant... You do this too often. Look, if you want to invite your friends do it the day I go to the Tech and, instead of hiring a baby sitter, you and your funny friends sit here, I don't care as long as the girls are asleep. But I am tired of cooking or serving or smiling for people I don't like.'

James took no notice and continue pleasing himself, he would bring home any occasional friend he'd met with, at any time, without previous notice to his wife and insist in sitting them at his table to share his food. Very generous maybe, or very mean to his wife. He was by this time very friendly with a couple Maria liked even less; her name was Patricia, a very suspicious name, he was John. They were married, so they said. She painted herself like a penny doll, eyes, hair, face, lips, nails, she had long and well shaped legs, showing them off almost to the groin. She was of a very joyful character, always telling jokes, rude jokes to make James laugh and Maria blush.

'Come, come,' Patricia said after telling a big one, 'you are married and loaded with children. You mustn't feel shameful.'

'To be married does not mean you have lost your decency,' Maria replied, annoyed.

And, as they all laughed at her, she felt her burning cheeks difficult to sustain and got up and went to the door to let the fresh air cool her face. The car was parked right in front of the entrance, she saw the keys in and, without a thought, got into it and let the hand brake off. Slowly the car slid down, she bent over the steering wheel with both arms, guiding it out to the road. She needed not make any effort, she felt a kind of comfort letting self and car go down remorselessly. Go down? That was exactly what she was doing, letting herself down. Good God! Why was she descending so low? Where was her intellect, her studies, her music? Her heart ached... Suddenly, a horn blowing alarmed her. A car overtaking, its occupant shouting something. Yes, what was she doing in the middle of the road with no light and engine off? She reacted quickly, switched on and controlled the vehicle, drove it toward a side lane leading into a field where she parked, remaining there for some time thinking in solitude upon the stillness of the night.

When driving back later, she found James furious.

'Where have you been? Do you think this is right what you did? Going without a word? They were waiting to say goodbye. They will think you have no manners.'

'I went for a bit of fresh air,' she answered, very calm.

'You are buxom!'

'Your friends, I don't like them, I have told you before, don't bring them here when I am in.'

EARLY DECEMBER, SNOWING. James, at the other side of the drive, had all the path cleared. Maria, with a spade in her hand, was watching the pile of snow she had just made. She bent again and eagerly attacked the white intruder. When the last shovel was thrown by the road she was sweating, then she looked at the side of the kiosk where it had been cleared first. It showed again a white mantel. If it kept on snowing the exercise would have to be repeated several times. Better, she thought; she wished for strenuous efforts.

The next day one of those currents of warm air coming from the Atlantic melted all the snow away. In the evening Maria decided to walk to Lindley. A client had an overdue account and had stopped calling for petrol. She went to see him.

She walked away from the lights and turned to the right, a lane sloping down a sharp bend. Her clouded spirit fancying shadows upon the shadowed night, she could only hear the sound of her steps; the rhythmic clash of her boots against the concrete was annoying. She was scared. A fear not entirely caused by the eerie place and hour, but the dreadful feeling she bore inside her, growing worse every day. Yes, those last few days had been of anguished recount. Working feverishly, running out to serve petrol, running back in. She played with the children more than usual, even at jumping ropes. She would take a hot bath and go to bed exhausted, to wake up the following morning and no further consequences.

She walked on. Nothing could be distinguished in front, then she glanced behind; the turning of her own eyes through a flush of feline light and a tremble of fright went all over her body, she speeded her pace just to see in front a darkest bulk to give her another shudder of fear. It was only the telephone box. What strange forms things take in the dark! She plodded on. Then the first lights of the village appeared, somehow dissipating her anguish; she turned her thoughts to her business. However, her client was not at home, she received excuses from the wife, but not her money.

She left the house and crossed the street, now she would take the upper lane, it was, if not less dark, less twisted. Up she walked, leaving the lights once more behind. As she walked deep into the quiet lane not calm, but turmoil, was over-powering the strange oppression over her senses. She had never feared the night before. Now the night was like a monster, titanic, its hands as big as her body, closing over, shunning her vision, hindering her breathing, hampering her walk. Her pace became doddery, she knew not where to put the next step.

Suddenly, taking her hands out of her pockets, she stretched them impulsively, as if to avoid a crash and cried, 'No, oh no, no, my God, no! Please no.'

But a little thin voice far into her depth answered: *Yes, yes,* so small yet terrifying, unacceptable yet swelling up her dearly to the paroxysm of real panic.

And she started to run, in little jumps like a frightened bird whose wings are wounded... Then she stopped. 'No, I am getting mad,' she uttered in despair; the echo of these words bounced on the wall of darkness resounding for few seconds, suspended till her senses picked them up, shaking her entire body violently...

She began to walk again. How could it be so? She did not want it so. She could not have it so! Then she raised her eyes to the sky searching for the stars, the eyes of God. None to be seen. Where are they? God was not looking down on her despair. No, dark, heavy, menacing the immense sky above her smallness.

'Oh God!, the God of my youth, the God of my parents! God of Abraham and Jacob. Where have you gone? What have you done with your blessings for the fertile woman? Your prophets who cursed the sterile, where are they? Her face twisted in ironic grimace, how bitterly she felt the scorn. False, all false. I am the cursed, I the fertile woman, I am the damned one with my absurd fertility, untimely, obtrusive, inconvenient, it is going to be impossible. I cannot have another child!'

And her sobs could move the stones but nothing else. And she would die, she would rather die. Why could not the night, that monstrous darkness, press harder on her, press her more, flatten her person on the soil like a road roller, and pass away leaving behind just a mark, only one spot over the path, a speck of dust upon dust, and no more.

It was evening, James was ready to go out.

'It is a very bad night,' his wife said. 'Why don't you stay in today?'

'I have to meet someone who might buy the garage. What you can do is to close. Nobody will call for petrol in this weather.'

'Well, you are out,' she replied. 'What I want is to speak to you.' He was putting his coat on. 'Don't go,' she continued impatiently, 'you must save and pay some bills, everything is overdue, the people who installed the heating are still claiming some money.'

'Let them, I told you, we do not owe them anything, they are mistaken.'

'But they are taking the matter to court... Besides, is not that only what I am worried about. I am pregnant again,' and suddenly, as if the statement struck at her, added with rage: 'You, you are to blame, you know very well I can't stand another lot of sicknesses. I have told you a hundred times to be careful.'

'Me? That's you girl, it is you the one who has to be careful.'

'No, it's you, who come full of spirit in the middle of the night and don't know what you do, you are a beast!'

'Don't be stupid, ignorant. The chemists are full of pills.'

He took the door and went out, she watched him abruptly start the car and speed down the road.

'Go, go, get lost, crash in the road,' she uttered between her teeth. 'So many accidents about and HE has to come back safe.' And the devil red and bright with eyes of fire entered like a thief into the heart of the woman.

Sauntering, solitary, around the Technical College, on the shadows of the buildings, her figure not to be seen, Maria had sat in the parked car waiting until seven o'clock had struck. Now she walked towards the building, her room would be empty. She eluded the porter and went upstairs to her Spanish class. She knew no one would be there. What she knew not is why she was there. Was it because of the routine of the past weeks? Or was it her inability to accept failure? Didn't she notice how the interest of the students had diminished in pace with her decline in mental agility, clarity and drive? As her problems were increasing, with her state of sickness becoming like illness, her capacity for teaching diminished so much, so her lessons were a disaster, until the head of department decided to close the class. Why was she there now like a spirit out of the grave?

The next week she did the same. Sat in the car. Her eyes wandering on the street lights, the building, the people, anxious to find some interesting company. She could stay there all evening; no one would care. Then she went back home because she had nowhere else to go, Carol the baby sitter being the only person surprised by her untimely arrival. Regarding her husband, he never noticed, not then, nor later, that she had stopped going to the Tech.

The woman was dragging on, clouded, lost the spirit, the strength, her vision narrowed to the present day, each hour, its toil and its effort, every minute, to keep looking after the children, trying to smile and give them some joy. Spasmodically reprimanding, shouting, surprising them with her unsteady humour, consequent with the alterations of her physical functions, so impossible to control, incomprehensible to the children and seen without sympathy by her husband. She had accepted the new life better than her luck. The sweetness of the mystery that will not fail to bring waves of wonder and love, caressing the soul with a feathery touch.

The man, rattled by his creditors, discorded by his wife, could not find other escape but his habitual going out, not realising precisely that his outings were more irritating to Maria than anything else. Yet she still would say, 'go out if you must, but don't come back so late. The later you stay, the more you spend, the later you get up in the morning, the less work you do. Why can't you see less work is less money and we are not getting on at all?' In her unbalanced state she would assess facts and pass from subtle persuasion to loud demands, her mind whirling incessantly round the same obsession. How could she make him realise his wrong doing and how she was suffering for it? Later on, she entered into a sobbing mood, well into her fifth month of pregnancy, feeling physically quite well, but for her bouts of crying, as if having a pool of tears behind her eyes ready to spill out at the least contrariety. Many nights, even without provocation, just her inner self so full of psychic substance which produced tears, the bitterly salted ones, would burst out, then she'd get from her bed to the sitting room and drop on the sofa sobbing, completely out of control and devoid of comfort.

One night James, moved by some remorse or something, went to her asking why she was so crying, coaching her to go back to bed. Yet this extemporary return of his care aroused her to even more tears which she was unable to explain, only saying: 'I am sad, how sad do I feel my God.' The bewildered husband tried still to take her gently up. 'Leave me. Please leave me alone' was her response and he went with the same old ignorance, leaving the same gap between them.

Another evening she decided not to go to bed. She'd waited for his return: busied herself with business papers, did the washing, folded the nappies, finished the ironing, then she sat down, the hours passed, then seemed to stop and the night became still, weighed like lead on her mind. To struggle against it, she stood up pacing the length of the room once, twice, many more times with increasing turmoil. She had torn again many papers into small pieces and her hands would not be still. At what time would he come today? And tomorrow what? No, she didn't want to think about tomorrow. She was feeling confounded. The intangible thing was hovering, menacing over her, ready to squeeze her so that no strip of light was she able to see. The minutes ticked on slowly. The children slept on.

'I'll put some obstacle to make him trip over as he comes in. I wish to see him flat on the floor. I'll place a pot full of water, perched up to drop over him and soak him cold. I'll take the poker and club his nape.' The little devil, growing bigger was looking through her eyes. Her mind, turbid, was searching for the ephemeral comfort of vengeance.

The kitchen clock showed three hours when Maria went to boil some milk. She filled the bottle, covered with an upside down glass and left it by the pot where the teat had been sterilised. Then she turned to the bedroom and began to dress, trousers over thick socks, then her boots, a jumper and a cardigan, took the duffle coat making sure the bunch of keys were into its pocket, her gloves into the other. In front of the door she remained, hesitating for a few seconds. Nothing that could be defined as thought or as impulse moved or unmoved her, yet she did not pass the door, she turned back to the sitting room and put off all the lights, then approached the window and stood upright, immobile, looking out.

The world was not going round any more that night; all was still, even the wind had dropped. James might not come back, she suddenly thought, as her brain emitted the wave quite clearly, her body shocked with strange coldness from her feet to her lips, parting them in a sigh of devilish relief. She remained there a long time until the sound of a motor car was heard. She quickly put on her duffle coat, then looked through the window: no, the car had passed by.

'Perhaps he will really not come back,' she repeated; this time with a little anguish.

The seconds were years. It seemed in fact as if he were not to return. Yet he came back, suddenly startling her because he came from the opposite side, from the top and in a second the car was stopped in front of the door. She saw him getting out, so much alive and full of health that he made her feel furiously vexed. Closing her teeth tightly, her hands pressing the bunch of keys, she rushed to the kitchen and fled from the house through the back door. Her legs were shaking so much, she had to lean on the wall. Soon the light of the kitchen went on; she, fearing being discovered, moved swiftly away, going round the house then run to the road.

Where was the wind today to take her, to push her down the hill? She went up. Walked into the night. Walked on as if with a purpose, head on into the dark as if light was there. At the summit she left the road and went into the fields as if she knew them well. And walked on as if she were light as a feather and never tired and walked still further as if the night were not cold: she was warm. Her mind fixed on the only wish remaining clear above all: that of getting free from the ties fastening her. Walk in vain. Nonsensical. The ties which fastened her to the house were her children, who lay now asleep, those ties like elastic ropes, stretching with the distance. Ah! If they should break, what sting. She'd bleed to death.

Stopping near the derelict stone wall she sat down and remained still, feeling the pull of the ties towards the home, although not so strong as to impel her to go back. Motionless, unable to tidy up her thoughts at that moment, dull like a desert, she stayed there till swiftly Aurora came, with her pinky face and her tender eyes blinking with dim light to give a new day. Would she bring some magic to lighten Maria's spirit? Her arrival is so soft and sweet, she goes slowly touching the land, hills and trees, houses, stones and weeds, every object upon the earth regaining its proper colour at the gentle touch.

Then Maria felt cold. Shocked herself upright. Some rocks slid down, a dog barked, so near that it gave her a start. She retreated quickly, somehow frightened. Where was she? By instinct she took the route home. Near the house she was not cold any more and began to walk slowly. Everyone would be asleep, the children innocently, the man: How could he? What was she doing at that hour? Where had she been? What had she done all night? James would ask and affirm she was already mad.

No, she would not enter the house. No, a bit more solitude. Better if they continue sleeping. The car stood in front of her, tempting for another run, the key in her pocket. A few seconds after she was driving down the hill. Yet her impulse, conditioned by a life of Christian discipline, brought her nowhere else but to Church. It was Sunday, before reaching Saint

Patrick's she was reflecting upon what she was doing. Seven o'clock Mass. Yes, good idea, at least today there will be no argument with James about going, she thought. She made an attempt to clean the mud off her boots and smooth her hair, although pondering sadly that no one would care how bad she may look.

She came out of Mass as she had entered: with her mind empty of answers and her soul darkened. Drove homeward through New North Road. This road she liked very much, especially in summer when the tall trees in full leaves provided a compact vault of moving green. Now the woven pattern formed by the still bare branches resembled a Gothic cathedral. A solitary run. Suddenly, she lifted her hands from the steering wheel to her head in a gesture of despair and cried aloud: 'He is killing my soul!' The inequity of that realisation fell upon her like a mallet, her whole body bent under the impact, her forehead resting on the steering wheel. Then, by the impulse of self-preservation, she pulled herself up and clutched the wheel, again putting her eyes on the road. The car could not stop on its own to help calm her sorrow, nor will life stop for us when it has become unbearable. Life is motion, stops for no one. We must continue the struggle and there is only one way, forward. The path behind is gone forever. The unavoidable needs of her life-link to James and the children overpowered any other preferment.

Mr Fursden had again distanced himself from the Moor's Garage, this time leaving debts. Maria asked James to call on him and request payment. Fursden's reply was that they were the ones owing money to him for the hours working in collecting for them, and the overtime, and the percentage etc. Maria studied the papers once more to make sure, concluding she was right. He was wrong, some money from petrol accounts was due to her. She was not prepared to lose it and consequently called him by telephone. The man's voice noticeably altered and he said *she* had to pay him.

'You come and I show you the papers, you'll see for yourself that there is money for petrol not paid for, you are mistaken.'

'I shall not come up there,' he pronounced in sharp voice and put the receiver down.

Later, Maria was retelling this to James.

'Do try to see him, he'll listen to you, he can't stand me,' she concluded.

'He is nutted,' he replied and quickly his mind went to his own problems. 'Tony is crazy too, now he wants me to pay him the share of the lorry. Now that he has sold it, he tells me I owe him money.'

'But, do you owe him money or do you not?'

'Nonsense! If we were to recount everything I am sure he would be the one who ought to pay to me.'

'Well, then perhaps you should settle this before the matter gets more embroiled.'

James shrugged his shoulders and continued doing nothing of that sort. He would work little and went out much, putting problems aside for the morrow. Maria's temperament, being the opposite, could not leave things morose. A problem in her mind had to be tackled today rather than tomorrow. She decided to go and see Mr Fursden.

He and his friend lived in a little cottage in the fold of a hill at the top side of the garage. From the lane leading to the bottom of the valley there was only a chimney throwing smoke against the ragged moor land. There was a narrow path from the lane to the door of the cottage, too narrow, thought Maria, so she left the car on the lane and, taking Mercè by the hand, walked towards the house. They were not halfway yet when Fursden appeared in the doorway, he must have seen them coming. With his arm stretched, his hand pointing to them, he began to shout as if he had seen the devil.

'No, do not come nearer. Stop there. You are not coming into my house!'

Maria stopped at once, shocked with surprise. She well knew he had no liking for her, but this greeting was unexpected. After all, he had entered her house whenever he pleased, always received as a friend. What was wrong with him now? That Maria was asking him to settle some accounts was not so terrible as to put him furious. Yet the man seemed to get mad at the sight of her, his eyes protruding as if to jump out of his head, his stretched hand shaking.

'You are not to step further into my property. Back out!'

'But Mr Fursden, don't get like that. I only came to show you the papers,' Saying this she moved forward a couple of steps, then the man became paler and shouted louder.

'Get out, get away from me. I shall take you to court.'

'Don't be stupid,' replied she with cold disdain. 'You will lose. It's better if you pay.'

'Pay you? You should pay me all the hours I've worked. You don't know what you are talking about.'

'It is you who know nothing. The judge will see, you'll go to court.'

Maria and the little girl had been slowly advancing, only few yards separated them.

The man, becoming red and purplish with rage, backing towards the door, glanced in and called: 'Jerry, Bruce, come!' The two Alsatian dogs rushed out. 'I'll set the dogs at you!'

Maria stood as nailed to the floor. Mercè, frightened at the sight of the large beasts, put her arms round her mother's legs, showing her state too evidently. Mr Fursden sent the dogs on.

'Jerry, Bruce, get them. Ar!'

The two Alsatians, barking ferociously, jumped forward to the group of mother and daughter. In one second they were to touch them. At the same instant Maria decided not to move, sure that if she turned her back to run the beasts would attack. Horrified, feeling the jaws of the dogs already in her flesh, she pressed her daughter closer with one arm and the other she stretched out in a desperate effort to be calm and said, 'Hello Bruce, Hello Jerry.'

These white magnificent animals had been up at the garage many times, although always inside the van, but she had been near enough for the fine noses to smell her. Now they stopped, their open jaws throwing vapour a few inches away, hesitating, waiting for their master's next command. Then Maria backed one step which infuriated the dogs, who began to bark furiously again, yet without advancing. Fursden stood in his doorway watching the scene. Would he give another order to the dogs? She looked at him, his eyes scanting, his face first pale then red, now green.

'If you don't call your dogs back I cannot go away,' she said at the same time, making another step backwards. But the Alsatians, still barking, made a step forward. Still Mr Fursden did not retract his dogs.

'Bruce, Jerry go, go to your master, come on go, go home, go.'

She tried to coach them gently, she didn't know what the animals were capable of. Her car down there seemed miles away. Then she tried another step backward, this time the dogs did not follow, then she backed another one.

'I don't want to see you here again,' shouted the man from the cottage.

'Sure you shall not see me again here, it will be in the magistrate's presence. Because if you don't I will take the case to court,' she replied, having increased the distance from the dogs and feeling safer. Holding Mercè still tight to her, she moved backward until they were near the car and safe to turn their backs to the man and his dogs.

Mother and daughter sat in the car still shaking with shock.

'Good Lord!' Maria uttered, 'this man is raving mad.' She couldn't take it in. It could not only be her state that made him so mad, it must be something else. James might not be taking enough notice of him. A man with his senses upside down, who knows how he sees sexual relations between man and woman, where his jealousy would lie. At that time one of the callers at the garage was Brian, young and handsome, whom James was befriending. Was it perhaps just that: 'the green-eyed monster which doth mock the meat it feeds on'?

MARIA HAD SOME calm days after the night spent in the open and the stormy encounter with Fursden. Now she was beginning to get nervous again about her husband's night outings. Unable to sleep well, the days felt long and heavy on her. Ready to complain, she often turned to James, begging, 'James look after the petrol for me, please! While I bath the baby!' or 'Please James, while I cook the dinner!' Other times she would ask to be relieved from the task of fetching the children.

'Please James do this for me...' trying meekly to win his sympathy, 'I am tired...I feel so heavy!'

'You are a nuisance my girl, you exaggerate your state.'

'If you had a thought for me, if you could anticipate what I need, I would not have to ask you so often.'

She was sitting on the sofa, it was midday.

'Now I only ask you to put the dinner at the table and serve it. I have cooked it and I am tired.'

'Well, what do you think I have been doing this morning? Brian and I have dismantled the engine of the Anglia. By the way, I told him to come in. Come on, get up and cook something for him.'

'No, I tell you I am tired. You invite him, *you* give him something to eat.'

At that moment the young man came in. James made his friends enter without knocking. He was tall and slim, fair and fine skinned; he had an elegant, easy manner and was well spoken. On seeing Maria sat on the sofa he made apologies immediately.

'Don't worry Mrs Martines, if you have an egg I'll cook it myself and that is enough, don't get up for me.'

But Maria had to get up to feed the youngsters and with a gesture sent the two men to the kitchen.

'James, tell him where the eggs are,' then proceeded with Alexandre who was still spoon fed. She kept silent until Brian finished his meal, thanked her and went out. Before James followed she stopped him sharply.

'No, you help me to clear the table.'

'You can do it yourself. I am very busy, we must assemble the engine anew this afternoon.'

'Well then, look after the petrol so I won't have to come out and can rest,' she said letting herself heavily on the sofa. She was really feeling drained of energy.

'No, it is better you come out. Is it not so that walking is good for the pregnant woman? It is said that moving about does you good. So up, get up and move about.'

'Move about? Is it not that, that I don't move enough? You do not talk nonsense to me. Do you hear? Don't be so stupid! Any woman in my state has to rest more than what I rest. Oh! How ignorant are you. I, eh, if I were a cow on the grass resting my big belly, you would say: Poor cow! No one would make her get up and follow the herd, would wait, let the animal get up on its own instinct. Poor pregnant cow! Not I, a woman, I have to rise and move and run to serve petrol. I have to move, even if I desperately wish to lay down quietly. Oh my God, why I am not an animal? I wish I were! If I were a goat or a bitch, men would have sympathy for me. There is no condition more miserable than mine!'

James had already gone but she kept on mourning to herself. Where was the woman's place in the great chain of beings? Do men still believe they are the first in the universe, women second? Men, unable to find a proof of their superiority have worked at it for centuries, tried to domesticate women as done with hens and mares. To deprive a woman of education, barring her from open knowledge, making her subservient to a man so her spirit would not develop. Using her fertile body in order to deprive her of liberty. Men have used and abused, turning a woman like a she dog that licks the hand battering her. That's the truth. Yet, why oh, why has a girl to be born with spiritual longings, with the anxious heart to look at open wide horizons, with the desire to reach high? The answer must be somewhere. Women cannot be the odd pieces out of Creation. Man and woman have the same destiny and must find the way to enter eternity hand by hand.

Maria was looking at the messy table, at the two children unable to care for themselves, herself in bondage... And if the bell rung she must go out.

On Saturday James went out as usual, returning after midnight. He went on Sunday, and Monday evening saw him going out again. Maria was feeling very upset. Patience and Resignation would have been welcome companions, but they were too far gone.

Since the realisation that now she was losing her soul, she could not resign to it. At the same time she could not see a way out. Her present pregnancy was the cause of that yearning for attention. She could use any discomfort for complaining. If she had back ache, if her legs swelled, no matter. The husband continued in his own way. Maria, instead of taking things calmly; after all, it was her fifth pregnancy. Why had she not adapted to the situation? No, her temperament would not accept the gross unfairness. Nonetheless, she persisted in her efforts, but it was like holding onto slippery and smooth walls, looking for hangers that were not there.

Why had she insisted in begging his company if he had better company outside? Why had she insisted the children belonged to both if he was convinced the responsibility of caring belonged to women? If she in her exasperation said she would leave him, he laughed, convinced too that she would not leave the children.

'I'll take them with me,' she would reply.

'Where will you go with so many?' he scorned, looking at her lost line.

And this laughing at her was more hurtful than Satan's forking. Ah! that is how he had tied her up. One thing was emerging clear in her mind:

this pregnancy was to be the last. Definitely the last. He was not going to bondage her further. How? She did not know yet, but she *knew* her strength was gathering to defend the liberty of her body, to fire and death if it need be.

With all these thoughts she was turning uneasy in bed, unable to sleep. What time will it be? James was not coming yet, very strange being Monday. Then she began to think about the practical things to be done: this summer she was sending the two eldest girls to Barcelona. At least with two less there won't be so much work, she thought. Must collect the passports – will be ready Friday. And the dresses for their First Communion. I'll buy sandals, be all right for the holidays. I am glad my sister comes, she'll look after things while I am in hospital, is not going to happen as last year when Alexandre was born. But what time will it be now?

Why is he not coming? That is too much... What could he be doing? she thought. She was growing nervous, very nervous. She better try to calm herself. Try to sleep. What about the court case? Fursden had taken her to court as threatened. Well, she had time to appear just before the baby was due. James had a notice from Tony's solicitors. And he had the fines to pay from the lorries to the court. And now what was he doing? Certainly not trying to solve his problems. She rolled her pillow and let her head sink on it. Sleep was definitely out tonight, her nerves were stretching so much, all the fibres of her body were tight and tense as violin cords.

When James came the bang of the door burst them, as a clash of lightning in a stormy sky, as thunderbolts flashed maddening her, spouting out through her eyes and her mouth.

'You are an animal, a beast!' she shouted coarsely. 'What are you doing so many hours out? Where have you been today? Don't you have enough with Saturday and Sunday nights? Tell me, where have you been?'

'Go to sleep and don't pester me,' he answered in a bad mood, sat on the bed and bent to take his shoes off.

At that point Maria was out of her senses. From her side of the bed she threw herself forward, and with closed fists began to attack him in a frenzied manner, repeating insults.

'You are jealous, stupid cow!' shielding himself with his elbow and pushing her back. 'You should know that I do not go out with women, they are all men.'

'I don't care if you are with men or with women, you are out hours and hours, and you leave me on my own. Well, then no more of that,' gathering momentum she continued, 'I can't stand any more, I don't want to! I don't...' She was going to attack him again with her fists when he raised his hand and gave her a hearty smack. The woman fell back on the bed.

'Let me alone, with you, with Tony and all together make me sick, stupid you are, stupid woman, damned the day...'

She was for few seconds paralysed, looking with horror at her husband.

'That is the last thing! Now I am done,' she got out of bed and left the room.

She passed through the corridor, went to open

the door and sure and steady like a somnambulist, walked outside barefooted with only a nightie on. The wind whistled around her, the gravel groaned under her feet, and she couldn't care. She walked down; nothing in the world she could care for, nothing absolutely, not even the infant in her womb. She walked steadily down, all the ties in this world severed. She could only feel the freedom of complete desperation. What must be like death. The total cutting of the bonds to earth when the spirit goes free. She walked on as if she knew at last where she was going.

Then a clamp on her arm, a voice.

'Where are you going? Mad, you are mad, where are you going like that?'

'No, no,' she struggled to go on, 'let me be!'

But the hand pressed hard, making her turn, retrace her steps, pulling her toward the house.

'No, let me be,' she cried, when she meant *let me die*, 'let death be me!' Now she began to feel the hard pebbles under her feet, the cold wind against her half naked body. The pain on her arm. How difficult it is to be alive! 'Let me go,' she struggled still, groaned, sobbed, like a wild beast trying to bite the hand that gripped her. Yet the man had a strong hand, perhaps harder than his heart, and did not let go, instead dragged her into the house, then he locked the door and after, not before, loosened his grip. She fell against the wall and like jelly slipped down on the floor in a heap. James went for her dressing gown, throwing it over her as one who covers a pile of rubbish.

However, Maria was not defeated for long. She sprang up and seemed as if she was going to attack him, but she went to the telephone. Still sobbing hysterically, she took the receiver crying: 'I need some help, I need some help!' James went to take it from her but she, moving aside, began to dial the emergency number. 'Let me, someone will help me! For the love of God someone will help me because I am utterly desperate!'

'To who you have to ask for help? To Storthes Hall I'll take you,' replied he, snatching the apparatus. She stretched to take it again, then he threw it on the floor in rage, the telephone emitted a click and a clack and became unusable.

'Mummy, mummy! What's happening?'

Elizabeth, awakened, emerged from the bedroom with wide wondering eyes.

'See what you have done? Woken up your children.'

Maria made a tremendous effort to control her sobs and told her daughter to go back to bed. Then she went to hers. She laid down but her nerves, broken into messes, jumping like little devils under her skin, did not let rest come to her.

After a while James entered the bedroom, proceeding to lie beside her. Then the woman, not yet reduced to submission, fiercely rejected him.

'If you get near me I shall go again, even throwing myself through the window.'

The threat sounded so determined that the husband left the room without a word and did not go near it for the rest of the night.

After a time of some drowsiness the voices of the children penetrated her brain. Theresa could not find her socks, rather one, she was asking her

mother where it was, she made a difficult movement leaning her elbow on the pillow and took her
legs out of the bed as if moving two bars of lead.
She gave Theresa a pair of clean socks. Mercè's voice
pleading for the sugar stopped, she had tried to
get it herself and spilled it over. James's voice
reprimanded his daughter while having breakfast.

Maria went into the bathroom, approached
the mirror and she made an instinctive movement
of retrogress. 'Who's that?' asked the image in a
shocked voice, moving now closer to it. The
eyes, reddish under swollen eyelids, mauvish deep
lines under, one side of the face coloured and the
other as pale as a thousand years of papyrus.

'Now I am really ill,' and she moved slowly
towards the bedroom.

'Good morning mummy!'

'Elizabeth, mummy is not well, tell daddy to
take you to school, I am going back to bed.'

She remained still with closed eyes. Heard the
car going. Baby Alexandre playing in his cot
waiting for breakfast.

Later, James and Mercè entered the room.

'Do you want some coffee?'

'No, prepare a bottle for Alexandre.'

The little girl climbed on the bed and began to
jump. Mother stayed still. When the baby had
the bottle, helped by Mercè, James asked again.

'Do you want anything?'

'No,' she answered, without opening her eyes
and hardly her lips.

He went out. The time ticked on while Maria
was asking herself from where could she get the
strength needed to move and carry on.

The human endurance to suffering is great.

It was two o'clock in the afternoon, when Maria was hanging nappies outside. There came Janet's mother to see her. Unusual visit, she thought.

'What brings you up?'

'I am sorry I could not come earlier,' the woman explained, somehow embarrassed, 'I haven't got the message till now.'

'What message?'

'Your husband has come down saying you were not well and asked if I could come up to help you.'

'Ah!' Maria didn't know what to make of it, why he went.

'Yes, I am not very well, but I am managing.' In answer of the woman's look she said, 'Men are the cause of all ills...men are.'

'Don't you want me to do anything for you then?'

'No, no thank you very much.'

Maria knew she had to look for help, this widow who had to queue at the Post Office every Tuesday morning for the S.S. money would not do. Yet she needed help badly and had reached the point where no more strength could be drawn from her own resources. She was empty.

That morning she believed she had been completely drained. Only the tenacity of life itself brought it back and she now was up. However, her spirit had taken too much battering.

'Hope had mourning on, drenched with tears, carved with Cares, Hope was twelve hours gone. Gone for ever!' she recited.

Hey! It wasn't. We know she still had the urge to look for help outside herself. She remembered having heard about a Marriage Council Bureau. She looked up the number and, as soon as the telephone was back in order, she asked for an appointment, pleaded urgency, and was given time for the morrow.

This counselling for married people was a social service run by the Establishment. The counsellor was a mature lady, tall and fair with a weathered face. Maria, explaining her sorrows, ended up in a pool of tears showing her bruises. The lady looked at Maria's arm like a person used to seeing all sorts of cruelties. The comfort given fell very short of Maria's expectation. It was just an appointment for next week.

Maria left more sunk than she went. She had taken Mercè with her and the little girl, seeing her mother cry, cried her heart out too. Nevertheless she went back, still with the vague hope of finding some help. She explained to the lady how that Saturday her husband made her go out with him to a cabaret, he had forced her to go when she didn't feel well, he had insisted, alleging she had to see for herself where he was going, she must see that he was not doing anything wrong. He made her go, made her to stand the company of his friend Patricia and the husband, who came into her bedroom, she was lying and made her get up and took her with them. And that in the cabaret she felt very uncomfortable, and before the end she felt sick and they had to take her outside and return her home. And that all in all was a torture she could not go through any more. What could the council do to help her?

The lady, who was listening very attentively, nodding her head as though sympathising with everything, after few seconds said, 'Have you thought he might be unhappy too?'

'It would be logical that he is,' reflected Maria. 'I would like you to talk to him, please!'

'If he comes we talk to him, but we do not go to see people, unless they want us to, we don't interfere.'

'He will not come here,' assured Maria bending her head, her last hope was disappearing.

'The state in which you are now causes these to be seen in a worst light. When you've had the baby we can talk again and try to find a solution to your problems.'

Maria did not raise her head again. It was useless to try to tell her that it was now, precisely now when things affected her so terribly, that she needed most help.

She got ready to go. Standing at the door the counsellor said, 'Be patient.'

Then Maria made a quick movement and was going to reply, 'Where do I get it from?' but did not open her mouth because she saw the eyes of the other woman, soft and full of sorrow; she was an old lady and her face was all wrinkled.

IT WAS SOME days since Maria had received the
notice from the Magistrate's Office alleging that
the Garage owed money to Mr Fursden and in
the name of justice she had to pay. Maria replied
with a counterclaim. Then she was asked for the
proof as a defence, which is generally done by a
solicitor who knows all the intricacies of the law.
As the case was plain and clear to her, Maria
decided to defend herself instead of wasting
money on fees.

Tony Kay had taken James to court too and
Maria urged him to fight his case, to look up
all his books and clear his accounts. However,
James kept on complaining how double faced
Tony was. He would not sit down to look
carefully at the concerning papers, ignoring the
Magistrate's letters.

One day came an envelope addressed to Maria,
demanding payment of a fine to the county court
of Snaith.

'James!' surprised, she showed him the letter.
'Was it not at Snaith where the police stopped you
for causing an obstruction on the railway? Or for
overweight? How is that? It was some time ago.'

'It was for the railway,' he replied.

'But, were you guilty? You didn't go to the hearing.'

'Too far away, it wasn't worth it.'

'Wasn't it? Well, there is a sixty pounds fine to pay. I think it is a lot. What I don't know is why they sent it to me. They probably think is the same business with the petrol. I'll write to them, I'll tell them there is a mistake. I have nothing to do with the lorries.'

James was moving away without a word when she stopped him.

'Look James, Galways Smith have taken us to court too. What can we do? Don't go yet, this is urgent, there is four hundred and sixty pounds owing, if we don't pay in seven days the Bailiffs will come. Look at the paper; it is a writ, we must take notice of it.'

'I have to go to Brighouse and I'll call the solicitor, he'll arrange something.'

'I am not so sure...' she muttered, shaking her head slowly while watching him go. 'He does not realise what a storm is gathering over our heads...'

She sensed that for some time, and now as her hopelessness increased the clouds thickened and darkened at a very alarming speed. Her efforts could only reach what she thought was more urgent. That afternoon she sat down to write a letter to the Snaith's magistrate to say there was a mistake.

Then she concentrated on her defence against Fursden. The hearing was fixed for the seventh of July, a week before her confinement was due. The solicitor, who was doing his best to stop the storm, advised them to write asking permission to pay Galways Smith by instalments. Maria wrote the letter and then paid the first instalment to delay the warrant.

James had tried after the drama of that night and, perhaps to justify himself taking her out, did not try again. Notwithstanding he continued going out himself, every night. She was unable to detach herself, her mood was turbulent, although she did not complain. In the evenings she went about the business of closing the garage on her own, putting things away, reading the pump numbers, counting the money, moving heavily with her bulky stomach, entering the house dragging her feet, leaning on doors and walls to reach the bed.

And the seventh of July arrived. She said to James: 'Today I cannot take the children with me, you must look after them while I am away,' she hesitated then added, 'I don't feel up to driving, I am sorry. Brian might take me to court. Can't he?'

The young man obliged immediately. He was really a nice lad, well educated. Maria couldn't understand how he had become so friendly with James. He wasn't his type. Brian could talk about books and music, and discuss social questions. He was a rebel without being a revolutionary or a communist. Simply, he was a youngster wanting to assert himself, out of the patronage of his well-to-do family, who had sent him to university, when his preference was to be a second-hand car salesman. Brian left her in front of the Queen Street building.

The room where she was led was empty except for a small group comprising Mr Fursden, his friend and another man. They looked sideways at her and continued whispering. She sat at the extreme opposite row of chairs, holding with both hands the bunch of papers. She felt very nervous. Was she going to come well out of it? Was she going to be able to concentrate? If there were words or concepts unknown to her? Was she going to manage? She was doing something a little unusual: a woman defending herself from the accusation of owing money, and heavily pregnant at that. Would the judge take notice of her? She was sure that a solicitor would be the proper person to be there, not her. The throbbing of her heart was so strong she feared it could be seen under her clothes.

A clerk came in, he was arranging his papers. Two other gentlemen entered, taking stands near the door. Then the magistrate came in wearing his black robe. He has forgotten his wig, thought Maria, and suddenly she realised everyone present was standing in a respectful attitude and she got up too. The clerk remained with his head bowed until the judge was seated.

While the case was read Maria, feeling her hand sticky, didn't know how to hold her papers. She was sweating, wishing to take off her coat, yet not daring to show her state even more plainly.

'Maria Martines, trading at the Moor Garage, who represents you?' the magistrate enquired.

'She represents herself, your honour,' answered the clerk.

She stood up and one of the men at the door moved to take her up to the defendant's place.

The magistrate looked intently at her for few seconds, then he said, 'Bring a chair for the lady.'

Maria made a quick gesture of excuse and desired not to be made a fuss of. But the chair was brought up.

Then she had to swear on the Bible.

'Religion?'

'Catholic.'

'Bring a Catholic Bible,' the magistrate ordered again.

The man near the door went out immediately, to come back in few seconds.

'There is not a Catholic Bible sir.'

'Look all over the place.'

The man went out, followed by the second man. Everyone remained in silence, waiting. After few seconds both men reappeared with sorry faces and no Catholic Bible. At that instant Maria was seized with a wave of confidence, as if that little incident could give her a kind of advantage over the others. She said in a clear voice: 'I shall swear over the Protestant Bible. I don't mind. And I can assure you that my truth will be the same.'

She reassuredly put her hand over the book presented to her and repeated the classic words. After that the Fursden solicitor began to read the accusation presenting all his arguments, a copy of which had been previously forwarded to Maria and she had it now in front of her well quoted, marked and numbered.

Mr Fursden's solicitor seemed to be less prepared and had to consult often with his client.

Maria, with lucidity and serene countenance was presenting her statement, showing clearly the unjust accusation. The solicitor was gradually becoming red, it might have been the heat of the room, or perhaps the embarrassment of being beaten by a woman who was not even a clerk.

The character of his client was coming to light, with the magistrate commenting on the oddity of two men living together, sharing everything including bank accounts and saying that it was not very becoming. (At that time homosexuality was an offence by law. The Act of Parliament making it acceptable was not till 1968.)

The judge resumed the case: it was proved that the debtor was Fursden. He was ordered to pay the cost of the hearing plus the fifty-three pounds to Maria for her counterclaim. The magistrate withdrew among the bended heads of the scarce concurrence. One of the doormen took Maria out of the room. No one congratulated her. She had gone on her own. It didn't matter, she felt very well, full of energy, with the newly found spirit of fight so long lost. Now she thought if only James were willing to cooperate she could fight his case against Tony.

She entered a telephone box.

'I have won the case,' she said to Brian.

'Good for you!'

'Where is James?'

'In the bungalow.'

'Who can come for me? I am waiting here in front at the tea house.'

Later, she was telling James how the hearing went.

'You must do the same with Tony,' she continued, excited by her victory. 'He wants to emigrate to Canada and now is trying to get as much money as he can.'

'But if I don't win, then to him I shall not pay and that's that.'

'No James, if you don't go to court and prove it. And that is what has happened. You didn't go so the court has given him the right. But you can still appeal, don't you know? And the case can be discussed again. Do it, James, fight him back. Don't you stay still doing nothing,' she insisted, eager to move him.

'I am not still,' he replied and, changing the subject, asked, 'at what time does your sister arrive? I shall go to the airport with plenty of time.'

Maria spent the rest of the day in tidying the house and preparing for the arrival of her sister. It would be past midnight. The children came from school, the last day, with their exercise books and drawings, showing them to Mum, and mother was active with an eye for everything.

Evening came and James went out as usual. When the children had their bath, their supper and were in bed, Maria went to sit outside to wait for the last customer of the day and the first stars of the night. In her solitude a wave of anxiety seized her. However, she soon shook it off. Her sister would be there, with news from home, would give her company; she had no reason to feel depressed again.

At eleven o'clock she went to the routine of closing the garage. Then James was coming up from the pub and both entered the house.

'Give me a clean shirt,' he asked, going into the bathroom.

'It is still early, you could...'

'It is quite a long run from here to Manchester and the airport,' he interrupted.

'Yes, if you find a pub on the way still more so.'

The woman was again left alone into the quietness of the place and the silence of the sleeping children. After checking the readiness of her sister's bed she went to lie down. It had been a long day and, in spite of the return of her energies, she felt very tired now.

Quietly stretched, she was drowsing when suddenly a sting of pain wakened her completely. Had she let the circumstances of the day deceive her? Or the counting of the days? Because all the energy she had, the eagerness to have the house clean were none but the maternal instinct of a doe rabbit cleaning her burrow and pulling her furs to build the nest.

She had felt that before, should not have been mistaken. Now the call of the baby was imperious. Broke the waters violently. Maria, taken aback by the urgency, made an effort not to panic, to think fast what she could do.

With a towel between her legs, standing by the telephone she waited for the reply.

'St. Luke's here.'

'Maternity, please,' she asked. 'No, it is not time yet but I am in labour...and is coming quick.'

'Come at once then.'

'I don't know how. I am on my own...the children are sleeping.'

'Tell the neighbours while we send the ambulance.'

'I do not have neighbours, the nearest one is ten minutes walk.' The pains were quite strong and she was worried. 'What am I to do?'

'I'll tell the police, you do not move, don't worry.' The voice was very calm.

Maria hung the receiver and went to the bathroom to gather the toiletries she would require. The telephone rung.

'Are you the lady in labour?'

'Yes, Maria Martines, Lindley Moor Garage.'

'A police woman is coming to look after your children. You do not worry at all – the ambulance is on its way. Will be there in two minutes.'

The two minutes had not yet passed when the noise of a motor could be heard stopping in front of the house. Two tall policemen entered, taking their caps off. Maria said she was ready, then a blue uniformed young woman came in a few minutes later. Maria was on her way to the hospital through the dark and solitary streets of Huddersfield, marvelling at the speed and efficiency of the English Establishment.

At the entrance of St. Luke's, the lights were on, bright and shining through the mist of the empty court. Two upright figures in white were waiting. One of them went forward with stretched arms to receive Maria, descending from the ambulance. The midwife greeted her as her own mother would and Maria, reclining on her arm, felt sheltered and helped.

The baby was born an hour later. It was a boy.

'How are you going to call him?'

'Benjamin,' she replied with a deep sense of relief. 'He is going to be always the youngest!'

The week Maria spent in hospital was like a drop of oil on the sea – calm, detached from her past weeks and the ones to come. She made it so on purpose, conscious that was the last opportunity to enjoy the pure maternal feeling. The garage business problems she put out of her mind, even the demands from the other children were distant. She hardly took notice of her husband's visits with his complaints.

Seven days later she was taking leave of the ward's companions and said to the one next to her, 'You are going home today aren't you? Your baby was born the same day as mine.'

'Yes, but I shall remain a few days more,' she added after a pause, 'I am getting sterilised.'

Maria looked at her with some anguish, mixed with admiration.

'My husband has to sign the papers,' concluded the mother. She was young, very young Maria noticed, and remained thoughtful for a long while.

James came to fetch them with a car he had just bought. Maria, busy greeting the children and talking to her sister, did not take much notice. It was sometime later that he wanted to explain his new buy.

'I've told you. I don't like the girls going to Spain on their own,' he said.

'Yes, but we have the answer to that, they'll go with Blanca.'

'Yes, but what about coming back? They are so young. It is better I go too, and like this, with the car, we save some money, so I leave the Vauxhall for you.'

'Do you mean that the car doesn't cost more? I don't see the need for you going to Barcelona now...' and for the help you give me, she continued in thought, 'it does not matter if you are here or there,' she shrugged her shoulders.

'I have engaged a mechanic who will look after the workshop and Brian will help you with the forecourt, he has done it all this week.'

She did not listen any more, the baby in her arms wanted his feed.

Eight days went by, the baby was baptised and the travelling for the girls was being prepared. James, up and down all day long, gave the impression of attending to everything while Maria, supervising the girls' packing, was thinking that, when they were all gone, she'd have some tranquillity to attend to the pending problems, the demanding letters, the writs and the like. James said she didn't need to worry about the new mechanic whom he had promised twenty pounds per week, but the man would earn his money as there were plenty of jobs waiting. Well, she would look into that later, now they could go.

James had his car in front of the bungalow and was loading it. Maria, coming back from the forecourt and passing the open boot, saw a tin box full of snapshots. The pack of their wedding caught her eyes and she instinctively took it, hiding it quickly into her pocket as he came out of the house with two folded eiderdowns.

'Why are you taking so many things?' she ask in wonderment. 'Why all the snapshots?'

'I want to show them to my family, they'll be happy.'

'As if you had not sent enough...' she sulked, entering the house.

The following morning, standing in the threshold with Alexandre in her arms and Mercè by her side, she waved them farewell as the car slipped away down the road. Maria watched the rear, so low it was almost touching the ground and doubtfully moved her head.

MIDDAY, THE WIND had calmed down to a soft breeze moderating the bright and hot sun. Maria took the pram out for the baby to sleep in the open air. She was smiling at him while adjusting the canopy. She gave a thought to the rest of her family, the ones going south, it would be hot inside the car, wishing James not to drive fast.

She raised her head. Two men were approaching, carrying papers in their hands.

'Good afternoon,' Maria greeted them with a smile.

Neither of them replied. One made a move as if to show her a paper, both glanced at her sternly and Maria's smile froze on her lips.

'We come by order of the sheriff to seize all the effects of the Moor's Garage.'

Bang! The sword so long hanging over their heads had dropped and was now over her head alone, while James was running towards the border, out of reach. These two men never touched her, nevertheless she felt four hands on her head and shoulders pressing down with force as if to bring her underground. Her legs bent, she could do nothing but crouch down.

At her feet was Alexandre, who had come out on his four looking for her. This little boy, just over one year old. Some weeks ago he had learned how to walk and run with his little feet and straight legs, carrying his round tummy about. Yet now he could not. His short history went thus: one day he saw his mother no more, then he saw her again: his mother, yes, but carrying another creature taking away his place. This shock was great and his little legs bent by the same tragic force bending his mother's legs just now. Maria picked up the infant and stretched up. As lightning, came to her the vision of James running, the car so low on its back. She understood.

Her blood began to circulate faster. Looking straight at the men she asked, 'What do you want? What do you have to do?'

'To take possession of all the valuables, furniture, clothing...everything.'

'How?' she glanced at the yard, no removal van was in sight.

'We are not taking it today; we just make a list and the sheriff will come to do the auction here. If you don't mind we shall start with the house.'

And without waiting to see if she did mind or not, they proceeded forward. Then Maria moved swiftly, situating herself in the middle of the open doorway.

'You are not going in.'

'Move aside lady, we have the warrant.'

The men were so near her she could feel their breath. She did not move an inch. With Alexandre in her arms and Mercè holding her hand, without shouting or moving her head she repeated, 'You are not entering my house.' She did not make any pathetic gesture, nor resembled the heroic Queen Boadicea. Only her eyes, full of supreme determination, subdued the two men; they retroceded, looking in wonder at the figure of the woman, small, unshaped still from the recent maternity. The only imposing menace was the dark fire from her eyes barring the entrance to the house.

A few seconds passed, the men glanced at each other, hesitating, while Maria felt the peculiar trembling of pre-battle. The hour has come, she was telling herself, no more time for weakness, for indecisions, for considerations or prejudices of any kind. I shall defend what is mine, even if I have to go against the law of this country. That was what the two men were saying at that moment: she was going to be charged with contempt to the law because they had their right orders.

'I don't care,' she replied, 'you go to the workshop garage and make your list there of the things my husband has left. But the house is mine and the forecourt too. You shall not touch anything here.'

She did not move until the men disappeared into the garage. Then she took the children in the house and, as if she were fearing for the baby, brought the pram back in and locked the door. She went straight to the bedroom, opening the wardrobe wide. Yes, there was the proof: empty of James's clothes, nothing left, even his winter coat was gone.

'No need for her to go and see the doctor,' she muttered, thinking about the woman in hospital being sterilised.

Later she came out of the house, locking the door again and put the key in her pocket. One of the men was sitting at her desk; he had the list in front of him and asked her to sign it.

'The compressor belongs to the forecourt, I do not want to sign.'

The man gave her a malicious look.

'You must sign. You are doing wrong.'

'I don't care. I shall not sign.'

'Do you think that if you don't sign we will not take everything we want?'

Then she replied quickly, 'Why do you want me to sign? Stupid!'

The man jumped up of the chair and with a sharp move gathered his papers, went out to his companion and both cleared out.

Then she passed to the workshop, straight to face the new mechanic. He was a grey man with insignificant grey hair, grey eyes, grey overalls. At that moment his skin was pale grey too.

'With what tools do you work?'

'I have mine, your husband has taken his.'

'Have you seen the sheriff men? Haven't you?'

'Yes, I am shocked.'

'You can go,' she told him sharply. 'I shall not pay you what Mr Martines promised you.'

'Oh! But...the point is that I have left my previous employment to come here...I have wife and children. I can't be without work.'

'Well, if you want to work for yourself remain.'

In the evening when Brian came she explained to him about the pending action, asking him in eagerness if he was prepared to help her.

'Yes,' he assured her.

'Even if you are to take risks?'

'What do you want me to do?' he assured without a blink.

'I want to save as much as I can.'

'Yes, but... he paused, hesitated.

'If you are scared, nothing, forget it.'

Brian began restlessly, 'I want to help you, yes, I do.'

'Come then, drive your van backward into the garage. We'll put in all we can, then you take and hide it where you can until the storm has passed, understand?'

Both dragged the battery charger, the hydraulic jack, the welding set, the sanders, drills and valve sets. Maria, with pencil and paper, was writing down each item. Thirty items, the van quite loaded, but the garage still looking full of things, Maria thought the sheriff men would have enough still. Then she sent Brian away, advising him not to tell anybody.

The following day the newspapers had the notice of the auction at Lindley Moor Garage with a handsome list of items, including household furniture. On reading it Maria closed her teeth so hard that the bones of her jaws showed below her ears.

She rang the solicitor at Brighouse, this gentleman affirmed that her situation was very bad and the best thing to do in order to quieten all the creditors who would now eagerly come forth would be to declare herself in bankruptcy.

'And then what?' she enquired.

'Not being a limited company it is everything seized.'

'All? The house too?'

'Yes, all but the clothes you are wearing.'

'And that is what you advise me to do? Don't think of that, what horror!' said she, forgetting she was still on the phone.

'What do you say?' the solicitor's voice sounded surprised.

'I said no. You write to the sheriff and tell him that the writ was against James, not against the petrol station or me. Tell him that the bungalow is mine and the petrol and the compressor are mine too.'

'Very well,' conceded the solicitor. 'You send me all the papers proving all that.'

But Maria replied, 'No, you write the letter and send it straight away - I shall go myself to see the sheriff and take the papers to him so to save time.' Then she hung the receiver. 'Bankruptcy and find myself with the three babies on the street! No certainly not, over my dead body they'll have to take my house!'

She started almost in frenzy to search for the documents and papers where her signature would be to prove her ownership. The licence to sell inflammables would be valuable now. The receipts of payments for the gas cooker, the washing machine; she gathered a good bunch of papers, put them in an envelope and waited for her friend Mrs Roberts to call.

She was not waiting long. Mrs Roberts had seen the news in *The Examiner*. She came straight into the house offering her help. Maria loaded the car with the typewriter, two boxes full of books, the most valuable of her possessions to keep for her and be secretive about it, then left her to the care of the house and children while she went to see the sheriff. Unfortunately he was not available in his office, so Maria left the documents and went back. Only a few minutes after Joyce Roberts had gone, there were two men in front of her door, coming for the payment for the installation of BBC2, done some time ago and not paid yet.

'My husband asked you to install, I'll not pay for it; he won't either because he has left the country. If you wish, come in and take it out, I don't need so many BBCs.'

The men began working. After a few minutes they left the set with the knobs gone, told Maria she could cover the holes with sellotape to avoid dust and went away. They had not left the garage yard yet and two more men were waiting to come in. They did without being invited, and curtly demanded payment for the fridge.

'We are tired of waiting, your husband bought it a year ago, it should have been completely paid by now.'

'I shall finish the payments as soon as I can,' Maria promised.

'Oh! No, you pay now or else we take it away.'

'No, wait! You sold to my husband a shooting gun didn't you? Worth more than the fridge. Wait!' she added, 'I'll give you the gun back.'

She went decidedly to the bedroom, remembering having seen the long case on top of the wardrobe. She climbed on a chair to reach...it was not there, she could only find a small one: the Browning automatic shotgun, valued at eighty pounds, had disappeared.

She went to the men with the small gun in her hands.

'I was looking for the other one,' she said, 'but take this and leave me the fridge please! My husband has taken everything he could,' she finished in a whisper, lowering her head.

'What do you think?' said one of the men grimacing. 'We do not want that. We shall take the fridge.' Making a sign to the other man, both entered the kitchen.

Maria followed them.

'You have no right to take anything.'

The men had already unplugged it.

'You hear? You have no right to. I shall ring the police. There is a lot of money paid already.'

The men were taking no notice of her and, with extraordinary rapidity, had emptied it out and were pushing it into the corridor.

'Well, take it then but you must pay me some money back.'

'All right,' said one, leaning his elbow over the fridge, 'we'll give you four pounds.'

'No, is not right because there are twenty pounds already paid,' protested Maria. The man took a cheque book out of his pocket and began to write.

'There you are,' he said in a very offensive tone, passing the bit of paper over her eyes. 'Have the five pounds.'

Maria took the cheque, feeling insulted as if she had been called a thief.

As soon as they were out she went to the telephone and called Tony Kay.

'Mr Kay, my husband is gone. What do you have against me?'

'Gone where?'

'To Spain, I don't think he'll come back.'

'I am not surprised.'

'Tell me, what do you have against me?'

'Against you nothing absolutely,' he assured. 'I only want the money James owes me.'

'But they want to take everything from me, they want to take the compressor, if so I can't make the pumps work without. They want to take all the furniture from the house, everything. Mr Kay, they'll leave me and the children without shelter. Do something please!'

'I am very sorry,' his voice sounded preoccupied. 'The point is that the matter is out of my hands now, it is my solicitor who takes care of it all.'

'Oh! But I am sure you could still do something, ring him urgently, tell him you have nothing against me, ask them to leave the compressor so I can earn some keeping money, also the furniture in the house. There are still plenty of goods in the garage to get the money to pay you. Do it please!'

'I shall try it, yes I'll do that. I am sorry for you, really, Mrs Martines,' and before hanging the receiver said in a low voice, 'curse him!'

The grey mechanic was still working and it was already dark. Maria was pacing up and down the workshop looking about intently, considering the quantity of parts and pieces accumulated during the years of work, building up the business. Was it all paid for?

'Mr Bell, how much do you think is all of it worth?' she asked, rolling her extended arm over the place.

'Hummm...few hundred pounds I would say...'

She knew not the man, she wasn't sure he was one to be trusted.

Nevertheless she said, 'I don't want them to seize everything, do you think we could hide something?'

The man stopped to look at her for few seconds, then he replied, 'I have noticed the battery charger was missing this morning.'

'Yes,' she affirmed, 'and now if you like you could get some batteries missing too. Behind the bungalow where the diesel tank is, under it there is some space hidden by the grass. I think there is also room for a tyre or two...understand?'

'Yes, yes,' he nodded and Maria left him alone.

She went to the house. The babies were much in need of her, and thinking about the other two girls, they would be by now reaching the South of France. The telephone was ringing when she entered, the men with the fridge told her not to bother to take the cheque to the bank because they had stopped it. Before Maria could reply a laugh was heard followed by the click of the phone. She was vexed. They had tricked her!

The following morning the post bought a pile of menacing letters. Amongst them, one to James from the bank saying his last cheque had been honoured, leaving an overdraft of fourteen pounds. 'Of course he had also scraped the bank,' she commented bitterly. 'Good thing he could not draw from my account.'

However, there was little money there, just enough to pay for the next petrol delivery. So how was she going to pay those creditors, demanding at once to be satisfied? She would write to them, each one of them...

The door bell rang, startled, she thought there would be another pair of men. No, there was a policeman who politely greeted her, taking his cap off.

'Mrs Martines?'

'I am, yes, but Mr Martines is not in.'

'You have to appear in court this afternoon, because of the fine from Snaith.'

'My husband has gone out of the country. I don't want any more complications. I have enough as it is...'

The policeman was very seriously watching her.

'I am here to make sure you have received the last notice to appear at court today.'

'No, I have not received it, well I don't know... you see, I have been in hospital...I haven't had time to look at all the papers yet.'

'You present yourself at two o'clock. You know where it is?'

'Yes, at Queen Street.'

'No, there is the civil court – it is at the criminal court in the town hall. You'll come?'

He seemed very anxious to make it clear. Maria trembled at the word criminal; what was it going to be? But she said, 'I shall go,' and let the policeman out.

He had come on his own but now there were two men standing by the pumps, forming a menacing group. Why were they coming two by two as if they had to face malevolent attacks, like nuns in the streets, like the animals into the ark for survival?

Carol's mother was coming up.

'A bit of luck,' said Maria, letting her in, 'I need a baby sitter for this afternoon, can you come?'

The two men were slowly approaching, they had been looking at Maria's car, they stopped in front of the door.

'We have come to speak to you about the Vauxhall.'

Maria's heart froze, what about the car? James had said it was for her, insured in her name and she had been driving it for some time.

'Come in, please, what about the Vauxhall?'

'The payments on it are so much in arrears that the time has come to repossess the car.' She was looking at them clearly not taking in what they were saying. The men continued explaining, 'The car is not fully paid for. Look at this paper, it's the H.P. agreement, the instalments to be paid have not been paid, in accordance to the contract the car is ours until fully paid, so if for three months nothing is paid we have the right, by law, to take the car back. Look madam,' the man was shaking the papers, 'this car is six months not paid for.'

'Why didn't you claim it from my husband before?'

'Oh! we have done it many times, but he always had some excuse or other, now we know he is gone, now we do not wait. You give us the log book and we'll take the car away.'

'Oh, no, no. Please tell me how much is there to pay and I'll pay. I can not manage up here without a car.'

'Two hundred and twenty-five pounds. How are you going to pay? When?'

Maria felt herself sinking. Why did James have to buy this car on hire purchase? Why by instalments and then not pay them? Typical of him, yes, nevertheless, ridiculous.

'How much is each instalment?'

'Thirty-five, but it is too late, the arrears must be paid. We must take the car now.'

She didn't even have the thirty-five pounds. Her troubled heart rose to her throat, shocking her. Her lips trembled.

'How?' and she sunk completely, her strength broken. Unable to control her despair, the sobs shaking her violently, she fled to the sitting room. The woman there passed her arm over Maria's shoulders and, with tears in her eyes, quietly let the unfortunate woman cry out her hopelessness.

The two men, moved by this sight, remained very still, not knowing what to do. After a while the old woman said to them: 'Her husband has left her with the children, look how young they are, the baby is only two weeks old,' pointing to the pram where Benjamin was sleeping, 'the action on top and you have to come and take the car from her, like a fallen tree everyone chops for wood! Why don't you leave her alone? Why don't you go?'

'All right,' conceded one of the men. 'We'll leave the car for now, but we shall come back next week.' Then, as if in a sudden hurry, they left the house.

Carol's mother went to the kitchen to make a cup of tea.

Still sobbing, Maria drank her tea. Oh, it was too much for her, she could not stand so much trouble, everyone was coming, pressing on her, she couldn't stand up to that struggle.

'Oh! Yes you can, you'll see how you can. Don't let yourself down, come now, finish your drink. You have to go this afternoon? I'll come and look after the children.'

'Yes, at two o'clock. I have to be there and I don't know what else is waiting for me.'

At that time Huddersfield had not yet its new modern court building. All cases were seen at the town hall courts. On a side door's top she read 'Court Sessions', through this door Maria went. A policeman looking at a list in front of him told her to go across to the other building, to the police offices. She went out along the building, turned and crossed the street.

As soon as she gave her name she was ushered into an office. The policeman was one she knew, he had been up to the garage several times. She smiled at him confidently.

'Good afternoon Mrs Martines,' he took some papers from his table, got up, moved away from his desk and watched Maria carefully without smiling, 'ah, yes, Mrs Martines...let's see...' He went to the door with bended head glancing at his papers. 'Let's see,' he repeated, 'we'll do what we have to do,' turned his head to look at her. 'Please follow me.'

In the corridor, upright behind a counter, there was a young policeman.

'Mrs Martines, give your handbag to the Sergeant.'

Maria, all her blood drained from her face, like an automaton stretched her hands holding the handbag. The Sergeant took it and began to search into it. Meanwhile, the other policeman made a signal over Maria's head who, bewildered, half turned and saw at her side a policewoman standing erect, with her arms along her sides, hands opened as ready to catch a thief, terribly serious. Nobody said, yet she knew she was detained in police custody. Good Lord! What had she done? With trembling lips, mute, fearing she would burst into tears, she followed the police. They went out onto the street, the blue uniformed woman walking at Maria's elbow. The way between one place to the other was short; it was the longest way she had ever walked as it left a lasting impression in her mind, the trotting steps of the two agents of the law walking close to her sides echoed like a thousand stanzas.

Sat on a wooden bench, she waited next to a woman who smoked constantly. Her escort was pacing up and down the corridor. There were other people waiting: men and women, even children, all looking at a door which, when open, policemen and grey dressed men carrying paper in their hands came out of. The place was foggy, or so it seemed to Maria, as she could see nothing clear, her eyes tarnished, her stomach to her throat, unable to utter a word. I must calm myself, nothing can happen to me, I shall go back home to the children, baby'll be wanting his feed, she thought. They can not put me in prison just for not paying a fine that is not mine, it's impossible. Oh my God, *Dèu meu*.

When her name was called she jumped nervously, the policewoman was immediately at her side and they entered the courtroom. This one was magnificent, nothing like the magistrates at Queen Street. Columns and arcades, the ceiling decorated with all the attributes of justice. Up on the stand the three watchers of the law were imposing in their black robes. The clerks sat below them. Plenty of policemen scattered about, lawyers and newspaper men.

Maria, standing with her face to the magistrate, was weakly answering the questions.

'Why have you not paid the fine, you had plenty of time.'

'I didn't know. My husband did know but he is gone without saying anything to me.'

'When is he coming back?'

'I don't know.'

'But you knew you had to pay the fine,' the man kept on accusing her.

'No, I didn't know,' she insisted in her defence. 'I mean yes, I knew because the papers were sent to me, but because the court at Snaith made a mistake, because I had nothing to do with the lorries, they were my husband's business, not mine.'

A silence followed while the judges looked at some papers, then one said, 'Yes, we know that you alleged that the lorry was not yours, but we have here the proof of the contrary: the Dodge, NOB 75 is registered belonging to Maria S. Martines,' declared the judge, holding up a piece of paper which passed over the judge next to him and this one passed to the other.

On hearing this Maria's mouth opened so wide, she instinctively took both hands over it to cover her horror and shame. How could James do that to her? How could he put the lorry in her name and deceive her as much? How could he let her write a letter to a magistrate telling him there was a mistake? How could he let her pass as a liar in front of the judiciary? Unbelievable!! She sunk on the seat, completely annihilated.

In the meantime the judges were conversing with each other, lowering their heads and voices.

When they were to address her again, the policewoman touched Maria's arm, she got up.

'Did you know that the lorry was in your name?'

'No, of course I did not know; the letter, I wrote a letter, sure, I...' she could not conclude, the sobbing rushed to her mouth, choking her, tears were running fast out of her eyes.

The court room was suddenly very quiet. Then the judge proceeded.

'We accept your word. However we can not rebuff the sentence of Snaith, we can not commute the fine, but we can give you plenty of time to pay, as much time as you need. There is going to be an inquiry on your income, also you shall have to present yourself to the court regularly until the fine is paid.'

He banged the table with his hammer: the hearing of this case was over.

The policewoman took Maria's arm and helped her to get out of the courtroom.

'You can go now,' with the other hand she gave her a handkerchief.

Maria wiped her eyes and blew her nose. 'Thank you.'

'I am going to fetch your handbag, wait here, please, cheer up,' she added not without some compassion.

Later, sitting at the steering wheel she felt the wetness of her breast, two marks appeared over her blouse. Benjamin would be crying as it was long past his feeding time. Letting this thought overrule all the others, she started the drive toward the garage. Her usual place for parking the car was taken by another. She stopped on its side, two men descended at the moment she got out of hers.

'Who are you?' she asked curtly.

'Woodhouse Furnishers.'

'Now I cannot listen to you, come back another day,' and she turned her back, going decidedly toward the house. But the men, unheeding, followed her. She had her hand on the door knob and it swung violently.

'I have to feed my baby. I can not attend you, go away!'

'We want only to talk to you,' said one of them, conciliatory, 'we have been waiting for some time.'

'Then you can wait twenty minutes more and if not please yourselves!'

She entered and resolutely locked the door.

'What do they think they are, all these people?' she commented, taking Benjamin from Carol's mother's arms to get him speedily at her breast.

The woman approached the window and said, 'They are not going. I told you what happens to a fallen tree and they think can take advantage of you because you are a woman. But never mind the men, you hold your own. I am sorry to leave you now, but I must go, my husband will be home for his tea.'

'I am all right now, you can go, and thanks very much. I'll see you later.'

With the baby over her shoulder, gently rubbing his back, she received the two men.

'The payment for the furniture is very much in arrears.'

'I know.'

'Well then, pay and we will go immediately.'

'No. Sometime ago I went to your shop to tell you not to send any more reminders to me. I told your boss to address them to Mr Martines.'

'We did that, once he paid one instalment but he has not paid any more for ages. We know now he will not pay.'

'I shall not pay either,' let them go to Patricia, she thought with anger, adding aloud, 'you can take them away.'

She turned to place the infant in the pram and they remained standing in the same spot. She, with a flaming light in her eyes, a subdued echo of great fury repeated, 'You can take them away this minute!'

The two men took an easy chair each and went out to load their estate car, then came back in.

'We will come tomorrow for the rest and will take the carpet.'

'Oh! No! the carpet you are not taking, that will do for what is already paid.'

'No, madam, the carpet is worth a lot more.' They all looked at it, good, beautiful and in good wear. 'We'll come tomorrow for this.'

Maria's anger burst out, she moved forward and got hold of one of the men's arms sticking her nails in, shouting through closed teeth.

'You are taking, now, the table and the chairs and the buffet and no more! Now this minute, you understand that; not tomorrow, not ever again set foot in this house, nor pester me for further payments!'

The man recoiled, trying to shake his arm off the grip of Maria.

She let it go, he looked at his companion and after a pause said, 'The point is that, well, there is no room in the car for everything, we'll come back tomorrow and we will talk calmly about the carpet.'

'I have said that I will not let you in,' her outburst spent, now she spoke with coldness. 'I shall keep the carpet.'

Her tone was so final that the men began to take the chairs out. They put the furniture in a pile in the yard and left. They came later with a van for it but they did not go to the house again.

What a long day that was, it seemed unfinishable!

Maria, absorbed in her problems was standing by the window, waiting for the end of it, for the calm the night would bring, wishing it would be quick so no more men in pairs would come. What could they come for, the gas cooker?

No it was paid for, remember? The washing up machine was not fully paid for. Suddenly she felt a tug on her skirt, moved her eyes from the outside to look in over the little figure who was pulling at her skirt. The three year old Mercè was looking up at her mother with a worried face, her eyes wide open, full of wondering sorrow.

'Mummy, mummy, smile...'

Maria, moved to the deepest of her soul, took the child into her to cradle her. How, how long, oh! How long since she last gave a smile to her daughter?

The day was coming to its end. 'At last,' said Maria to herself, glancing at her watch, 'nobody else will come today, ten to eleven.' It was already dark outside, she'd lock up exactly at eleven, no one was in the workshop.

At that moment the telephone rang.

'Maria, I'm James, we have arrived well,' his voice was happy, careless, its sound made Maria shake so that her bones almost bumped each other. 'Don't you hear me?'

'Yes.'

'We have been so boiling hot all the way through France, terribly hot. This morning we have passed the Pyrenees. I have left the girls in Blanes at the beach with your sister, they are very happy. Don't you hear me?'

'Yes.'

'I am at home in my parents house. Here in Spain is fantastic, you know?'

'What?'

'Everybody lives very well.'

'Yes.'

'What are the little ones doing? You say nothing to me.'

'The sheriff, it is going to be an auction for Tony's case. They have come to seize everything.'

'Oh! Let them do, here...'

'They have taken the fridge, the furniture, the car...'

'Tell the solicitor to solve everything and you take the babies and come to me. That is what you have to do come to Spain.'

'Do you want me to flee as you have done? No. I am not a coward.'

'What do you say?'

'I say no. I say with you I do not go or come anywhere else. Never again in my life. Goodbye.' She hung up the receiver.

A car had come into the yard, she had heard the bell and went out. There was a car stopped by a pump and a tall, massive figure was pacing the forecourt.

'I am sorry to keep you waiting Sir. How many?'

'Oh, I am not in a hurry, put me in two Super please.' The gentleman was looking at the garage building very attentively.

'Twelve shillings please.'

He fumbled in his pockets, saying, 'I believe this garage was for sale sometime ago, wasn't it?'

'Yes, sir, it still is,' she answered without enthusiasm.

'I have three sons, we all are interested in the motor car business. I'll have a garage for each one of them, in time. Is the bungalow included?'

'Yes, and the land is freehold.'

'How much are you wanting?'

'I want five thousand pounds clear, the mortgage apart.'

They had been walking toward the house, the telephone could be heard ringing.

'I could come to speak to your husband.'

'No, he is not here. You'll have to talk to me.'

The telephone still ringing.

'Excuse me, I shall have to answer the phone, come back some other time please!'

'All right. I will come back.'

The man stopped to turn and Maria, making a gesture of dismissal, went in to take the receiver.

'What are you doing?' James's voice asked, very annoyed. 'Where have you been?'

'Outside, there was a customer waiting.'

'Oh! Let them bugger off. I was speaking to you, that is much more important, what I was saying is more important than the petrol and all things there. Do you hear me? Your duty is to listen to me, your duty is to come to Spain, to your husband, that is what you have to do. I had not finished talking.'

'Yes, James,' she replied calmly. 'Yes *we have finished*, talking and everything. I have nothing else to tell you,' and she stopped shuddering, cold, the cold of death coming over her.

At that moment in her life something had just died. Died completely and finally forever more. She had nothing else to tell the man with whom she had lived for ten years. Nor she had anything else to listen to from him. She felt deadly tired of his voice and slowly took it away from her ear, placing the receiver carefully back to its place.

THE
END

LaVergne, TN USA
19 April 2010
179696LV00007B/1/P